The Stationmaster's Daughter

KATHLEEN McGURL

ONE PLACE. MANY STORIES

HQ
An imprint of HarperCollins*Publishers* Ltd
1 London Bridge Street
London SE1 9GF

This paperback edition 2019

First published in Great Britain by
HQ, an imprint of HarperCollins*Publishers* Ltd 2019

Copyright © Kathleen McGurl 2019

Kathleen McGurl asserts the moral right to be
identified as the author of this work.
A catalogue record for this book is
available from the British Library.

ISBN: 9780008331115

Printed and bound in Great Britain by
CPI Group (UK) Ltd, Melksham, SN12 6TR

For my brother Nigel
who provided much of the inspiration for this novel

Prologue

For a moment he was frozen, unable to move, unable to react to what had just happened. Time stood still, and he stood with it, not seeing, not hearing, doing nothing.

And then as his senses returned he registered screams of horror, followed by the sight of that broken and twisted body lying at the foot of the stairs. How had it happened? Annie was screaming, lung-bursting screams of pain and terror. His instinct was to rush to her, gather her up and hold her, but would that make things worse? There was no going back now. No returning to how things used to be, before … before today, before all the horrible, life-changing events of the day. It was all over now.

The screams continued, and he knew that the next minutes would alter his life forever. He knew too that even without the broken body, the screams, the fall, his life had already changed irrevocably. The door to a future he had only dared dream of had been slammed shut in his face.

He allowed himself a moment's grief for what had been and for what might have yet been, and then he shook himself into action, hurrying down the stairs to deal with it all. Not to put it right – that wasn't possible – but to do his best. For Annie.

Chapter 1

Tilly – present day

It was her dad's voice that Tilly Thomson could hear, outside the room she'd been sleeping in. Her dad. What was he doing here? She rolled over and buried her face in her Disney Princess pillow. She didn't want to see him. No, that wasn't true, she *did* want to see him – she wanted nothing more than to be scooped up in his strong arms, and for him to take all the pain away. But she didn't want him to see her like this. Broken, sick, deep in a pit of despair. No parent should see their child in this sort of state. Even if that child was 39.

There was a tap at the door, and then Jo entered. Jo was Tilly's best friend, the person who'd saved her life and given her a place to stay. She'd moved her two little daughters into one room to make space for Tilly, after she was discharged from hospital.

'Tils? Your dad's here.' Jo stepped into the room, her face taut with worry. 'I know you said you didn't want to worry him, but listen, mate, he's your dad. So I phoned him. Don't be cross at me. Let him help.'

Before Tilly could summon the energy to answer, Jo stepped

aside and Tilly's dad, Ken, entered the room. He looked stressed, much older than when she'd last seen him. That would be her fault, she supposed.

'Hey, Dad,' she managed to croak.

'Oh, pet. What's up? Jo said you were in a bad way?' He looked about for a place to sit down, and pulled out a small stool upholstered in pink to perch on.

'I'll, um, leave you two to talk,' Jo said. 'Did you want a cup of tea, Ken?'

'Thanks, Jo. I'd love one.'

Jo closed the door quietly behind her. Tilly took a deep, shuddering breath, and closed her eyes. The pain on her father's face was too much to bear.

'What's up?' he said again, his voice hoarse. He was fighting back tears, she realised.

'Just … all got a bit much for me, I suppose,' she whispered. She couldn't tell him the whole truth. Not now. Not yet.

'You should have talked to me! I'd do anything for you, you know that, pet? Jo said you were … having a breakdown of some sort. God, when I heard …'

Tilly didn't want to think about how he'd have felt. A pang of guilt coursed through her, adding to the pain, pushing her deeper into that dark pit of misery. 'Sorry, Dad. I … didn't want you to be worried.'

'Of course I worry. Just want my girl to be happy again.'

She forced a weak smile to her face and reached for his hand. Her lovely dad, just trying to do what was best for her. But he wouldn't be able to fix everything. 'I know you do. Thanks.'

'Look, pet, we have a bit of a plan. I think you should come home with me. Down to Dorset. I'll sort out the spare room for you, and then you can rest and relax as much as you need. Jo's been so good, but you can't stay here forever. She's got her own family to look after.'

Tilly tried to imagine life with her dad in his bungalow by

the sea. He'd lived on his own since her mum died nearly three years ago. He spent all his spare time helping with the restoration of an old railway. He'd probably try to get her involved in it too, but right now, she couldn't imagine doing anything other than lying in bed, under a thick duvet to insulate her from the rest of the world.

'It'll be good for you, pet. Sea air. The views from the cliff top. Getting away from London and all … everything that's happened.'

'He's right, Tils.' Jo had come back in with a couple of mugs of tea. She handed one to Ken, put the other on a bedside cabinet then perched on the end of the bed and took Tilly's hand. 'Listen, mate, you know you can stay here as long as you want. I'm not chucking you out. But have a think about it. New surroundings, living by the coast in Coombe Regis, a slower pace of life a long way from Ian and the rest of it. Might help get your head straight.'

'I'm not sure it'll ever feel straight again,' Tilly said, but regretted it when she saw Ken wince. He didn't know all of it. Unless Jo had told him.

'It will, in time. Believe me.' Ken put his tea down on a plastic toy crate and slid to his knees beside the bed. 'Come here, pet. Let your old dad give you a cuddle. Can't promise to make it all better in one go, but the Lord knows I'll give it my best shot.'

And then he scooped her up into a sitting position, wrapped his arms around her and held her tight. Tilly held on to him, letting his strength seep into her, resting her head against his shoulder and finally giving in to the urge to cry – huge, ugly sobs that shook her body and wracked her soul, but which somehow he seemed to absorb, so that when she finally calmed herself and pushed him gently away, she felt just a tiny bit better, just a touch more able to face the world. Perhaps he and Jo were right. Perhaps a stay on the Dorset coast with Ken would help. It certainly couldn't make her feel any worse.

*

5

Ken slept on Jo's sofa for the next two nights, until Tilly felt ready to face the journey. She felt scared to leave the cocoon of Jo's house, that comforting little pink bedroom in which she felt like a child being cosseted as she recovered from a bout of chicken pox. But 5-year-old Amber deserved to have her bedroom back.

At last it was time to leave. After dropping her kids off at school and nursery, Jo had made a trip to the house Tilly had once shared with Ian, and filled a suitcase with clothes. 'I picked up mostly jeans, T-shirts, fleeces,' she said. 'I guessed you wouldn't want your smart work clothes. If you need anything more I'll go and fetch it, and bring it when I come to visit.' She hugged Tilly. 'Which won't be too many weeks away, I promise.'

Tilly's eyes filled with tears. Jo had been such a good friend to her through all this. There was no way Tilly could have faced returning to her old marital home to pack, even when Ian wasn't there. And although Ken had offered, Jo had insisted he stay with Tilly rather than risk a confrontation with his son-in-law, which would almost certainly end badly. 'Thanks, Jo. I can always buy anything else if I feel I need it.' Though right now all she felt she'd need was a few pairs of warm pyjamas and maybe a dressing gown.

With effort, she dragged herself into the shower, washed her hair, and dressed in some of the clothes Jo had fetched. When she came downstairs, she found her father and Jo sitting in the kitchen, talking seriously. About her, no doubt. They cared, she reminded herself, even if she no longer cared about herself.

'There you are. You look better for having that shower,' Jo said, with a smile. 'Cup of tea before you go?'

Tilly shrugged. Recently she'd found it impossible to make even the simplest decision. Ken put out a hand to her and squeezed her arm. 'Thanks, Jo, but I think we'll get going. It's a longish drive, and I want to get home before the evening rush hour. Ready, pet?'

She nodded, numbly, and allowed him to shepherd her out to the car. Jo gave her a hug. 'Look after yourself, Tils. Listen to your dad. Do whatever he suggests, promise me. I'll be down to see you in a couple of weeks, I promise. Love you, mate.'

'Thanks, Jo,' Tilly managed to say. The words seemed inadequate, but the effort required to find more was too much. She climbed into the car, put on her seat belt and leaned back against the headrest. Outside, Ken was hugging and thanking Jo, and loading his bag and Tilly's suitcase into the boot. And then he was in the driver's seat beside her, starting the engine, and they were on their way, leaving Jo standing on her driveway, dabbing at her eyes with a tissue. Even Ken's eyes looked suspiciously moist. Far too much crying was going on, Tilly thought, and all of it her fault. But right now, she didn't feel she could do anything about it.

*

The journey passed uneventfully. Ken found a classical music station on the radio, and Tilly let the music wash over her as she stared out of the window at the passing countryside. It was February, the fields were brown and bare and the sky was a dismal grey. The scenery and weather were a perfect match for her frame of mind. Soon it would be spring, there'd be new growth in the fields and hedgerows, birds would sing and lambs would be born, and everyone would look forward to the warmth of summer. Would she? Was there anything to look forward to? She'd lost her job, her husband, her chances of having a family. But now she was here, with her dad, and somehow she had to find a way forward.

She knew she shouldn't dwell on these thoughts. All it did was make her more miserable. She fumbled in her jeans pocket for a crumpled tissue, but it wasn't enough to soak up her neverending tears. Ken glanced over, then rummaged in his pockets and pulled out a cotton handkerchief. 'Here, pet. It's clean, and it'll be easier on your skin than those tissues.'

She took it gratefully. The cotton was soft from having been

7

washed hundreds of times. It had been folded in four and ironed, just the way her mum always used to iron handkerchiefs. An image of her dad standing over the ironing board, carefully ironing and folding hankies flitted through her mind, and despite her misery she found herself smiling faintly.

'That's better, pet. Breaking my heart to see you so upset. When we get home I'll make up the spare bed for you. Then I'll make us shepherd's pie for tea. You always loved your mum's shepherd's pie. I've learned to cook since she … went.' He bit his lip. 'I've had to.'

Tilly reached out to pat his shoulder. Dad had never cooked so much as beans on toast the whole time she was growing up. Mum had done everything. When she died, Tilly had wondered how he'd cope on his own, but she'd been so caught up in her own problems at that time that she'd never asked. To her shame, she realised this was her first visit to Dorset since the funeral. And this wasn't so much a visit – more like a rescue.

'Thanks, Dad. Looking forward to it.' Looking forward. Well, it was a start.

The roads became narrower and more twisty as they drove deep into Dorset. Not far from Coombe Regis Ken slowed down as they passed through a village. 'That's Lynford station house,' he said. 'The first station the restoration society bought. We've laid some track here and we're open at weekends and school holidays, running trains up and down.' Tilly glanced across at the building he was indicating, and saw a sign: *Lynford station: Home of the Michelhampton and Coombe Regis Railway.*

'Is that where you spend your time?' she asked.

He nodded. 'Well, there and Lower Berecombe, which is the next station on the line. Actually, I'm usually at Lower Berecombe. We've not owned it as long, and there's more to do there. Anyway, I'll give you a tour of both as soon as you feel up to it.'

She forced herself to smile at him, then stared out of the

window in silence for the remainder of the journey. Thankfully they were soon in the outskirts of Coombe Regis. She'd been here before – her parents had bought their cliff-top bungalow after they retired, and she and Ian had visited a few times.

Ken drove down a steep street that she remembered, that led straight down to the tiny harbour in the heart of the little town. There, they turned right, past some shops and a small beach, and then through a residential area, heading uphill once more to the cliffs on the west side of town. This part was familiar from her previous visits, and soon they turned into her dad's driveway and she saw the stunning view across the cliff top to the sea. Even with the low grey cloud and sporadic rain, it was beautiful.

'Here at last, then, Tillikins!' Ken jumped out and began unloading the luggage from the boot.

'Great,' she replied, turning away. His use of her old childhood nickname had made her eyes prickle with tears.

She got out of the car and followed Ken inside. It was exactly as she remembered it – exactly as it had been when her mother was alive. A small table stood by the front door, with an over-grown spider plant on it, its offspring dangling down to floor level. Her mother's deep-red winter coat still hung from a hook in the hallway, and as she passed, Tilly reached out to caress it.

'I should send that down to the charity shop, I suppose,' said Ken, noticing her action.

'Not if you're not ready to,' she replied, and the way her dad turned quickly away told her he wasn't.

'Go on into the sitting room,' he said. 'Give me ten minutes to sort out a bedroom for you.'

She did as he said and sat on a sofa that was angled to make the most of the view of the cliff top and sea. There was some-thing calming about resting your eyes on a distant horizon, she thought. It would help, being here.

A few minutes later Ken came back. 'So, you're in this room,' he said, leading her along the corridor and into the guest bedroom, the same one she'd stayed in before with Ian, but her father had decorated it since she'd last been here. It had a double bed with crisp white bed linen, pale-blue painted walls that on a good day would match the sky outside, a dark oak chest of drawers and a chair upholstered in vibrant blues and greens. The floor was a pale laminate, with a fluffy cream rug beside the bed. The whole effect was restful and calming. Ken had put her suitcase on a low table and laid a blue-and-white striped towel on the end of the bed.

Tilly felt tears come to her eyes again. 'Thanks, Dad. This is really nice.'

'I tried to think of what your mother would have done, and did the same,' he said.

'She'd be proud of you.'

'Thanks, pet.' A gruffness in Ken's voice betrayed his usual discomfort with emotional scenes, so Tilly said no more, but set to work pulling clothes she had out of the suitcase, putting her wash bag on the chest of drawers and tucking her pyjamas under the pillow.

'Right then, a cup of tea, and then dinner in about an hour?'

'Got anything stronger? I feel the need … well, it's been a long day.'

Ken nodded. 'There's some wine, but are you sure, after—'

'I'm fine. I won't overdo it.'

A few minutes later, with a glass of buttery Chardonnay in her hand, Tilly was standing by the picture window in the bungalow's sitting room, gazing at the view. The rain was beginning to clear, and dusk was falling. To the west, over the sea, there was a strip of clear sky, turning ever deeper red and purple as the last of the light faded. There was a path along the cliff behind her father's garden.

'Did Jo pack your walking boots or a pair of trainers? It'd be good for you, to get out there and walk along the cliffs. Helps

10

put things in perspective. Well, it helped me, after … you know.'
Ken had come to stand beside her, watching the sunset.

'Yes, maybe I will. Some day.' Tilly topped up her wine. Right
now, the only thing she wanted was to drink enough to blot out
the world and then crawl under a duvet.

Chapter 2

Ted – 1935

Ted Morgan, the stationmaster at Lynford station, had reached the not-insignificant age of 40 years without believing in love at first sight. Indeed, he wasn't sure he believed in love at all; that is to say, not the romantic variety. You loved your parents, your siblings, and children (if you had any), of course. And you could be *infatuated* by a member of the opposite sex. But romantic love was a notion he'd had no experience of, and therefore was disinclined to believe in.

Until, that is, he'd first laid eyes on Annie Galbraith, and love – he could not call it anything else – hit him between the eyes with all the force of a Manning Wardle 2-6-2 tank engine.

Annie was slim, shorter than him by a foot, blonde of hair and blue of eye, her face shaped like a perfect heart. She held her head high as if to make herself taller, giving the impression of someone who was superior, as she was to him, in every way. She arrived each morning on the 08.42 from Michelhampton, strode purposefully through Ted's little branch-line station with a neat black handbag hooked over her arm. In the evenings she returned three minutes before the 17.21 was due to depart. She sat in first class – where else for such a goddess? – in a seat on the left-hand side, one which afforded the best views across the Dorset countryside, on the forty-minute journey to Michelhampton. She had been travelling on these trains every weekday for the past four months, and in all that time he had only ever said three words to her. The same three words, over and over. In his head they were, 'I love you', but they came out of his mouth as 'Thank you, ma'am,' when he inspected her ticket each day. The weekly ticket that, he knew, she bought from the ticket office at Michelhampton, from the lucky, lucky clerk there, who had the pleasure of the longer and more involved interaction associated with purchasing a ticket.

Still, gazing at the ticket, holding it when it was still warm from her own fair hands (that were sometimes encased in soft leather gloves, though not now that the season had progressed towards spring), was a thrill in itself. And then, when he'd completed his check, he could raise his eyes to hers, smile, and say those three words, and she'd nod and take the ticket from him, then turn and hurry onto the platform where the train was waiting. Once, she almost smiled back at him. Twice, she'd said thank you. And on another occasion, when she was a minute or so late, he'd held the train and ushered her onto it as she scurried through the station, her heels clip-clopping on the station's tiled floor. He'd waved her away as she reached for her ticket, and she'd smiled for sure that time before wiping the back of her hand across her brow as she boarded the train as if to say phew! Thank goodness she'd made it, and all thanks to Ted!

He'd discovered her name a month or so after she'd begun commuting regularly. He knew the names of most regulars; certainly those who lived in Lynford or Berecombe, and many of those who lived in Coombe Regis. Michelhampton was larger, further off, and not a place he'd regularly visited himself, so he wasn't as well acquainted with passengers who came from there. In the summer season, most of his passengers were holidaymakers and day-trippers, changing onto the branch line from the main line at Michelhampton.

He wasn't proud of the way he discovered her name. It was a quiet Monday morning, and she was the only passenger alighting from the 8.42. He'd watched her from the door of the station as she walked up the lane towards the village. Then, on a whim, his next duties not being for thirty minutes when a goods train was due, he locked up the station and followed her, at a respectable distance, telling himself he needed to buy some bread and a chop for his dinner, and now was a good time to visit the village shops. She was a little way ahead of him, and he turned a corner only just in time to see the hem of her dress disappearing into the National Provincial Bank. Did she work there? Ted *had* to know. He removed his stationmaster's peaked cap and followed her inside. Perhaps he could pretend he had some banking business to do, ask about opening a savings account or the like. He usually did his own banking at the Midland Bank, a little further up the High Street.

'Hey, Annie! How was your weekend?' Ted heard a girl cashier call out, as the object of his attention disappeared through a door marked Private. A supervisor came up behind the girl. 'Now then, Muriel, attend to this gentleman. You can catch up on Miss Galbraith's gossip during your lunch break.'

Ted suppressed a smile. So his angel's name was Annie Galbraith. He stepped up to the counter and spoke to the cashier for a few moments about the interest rates available on savings accounts. He was furnished with a leaflet, and left, promising to think about it and return at a later date. He had no further glimpses of Annie, but it was enough. He knew her name. This evening when he checked her ticket, he could say to her, 'Good evening, Miss Galbraith.' If he could pluck up the courage to do so, that is.

Eventually, he did, but not until about a week later, when an unseasonably warm day had filled him with vigour, emboldening him just a little. He'd felt himself blush to the roots of his hair as he'd greeted her from the morning train, with a cheery, 'Good morning, Miss Galbraith.' She'd stared at him for a second, then recovered her manners and nodded an acknowledgement with a smile, before hurrying through the station as usual.

That smile. He treasured it. Every tiny, brief second it had been upon him.

*

Ted had been stationmaster at Lynford for fifteen years. He'd worked on the railway for eleven years before that – starting as a porter up the line at Rayne's Cross when he left school aged 14, before being promoted to stationmaster aged 25, the youngest and proudest stationmaster in the whole of Southern Railway at that time. Then, he'd moved to Lynford, where a single building functioned as both station and stationmaster's house. There was a ticket office where his Stationmaster Certificate hung proudly behind the counter, a ladies' waiting room, ladies' and gents' water closets, a small sitting room, kitchen and scullery downstairs. Off the sitting room a narrow staircase rose, twisting back on itself to reach a tiny landing, which led to two small bedrooms. Ted slept in a single bed in the larger of the two, and used the other one for storage, though he cleared it out whenever his sister and her children came to visit. It was a small home, but adequate for his needs.

Behind the station was a goods yard – a siding ran off the main line and stopped inside a large shed. Here, the daily goods trains were shunted and the goods unloaded from wagons directly into trucks, to be delivered locally. Coal came once a week, and the other days brought various different commodities – groceries, goods for the various Lynford shops, occasional livestock bought at markets by local farmers. A larger station would have employed a dedicated goods yard manager, but here, it was Ted's job to organise the goods yard, marshalling the trucks and carts as they turned up to deliver or collect goods, operating the hoist that was used to lift crates off wagons and onto trucks. He was aided in these activities by Fred Wilson, a skinny, sallow, surly lad of 18, who was officially employed as a porter, but in reality took on any job that needed doing, albeit usually with poor grace. 'I'm supposed to be a porter,' he'd grumble, when Ted called on him to help unload a goods wagon. 'If I gets me uniform mussed up on the wagons, Ma will have me guts for garters. And that'll be all down to you, Mr Morgan.'

'Take your jacket off then, lad,' Ted would reply, every time he heard this grumble. 'And put on a set of overalls.'

'They're as mucky inside as the wagons are on the outside.' And Ted would roll his eyes at the boy and get started himself on the task at hand. Fred would soon join in, still muttering but eventually getting the job done.

Every day the post came by rail, too, and Ted brought them into the ticket office, where the Lynford postman collected them for onward delivery. A bundle of morning newspapers arrived on the 07.42, and was left in the ticket office until the newsagent's paperboy collected them on his bicycle with its enormous wicker basket balanced on the back.

There was always something that needed doing, from early morning till mid-evening, in and around the station and goods yard, and of course all of it had to fit around the arrival and departures of the dozen trains a day between Michelhampton and Coombe Regis. Some services were quiet, almost empty, in the winter months, but summer brought an influx of holiday-makers and day-trippers. Most went through to Coombe Regis, but some would stop off at Lynford for a few hours, or maybe overnight, and visit the village's fourteenth-century church and ancient witch's dunking stool that overhung a stream, or spend a day walking over the hills between Lynford and Coombe Regis, which rewarded the more energetic visitors with the best views of anywhere, in all of southern England. At least, Ted thought so. He'd lived all his life in this area and could not imagine a more beautiful place. Why would anyone want to leave? He had no interest in going anywhere. Michelhampton was the furthest he'd been, other than a couple of railway training sessions held in Dorchester. That was a big enough city for his taste. Why anyone would want to go somewhere like London he couldn't understand.

No, Ted was content with his life here in Lynford. Contented and happy for it to continue as it always had – up until the moment he'd fallen in love with Annie Galbraith. Suddenly, making sure the trains ran on time and the railway functioned smoothly seemed no longer enough, and he found himself fantasising about another life, one with Annie by his side, a clutch of children at their feet, a home away from the railway with roses around the door …

Chapter 3

Tilly

Tilly awoke, wondering for a moment where she was. A bright, blue room, with white bed linen. Not her bed with Ian, not Amber's pink princess bedroom. Not the hospital bed she'd spent a few days in either.

It came back to her slowly. Her father's bungalow. Of course. He'd driven her down to Dorset, made her shepherd's pie, and she'd then polished off a bottle of wine. Or was it two? She'd cried a lot, as well. And her dad had loaned her his soft, neatly ironed handkerchiefs and let her cry as much as she needed to.

Her eyes felt sore and her mouth was parched. She needed cold water on her face, a thick coating of moisturiser and about a gallon of tea. As if he had heard her silent cry for help, at that moment Ken tapped on the bedroom door and entered, carrying a large mug.

'Thought you might be in need of this, pet,' he said, placing it on a coaster on the bedside table.

'Cheers, Dad. Did I embarrass myself last night?'

'Not at all. You cried a lot. I hate to see you like that. But I know what I was like, after your mother …'

He turned away, uncomfortable with the intimate talk. 'Want me to open your curtains? Or are you going to go back to sleep? You can do whatever you want, you know. No need to get up for ages. I thought – when you do get up – we could go to Lower Berecombe. To the station. I'll show you what I've been spending all my time doing.' He shuffled towards the door.

'I'll be up soon,' Tilly called after him, as he gently closed the door. Her instinct was just to drink the tea then crawl back under the covers and stay there for the day. But she knew that wouldn't help.

'Promise me,' Jo had said, as she waved Tilly off the day before, 'that'll you let your dad help you. Don't shut him out. Do whatever he suggests, go out with him, look at all his railway stuff. I think it'll help. You said it helped him, after your mum died. Gave him something to do, something to be interested in.'

She'd nodded at Jo, promising she would, and that meant she'd have to make the effort today to get up and dressed and go out with her dad.

*

It was late morning before Tilly was finally up, showered, dressed, with a fried egg on toast and several cups of coffee inside her, at last feeling ready to face the day. She'd spent a few minutes looking round Ken's house, seeing everywhere the evidence that he'd not been able to move on at all since her mother's death. As well as that coat by the front door, her phone still lay on a bedside table, constantly charging although it would never be used again. The smallest of the four bedrooms was still kitted out as her mum's crafting room – the sewing machine set up and threaded ready for use, scraps of cloth for a patchwork quilt strewn over the bed, a pile of craft magazines with Post-it notes marking interesting pages on the floor.

If he hadn't managed to move on yet, what hope was there for her?

'Ready, pet?' Ken said, from where he was standing by the front door, cap in hand, ready to take her out to his beloved station.

'Yeah, sure,' she replied, trying for his sake to summon at least the appearance of enthusiasm.

*

It was just a tumbledown cottage, was Tilly's first thought, as Ken parked outside Lower Berecombe station house. She climbed out of the car and stood for a moment, looking around. Not much to show for the restoration work, she thought. You could just about see that there'd once been a railway through here – behind the station house was the remains of the trackbed, and a straight, flat footpath led off in one direction, signposted 'The Old Station Inn – 5 miles'. A couple of sheds stood to the side of the main building. One, looking just big enough for a man to stand up in, looked as though it had once housed signalling equipment.

'So, this is it,' Ken said, sounding excited to be showing her around his pride and joy at last. 'Obviously Lynford's in better shape but this place is coming along nicely too. Come on in.'

Tilly followed him into the building. Inside the old station was a mess. There was no other way to describe it. Debris everywhere, broken stepladders, ancient pots of paint, mouldering boxes containing who knew what. Ken led her through to a small room that had a hideous orange floral carpet and an old brown velour sofa on which a tabby cat lay curled up, sleeping.

'Sit down. I'll put a pot of water on to boil. We can have a cuppa.' On a rickety-looking table in the corner was a Primus stove, a five-litre container of water, a box of teabags and a couple of chipped mugs. He set to work while Tilly sat down. The cat sniffed at her and then stood, stretched and calmly walked across and onto her lap, where it settled down once again, purring happily. She stroked it, discovering a feeling of calm as she rhythmically smoothed its fur.

'Ah, you've made friends with our resident moggy,' Ken said, looking over his shoulder at her. 'We've no idea where she came from. She just hangs out here, and any railway volunteer that's here feeds her.'

He handed her a mug of tea and sat beside her on the old sofa, chattering away about the railway restoration while Tilly drank her tea, stroked the cat and tried to keep herself composed. Ken seemed totally at home there. He'd been an area manager for a railway company before he retired. 'Glorified stationmaster, essentially,' he'd always said, with a laugh. Railways must be in his blood, Tilly had realised, for as soon as he'd retired and moved to Dorset he'd involved himself in this railway restoration project.

'So, bring your tea with you, and I'll give you a quick tour,' he said, clearly longing to show off what he'd been up to.

She pushed the cat off her lap and stood up. 'Is this where you spend all your time, then?'

'Mostly, yes. This was one of the stations on the line. The Society – the Michelhampton and Coombe Regis Railway Society, that is – bought it a few months ago. It had stood empty for years, after being used as a holiday home back in the Sixties and Seventies. As you can see there's an awful lot of work to do here. Come on, I'll show you.'

She followed him out through a set of double doors that led into what had once been a garden. He stopped a couple of feet away from the door. 'You're now standing on what was once the "down" platform. It was only ever a low platform – about a foot above the height of the trackbed. See the step down?' He walked forward and down a muddy step, and Tilly followed. 'Now we're on the trackbed. Look that way' – he gestured to his left – 'and you can see the footpath that runs along the trackbed from here to Rayne's Cross and the reservoir. It goes over the old viaduct which has amazing views, so it's quite a popular walk. And Rayne's Cross station is now a pub, the Old Station Inn. Lynford is in that direction.' He pointed to the right where a fence ran across the trackbed and there was no footpath.

Tilly turned and looked back at the station house. There were missing roof tiles, the brickwork looked in need of re-pointing, the paintwork was horribly peeling, and the remains of the platforms and trackbed were muddy and overgrown. It looked the way she felt, she thought, feeling a weird kind of empathy with the building.

'Why don't the trains run all the way from Lynford to here?' she asked.

Ken pulled a face. 'We'd love to do that, but we've had to buy back the trackbed from local farmers, bit by bit. Unfortunately, we've been having trouble buying that last piece of the trackbed. Owner won't sell up.' He pointed once again to the fence.

'Why not?'

Ken shrugged. 'Who knows? She's got some sort of long-standing grudge against us but no one really knows what it is. Anyway. Come on, come and see my workshed.' He walked along the old trackbed to just past the station house. Tucked in behind was a large metal shed – it looked like a shipping container. The doors at one end stood open, and inside was what Tilly instantly recognised as paradise for her father. There was a workbench strewn with tools along one side, a couple of rusty railway signals lay on the floor on the other side, and the far end held a large container filled with more rusty metal pieces. Ken picked one up and turned it over, lovingly.

'This is a track spike. These are used to hold the rail to the wooden sleepers. We've acquired thousands of them over the years, and they all need cleaning up before we can use them on a new section of track. And those signals there, those are my next job. Clean them up, get them in working order, repaint them. If we ever manage to buy that bit of land, we'll be wanting to extend the line to here as soon as possible, and then beyond to Rayne's Cross. The owner of the pub there can't wait for us to link up.'

Tilly was only half listening. Her mind was in no state to take in the details of railway restoration. She was gazing instead at the countryside, the gentle rolling hills, copses and hedgerows. 'Dad? Mind if I go for a walk?'

'Er, sure. Shall I come with you?'

She shook her head. 'No thanks. I kind of want to be by myself for a bit.'

'OK.' He looked around at the rusty equipment and greasy tools. 'I suppose this kind of thing isn't really your cup of tea. Go on then. You could walk the old trackbed towards Rayne's Cross, then there's a footpath off to the left through some fields and along a lane that loops back round to here. Takes about an hour. You'll be all right on your own?'

She heard the unspoken words – *you won't do anything silly, will you?* – and nodded. 'I'll be fine. See you back here in a bit, then.'

She headed off along the old railway track, half-heartedly trying to imagine what it might have looked like eighty years ago when steam trains ran a regular service on the line. The path was straight and level, its surface a mixture of grass and gravel. It was flanked by overgrown bushes, some overhanging the trackbed. If ever her father and his restoration society managed to extend the track in this direction, they'd have a job to do to keep the foliage under control.

After a while she came across a gap in the hedge on the left, and a stile set into a short piece of fence. Deciding this must be the place her dad had suggested she leave the trackbed, she climbed over, and headed off across the fields, clad in their winter brown and dull green. Here and there a few sheep grazed on the short grass; in the next field two horses in heavy winter rugs stood dejectedly nose to tail under a tree. Tilly's mind wandered as she walked. She found herself reliving the events that had brought her here to Dorset. It wasn't healthy to do this, she knew – she should look forward rather than back. But her future was too uncertain to dwell on. It was too depressing to think of it. And so she found herself thinking about Ian, the way he'd left her, her redundancy, and her miscarriages. The way it had all come to a head one day and she'd felt there was no way forward. Her dad didn't know about all of it, yet. One day maybe she'd tell him the details, perhaps when she felt strong enough to talk about it.

She crossed a couple of fields, following a lightly trodden path. Ken had said it came out on a lane and looped round back to the station. She stopped and looked around, and realised she had no idea where she was, or what direction the station lay. Where was this lane? The weather was deteriorating – grey skies were becoming darker and the threat of rain hung heavy in the air. She'd been walking for over an hour. She pulled out her phone to call Ken for directions but there was no signal.

A little further on there was a farmhouse. That must have an entrance onto a road, she thought. Maybe from there she'd be able to figure out the way back. She headed towards it and realised she was approaching it from the back, through the farmyard. There were a couple of near-derelict barns and a rusty old tractor sat forlornly to one side, its tyres flat and weeds growing up around it. Not a working farm anymore, then. She headed round to the front of the house, to the gravel track that led to a lane, but then she wasn't sure which direction to walk once she hit the lane.

The farmhouse looked scruffy and uncared for, its front door painted with peeling dark-red paint, but there was a light on inside so it was clear someone lived there. Tilly sighed with relief and knocked on the door to ask for directions.

The door was opened by a stooped woman who looked to be in her eighties. She was wearing an old-fashioned pink nylon housecoat, of a type Tilly had last seen on her own grandmother thirty years before.

'Er, hello, I am sorry to bother you, but could you tell me the way back to Lower Berecombe?' Tilly asked. 'I seem to be a bit l-lost.' To her horror she found her eyes welling up with tears as she spoke.

'Of course, dear, it's not far, but – you look upset? Won't you come in for a moment until you feel better? A cup of tea, that's what you need. And I have a pack of chocolate biscuits somewhere.'

'Oh, but I m-mustn't disturb you,' Tilly said, fumbling in her pocket for a tissue.

'Nonsense. Disturb me from what, daytime television?' The old woman scoffed and rolled her eyes. 'Come on in, dear. I'm not turning away a crying stranger.' She stood back with the door wide open, and Tilly followed her inside. Perhaps a cup of tea was what she needed. Some time away from her thoughts, with someone who knew nothing about her or her troubles.

The old woman had gone into the kitchen – a clean but tatty room that looked as though it had last been refitted in the Seventies. She filled a kettle, switched it on and dropped a couple of teabags into an old brown teapot. 'Sit down, do,' she said, gesturing to the group of mismatched chairs arranged around a battered Formica-covered kitchen table. She took a box of tissues from a work surface and put them in front of Tilly.

Somehow this quiet gesture was too much. As if she hadn't cried enough over recent weeks, Tilly found herself with tears coursing down her face once more. She pulled out a couple of tissues and tried to compose herself while her host finished making tea and laying biscuits on a plate.

A few moments later the old woman put a cup of tea in front of her and sat down. 'I'm Ena Pullen,' she said, pushing the biscuits nearer to Tilly.

'Tilly Thomson,' Tilly replied, taking a biscuit. 'Thank you so much for inviting me in.'

'You look like you are having a tough day,' Ena said. 'I'm not going to ask you what's wrong, but I hope when you leave here you feel a little better than when you arrived. If you do, I'll have done my job.' She smiled, and it was all Tilly could do not to begin crying again. Tea and sympathy always set her off.

Ena chatted about inconsequential things – whether her favourite contestant would win the latest TV reality singing competition, the likelihood of the summer being warm or not, the different types of birds who visited her bird-feeder over the winter months. Tilly listened and nodded but said little in return, allowing the trivial topics to fill her mind, pushing everything else out.

When her tea was drunk, Tilly reluctantly got to her feet and shook Ena's hand. 'Thank you so much. I feel a lot better now, but I'd better get going. Dad will be wondering where I am. Could you just point me in the direction of the old station at Lower Berecombe?'

'The station?' Ena's expression darkened. 'Don't say you are anything to do with that old railway?'

'Well, no, but my dad is … he's part of the society trying to restore it.'

'Is he now …' Ena pressed her lips together and led Tilly out of the kitchen. 'Well, Tilly, as you said, it's time for you to go. Turn left along the lane, keep walking for about ten minutes and you'll reach the village, then go right by the church until you see the station.' Her tone was noticeably colder.

'Is everything OK?' Tilly asked hesitantly as she stepped through the front door.

Ena's previously friendly expression was harsh. 'That railway was the death of my father, and that society's trying to rebuild it. It's all wrong. I want it stopped.' With that she shook her head and closed the door behind Tilly.

*

Tilly found her way back to the station, where Ken had changed into grimy blue overalls and was busy removing rust from one of the old railway signals. He looked up as she approached.

'I was about to send out a search party. Where did you get to?' His tone was joking but she could sense his worry behind it. She told him about her meeting with Ena Pullen and he made a face.

'Oh, her. She's the one who won't sell us that length of trackbed. The death of her father? Rubbish. She's just a miserable old so-and-so who doesn't like change.'

Tilly frowned. She didn't agree with her dad's opinion of the old woman. Ena had seemed kind and caring, right up until the moment when Tilly had mentioned the railway. She wondered idly what could possibly have happened to have elicited such a change.

Chapter 4

Ted

It had become an annual event for the last few years: during the school's October half-term break Ted's sister Norah would arrive with her three children to stay for a few days. They lived in London and loved coming to the country. Norah's husband couldn't spare the time off work, so she'd bring the children by train, herself.

It meant Ted had to clear out the second bedroom so that Norah and her 5-year-old daughter Margot could sleep there, but he didn't mind. It was always a delight to have company. The two boys, Peter aged 12, and Tom aged 10, would sleep downstairs in the parlour. It was a squash in the small house, especially when they all sat around Ted's tiny table at mealtimes, but somehow it worked. Norah would take over cooking duties while she was there, and Ted relished the break from having to do it himself. Plus, she was a fabulous cook, and he always ate well when she was there – her pies, pastries, roasts and desserts were delicious.

Norah arrived on the 14.25 from Michelhampton, one sunny but chilly afternoon. As she alighted from the train amid a cloud of steam, Ted doffed his cap to her but otherwise stuck to his duties. It was most important to ensure the other passengers disembarked safely and that the train left on time, having taken on more water from the water tower. He knew that his sister understood that his duties came first, and indeed, he saw that she had herded the children together and sat them on a bench on the platform, with their luggage beside them, while they waited for him to be free.

At last the train was ready to leave; Ted checked all doors were closed, blew his whistle and waved his flag. He stood watching it until the last carriage was beyond the end of the platform, and then turned to Norah with a smile.

'So good to see you! I trust the journey was pleasant?'

'Ted!' Norah placed her hands on his shoulders and kissed him on both cheeks. 'Yes, it was. We were six minutes delayed reaching Michelhampton from London, but the Coombe Regis train was held for us.'

'Bill must have made good time then, on the way here,' Ted replied. 'Come along then, scallywags. Let's see if Uncle Ted has some biscuits hidden in the cupboard for you.' He picked up Norah's suitcase and holdall and led the way inside, followed by the three whooping children.

A few minutes later the children were sitting around the little kitchen table, each with a glass of orange squash and with a plate of biscuits in the middle. They were arguing at full volume about whether custard creams were nicer than Bourbons, or whether Garibaldi were the best biscuits of all. Ted was pleased he'd made the effort to buy a selection from the village shop. It wasn't something he normally treated himself to, but having always assumed he'd have no children of his own, it was fun to spoil his nephews and niece. He took the cases upstairs and came down again to find Norah had put the kettle on for a cup of tea. He smiled to see her making herself at home. Really, she was the easiest guest in the world, even if she was accompanied by three boisterous children.

'So, Ted, any news?' Norah asked, as she took his brown pottery teapot down from its shelf and spooned tea into it.

It crossed his mind to tell her about Annie, about how he felt every time he saw her, about his crazy dreams that one day Annie would feel the same way about him. Ted had always confided in his big sister. But somehow, this felt too private. Norah would get the wrong idea, and would assume he was walking out with Annie, when he'd never even had a conversation with her. 'Nothing new, no. We had a good summer season, plenty of day-trippers. The line's quiet again now, though. Had a train through yesterday with not a single passenger on it, right through.'

'Does that worry you?'

Ted shook his head. 'Not really, no. The line makes money in the summer. It provides a good service for this area.'

'But if it's not making money all year round, I'd be worried the railway company might be thinking of … I don't know … cutting back, or something? There's a station near one of my friends, up in Yorkshire, that is unmanned now. You have to tell the guard if you want to get off there, and wave a flag if you're at the station and want the train to stop to pick you up. Do tell me to stop fretting, but I'm worried for your job, Ted.' She passed him a cup of tea and they went into the parlour to sit down.

'Bless you, Norah, for worrying about me. But this line is a goods line too, and there's plenty of trade still coming by rail. Lots of work for me here, managing the goods yard.' He reached over and patted her knee. 'My job's safe enough, don't you fret. Now then, what are your plans for the week?'

She smiled. 'Margot wants to feed the ducks in Lynford's pond, and see the witch-stool, so that's all easy enough. The boys want you to show them how to operate the signals. They said you promised as much, last year. And I want to walk along the cliffs at Coombe Regis and have an ice cream sitting on the harbour wall.'

'Might be too cold for that last one, at this time of year,' Ted laughed.

'I don't care. If I'm at the seaside, I want an ice cream, any time of year. I suspect the children would be happy to have one too.'

'Did someone say ice cream?' yelled Peter, from the kitchen. 'Yes please! When, where?'

*

It was Wednesday morning, halfway through Norah's visit. She'd taken Margot off into the village, for some 'girl time' as she'd put it, to feed the ducks and look for squirrels in the park, and do all the things Ted supposed little girls liked to do. Peter and Tom were left in Ted's charge, on strict instructions to behave, not fight each other, and do exactly as their uncle told them, or they'd miss out on the planned trip the next day to Coombe Regis.

'Show us how to operate the signals, Uncle Ted? You promised us last year you would.' Peter was jumping up and down with excitement, as soon as his mother and sister had left.

'All right, then. We've got some time before the next train is due to come through. Now then, you see how there are two tracks running through this station?'

'The up line and the down line?' Tom said, looking at Ted for confirmation.

'That's right. But actually for most of this line, there's only one track. This station is one of the passing places along the line. So if a train coming up from Coombe Regis is late, we have to hold the down train from Michelhampton here, because they can't pass further along. So the signal must be set at stop until the up train has arrived and we know it's safe.'

'What if you've forgotten whether the up train's been through or not? I mean, what if you were in the lav or something, when it came through?' asked Tom.

'Don't be stupid. Why would he forget?' said his brother, but Ted held up a hand.

'It's not a stupid question. You're right, it's essential that there's

31

only one train on the track from here to Coombe Regis at any one time, and also only one from here to Rayne's Cross, the other passing place. And the train drivers need to be certain that the way ahead is clear. So we use tokens.'

'Tokens?' Peter looked confused.

'There is an engraved token for each of the three sections of the line. The train driver cannot progress onto the line until he has the token for it in his possession. So the driver of the train that's now coming up from Coombe Regis will hand me the token for that section of the line, and I'll hand it on to the next down train. He can't leave until he has the token.'

'Clever!' Peter's eyes were shining. 'Can I hand the token to the driver?'

'I don't see why not.' Ted smiled. Such a little thing, but so exciting. He remembered being 12 himself, longing for the day when he could leave school and come to work on the railway himself. It was all he'd ever wanted to do. 'We don't always need the token system, strictly speaking, as often there's only one train running up and down the line. Though we'll generally use it anyway. In the summer when it's busy we run more trains, and they need to be able to pass safely, so the token system is essential then.'

He led them along the side of the track to where the little signal box stood, and ushered them up the few steps inside it. There were four signal levers – one each for each track and each direction. And two points levers, to switch the points where the two tracks became one, just beyond the station in both directions. He showed them all these, and demonstrated how the levers worked – the way to grip them to release the lock and pull down hard until they slotted in place. 'It's important they click into position, so they can't accidentally slip out.'

'Cor, what would happen if one did slip out of position?' Tom asked.

'Could cause a crash, couldn't it, Uncle Ted?' said Peter, always wanting to be the one who knew the most.

'It could. But it's part of my job to make sure that all signals and points are in the correct positions before I leave the signal box. So look, we've got the 11.42 up train coming through soon. The points are set right, but we need to set the up signal to stop. Can you do that, Peter?'

The boy's eyes shone as he leapt forward to the signal lever and got ready to pull it. Tom's lower lip quivered, and Ted ruffled the younger boy's hair. 'Don't fret. You'll get to set the signal to go, when the train's ready to leave.' It did the trick, and Tom grinned happily.

Peter managed the signal with no problem. 'Now then, we need to go back to the platform and get ready to swap the tokens over.'

'Uncle Ted, can I stay here with the signals, ready to change it to clear?' Tom was standing to attention, his hand on the signal lever.

'If you like, but don't touch anything else. I'll give you a wave when it's time to change the signal. All right?'

'Yes, sir!' Tom saluted.

Now it was Peter's turn to pout. 'I didn't get to change a signal all by myself, Uncle Ted. I only did it when you were with me. And as I'm the oldest I should have been given more responsibility, not him.'

Ted sighed. He never did quite understand the children's fine-tuned sense of justice. It was so hard to ensure they were both happy. 'Well, you can have another turn this afternoon. We'll keep things fair.' He led Peter back down to the platform to await the train. It was right on time, and Peter proudly handed over the token to Bill Perkins, the train driver.

'Good lad. We'll make a stationmaster of you yet, won't we, Ted?' said Bill, grinning.

There was only one person alighting from the train, and no one to pick up, so in no time at all Ted was waving his flag to allow the train to move. But the signal was still at stop. He waved again, and saw little Tom's answering wave from the steps of the signal box. But still the signal didn't change.

'Why doesn't he change the signal, the silly boy?' muttered Peter. 'Shall I go and see?'

'Give him a chance,' said Ted, watching the signal box carefully.

'What's the hold up?' Bill leaned out of the cab to ask.

'My younger nephew's in charge of changing the signal.'

'Ha ha! Maybe the poor little nipper can't manage the heavy lever. You'd best go check on him, Ted, or the train'll be late and we can't have that!'

He had a point. Ted hurried up the platform and into the signal box where, sure enough, Tom was pulling on the lever with all his might, leaning all his weight into it and grunting with the effort. 'I can't make it change, Uncle Ted! It's too heavy!'

'Squeeze the handle, like I showed you, lad. That releases it.'

'Nnghh!' Tom did as he was told and the lever released easily, sending him flying backwards across the shed. With a whistle the train shunted forwards. 'I did it!'

'You did indeed, young Tom. Well done.'

Ted was sweating. That was the last time he'd let a child handle the signal levers alone. The train had been two minutes late leaving! He'd have to log that, in his notebooks that contained details of every train that passed through – but he wouldn't log the reason why.

*

Norah and Margot were back at five o'clock. Margot had a bag of sweets in her hand from the village grocery shop, and Norah had a sherbet dip for each of the boys. 'I hope you've been good for your uncle,' she said, and Peter and Tom both nodded solemnly.

'Well, off you go inside and play quietly now till teatime,' Norah told the children, who ran off to the station garden. 'You're so good with the children, Teddy. You'd make an excellent father. I'll put the kettle on for a cuppa.'

'Thanks, Norah. There's a train coming through shortly so I'm busy for a bit.' It was the 17.21. Annie's train. She'd be here soon, passing through the station, and he wanted to be ready for her, with his hair smoothed down, cap on straight, uniform brushed.

'I'll bring the tea through to you,' Norah called, as she made her way to the little kitchen.

Ted busied himself around the station, emptying a litter bin, straightening chairs in the waiting room, stacking the pile of used magazines. The signal was already at stop, so there was nothing more to do. He went out to the platform and looked along the line – no sign of the train yet, but he didn't expect to see it. Back in the ticket office he paced up and down until Norah brought through his cup of tea.

'Here you are, then,' she said, as she handed it to him.

It was at that moment that the station door opened and in came Annie, wearing her deep-green coat that had a pinched in waistline and a matching neat hat. She nodded to him, pulled out her ticket to show him as usual, and then walked through to the platform. It was a fine day so she sat on a bench on the platform rather than use the ladies' waiting room that he'd just tidied up for her. His eyes followed her as always, and it was only when she'd taken a seat that he came back to himself, and realised he was holding his tea at an angle, spilling some over his boots.

'Who is she?' Norah asked, quietly.

'Er, her name's Annie Galbraith, I believe. She works in the National Provincial Bank in Lynford.'

'You like her, don't you?'

He turned to stare at his sister. 'I … I barely know her.'

Norah smiled. 'You don't have to be well acquainted to know how you feel about her.' She took a step closer to Ted and punched his arm, playfully. 'If I didn't know better, I'd think my little brother is in love, at last!'

'I … no … what do you … I mean … well. She's very beautiful.' Ted spluttered as he glanced out to the platform where Annie still sat waiting patiently. She looked up, caught his eye and smiled.

He was blushing furiously, he knew it, but it was time for him to be on the platform too. The train was due in one minute. 'Ahem. We'll talk about this later, Norah.' He put down his cup of tea on the ticket-office counter, straightened his jacket and strode out to the platform just as the train pulled in. He dared not look at Annie as she climbed aboard the first-class carriage, and was for once thankful when all were aboard, he'd set the signal to clear, handed over the token and waved his flag.

Norah joined him on the platform as the train puffed away. She laid a hand on his arm. 'I'm sorry if I embarrassed you. It's just, when that woman walked in – and yes, she is very beautiful – I could see you were smitten. You're my little brother, Ted. You can't hide anything from me! Now then, I noticed she didn't say anything to you. If that was due to my presence, I am sorry.'

Ted shook his head. 'No, we don't as a rule hold any conversations when she passes through.' As a rule? Who was he kidding? He could count on one hand the number of words she'd ever spoken to him.

'Well, I think you should rectify that,' said Norah, with a smile and raised eyebrows. 'Next time you see her, pay her some little compliment. I think she likes you, judging by that lovely smile she gave you. And smile back at her, for goodness' sake! You stared at her today as though she had two heads!'

Had he really? And would it work, if he overcame his shyness and actually spoke to Annie? He only knew her name and where she worked by following her that day. He couldn't very well do that again. Norah was right. It was time he struck up a conversation with Annie. He had nothing to lose. In a few days, when Norah and the children had left, he would try it.

Chapter 5

Tilly

The day after their visit to Lower Berecombe, Ken drove Tilly out to Lynford station. It was a cold but fine day, the smattering of frost that had covered everything overnight was beginning to melt. It was the kind of day, Tilly thought, as they drove along the country lanes between fields dotted with sheep, when in years gone by she'd have felt glad to be alive, joyful just to be a part of such a beautiful world. Maybe one day she'd feel like that again, but it seemed a long way off yet.

'So if you look over there,' Ken was saying, dragging her morbid thoughts back to the present, 'there's a little glimpse of the viaduct. It's miles away but just there, see it?'

She looked where he was pointing and yes, way off in the distance she could see the arches of the viaduct spanning the valley. They were high up here, the road winding around the side of a hill before it dipped down to Lynford village. 'Yes, I see it.'

'I love that view,' he said. 'After your mum died, I used to come here, park just up that lane there, and walk up the hill from where there's an even better view. Something about gazing into the distance helped put everything into perspective. It made me realise life went on, despite all that had happened to me. I always felt more – well, grounded I suppose – after going up there. Ah, pet. I'm probably talking rubbish, aren't I? Maybe one day I should take you up there, for a walk. If you'd like to. It might help.'

'Yes. I think I'd like to,' Tilly said quietly. She'd never heard her father talk in this way before. He'd never opened up about his feelings after her mum died, or how he'd coped. She should do what she could to help him, but how could she do that when she couldn't even help herself?

'So, we're nearly there,' Ken said, as he drove down the hill, and through the little village. 'Worth having a stroll around here too, when you get the chance. Some quaint old buildings. That café there' – he pointed at an imposing building on a corner – 'used to be a bank. And down there's a path to the river Lyn, and there's a little park and an old witch's ducking stool that supposedly dates back to the sixteenth century. I reckon it's a Victorian copy, myself. Anyway, it's worth a look, and the café does a fantastic range of cakes. I miss the cakes your mum used to make.'

'She was such a good baker,' Tilly agreed.

Ken turned into a small car park beside the red brick station building. 'So. Lynford station. Here we are! There are no steam trains running today – we only do school holidays and weekends from Easter to October. But the station's open to visitors, and we have a little tea shop, selling cakes.'

Tilly climbed out of the car, and let her father show her proudly around. 'They'd just begun opening to the public when we first moved here, and I got involved. I couldn't help but join the society. Your mum laughed when I told her. "You've just retired from the railways," she said, "and now you want to work for them again!" Ah, but this is different, I told her. This is fun. Old-fashioned station, steam trains, tinkering with bits of equipment. None of your automated systems we ended up with.' Tilly smiled at the story. She could so easily imagine her mum teasing him about his railway obsession.

'So, in here.' He led her inside. 'This is the old station. A ticket office that we've restored, ladies' waiting room, and through there – that's now the tearooms but would have been the stationmaster's private rooms. He'd have lived here. There are two bedrooms upstairs.'

The station was nicely done up, with a collection of old tables and chairs in the tearooms and a modern kitchen behind. 'Want to see upstairs?' Ken asked. 'It's just used for storage now, but back when the railway was operational it's where the stationmaster and his family would have slept.'

Tilly followed him dutifully upstairs. There was a worn-out carpet on the stairs, and peeling gloss paint on the walls. Someone had stuck photos of the restoration work up with Blu-tack. At the top was a tiny landing with two doors leading off. One was filled with boxes, stacked higgledy-piggledy across the floor. The other contained a single bed with a stained mattress, and more boxes, mostly containing papers and magazines. An electric fan heater stood on top of an old wooden crate.

'Sometimes if a volunteer wants to work here late in the evening they might kip here, in a sleeping bag,' Ken explained, as Tilly looked around. 'Not often, though. There's rumours of a ghost.'

'A ghost?'

Ken chuckled. 'Ah, it's all rubbish. Just an old building creaking a bit at night. Someone died here once, but I don't know any details. They say the ghost of that person haunts the building. Alan'll tell you more about it, if you're interested. He should be around here somewhere. I've never spent the night.'

Tilly shuddered. Nothing would entice her to sleep here, ghost or no ghost. Ena's words – *that railway was the death of my father* – ran through her mind. Could this be what she was referring to?

She laid a hand on the nearest crate. 'What's in all the boxes?'

'That's our archive.' Ken pulled a face. 'There's probably loads of great stuff in there. But who knows? It's all in such a mess, and no one with any time to sort it out.' He looked thoughtful for a moment, then turned to Tilly with a querying expression. 'Don't suppose you'd like to take it on, pet? Go through it, pull out the interesting bits, throw out the rubbish? You're good at that kind of thing. We've got a website too, that needs someone to keep it up to date. Could be something to ... get your teeth into. Help take your mind off ... everything.'

Tilly glanced again into the bedrooms and the daunting piles of boxes and papers. 'I don't know. Not sure I could.' Not sure? The way she felt now she was absolutely certain she wouldn't be able to summon up the energy to root through loads of dusty boxes.

'All I'm saying, love, is if you want to, there's a project for you. This railway, it was the saving of me. Working on it after Margaret was gone was the only thing I was getting up for, each day. I just wonder if it could help you, too. You never know.'

*

Back downstairs, Ken led Tilly through the tearooms and into the ticket office. There were a number of tools strewn about and a barrier blocking off the ticket counter. A table had been set up on the opposite side of the room as a makeshift counter.

'We had all this up and running, but it seems there's some problem behind the ticket counter,' Ken explained. 'An old pipe in there must have corroded and is leaking. Took us ages to see where the water was coming from. Now we're going to have to strip back all that original panelling, get at the problem, replace the pipe, dry it all out and replace the panelling.' He shook his head, but he was grinning. 'One problem after another, in these old buildings.'

Tilly smiled too, despite herself. His enthusiasm was catching, and it was good to see him happy. 'You love it, don't you, Dad?'

'I do indeed, pet. You know me. Never happier than when I've got a bit of DIY or an engineering challenge in front of me. Ah. There's Alan. Come on. I'll introduce you.'

Tilly followed him out onto the station platform, where an old-fashioned luggage trolley, loaded with a couple of battered old leather suitcases, was artfully arranged beside a vintage bench and a restored Fry's chocolate machine. A man who looked to be a few years older than her father approached. He was wearing blue overalls just like the ones Ken had worn yesterday. He had a shock of grey hair and kindly eyes. Tilly warmed to him instantly, despite not really feeling up to meeting new people.

'Ken, lad, this your daughter then? Very pleased to meet you. Going to keep your old man under control, are you?'

Ken chuckled. 'Yes, Al. This is my Tilly. She'll be stopping with me for a bit.'

Tilly shook Alan's hand, and then the two men began chatting about the latest work done on the railway. It was good that her dad had a proper friend here – someone with similar interests to himself, someone he could have a laugh and a joke with, and presumably the occasional pint with, in the local pub. Friends were important when life had thrown you a curve ball.

She tuned out of Ken and Alan's conversation and gazed around at the restored station. It was built of red brick, with grey slates, in a chalet style. Upstairs she could see a window of one of those little bedrooms, while the downstairs was much bigger, incorporating the ticket office, waiting room, and stationmaster's quarters that she'd seen. The outside of the building was immaculate; the society had done a fantastic job restoring it. On the platform, period advertising signs and a departure board had been lovingly restored and displayed. As at Lower Berecombe, the platform was only about a foot above the trackbed. But here the platform was neatly edged with grey bricks and there were rails laid, extending in both directions, with sidings branching off just past the station.

'What do you think?' Ken asked.

'Looks great. Do you get many visitors?'

Alan nodded. 'Oh aye. On the gala days we get thousands. And during the school holidays we do very well, too. Have you shown her the engines? And the museum?'

'There's a museum?' Museums were Tilly's thing. She could spend hours peering at old photos and artefacts, reading up on the history of a place. Maybe there was something she could get interested in here, after all.

'Well, sort of,' Ken said, with an expression Tilly couldn't quite read. He was plotting something, she thought. 'It's over here. I'll catch up with you later, Al.'

'Cheers, mate,' Alan said, as he loped off around the back of the station.

Ken led Tilly along to the end of the platform then around the side of the station building to where an old railway carriage stood on a siding. A set of wooden steps led up to the door at one end. Inside, the seats had been removed and a motley collection of felt-covered boards displayed curling photographs with faded handwritten captions pinned beside them. A handful of old books about steam railways in Dorset lay on a plastic garden chair.

'It's not much. You saw our archive, Tillikins. The society is desperate for someone to go through it all and put together some decent displays showing the history of the railway. We're planning on painting this coach and fitting it out as a proper museum. We've no problem doing the practical work, but those boxes of paperwork just scare everyone off. That's why I hoped ...'

'That I'd take up the challenge?' Tilly shook her head. The thought of spending the next few weeks rummaging through those boxes, piecing together an enticing tale of the railway would have appealed to her once, but now ... no. It was too big a job, too daunting. 'Not sure, Dad. I feel at the moment like I couldn't concentrate on something like that. Maybe later on, I could give it a go.' When she felt she could last more than twenty minutes without crying, perhaps.

Ken hugged her. 'That's fine by me, pet. In your own time. Come on. I need to show you the engine shed. We've got a replica of one of the original engines in there. *Coombe Wanderer*, she's called. Built by Manning Wardle, the same company that built the originals, believe it or not. She's a beauty. We'll have her in action at the next gala day.'

*

Tilly spent much of the day with Ken at the old station, mostly just sitting in the sunshine on a restored wrought-iron bench painted in Southern Railway green, on the platform. Ken handed her a cup of tea from the station café and a couple of editions of the Michelhampton and Coombe Regis Railway Society's magazine to flick through, but she struggled to concentrate. She'd read a few sentences then find her mind wandering off over the events of the last few weeks. And then her eyes would fill with tears again, and she'd have to raise them from the magazine and focus on her father and Alan, who were tinkering with a railway signal on the opposite track.

Ken drove her home in the mid-afternoon and began work on preparing the dinner for that night.

'While I do this, pet, you go out for a walk. It'll do you good. Just head out that way along the cliff path as far as you like, then turn around and come back. As long as you're back before it gets dark.'

'Maybe tomorrow,' she protested, but Ken would not listen.

'Tomorrow it's due to rain all day. Today's a better day to go. Just ten minutes, if that's all you're up to, but believe me, it'll help.'

It was easier to go along with his suggestion than not. Tilly put on her trainers and headed out along the cliff path that ran behind Ken's bungalow away from town. It rose steadily, first fenced on both sides but once she was away from the town there was a fence only on the inland side, keeping walkers out of the fields. There were a few metres of grass between the path and the cliff edge. Tilly took a few steps nearer the edge and peered over. The stony beach was a long way down, with waves crashing onto it. She wondered if the fall would kill a person instantly, or just leave them broken and battered in hospital for months.

Feeling suddenly alone and scared of her own thoughts, she pulled out her phone and punched in Jo's number.

'Hi, Jo. Just letting you know … everything's OK so far.'

'Great! Where are you now?'

'I'm on a walk. On the cliffs. Dad sent me out.'

'Sounds good. It'll help, if you'll let it, Tils. Describe it to me?'

Tilly looked around and searched for the right words. 'The sky's blue, fading to pink, the sea's shimmering in the sunshine, and there are rabbits ahead of me on the path.'

'Sounds glorious. Take me on that walk when I come to visit.'

'Sure.' Tilly took a deep breath. Her friend's voice, making plans for the future, had helped calm her. Jo's visit was something she felt she could look forward to. 'You were right, Jo – it's going to be good for me, living here with Dad for a bit. I'm glad you phoned him and told him.'

'You're doing so well, mate,' Jo said. 'I can't wait to see you again. I'll be there in a fortnight. Sean's happy to stay home with the kids.' Tilly felt a surge of pain and bit her lip at the mention of Jo's children. Her children would have been the same ages as Jo's. They'd have grown up together, gone to school together, played together.

With her first pregnancy, she and Ian had been ecstatic when the blue line showed up on the pregnancy testing kit. They'd only been trying for a couple of months, and Tilly had schooled herself not to be disappointed if they had no luck for ages. But it seemed they were both fertile, and a baby was on the way already. There'd been no sickness, and only a tenderness in her breasts to show that something was different.

And then, at around ten weeks, she began to feel a dull pain, low on the left side of her abdomen. There was a little bit of bleeding too. Tilly came home early from work, tucked herself up on the sofa with a rug and a soothing cup of tea.

'I think I might be losing the baby,' she said to Ian, when he arrived home.

He dropped his bag and sat down heavily opposite her, looking down at the floor. The pain in his eyes when he finally raised his eyes to hers broke her heart. 'How come, Tils? How has it happened?'

She shook her head. 'I don't know.'

'Should we go to hospital?'

'Don't think there's any point, right now.' She reached out a hand to him. 'It might not be a miscarriage. Sometimes people bleed in pregnancy and it turns out to be OK. But not always. Jo lost her first one. She sighed. 'If it's going to happen, it'll happen. I don't think there is anything they can do, in hospital. I'd rather stay here.'

'Can't you do *anything*? Rest or something, try to keep it?' His voice was hoarse with emotion. He really wanted this child, she realised. She hadn't thought he felt so strongly about it.

'I am resting,' she replied. Why wasn't he asking her how she felt; whether she was in any pain?

Later that night the pain increased severely. Tilly was doubled up in agony. This was more pain than Jo had described experiencing. This was far more pain. Tilly couldn't function, couldn't think straight. Ibuprofen made no difference. While Ian paced, muttering about how she must have done something wrong to cause this, she called the out-of-hours doctor's number. Between spasms of pain she described her symptoms.

'You need to go to hospital, right away,' the doctor told her. 'Call an ambulance if there's no one who can drive you.'

Ian had drunk a couple of glasses of wine with his dinner, so she took the doctor's advice and called an ambulance for herself. Thankfully it arrived very quickly. She was diagnosed with an ectopic pregnancy; her fallopian tube had ruptured, and she was in surgery within thirty minutes of being admitted.

'Can you still get pregnant?' Ian had asked, sitting at her bedside after the operation.

'Yes. Though I'll only be firing on one cylinder, as it were, so might not be fertile every month.' It's what she'd been told when they'd prepped her for surgery.

Ian had grimaced. 'Well, as long as we can still have children, I suppose that's all right. How soon until we can try again?'

Tilly put a protective hand on the surgery dressing and winced. 'Give me a chance. They say a couple of months, at least.'

'OK. Well, get well soon, and all that.' Ian had patted her shoulder. It was as much sympathy as she was going to get from him, she'd realised. At the time she'd just excused it as his way of expressing his sadness at their loss.

Six months later, she was pregnant again. Ian had wanted to wrap her up in cotton wool. 'Don't go to your Zumba class. Don't go running. Make sure you get a seat on the bus. This baby is precious to me.'

'And to me!' she'd protested. It was so precious. She wanted children at least as much as Ian did.

But that pregnancy never felt quite right. She couldn't explain why, but it was as though her body didn't want this embryo. At just seven weeks the bleeding started, accompanied by what felt like bad period pains. She knew she was losing the baby, but this time had no chance to tell Ian until it was all over. He was away on a training course with work, and this wasn't something to tell him over the phone. When he returned, and she told him, his first reaction was one of anger.

'Not again! Bloody hell, woman. Having a baby's a natural thing. Why can't you do it?'

She'd been calm throughout the miscarriage, dealing with it with a resigned efficiency. But Ian's outburst was the last straw. She crumpled, throwing herself down onto the sofa, wrapping her arms around her face. 'It's not my fault, Ian! It just … happens. This time it wasn't ectopic. Maybe next time will work.' God, she hoped so. She was 37. They'd left having children until they'd established their careers and bought a big family home. Now Tilly was regretting those decisions. Perhaps in her twenties her body might have made a better job of growing a baby?

It was another year before Tilly became pregnant again. She'd insisted on waiting six months before trying, and then it just took a long time. Ian had been getting more and more frustrated each month, when she told him that no, they'd had no luck this time.

When it finally happened, they were both thrilled, and the news gave a much-needed boost to their relationship. This time the pregnancy felt right. There was breast-tenderness, sickness, a small but definite bump low down on her abdomen.

'This time it'll work. This time we'll end up with a baby,' she told him, and they made plans to decorate a bedroom in readiness, and started looking at catalogues of prams and cots and car seats.

The twelve-week scan showed a tiny but recognisable foetus, waving its little arms around, its heart beating strongly, and they were ecstatic.

Then when the bleeding had started two weeks later, it was Tilly who reacted with anger and disbelief, while Ian was the resigned one.

'How can it be happening again?' she screamed at him. 'Twice is enough. How much more bad luck are we due to have?'

'Shh,' he said, taking her into his arms and patting her back, as though she was a child crying over a broken toy. 'It'll be all right.'

But it wasn't all right. The bleeding continued, the pain intensified and at three o'clock in the morning she had a miscarriage on the bathroom floor. She sobbed, unable to believe that the same happy little person she'd seen on the ultrasound scan a fortnight ago could now be lying here cradled in the palm of her hand, dead.

Ian hadn't wanted to see it. She'd buried the poor thing, a boy she thought, in the garden, as though it was a dead pet. Better than a hospital incinerator. At least this way she could feel close to her child. She took herself to hospital as an afterthought, and was advised to come back only if the pain or bleeding continued longer than seven days. It didn't.

'We should get some tests done,' she said to Ian, 'to find out why I keep miscarrying. Perhaps there's something that can be done.' She was thinking of a friend of a friend, who apparently had a rare blood clotting disorder, that meant tiny blood clots formed. Harmless for the mother but fatal for tiny embryos.

'Sure,' Ian replied, but there was no conviction in his voice. It was as though he'd given up trying, she thought. And yet he'd been the one who most wanted a family.

They'd drifted apart after that. There'd been no discussion of when to start trying again. Tilly had withdrawn into her grief, for the babies that hadn't had a chance, for the family she'd hoped and expected she'd have with Ian, for their relationship, which never recovered from this final disappointment.

*

Tilly had been so caught up in memories that she hadn't realised how far she'd walked. The path had risen well above sea level then dipped down the other side, and she was now walking into a small village that nestled between two high cliffs. Beremouth, it was called, according to signs on the footpath. Tilly felt strung out again; remembering her miscarriages had drained her emotionally. She glanced at her watch. Ken was expecting her back for dinner – but he was cooking a roast and had said it wouldn't be ready till eight o'clock. It'd take her an hour to walk back, and that left her another hour spare before it became dark. She could do with a drink.

Tilly headed on into the little village and found a small pub overlooking the little harbour. It was the kind of place that sold more wine than beer, and served enticing-sounding light meals to visitors. She went inside and ordered a large glass of Pinot Grigio and a bowl of homemade vegetable crisps, and sat at a small table with a view of the sun sinking over the sea. She'd done the right thing coming to stay with her father, she knew. But she needed to somehow keep her mind off all that had happened. Just wallowing in the memories of her miscarriages had set her back. It wouldn't take much to give in to it, and she'd find herself curled on the floor, crying her eyes out. That wouldn't do, in this pub where no one knew her or where she lived.

She knocked back the last of the wine. That had disappeared very quickly. Was there time for another? The sun was just above the horizon now, and with an hour's walk back, perhaps she should leave, rather than risk having to walk the cliff path in total darkness.

As she left the little pub, she realised there was a small corner shop across the street. Without quite realising what she was doing, she crossed over to it, went inside and bought a screw-top bottle of wine. 'To have with dinner,' she told herself, but she'd unscrewed the top before she'd even left the village, and spent the long walk back swigging from it.

Arriving back at Ken's in almost complete darkness, she dropped the empty bottle into his recycling bin and went inside. A roast dinner would help soak up the alcohol. With luck, Ken would have another bottle open.

Chapter 6

Ted

It was lonely without Norah and the children around, but at the same time Ted appreciated having his home back again, the peace and quiet and the return to routine. How on earth one got used to children being always around, he had no idea. Norah seemed immune to the constant noise and bickering, especially that produced by the two boys. Maybe it was different when it was your own flesh and blood. He supposed he'd never know. The chances of him ever having a child seemed very remote. This had never bothered him before, but for some reason now it made him feel sad.

He hadn't forgotten his conversation with Norah about Annie. Indeed, he'd spent many a sleepless night running over scenarios in which he finally plucked up the courage to speak to Annie, to say something more than simply 'thank you' or 'good morning'. Endless scenarios, in which sometimes she'd scorn him and other times she'd smile and stay chatting with him, missing her train to prolong it, accepting the offer of a cup of tea. In one fantasy, she leaned towards him, put a hand on his arm, and kissed him, just lightly, on the lips. He'd been shocked at his reaction to this little daydream. He shouldn't think of her in such a way, not before he'd even spoken to her. It wasn't right.

And still, Monday to Friday, morning and evening, Annie passed through the station on her regular trains. The year was drawing towards its close – it was dusk by mid-afternoon. Ted made sure the station's electric lamps were switched on well before Annie arrived for her train. He also lit a fire each afternoon in the ladies' waiting room, in case she arrived early and wanted to sit in there. It was an extravagance, he knew, as there were so few passengers passing through. But he'd do anything for Annie.

It was a Friday morning, the week after Norah's visit, when he finally took his chance. Annie alighted from her train wearing a bright red coat, matching hat, black stockings and heeled shoes. Her lipstick was the same shade as her coat. Her hair curled around her face, framing it to perfection. Ted held open the ticket-office door for her to pass through, and almost without realising what he was doing, said, 'Good morning, Miss Galbraith. Might I say you look very lovely today. That colour brightens the day for all who see it.'

He felt his cheeks blush to a shade that probably matched her coat as she smiled in response – a gorgeous, wide smile, showing perfect pearl-white teeth. 'Why, thank you, Mr Stationmaster. It's most kind of you to say so.'

'M-my name is Edward Morgan. M-most people call me Ted.' But by the time he'd got the words out, she had gone.

Nevertheless, he'd done it. He'd spoken to her. Complimented her. And been rewarded by a smile and a thank-you. She wouldn't have heard him mumbling his name. But it was a start. Something he could build on. And what a smile she'd given him! He knew he would never forget it, even if he never saw it again.

Ted spent the rest of the day smiling broadly, watching the station clock as it ticked away the minutes until Annie would return for the 17.21. He had the station at its best by mid-afternoon. The platform swept clear of dust. A roaring coal fire in the ladies' waiting room. Flowers – a tiny posy of winter jasmine in a jam jar – on the waiting-room mantelpiece and a cushion, borrowed from his parlour and placed on the best waiting-room chair, completed the setup. His hair was combed and uniform brushed.

But it was 5.20 and there was no sign of Annie. The train pulled in, and Ted asked the driver – it was Bill – to wait a moment. 'A regular, she must have been held up.' He darted out to the street and looked up and down it. The dim streetlamps meant it was hard to be sure, but he could not see anyone approaching. He waited a minute and checked the station clock. 5.23 p.m. Another minute. She'd be here.

But she didn't arrive, and Bill was impatient, and he couldn't hold the train forever. With a sinking heart he set the signal to clear, waved his flag (red, like her coat) and the locomotive released its brakes and puffed out of the station.

Ted was worried. Should he run down to the National Provincial Bank and check if she had left, or if there was some problem, something he could help with? It felt like something that ought to be part of his duty as stationmaster, to ensure regular passengers were safe, and caught their trains. He was on his way out, locking the station door, when he stopped. He wouldn't do this for any other passenger. He'd just assume they'd made other plans. Maybe Annie was working late today, or going out with friends in the village. Maybe she'd be travelling home on a later train. Yes, that was it. She'd be here later. He'd keep the fire going in the waiting room, just in case.

Three hours later, when the last train had passed through the station, Ted doused the fire in the waiting room, threw the little bunch of flowers out onto the track, and locked up. Annie had not caught a train that evening. He spent a sleepless night worrying about what had happened to her.

*

It was Monday before Ted saw Annie again. She was on the usual train in the morning. His heart leapt to see her, and he rushed across the platform to open the carriage door and assist her down from the train.

'Thank you, Mr Stationmaster,' she said, with a smile.

So she hadn't caught his name when he'd spoken to her last week. Or at least, she'd not remembered it. Never mind. He opened his mouth to say something, but at that moment she squealed and stumbled, tripping on a scarf that was trailing out of her bag. He caught her by the arm, saving her from falling headlong out of the carriage onto the platform.

'Miss Galbraith! Are you all right?' he said, as he helped her to regain her balance. He bent to pick up the scarf – a flimsy, lacy affair that could not provide much warmth, he thought.

'Oh no! Look, my coat sleeve!' She was wearing the red coat again, the one he'd complimented her on. She must have caught it on the railway carriage door as she tripped. It was torn – a gash of about three inches from elbow to wrist.

'And you are hurt, too,' Ted said, noticing blood on the silky blouse sleeve that showed through the rent.

'Am I?' She twisted her arm around. 'Oh! I'm bleeding!'

'Come, sit down, Miss Galbraith.' Ted led her gently into the ladies' waiting room. There was no fire lit at this time of the day. He bade her sit in the best chair, which still held the cushion from his own parlour.

'Wait, I need to take this off,' Annie said, unbuttoning her coat, which she removed before sitting down. She then rolled up her torn blouse sleeve. Ted knelt at her side to look at the injury. It was superficial – just a scraping of the skin – but looked sore.

Outside, the train whistled. Bill must be impatient to be off. Ted glanced at his watch and realised he needed to change the signal and let the train leave, or it would be late. 'Wait here. I'll be back in a moment. And I'll fetch something to bathe and dress the wound,' he said.

Once the train was dispatched, he fetched first-aid items from his kitchen and returned to the waiting room. He bathed Annie's wound with as much gentleness as he could muster, inwardly cursing his rough hands and lack of nursing experience. He covered it with a bandage. 'There, Miss Galbraith. That should sort it.'

'You are very kind, Mr Stationmaster. Oh, I cannot keep calling you that. You told me your name last week, but I confess I have forgotten it.'

'E-Edward Morgan,' he stammered. 'But most people call me Ted.'

'Then I shall, too, if you don't mind,' she replied. 'I must ask you, though, how did you know my name?'

Ted felt himself redden. Why did his skin always let his nervousness show? 'I – I heard someone say your name. I was in the bank, where you work ...'

'Ah, yes. I see. But now we are acquainted, please call me Annie.' She smiled and touched his arm as she spoke.

Was it possible for his face to burn any more? 'Y-yes. Thank you. I shall.'

'I should get to work,' Annie said, rolling down her blouse sleeve and buttoning the cuff. 'Too bad about that tear. I have another blouse left in the office I can change into. But my coat! It's new, and look, it's ruined.' Her voice cracked, as though she was fighting back tears.

Ted inspected the rip. It was close to the seam. 'With careful mending that wouldn't show too much, I dare say.'

'I am terrible at sewing. I paid no attention to it in school.'

'Miss Galbraith – Annie, I mean, I could mend it. I do all my own mending, My sister taught me. Perhaps if you borrow an overcoat from me for today – it won't fit but will keep you warm – y-you could leave your lovely red coat here, and I could ...'

'But surely you won't have time to do any sewing? You must be such a busy man.'

'Th-there are gaps, between the trains. I will make the time. Leave it with me. It would be my pleasure.'

She smiled. 'Very well, if you insist.'

He took the coat through to his parlour and collected his own overcoat for Annie to wear for the day. The thought of her arms slipped inside the sleeves where his arms had been, her perfume rubbing off onto the coat's collar – he had to shake his head to stop those thoughts. He took it out and held it out for her to shrug on. It was far too long, the sleeves hanging past her hands, the coat so wide it would fit two of her.

'How does it look?' she asked, twirling round, a shy smile playing at the corners of her mouth.

'Well, it will keep you warm at least,' he replied, and she burst out laughing, a tinkling, rippling sound that went straight to his heart. If he could hear that laugh every day of his life, he'd be a happy man.

'Thank you again, Ted. I shall be back here for the 17.21 as usual. And please don't worry if you find you don't have time to mend my coat.' She picked up her bag, wound the scarf that had caused all the trouble around her neck, and went on her way, leaving Ted standing in the waiting room, with the stupidest grin on his still-blushing face.

*

Annie arrived back at the station a good ten minutes before the 17.21. Ted was busy doing some accounts in the ticket office, and looked up as she walked in. She was smiling as she greeted him – a smile that lit the room.

'I've mended your coat,' Ted said, blushing as he put down his books and came out from behind the counter, bringing her coat. He'd spent hours on it, on and off, all day. He'd had to undo the lining to sew up the tear from the inside, and then re-stitch the sleeve lining into place. He'd taken care to use the smallest possible stitches, working as neatly as he could, silently thanking Norah for teaching him to sew as a child (in return for which, he'd tried to teach her the names of all parts of a steam engine, but she had not been interested in learning them). He'd made a good job of the repair, he knew. His pernickety, perfectionist nature had made sure of that. So what if two or three times he'd lifted the coat to his face and tried to breathe in Annie's scent from it? So what if he'd lovingly stroked the fabric? He'd done what he'd promised.

She took the coat from him and inspected the repair. 'Oh, Ted. That's marvellous! One would hardly realise it had been torn. I could never have managed to do that so neatly. It must have taken you ages. I insist on paying you for your time.'

'I won't hear of such a thing,' Ted objected. 'Let me help you on with it.' She took his overcoat off and draped it across the ticket-office counter, while he held her coat ready for her to slip into.

'Thank you.' That smile, again.

'How is your arm?' he asked.

'Much better. It's only a scratch. I shall take the bandage off tonight. You've been very kind, Ted. I do appreciate it. Oh, here is the train, already!'

For the first time in his life, Ted felt disappointed to see a train pull into his station on time. Why couldn't it have been late, just this once? And was that a little sigh of disappointment from Annie too? He went out onto the platform, watched over the two or three people alighting and offered his hand to Annie to help her climb aboard. She took it, and he relished the feel of her small, soft hand in his. 'Why did you miss the train on Friday evening?' The words were out of his mouth before he realised he was going to say them.

'Friday? Oh, yes, Friday.' She looked suddenly awkward, as though reluctant to answer his question. 'A ... well, a *friend* picked me up from the bank in his motorcar.'

The train whistled, and Ted had to step away, closing the

carriage door. Bill was leaning out of the locomotive's cab. 'Second time today I've had to hurry you along, Ted! What's going on?'

'Just looking after our passengers,' Ted replied, as he ran along the platform to the signal box. Looking after one passenger, at any rate. He pondered on the way Annie had said the word 'friend'. An acquaintance or family friend? He felt insanely jealous of the unknown man. Whoever he was, he'd had the pleasure of Annie's company for an entire evening. He wished he'd never asked her about Friday. If only he hadn't. It would have been better to have remained in blissful ignorance.

Chapter 7

Tilly

Waking up with a hangover was already becoming a habit. Ken brought Tilly tea in bed again, and put it beside her without a word. But she could feel he disapproved of the amount she was drinking. Hell, she disapproved of it herself, in the mornings, when she was suffering from the fallout of the night before. But it helped her forget, and for now, forgetting was what she felt she needed to do.

She crawled out of bed around eleven o'clock. For the first time she thought it was as well she'd lost her job at the same time as losing Ian. How she'd have been able to carry on going to work in this state she didn't know.

It had happened three months after her third and last miscarriage. Tilly knew something was up at work – there'd been talk for nearly a year about a restructuring. But the company would always need payroll administrators, so she'd assumed she was safe. It'd be just a reorganisation – combining a couple of departments, a manager leaving and not being replaced, something like that.

It always was. She'd worked there for fifteen years and it was the third reorganisation she'd been through in that time.

But then she, along with her team of four admin assistants, were called into a meeting in the management offices. There was a brief presentation about how the poor exchange rate, the uncertainty of Brexit, and the rising cost of imports all meant the company had to become leaner and more efficient or else it would go under. And then had come the news that payroll administration could be covered by outsourcing to a third party, who would bring expertise and economies of scale, and so with great regret the company had decided to put all those in the payroll team into a consultation process. They were invited to apply for a job elsewhere in the company, which would entail relocating, or take voluntary redundancy. The redundancy terms were outlined and they were generous – with Tilly's length of service she'd be entitled to eighteen months' pay.

But it was a blow. She'd been good at her job, and the company had been sympathetic to her when she suffered the miscarriages. She'd been coasting since the last one – doing the minimum, trying to get herself back on her feet.

She had no intention of relocating, so had agreed to take the redundancy package. Maybe the time it would give her would allow her to come to terms with her losses and move on. Maybe not having a job would let her focus on her marriage, and try to restore to it some of the joy they'd once had. Eighteen months' pay meant she could afford to wait a good while before doing any job-hunting. Which was just as well, because the very thought of trying to find something else filled her with terror. It had been a very long time since she'd had a job interview or updated her CV.

*

Today, the weather was completely different to the day before – grey, with low clouds threatening rain at any time, and a cold wind off the sea.

'Cliff path doesn't look so enticing today, does it?' Ken commented, as Tilly gazed out of the kitchen window over her late breakfast. 'Good job you had your walk yesterday.'

'Mmm. I think I'll just veg around the house today,' Tilly replied. She could read, perhaps, or watch daytime TV. Ken would no doubt want to go to work on the railway, de-rusting more of those track spikes or whatever they were called, up at Lower Berecombe station.

'Or ...' Ken said, with a shifty look in his eye. 'You could make a start on this.' He went out of the kitchen and returned a moment later with a box. 'Brought it back yesterday. Just in case ...'

'It's one of the ones from Lynford station, is it?'

'Yes, pet. No need to look at it today if you don't want to, but if you get bored ... maybe you could make a start. I thought you could use the dining-room table – spread everything out in there as much as you like. We're all right eating at the kitchen table, aren't we?'

'Sure. You might as well put the box in there. Not promising I'll look at it though.' Tilly wasn't sure how she felt about it. Perhaps if her pounding headache eased up, she could start rummaging through. Right now, she needed a shower. And coffee.

'No problem. When you feel up to it,' Ken said. He said his farewells and headed out, leaving Tilly with the TV remote control and a large mug of black coffee.

*

Ken came back in the mid-afternoon, still in his blue overalls, and with another box of archive material tucked hopefully under his arm. Tilly was dozing on the sofa when he came in, a colourful knitted blanket that her mother had made draped over her.

'Hey. Good day?'

'Yes, pet. Got lots done. Another old signal is ready for use.' He put the box of archive material down on a coffee table.

'More papers? I'm sorry, Dad, I didn't feel up to starting it today.'

He looked disappointed but didn't push the matter. 'No problem. I brought you something else as well. I bought a whole chocolate cake for you, from the Old Bank teashop. Two ticks and I'll bring you a slice along with your cuppa.' Ken went through to the kitchen and came back a little later with the tea and cake which he set down on a side table beside the sofa.

'Thanks, Dad.' Tilly pushed herself upright so she could eat the cake, which was delicious.

Ken was watching her thoughtfully. 'You know, pet, I think it'd be good for you to give yourself a bit of a challenge. Why not have a go at sorting out these boxes? It'll take your mind off … things. The other thing you could consider taking on is—'

'For goodness' sake, Dad.' She fell back on the sofa. 'Stop giving me jobs to do! I'm … not well. I'm not up to all that research and everything. God, I know it helped you after Mum, but I'm not the same. I don't want – I just can't – leave me alone, all right?' She stood up and stormed off to her bedroom. She knew she probably sounded like a petulant teenager, but so what? He was pushing her too hard, too fast. It'd take time to recover from all that had happened. If she was even able to recover, that was.

*

Tilly spent the week doing very little other than lying on the sofa, reading or watching TV, and going for the occasional cliff-top walk. She made no effort to start looking at the archives, and thankfully Ken made no more comments about them. He gently tried to interest her in another visit to the railway, but she declined. The one thing that was keeping her going was the thought that Jo was due to visit at the weekend. She felt more than ready for a top-up of her friend's support and advice.

On Friday at around three o'clock, her phone rang. Assuming

it was Ken asking if she needed anything from the shop on his way home or similar, Tilly answered with 'Hey, Dad!' without even glancing at the screen.

'Tils, mate, it's Jo.' Her friend's broad Yorkshire accent brought a smile to Tilly's face. She couldn't wait to see her.

'Jo! I've got your room all ready, and we've got crispy spiced salmon tonight for dinner. With new potatoes, or would you rather baked? Can do either. Broccoli or salad? Dad wants baked beans but I told him no.'

'Tils, listen. I'm so sorry, but I'm going to have to call it off for this weekend. It's Amber. She's got chicken pox. Caught it at school. Poor little mite's covered in spots and feeling very sorry for herself. Bryony will no doubt get it in a few days' time as well.'

Chicken pox. Tilly's heart sank. She was going to miss seeing her friend because of a bout of stupid chicken pox. She felt a sudden irrational surge of jealousy that Amber would be the one to have Jo near, caring for her this weekend, instead of Tilly. But she pulled herself together. Of course, Jo's children were more important. She forced herself to sound sympathetic, when all she wanted to do was curl up and cry.

'Oh, Jo. I'm so sorry. Poor Amber. Of course, you must stay home and nurse her. Give her a hug from me.'

'I will, mate. Can we rearrange for a few weeks' time, when they're both over it? Actually, it'll have to be after Easter as we're going away then … God, it's such bad timing, but poor Amber. I hate seeing her so poorly.'

After Easter! Tilly fought to keep herself sounding positive. 'Can't be helped. Email me whatever weekends you're free and we'll book in another date.'

'So sorry, mate. I wish I was able to come and see you but, you know.'

'Your kids have to come first. No worries. There'll be another time.'

When she'd hung up, Tilly sat down heavily on the nearest

chair. No Jo this weekend. The one thing in her life she'd been looking forward to. More than looking forward – *depending* on Jo's company this weekend. It would be ten days since she'd arrived at Ken's. She wanted to take Jo on the cliff-top walk, go with her to one of Ken's stations and see what she thought of the railway, get drunk with her and hear her advice on what to do in the long term. She couldn't stay here forever, she knew, but how long would be all right? Ken would say no problem, stay as long as you like, of course, but Jo would be able to advise her what was best. A month here? Two, Six? Or take it week by week?

Tilly had met Jo at university, in their first term. They were next-door neighbours in a hall of residence, sharing a kitchen. Tilly had loved Jo's gruff Yorkshire accent and her no-nonsense Northern personality. They'd hit it off immediately and been inseparable for the following three years. They'd been each other's bridesmaids. Tilly was godmother to Jo's eldest daughter. They'd met up every week while Jo had lived in London, for a drink and a catch-up.

And now Jo couldn't come for her visit. That bottle of Prosecco Tilly had put in the fridge to chill was all for nothing. She might as well put it back in the cupboard. Tilly stood up with a sigh, went to the kitchen and took out the bottle.

Or maybe she should open it anyway. Ken didn't like sparkling wine but there were a few bottles of his favourite real ale that he could drink. Tilly found herself peeling off the foil, untwisting the wire that held the cork in, and easing the cork out with her thumbs without having made a conscious decision to open it.

The cork emerged with a satisfying pop, and Tilly grabbed the nearest thing to hand – a teacup from the draining board – to catch the frothy overflow. She poured herself a large measure into the teacup and drank it, enjoying the way the bubbles tickled her nose.

Her mum would have had a fit, seeing her drink out of a teacup. She fetched a cut-glass champagne flute from the glass cabinet in the dining room. It was from a set that had been a wedding present to her parents, she recalled. As a child she'd never been allowed to touch any of the glasses from the cabinet. Pouring herself another glass, she wondered what would happen to all the wedding presents she and Ian had been given. And all the furniture they'd bought jointly for their house. She supposed he'd want to keep it. Was there anything she wanted? Did she even care? She downed the Prosecco and poured herself more.

*

Tilly had polished off the Prosecco and was halfway through a bottle of red wine, by the time Ken came home at six o'clock.

'Tilly pet, what time is Jo arriving?' he called from the hallway, as he hung up his coat.

'She's not coming.' Tilly suppressed a hiccup. The kitchen was a mess. She'd spilt some wine in her hurry to open another bottle. Her lunch dishes were stacked unwashed in the sink.

'Not coming? Oh no, why?'

'Her kid's got chicken spots. Pox. Chicken pox, I mean.' Tilly waved her hand as she spoke and too late, realised she was holding her wine glass in that hand. A neat arc of red wine sprayed across the kitchen wall.

'Watch out!' Ken leapt forward to take the glass from her. 'Oh, pet. Sorry she's not able to come. Is that why you've started drinking? It's a bit early. And what's this?' He picked up the empty Prosecco bottle and turned to her with a look of concern. 'Tilly, I don't like to say this, and I'm not judging you at all, but don't you think you're drinking a bit much?'

'No, not drinking too much. Just drinking 'cos it helps me forget all the shit.' She put her head down on the kitchen table, face in her arms.

'You've been through a lot. Ian leaving, losing your job, and that miscarriage. I wish I could help, but honestly, I don't think all this drinking does you any good. I don't want to lecture, I know you're a grown-up, but even so. I have to say something. I lost your mum, but I didn't turn to the bottle.'

Tilly shook her head. He didn't know the half of it. 'Three of 'em,' she muttered.

'What, love?'

She raised her head and gazed at him. 'Three. Three bloody miscarriages, Dad! I only told you about the first one. Didn't want to upset you, what with Mum and everything. First one – the ectopic one – you know about that. Then an early one. Seven weeks. Then the third – God, I was about to tell you I was pregnant. Was waiting until it felt safe, and it just about did, we'd had a scan, and then suddenly, all that pain, then the bleeding, and then … Dad, it was a … a boy.' And suddenly she was grieving all over again, for those three babies, who would have been Ken's grandchildren had they lived. She crumpled, head in hands, over the table again, and was only dimly aware of Ken coming to kneel beside her, his arms around her, stroking her hair, as she grieved once more for her lost babies.

'Shh, pet. Your dad's here. I'll do everything I can to help, you know that, pet, don't you? I'm sorry I had a go at you for drinking. I'm sorry I didn't know about the other two miscarriages. I see why you didn't want to tell me at the time. You had Ian still, then. And I suppose you told Jo. Does talking about it help? I'm no counsellor, no good with it all, you know that, but God knows I'll listen and hold you while you cry and whatever else I can do. You're still my little girl, Tilly.'

Did she want to talk about it? Yes, suddenly she did. Not the miscarriages. What was there to say? The babies were gone. But Ian. Ken didn't know the full story of Ian leaving, what he'd said, what his reasons were for wanting to end their fifteen-year marriage. And now – maybe it was the wine, maybe it was the disappointment of not having Jo here to talk things through with, probably it was the combination of the two – but now she wanted nothing more than to talk to Ken. To tell him all about that horrible day when Ian made his announcement. It had been the straw that had broken her.

'Yeah, Dad. It might help to talk.'

'Go on, then. Talk away. Want a cup of tea?'

She sat up, grabbed a tissue to mop her eyes and nodded. And then she told him the entire story of how Ian had dropped his bombshell.

*

His timing couldn't have been worse. It was her last day at work, a month after the redundancies had been announced. There'd been a demoralised attitude in the office ever since the big announcement, and no one had felt up to going to the pub or celebrating in any way. Tilly had switched off her computer, gathered up the few personal items she'd kept on her desk, put on her coat and left, nodding goodbye to her erstwhile colleagues who were all doing the same thing. On the way home she decided she'd at least open a bottle of bubbly with Ian – call it a celebration of being out of the rat race, for a few months at least.

When she reached the three-bed semi she shared with Ian, she realised his car was outside. He normally didn't come home until an hour or more after she did, and often not till much later. There always seemed to be something keeping him at work, a problem, a late meeting, or some office do he needed to attend.

He was in the kitchen, sitting at the table with a cup of tea in his hands. He didn't smile when she walked in.

'So, that's me done, then,' she said, trying to sound cheery though inside she felt like crying. 'No more work. I'm going to give it a couple of months then start job-hunting.' She opened the fridge and took out a bottle of Prosecco that had been chilling there for weeks. 'Fancy celebrating my freedom?' Without waiting

66

for an answer, she tore off the foil, untwisted the wire and popped the cork.

He watched her, unsmiling. 'Tils, there's something I need to talk to you about.'

She took two glasses out of a cupboard and filled them, passing one to Ian. 'Sure. Well, cheers, here's to my freedom.'

He pushed the glass away, untouched. 'Not for me, thanks.'

Great. So she'd be 'celebrating' alone. 'Sure you won't have some? Go on, keep me company. No one in the office felt like going out.'

'No. Listen, Tils, I guess the timing's not great for what I need to say to you, but then again, there's never a good time for this kind of thing.'

She felt suddenly cold inside. 'What kind of thing?'

He sighed. 'We've wanted a baby for so long. I've wanted one since the day we married, but I was happy to wait until you felt ready. I can't wait anymore, though.'

'I guess we can start trying again,' she said. It had been several months since the last miscarriage. Long enough, she supposed.

Ian shook his head. 'I can't put you through the pain of any more miscarriages. It's not fair.'

'What, then?' Was he suggesting they adopt a child, perhaps?

He picked up a coaster and began flipping it around his fingers as though it were a cheerleader's baton. It meant he didn't need to look her in the eye as he spoke, she realised. 'The thing is, I want children so much. If I can't have them with you ...'

'What?' she said again, her voice emerging in a squeak.

'... I'll have them with someone else. Well, with Naomi, to be precise.'

'Naomi?' Tilly had heard the name, and vaguely remembered meeting a pretty blonde at one of Ian's Christmas work parties.

'Yes. Listen, Tils, I'm sorry. It shouldn't have happened like this, but, well, it has. We've been seeing each other for a while now. And ... she's pregnant. Sixteen weeks. All looking good on the scans and everything.' He smiled. 'This time it's going to work. I'm going to be a dad.' He picked up the glass of Prosecco and took a swig.

'She's having a baby?' Tilly whispered. It wasn't making sense. What did he want – for them to adopt Naomi's baby?

'Yes, she is. Well, she and I are having a baby. I know it's difficult, what with you losing your job and all, but there's no great hurry. Move out in a month or so, perhaps? That'd still give us time to get her settled well before the baby comes.'

'Move out?'

He looked sheepish. 'Well, yes, you can hardly stay here when Naomi moves in. We can sort out the legal stuff later. It's OK – you can name me as the guilty party. The house is in my name anyway. I know you've paid something towards the mortgage, but I can compensate you for that, I guess.'

'You're divorcing me?' Tilly stared at him. What he was saying was just not sinking in at all.

'Technically you'll divorce me, for being unfaithful. But yes. This is the end, for us. This children issue – or lack of children – it's so important. If only we'd known you couldn't have them sooner, we could have—'

'Divorced *sooner*?' She spat the words out.

'Well … No, I don't mean it like that. I loved you. Still love you, I guess. But I want children. And Naomi can give me that.'

'Do you love her?'

He hesitated for a moment before saying, 'Yes. Yes, I do. She's glowing in pregnancy.'

'Well *fuck you*, then,' she shouted, grabbing his Prosecco out of his hand and throwing its contents over him.

'I deserved that, I suppose,' he said, his tone infuriatingly mild as he brushed the wine out of his eyes. 'I'll go and stay in Naomi's flat for a few weeks. Just until you're able to find somewhere else.' With that he stood up and left the kitchen, leaving Tilly staring at the chair where he'd been sitting. A few minutes later the front door banged shut, and she realised she was alone. Alone with an almost full bottle of Prosecco to 'celebrate' her new, unwanted freedom from both job and husband. She topped up her glass and stayed sitting exactly where he'd left her, her gaze fixed on her bleak, lonely future.

*

When she'd finished telling her story, she picked up the cup of tea Ken had quietly placed in front of her and sipped it. Ken was silent, but she could see a muscle twitching in his cheek, as though he was clenching and unclenching his jaw. He lifted his own cup of tea but before it reached his mouth, he put it down again, hard, so that some spilled and joined the red wine that already puddled on the table.

'I can't believe it. So he'd been cheating on you with this Naomi. And now she's pregnant. And I'd thought I liked the man.' Ken reached for her hand. 'Tilly, pet, you are definitely better off without him, although I know it might not feel like it right now.' He looked distraught.

'You're right, Dad, I am. Not that I had any choice in it. But I can see now that we'd been drifting apart, after that last miscarriage. I guess there are some things a relationship can't cope with.'

'For some people, it'd make them closer. Shared tragedies.'

'Not us, apparently.' She drank more of her tea. Her half-drunk wine was still there, on the table, but she no longer wanted it. 'Thanks, Dad. For listening. It's definitely helped.' It had, she realised. He knew nearly all of it now. Not everything – but he knew about the miscarriages and Ian, and somehow that made it seem just a tiny bit easier to cope with.

Chapter 8

Ted

Ted was planning to spend a quiet Christmas on his own at Lynford station, as he'd done for so many years. Norah always spent the festive period with her husband and children – there was not enough space for them all in the station anyway, and Ted was not able to go to visit her. He was entitled to a couple of weeks' holiday each year, but never took them. If he'd had a wife and family maybe he'd feel differently, but his life was here, at Lynford station, and he wanted no other. Or at least, that had been true until he'd fallen in love with Annie Galbraith.

The last train before the short closure was to be the 17.21 – Annie's usual train. She was working that day. He'd seen her as usual in the morning, when she'd flashed him a smile and waggled her fingers at him as she hurried through the station in her red coat. Ted had taken pains to make the station look welcoming and festive, festooning the mantelpiece in the waiting room with sprigs of holly, and attaching paper-chains around the edge of the ticket counter. It wasn't much but it was more than he normally did, and it was all for Annie.

To his surprise she returned early that afternoon – just after half past four. Ted was in the process of setting a fire in the waiting room. She sashayed in, humming a Christmas carol, and sat down on one of the chairs.

'Well, Ted, the bank closed early today and we've been sent home. But my father is not expecting me until the usual time, so I wondered – what shall I do for the next half-hour or so? I know, I thought to myself, I'll come and see my favourite stationmaster. So here I am!'

'A-Annie! You're very welcome. I'll just light the fire, and then w-would you like some tea, perhaps?'

He was rewarded with a smile, that lit up the room like a Christmas tree. 'I'd love a cup, but only if you've time to sit and drink one with me.'

He tried to reply but could not trust himself to speak. *But what about your gentleman friend,* he wanted to ask her. *The one with the motorcar.* Instead he simply nodded and hurried off to make the tea, placing his best cups and saucers on a tray, finding a few biscuits to put on a plate. He brought it through and set it down on the waiting-room table, then sat down in a chair beside Annie's. Half an hour in her company! He willed the station clock to slow down so that he could relish every second of it.

'Oh, this is perfect,' Annie said. 'Shall I be mother?'

He was confused for a moment, until he realised she was asking if she should pour the tea. He swallowed and nodded. It was so good to be sitting beside her with little to do until the 17.21 was due.

'Are you staying here for Christmas, Ted?' Annie was asking. 'Or are you visiting someone? That family who stayed here, perhaps?'

'My sister? No. I have to stay here to run the station. There is only one day with no trains. Services restart on Boxing Day.'

'You won't be alone, surely?' Annie put down her cup and

71

placed a hand on his arm. He felt the warmth of her fingers burning through his jacket sleeve.

'I-I … yes. I will be alone. But I have a joint of ham to cook and a book to read and the wireless to listen to.' He did not want her to feel pity for him. He wanted her to love him.

She sighed. 'Poor Ted. I wish I could come to visit you.'

'I would n-not expect you to visit me. I mean, it would be lovely to see you, but of course you will be with your family.' He knew he was blushing as he always did in her presence.

'Just my father.' She pulled a face. 'It won't be the most festive of occasions. To be perfectly honest, I really would much rather spend the day with you tomorrow. But of course, there are no trains so I can't get here.' She gazed into her teacup, apparently deep in thought.

'Y-your father.' Somehow that was all he could say.

'Yes. There's just the two of us at home. Mother died five years ago. Father's a businessman. We have a large house for just the two of us. Sometimes I think I'd prefer to be in a cosy cottage. Or even a little station house!' That laugh again.

'W-will you see anyone else tomorrow? Any f-friends?' He was desperate to know more about the man who'd collected her from work that day.

'No. Just me and my father.' It was as though she'd read his mind. Ted felt a surge of relief that she would not be seeing the other man on Christmas Day. Surely then it could not be anything serious? A small smile came unbidden to his lips.

'Ah, Ted. It would be so wonderful to spend Christmas Day with you. You're such a lovely man. But it's just not possible … this year.' She tilted her head to one side as she gazed at him for a moment, and then glanced at her watch. 'Oh, look, it's almost time for my train. You have signals to set and flags to wave. I must wish you a merry Christmas, say thank you for the tea, and let you be away to your duties.'

And then she stood, bent over him where he still sat in his

72

chair, and kissed him on the cheek, before waltzing out to the platform leaving Ted feeling happier than he had ever felt in his life before.

*

After Christmas, once a week or sometimes more, Annie would arrive early enough to spend a few minutes sitting and chatting with Ted before catching her train. Ted's good spirits lasted right through to mid-January, but then a letter came that changed everything. It was addressed to the stationmaster, type-written on official Southern Railway notepaper.

Please be advised that Mr Gerald Hornsby, Southern Railway's Dorset Area Manager, will be paying a visit on Tuesday 21st January. All staff employed at Lynford station to make themselves available for an important announcement. Mr Hornsby will arrive at approximately eleven o'clock.

Ted frowned as he read it. Arriving eleven o'clock? There was no passenger train due at Lynford in either direction at that time. How could Mr Hornsby arrive then? He had only met the area manager on one previous occasion, when, shortly after taking the job, Hornsby had made a tour of all the stations under his control. Then, he had arrived by train, spending a day visiting each of the stations on the line, alighting from one service and resuming his journey on the next. Ted recalled a short, portly man in his early fifties, with Victorian-style whiskers. A career-man, Ted had thought. One whose aim was to advance up the management ladder, as quickly as possible. Not someone who loved the railways. Hornsby could have worked for any company – he was a pure bureaucrat.

He went out to the goods yard, where Fred Wilson was busy supervising the transfer of a wagonload of coal onto a truck that would deliver it to homes in and around Lynford.

'Your attention for a moment, Fred. I've had word that next

Tuesday morning we have the area manager paying us a visit. There's to be an important announcement. I need you to be here, just for that meeting. In your best uniform, smart as you can manage, if you please.' Fred had a habit of turning up with food stains on his jacket, his hair unwashed, his hands filthy. While it didn't matter if he was working in the goods yard, at times Fred was needed on the platform, acting as a porter. His unkempt appearance gave a bad impression to passengers, Ted thought, especially in the summer months when they were busy with holidaymakers. He'd seen some wrinkle their noses as Fred, his expression surly, loaded their suitcases onto the small luggage-van that was part of the last carriage of every passenger train.

'Supposed to be my day off,' said Fred, flinging a sack of coal onto the truck.

'I know, and I'm sorry. But the letter says all staff are to attend the meeting. It'll probably only take a short while. Let's make a good impression, eh? You never know, could be a pay rise for us, in the pipeline.' Unlikely, Ted knew, but saying that might help get Fred to attend the meeting, properly attired.

'Huh. Been a long time since I had a pay rise. All right, I'll come. Only for an hour, mind. Then I'm off. Promised my girl I'd take her out in the afternoon.'

'Good. Thank you.' How Fred had managed to get himself a girlfriend, Ted would never know. But he'd been courting for a while, now. There was someone for everyone, Ted supposed, though he'd always assumed he himself was not part of that 'everyone'. Could Annie be his 'someone'? He doubted it. Even though they were spending more and more time together, there were still those days when she was not on the evening train. The thought of her *friend with a motorcar* made Ted press his lips together. How was it possible to be so envious of someone you'd never met?

*

A little later that day, when the 14.25 arrived slightly early, Ted took the chance to talk to its driver, Bill Perkins, about the mysterious announcement.

'I don't know what it is, Ted. But funny thing is, the other stationmasters have had the same letter. Sounds like Hornsby is going to be paying a visit to all the stations next week. And us drivers and firemen have been called to a meeting up at Michelhampton, at the end of the day. Must be something big.' Bill was still in his locomotive's cab, while Ted stood on the platform, one foot on the cab's footplate.

'Perhaps they're expanding the line? There was always talk about running another branch off it, down to the coast at Beremouth.' The original plans, from the 1890s, had included this second branch, with a junction just outside Lynford station. If built, it would do for the sleepy coastal town of Beremouth what the existing line had done for Coombe Regis – bringing in thousands of day-trippers all summer long.

Bill laughed. 'You think that's likely? Sorry, Ted. More likely my lovely *Coombe Explorer* here' – he patted the locomotive's cab – 'will grow wings and fly. We carry barely enough passengers to keep this branch going.'

'We're full to bursting during summer weekends!'

'But is it enough to finance the rest of the year?' Bill shook his head. 'Sometimes I run end to end completely empty, carrying nothing but the post. An expensive way to deliver a few letters. You're closer to the accounts than I am, Ted. You tell me. Does this branch line make money for Southern Railway, overall?'

'I only know the figures for Lynford,' Ted replied. 'And most people buy their tickets at Michelhampton or Coombe Regis. I hope to God you're not right. How would this area survive without a railway? How would the goods get through? Coombe Regis owes everything to this line. It was nothing before the railway came, and if the railway closed, it'd decline again.'

'You're living in the past, Ted, mate. The roads are so much better now than they were last century. The goods would be moved about by road. The tourists would still come – by omnibus. There's a new service just started, that's going to run from Michelhampton to Coombe Regis all year round. My neighbour tried it out and said it's quicker than the train, and stops in all the village centres, so it's more convenient, too.'

Ted didn't know how to respond to that. The railway was his life, and he'd assumed it was the lifeblood of the whole area, too.

'Well, then, Ted. Right now we've still got a railway to run, and I think I'd best be off, now. We'll hear soon enough what's in store for us.'

'Indeed we will.' Ted nodded to Bill, stepped away from the train and went off to change the signal and do the final checks to allow the train to depart. There were a half-dozen passengers on board. Not bad for middle of the day, on a Wednesday in January. The railways surely couldn't be in such a bad way that the company were considering closing it. Bill Perkins must be wrong. Ted certainly hoped so.

*

It seemed a long wait until Tuesday finally rolled around. Ted had spent all his spare time on Sunday making sure the station was in the best condition possible. He'd swept the goods yard, weeded the track-sides, repainted the windowsills on the front of the station, cleaned the station signs, polished the ticket-office floor. He'd also ensured all the trains – the reduced service that operated on winter weekends – ran on time. Like clockwork. He was good at his job, he knew. It was all he'd ever wanted to do. If the railway did close, what on earth would he do then? Look for a job as stationmaster on some other line, he supposed, though the thought of moving away from Lynford – away from Annie! – filled him with horror.

And that's when it really hit him. If the railway did close, even if he found another job locally, he would no longer see her twice a day. Their occasional chats when she came early for her train would end. There would be no chance of a repeat of that magical Christmas Eve, when he had felt the softness of her hand and then her lips against his cheek. Those moments that he lived for and could no longer imagine life without.

No, the railway could not close. He could not contemplate losing this way of life.

On Monday evening Ted switched on his wireless to listen to the day's news. A statement from Sandringham House, where King George V lay dying, was read out. 'The King's life is moving peacefully towards its close,' the king's physician had said.

'God bless him,' Ted muttered to himself. 'And I pray that the Michelhampton and Coombe Regis Railway is not going the same way.'

The first train of the day on Tuesday, the 07.42 from Michelhampton, brought the day's newspapers as usual. 'Heard the news?' Bill shouted from the cab, as he threw the bundles of newspapers onto the platform. For one heart-stopping moment Ted thought Bill had heard something about the railway, before Mr Hornsby's big announcement, but then he saw the newspapers' headlines: *DEATH OF THE KING*, above a full-page picture of the late George V.

'He's gone, then,' Ted said.

'Heard it on the wireless yesterday that they didn't expect him to last long,' Bill said. 'Very sad. End of an era.'

'It is, that,' Ted replied, praying again that another era wasn't about to end.

Fred turned up at five minutes to eleven, looking just about respectable. 'We'll use the ladies' waiting room for the meeting,' Ted said. 'Unlikely to be any ladies needing it for the next half-hour. Make yourself useful, Fred, and bank up the fire in there.'

'It's my day off,' Fred grumbled. 'I'm not working. I'll go and sit down till the big-wig gets here.'

Ted rolled his eyes but didn't push the point. The waiting room was ready, anyway. He stayed in the ticket office, from where he could keep an eye on the street outside. Why Mr Hornsby was arriving by road and not rail, he couldn't understand. It'd cost the company more to lay on a car and driver for him, when he could use his own company's trains for free.

At last, at just after eleven, a Bentley pulled up outside. Its chauffeur got out and opened the rear door for Mr Hornsby. He was carrying a briefcase and his expression was grim. He was accompanied by a nervous-looking younger man Ted had not seen before. The two men entered the station and at Ted's invitation, followed him through to the ladies' waiting room.

'I thought we'd be most comfortable in here,' Ted said, throwing a few more lumps of coal onto the fire. It was a chilly day.

'As you wish. This won't take too long. Just you, Morgan, and the lad here, is it?' Mr Hornsby said, indicating Fred.

'Yes, just us.'

'Right. Well, you'll have realised, I suppose, that times are tough for railways right now. Every year the roads improve, bus services increase, people buy private cars and stop using the trains. Especially somewhere like this, where the countryside works against the railways. Trucks and motorcars can get up and down hills far easier than trains, as you well know.'

Ted nodded. He did not like the way this was going.

'As a company, we have to be efficient. We're here to provide a service, of course, but we're also here to make money for our shareholders. And I'm sorry to say that the Michelhampton and Coombe Regis line does not do that.'

'But, in the summer—' Ted began.

Hornsby held up a podgy hand. 'In the summer, of course it does well. But six weeks of full trains does not earn the company enough to subsidise the rest of the year.'

'So what—'

Again the hand was raised, and this time Hornsby glared at

Ted. 'I'm getting to that. The company board has decided, and rightly so, in my opinion, that we have no choice but to close this line. We will keep it open for one more summer season, and then close the line in September. All employees will of course receive severance pay, and every effort will be made to help you find new employment. For some, such as train drivers, jobs will be offered elsewhere on our network.'

'But ... will the line open again next summer?' Ted could not believe it. He glanced over at Fred to gauge his reaction, but the boy looked unconcerned, more interested in what he'd picked from his nose, that was now stuck to the end of his finger.

'No, the line closes for good, this September.'

The King dead, and the railway receiving its death notice, on the same day. 'Would some other company not consider buying it? It could be made profitable, I'm sure—'

'Morgan, do you not think the company has explored all angles? The decision has been made, and that's final. I have here' – he pulled a document out of his briefcase and handed it to Ted – 'a paper explaining the details of the closure and the reasoning behind it. Read and digest it. Nearer the time, I shall visit again to talk about plans for dismantling the railway. You may leave the company's employ on the last day of operation, or if you prefer, there will be a little more work after that overseeing the disposal of assets. Of course, when the station house is sold, you will need to find alternative accommodation.'

Ted felt the words hit him like a punch to the gut. He was to lose his home, his job, his beloved railway, all in just a few short months. He'd lose too, any chance he had, however slight, of a relationship with Annie. Everything would change. He had never coped well with change, and this time there was so much more at stake than ever before. He tried to imagine what his future might hold but beyond September it looked like a dark and featureless void.

Chapter 9

Tilly

Tilly spent the next day in bed. Although talking to Ken had helped, she still felt the absence of Jo like a bereavement. The day was a fine one, and if Jo had been there, they'd have walked the cliffs, talking non-stop. Tilly would have delved deeply into her feelings, and Jo would have listened and advised and helped her make sense of it, come to terms with it a little.

It was tempting to reach for another bottle of wine, but she resisted, ashamed of her behaviour the day before. Ken would hate it if she got drunk again. She had to try to find another way. But somehow today she could not bring herself to get up and dressed, and instead indulged herself in an all-day lie-in, reading books, leaving her bed only to make cups of tea or forage for junk food in the kitchen.

The next morning, Sunday, Ken stood in the doorway of her room with his arms folded.

'Right, pet, one day in bed is enough. There's something I want to show you. I'm going to make us a cooked breakfast, and then

I need you up and dressed and ready to go out by ten o'clock. In walking gear. All right?'

Tilly nodded mutely. He was sounding like Jo. She wondered if perhaps he'd rung Jo to find out how best to deal with her. But he was right. One day was enough. She hauled herself out of bed and into the shower, wondering what it was that Ken wanted to show her. No doubt something related to the railway. She steeled herself to pretend to be interested in it, for his sake.

*

An hour later, at Lynford station, Ken parked his car and opened the passenger door for Tilly. Such an old-fashioned gent, she thought, smiling her thanks. Instead of going into the station, Ken led her around the back, past the engine sheds and onto the trackbed that led northwards from the station, the opposite way to the rebuilt part of the line.

'So we're heading towards Lower Berecombe station here. If only that woman could be persuaded to sell her bit of trackbed, we'd be extending the line to join up the stations in no time,' Ken said, as they began walking. 'We already own this part of the trackbed, but there's no point extending until we can link up to Lower Berecombe. There's nowhere along here we could even build a temporary halt.'

As they walked, Tilly could see what he meant. This part of the line was in a cutting that became gradually deeper. The steep sides were covered with a dense mix of bramble and gorse, some of last year's blackberries rotting on the stems. The new season's gorse flowers were just beginning to emerge, adding occasional vibrant splashes of yellow to the banks and a vanilla scent to the air.

'People used to lean out of the carriage windows plucking blackberries as the train passed through this section,' Ken said. 'Imagine – no health and safety regulations back then!'

'Where are we heading, Dad? What did you want to show

me?' It was nice enough being out on a pleasant if cold day, but they'd been walking for some time in the cutting, with no view.

'Just around this next bend, you'll see,' Ken said.

Around the bend the cutting grew even deeper, and then ahead of them a tunnel came into view. It looked dark and forbidding.

'That tunnel? Is it safe?'

'Yes, perfectly safe. We own it, and we've had it inspected by engineers. It was built to last. Just the other side of it is Miss Pullen's land. Anyway, in you go.'

'Inside?'

'Yes. I suppose I should have brought a torch.'

'I'll use my phone,' said Tilly, pulling it out and switching on its torch function.

They walked on, and about a third of the way in on the right Ken stopped. 'Shine the light on the brickwork here, about head height.'

She did as he asked and watched him as he peered at the tunnel wall. 'Maybe a bit further on.' He walked on a little way then stubbed his toe on a rock that lay at the side of the tunnel. 'Ouch. Oh yes, I remember now. I put that there to mark the spot. Here, shine the phone this way, pet.'

And there, carved into the brickwork of the tunnel wall, were some words. Tilly moved closer to read it, running her fingers over the words. 'Annie Galbraith. I will love you forever. T.M.' she read. 'Wow. A love letter deep in a tunnel. Who were they?'

Although she couldn't see him, she knew Ken was smiling as he replied. 'We don't know. The engineer discovered the carving when he inspected the tunnel. I'm hoping … it might inspire you … to do a bit of investigation?'

'They could be anyone. Could be kids. Could have been carved any time since the tunnel was built.'

'We think it's quite old. The engineer scraped off a lot of dirt to make it clearer to read.'

'Well, if I ever start looking at those archives I can see if the name or initials crop up anywhere, I guess. Or Google them, see if anything turns up. Not promising, though.' Tilly flicked her phone into camera mode and took a few photos of the carving with flash. 'Intriguing.'

'I was hoping you'd think that,' said Ken, as they began making their way out of the tunnel.

*

Tilly spent the following week trying not to brood on her problems, trying not to drink too much, and endeavouring to get out for walks as often as she could. It was only when out in the fresh air that she was able to feel there could be some way forward for her. She made a new arrangement for Jo to visit – sadly not for several weeks as Jo's husband worked shifts and had no free weekends to allow him to look after their children while Jo visited Tilly.

'But we can talk on the phone every couple of days, mate,' Jo had said, her no-nonsense tone of voice helping to ground Tilly. 'And you phone me if ever you feel things are getting on top of you again. Day or night, I'm there for you. God, I'm so sorry about last weekend. I should have stayed on the phone longer with you. Had no idea it'd set you back. I felt awful when your dad rang to tell me.'

'I had no idea that would happen either,' Tilly had replied. 'I guess I'm still a long way off feeling well again.'

'Takes time, mate, takes time.'

There was to be a gala weekend at Easter, to mark the start of the new opening season for the railway. Ken spent every dinner time discussing plans for it with Tilly, and despite herself she found herself getting caught up in the excitement of it.

'You'll come along, then? Maybe help serving teas or something?' Ken said.

'OK. It'll take my mind off things, I suppose.'

He smiled. 'It will, that. It'll be so busy you won't have time to think of anything else.'

*

The gala ran over the three days of the Easter weekend – Saturday to Monday. The Society ran a steam train every half-hour along the track at Lynford. A marquee had been erected in the Lynford station grounds, to allow for more café seating. Visitors could come in to look around for free or could pay for a trip on the train. A popular option was the 'full MCR experience' – a trip on the train, a guided tour of the engine shed and the chance to work the signals, plus a complementary hot drink and a cake.

Tilly had agreed to work as a waitress for the three days, and Ken was busy taking the guided tours and supervising people in the signal box. Alan was driving the trains. Despite an unpromising forecast, the rain held off for all three days, and visitor numbers were exceptional.

On Monday, the final day, Ken and Tilly took a break together, eating a late lunch in a corner of the marquee.

'Glad it's nearly over, pet?' asked Ken.

Tilly smiled. 'It's been hard work, but I've kind of enjoyed it. Makes a change from watching daytime TV. How's it been for you?'

'Busy. I'm exhausted. Had a bit of fun today, when a young lad on the full MCR experience couldn't quite work the signal. It was too heavy for him. He was desperately trying to pull the lever to change the signal, wasn't squeezing it fully, refusing to let me step in to help. Did you hear the train whistle? That was to hurry things up – Alan's not supposed to move until the signal's set at clear.'

'Yes, I heard the whistle and thought it was just Alan showing off. So what happened in the end?'

'Eventually he listened to me telling him to squeeze as well as pull, and the lever moved so easily then he ended up falling

84

backwards across the signal box. Thankfully didn't hurt himself, though. Might need to put a minimum age limit for children handling the signals in future galas.' Ken chuckled. 'Ah well. He won't forget that experience in a hurry. Kids love changing the signals and seeing how it all works.'

'You love showing the kids round, don't you?' said Tilly. He'd have made such a good grandfather. The best, like he'd been the best possible father. And still was. But now that she was 39 and in the process of getting divorced, it didn't seem likely he'd ever get the chance.

'I do, indeed.' He smiled. 'Listen, a few of us were talking about going to the pub, the Angler's Tavern down in Coombe Regis, to celebrate the end of the gala. Want to come along? Only for an hour or so, mind.'

He was still keeping an eye on her drinking, she knew, but for the last couple of weeks she'd only had a glass or two of wine with dinner. She'd had no more blow-out sessions, and had not drunk alone, only when Ken was joining her. And she'd not broken down in tears, either. Well maybe once or twice at night, in bed, alone. But Jo had said that was normal, and better to cry a little than bottle it up.

*

There was quite a gang of Society members in the Angler's Tavern that evening. The gala weekend had been a huge success, and everyone was tired but elated.

'First round's on the Society,' announced Geoff Hill, the society's chairman, as he took everyone's orders.

It was the first time Tilly had been in a pub since going into the one along the coast in Beremouth alone in her first week at Ken's. That night had not gone well. She'd be all right today, she thought. Ken was here, and Alan, and the rest of them. She'd just sip her wine slowly and have no more than two glasses. She and

Ken had gone home to change, and then walked down the hill to the pub that was situated right on the quayside.

'Cheers, then!' said Ken, clinking his pint glass against Tilly's and Alan's. 'Here's to a job well done.'

'Imagine in a few years,' said Alan, 'when old misery-guts has sold her bit of land to us, and we've linked Lynford through to Lower Berecombe.'

'She's not a misery-guts,' Tilly said. 'She was kind to me when I called at her house, that day I was lost.'

'Well, I don't know about that but she's certainly miserable when it comes to the railway. If she'd sell up, we could extend the line right the way to Rayne's Cross. The owner of the Old Station Inn there is desperate for that to happen. Loads of visitors would get on the train at Lynford, up to the Rayne's Cross for a pub lunch before coming back again. We'd be raking it in, and so would he!' Ken's eyes were gleaming.

'And the line would go through the tunnel and over the viaduct. So much more to offer.' Alan sighed and shook his head. 'Don't suppose it'll be any time soon, sadly.'

'Didn't your uncle have something to do with the railway?' Tilly asked Alan. 'Dad was telling me.'

'Yes, he was employed on it. Not entirely sure what he did – porter or something. I've been more involved in the practical side of things, driving engines and such, than looking into the history. I'd love to know, though.'

'Do you know what happened to him when the railway closed?'

Alan shrugged and shook his head. 'Died when I was tiny, and Mum never spoke about him much. I'm the youngest of four. Only the three oldest ever met him. My brothers have memories of coming to stay in a station house, where they had to sleep on the sitting-room floor. They loved it.'

The evening passed quickly and enjoyably, and it seemed no time at all before Alan was putting on his jacket and bidding them goodnight. Ken looked at Tilly. 'Well, pet, it's gone ten, and I'm in need of my beauty sleep. Shall we go?'

Tilly looked at her glass. It was her third, all had been large ones, and she still had half of it to drink. 'I'll stay and finish this. There are some other Society members still here – I'll go and chat to them. See you later, Dad.'

He looked a little worried. 'You sure? Don't be too late back, will you? You've got your key?'

She patted her pocket. 'Yes, got it. Bye then, Dad.'

As Ken left, Tilly got up and went over to join the other Society members, and before long was laughing and bantering with them as though she'd known them for years. She accepted another drink from someone, and then as that party gradually thinned down, she looked around the pub to see if there was anyone else from the railway. She couldn't remember having enjoyed an evening so much for a very long time.

'Lost someone?' asked a man who'd seen her scanning the pub. He had a pleasant, open face and attractive dark-blond curls.

She shook her head. 'Just wondering if there's anyone left I can have a drink with,' she replied.

He smiled. 'How about me? My mates have just left. I was going to call it a night, but if you'd like to sit and chat ... I'm all yours.'

She hesitated for a moment. She should go back to her dad's, really, but, it was still well before midnight, she'd only had four glasses, and she was having a good time. She deserved a good time, didn't she, after everything? 'Yes, why not? I'm Tilly, by the way.' She held out her hand and he shook it. His palm was warm and dry.

'Pleased to meet you, Tilly. Rob Coogan. Now then, what can I get you?'

'A glass of Pinot Grigio would be lovely.'

As he went to the bar, she sat back down at the table recently vacated by the Society members. Rob was tall, she noticed, and well built, with muscular shoulders under his dark-blue shirt. He was what she would have called 'her type', back in those pre-Ian days when she would go out on the pull with Jo.

'Here you are.' Rob placed her drink in front of her and pulled out a stool to sit on. 'Well, cheers. You were with the Lynford railway crowd, weren't you?'

'Yes. Celebrating the end of a long and hectic gala weekend.'

He smiled, and asked questions about her involvement with the society. Then he told her about his busy weekend working at a nearby sports centre. Before long they were laughing together like old friends. Tilly felt young again, younger than her thirty-nine years, anyway. He was fun, easy to get on with. She bought the next round, staggering slightly and spilling part of his pint as she returned to the table.

'Oops!' She giggled. 'Must be getting a bit tipsy!'

'Perhaps this is the last one, then,' he said, taking the drinks from her before she sat down.

'Aw. But we're having such fun!' Even as she said it, the bell for last orders rang. It was half past twelve.

They stayed another fifteen minutes drinking up, then left as the bar staff began clearing up around them. 'You know you're no longer welcome when they start stacking chairs on top of the tables, don't you?' said Rob. 'Guess it's time to go.'

'Guess so.' Tilly found she didn't want the evening to end. For once she had managed to completely forget about everything that had happened. Everything. The miscarriages, the redundancy, Ian ... all of it. She stood to put on her jacket and almost overbalanced.

Rob caught her. 'Steady, now.'

'I'm all right.' She regained her balance, and they left the pub.

'Which way are you going? I'll walk you home,' Rob said.

'Well I'm living with my dad, and he's – oh God. He's all the way up the hill. I can't face it! Can we go to yours? I could do with a coffee before tackling that ascent.' She remembered he'd said the pub was his local, so he couldn't live far away.

Rob laughed. 'Sure, why not? I'm not working tomorrow. I'm just around the corner here.'

Tilly tucked her arm into his, enjoying the feeling of warmth and strength from him. He lived in an old fisherman's cottage, in one of the jumble of lanes behind the harbour. Its brightly painted blue door opened directly onto the street, and she giggled as he ducked a little to get through it.

The door opened directly into the sitting room, which was low-ceilinged with exposed beams, and starkly furnished with only a large TV, a leather sofa and dark wood bookcase, but a couple of throws and cushions made it feel cosy.

'Coffee, then,' he said. 'Make yourself comfortable.'

He disappeared through a door at the back of the room. Tilly perused his bookcase for a few minutes, but the light was dim and her eyes didn't want to focus. She'd probably drunk more than was good for her. But the fact she was aware of that, meant that she was sober enough, didn't it? The room wasn't spinning, she didn't feel sick …

On an impulse she followed Rob through to a small, neat kitchen at the back of the cottage. He was spooning ground coffee into a cafetière. She stood behind him and wrapped her arms around him.

'Hey! I'll spill this coffee!' He twisted round and returned the hug. It felt nice, being held by a man. It had been a long time since Ian had hugged her. It had been a long time since she and Ian had … and suddenly, without warning, Tilly was filled with desire. She wanted this man. She wanted him, right here, right now. She turned her face towards him, reached up and kissed him, pressing herself against him, her hands running up and down his back.

He kissed her back, cautiously at first and then with more urgency, and she felt him harden against her.

'Shall we go upstairs?' she whispered between kisses, and word-lessly he let go, took her hand and led her up the narrow stairs to a room at the back of the cottage that was dominated by a huge bed, with a deep-red duvet cover and plenty of pillows. They stood beside it, hurriedly pulling off each other's clothes, before collapsing onto it, kissing urgently, exploring each other's bodies with their hands. At last Rob rolled her onto her back.

'You sure about this?'

'I'm sure. It's all right,' she gasped in reply, desperate to feel him inside her, to lose herself in the act.

And then it was happening, and she moved with him and felt herself give in to the intoxication of the moment. There was only now, there was nothing before, nothing after, and none of the bad things had happened. Nothing had ever happened; only this. This moment. This man, and her, and what she could smell and feel and taste right now, and nothing more.

Chapter 10

Ted

The evening after Mr Hornsby's visit, when Annie arrived for the 17.21, Ted felt too shell-shocked to talk to her. He needed time alone to process what he'd heard, to make sense of the fact that his world was changing and that he'd need to find a new job, a new home. A new life. He wanted to talk to Norah – she'd be able to advise him, help him. She always had, ever since he was a boy, struggling to get along with his peers in school, not understanding quite how the world operated. It was always Norah who'd explained things to him, slowly and carefully. Not the academic work – he found that easy enough. But how to deal with people, bullies, teachers, boys who simply wanted to be his friend. And how to cope with change – moving to a new classroom, a new teacher, handling the house move that had happened when he was 10 years old. Norah too had helped him get his first job on the railway, and advised him to apply for the stationmaster's job, fifteen years ago. She could help him work out a way forward now.

But Norah lived far away, and she had no telephone at home. Ted had not had a chance yet to sit down and write a letter to her, or even work out what to put in such a letter. It would take him a while.

And meanwhile, it filled his head. The railway's going to close. The railway's going to close. Like a mantra, going round and round, leaving no room for other thoughts.

So when Annie arrived, smiled her world-beating smile and said a cheery 'good evening Ted!' to him, he just looked away. He turned his back on her, walked along the platform, away from her.

'Ted? What's wrong? What have I ...' he heard her call after him, but then the 17.21 arrived and drowned out her voice. He kept his eyes averted from her, dealt with the signal, stayed away from the cab (Mr Hornsby had instructed him and Fred to say nothing of the closure to any other railway employees until the following day, when they would all have had the chance to hear the news first-hand) and was relieved when it was time to wave his flag and send the train on its way.

He would find a way to apologise to Annie another time, when he felt ready to explain to her about the closure. If he'd tried to say anything today, he'd have feared breaking down and sobbing, and that was hardly the done thing for a man of his standing.

*

The next morning, after a night spent tossing and turning, wondering what his future would hold, he'd come to a set of decisions. One: he'd write to Norah that evening, telling her his news, inviting her to come to visit for one last time, perhaps in the summer holidays bringing the children, or perhaps on her own sooner than that if she could manage it. He'd also ask her to telephone him at the station at her earliest convenience. Two: he'd apologise to Annie as soon as she arrived on the 08.42. Three: there was still a railway to be run, his regular chores to do, and he was damned if he'd let standards slip over the final eight months or so. Four: he'd find out what Bill Perkins was planning to do after the railway closed. Perhaps that would give him some ideas of a way forward.

When Annie alighted from the train that morning, he was waiting on the platform for her. He took a pace towards her, but she stepped around him, holding her head high, a look of confusion in her eyes. 'Annie, wait, please. I'd like a word with you, as soon as this train has left,' he said as she passed.

'Oh, *today* you want to talk to me.'

'Annie, I'm sorry. I need to explain. I was upset …'

'Because the King died?'

'No, not that, well, that's sad but … wait a moment, please.' Bill was leaning out of his cab, pointing to his watch. The train had arrived a couple of minutes late and he clearly wanted to make up time.

Ted checked the platform, passed over the token, jogged along to the signal box, set the signal to Go and waved his flag. The train left, Bill waving cheerily out of the cab as he passed. Well, there was someone who didn't seem too perturbed about the news.

Annie was nowhere to be seen. Ted's shoulders slumped as he walked back to the ticket office, but then he brightened as he realised she was inside, waiting for him.

'What's upset you, Ted?' she said, patting a space on the bench where she was sitting.

He joined her and took a deep breath before answering. 'The railway's going to close. In September. It's not public knowledge yet, so I'm probably not supposed to have said anything.'

'Oh no. That's awful. You'll need to find another job.'

'And you'll need another way to get to the bank.'

'Well, I might not be working in Lynford by then,' she said, with a grimace. Ted was not sure what she meant. Perhaps she'd been offered a job in another branch of the National Provincial Bank. Perhaps she'd been promoted.

'We won't see each other anymore.' The words were out before he could stop them.

She took his hand in hers. The contact was unexpected – it was the first time they had touched since Christmas Eve. 'Please don't say that. We'll keep in touch, no matter what happens. Besides, September is a long way off yet. Who knows what might happen between now and then? And you'll have no problem finding another job. A good man like you, you'll be snapped up in no time.'

He barely listened to her words. His focus was all on her touch, the warmth of her fingers, the nearness of her leg beside his, on the bench. All too soon it ended. She let go, stood up, shuffled her bag strap higher on her shoulder. 'Well, I must go. I mustn't be late.' She smiled, blew him a kiss, and then she was gone.

Ted looked at his hand, the one she'd held, and tried to remember what she'd said. They were friends. They'd stay in touch, *no matter what*. He hoped with all his heart that was true.

*

From that day on, Ted noticed that Annie began regularly arriving at the station a little earlier each evening. Almost every day now she arrived at ten past five, or even earlier. As a result, they had time to sit on a station bench and chat for a few minutes before the train came, if there was no one wanting to buy a ticket. Ted looked forward to these few minutes. Sometimes she'd even hold his hand as they sat together. Once, when no one was looking, she'd kissed his cheek just as she had on Christmas Eve. He'd wanted to kiss her back, on the lips, but was afraid of how she might react, let alone what would happen if Fred Wilson appeared at the end of the platform and saw them.

He'd written to Norah, telling her he had important news and urging her to telephone him at the station one evening, whenever she was able to. She had no telephone in her home, but he knew she had a neighbour who did, and there was a public telephone nearby. He was desperate to hear her calming voice, her wise words advising him on how to deal with this crisis.

But meanwhile, while he waited to hear from Norah, it was Annie he'd turned to. Annie who'd listened to his worries that he might never find another job, that he'd be homeless and poor and friendless. Annie who'd soothed him, and told him she'd never let that happen, and that he'd have his pick of jobs as soon as he started hunting for one, and anyway, most likely Southern Railway would find him another post at a station on another line. There was plenty of time, she said, and no doubt they'd be in touch with offers of appointments for him over the summer.

And then she'd had to calm him down as he fretted and worried about how he'd cope with living in a new place, managing a new station where he knew no one and would have to learn a whole new timetable.

'Ted, you are too hard on yourself. Yes, it'll be a challenge, but you can do it. You can do anything, you know, if you put your mind to it. We all feel a little nervous about the idea of things changing, and some feel it more than others. I think, Ted, you are one of those people. But please try not to worry. You're a good, kind, hard-working, intelligent man and once you've got yourself settled in a new situation you'll be just as happy as you have been here.'

Only, he thought, if she was nearby too. Only if he could see her every day. But he'd kept quiet, smiled at her, accepted her kindly pat on the shoulder and agreed with her that the closure of the railway could be seen as an opportunity for him to move on to something bigger. Even though inside he was in torment, his mind a scrambled mess, with his routines and life's structures crumbling about him.

It was a Thursday evening, the end of a sunny day in February and still light as he and Annie sat awaiting the 17.21. The kind of day when spring feels just around the corner. When it's warm enough to sit outside, and the seasons ahead feel full of promise. The kind of day when Ted could begin to believe that the end of this summer would not be the end of life as he knew it. Just a change, and who knew, it could be a change for the better. He looked sideways at Annie and wondered. Would she, could he … was it possible they might have a future together, somehow? Was there something he could say, some way of asking her if she possibly saw him as anything more than a friend? How did one start such a conversation? He had no idea, but knew he must try. He must find a way.

There were still ten minutes to go before the 17.21 was due, and no other passengers. There was time enough to talk. But just as he plucked up the courage to do so, the door to the station banged open and a man, dressed in a pinstripe suit with a mustard-coloured tie and trilby hat, came striding onto the platform. Annie leapt to her feet at once, as the stranger approached her.

'Bertram! Oh! I didn't think we were meeting until tomorrow! Have I got it wrong?' She was patting her hair and smoothing her skirt, and seemed altogether flustered by the man's arrival.

The man put his hands on her shoulders and kissed her. She did not kiss him back, and Ted thought he saw her flinch slightly.

'Anne, my dearest, no, you haven't got it wrong at all. I thought I'd surprise you. I was able to leave the office early today and there's a new restaurant opened in Michelhampton, and I thought we should try it out. What do you say?'

'But …' She frowned and glanced at Ted, biting her lip. 'I'm in my work clothes. I need to change.'

'You look perfectly lovely as you are. I have the car outside – we can drive directly there. No need to wait for the train. Shall we?' The man began to walk back through the station building but Annie pulled back. She turned to Ted with an apologetic expression.

'Oh! But just a moment. Bertram, this is Ted Morgan. He's the stationmaster here and he's become a great friend of mine. Ted, this is Bertram Clarke-Watson.'

Bertram stuck out his hand. 'Pleased to meet you, Ted.'

Ted felt flustered and anxious. This was the man he'd been so jealous of, the *friend* with the motorcar, and now polite convention dictated he must shake hands with him although it was the last thing he wanted to do. He put out his hand but misjudged the distance and ended up sliding his hand up along Bertram's forearm. 'Hello, Ted, um, I mean, hello, Mr Watson, Clarke. Nice to see you. Meet you, I mean.' He felt the familiar blush rise up his face as he spoke.

Bertram grinned, as though amused by Ted's gaucheness. 'Well, Ted. Nice station you have here. Sorry we can't stay to chat. Anne, shall we?'

'Ted, I'll see you in the morning. Bye, now.' Annie gave him one last desperate glance, and then let Bertram pull her back through the station building. The 17.21 was just approaching. No matter how he felt, no matter that it seemed as though all his hopes and dreams now lay in tatters around his feet, Ted had duties to attend to.

*

Once the train was safely dispatched, Ted sat down heavily on the station bench to compose himself. So that was Annie's 'friend'. A little shorter than Ted, and certainly younger – he looked about 30, closer to Annie's own age. Smart. A bit flash, Norah would describe him. Confident. Good looking, he supposed, but he was no judge.

Perfect for Annie, no doubt.

So why did he feel a rush of rage towards the man? Why did he feel like he wanted to pick a fight with him, punch him, hurt him? If he was perfect for Annie, and Ted wanted only the best for her, then surely he should feel pleased that she'd met someone she obviously liked a lot, and who clearly liked her? Those times she'd kissed Ted's cheek and held his hand – that was just her natural affectionate nature. He had obviously read too much into it. She'd probably kissed this Bertram, too. Properly, on the lips. The way Ted could only dream of.

Ted had never been good at understanding what people really meant by their actions. He'd been stupid to think he might have a chance with her. Of course she wouldn't want a lowly stationmaster who was soon to lose his job. This Bertram looked as though he had money – money that would enable him to support a wife.

Ted needed to talk it through with someone. If only Norah would telephone him and help him make sense of it all.

*

Norah telephoned him that evening. It was just as well, as Ted couldn't settle to anything. After closing the station he'd made himself some dinner, been unable to eat it so had thrown it out, sat down to read the newspaper, couldn't concentrate so tore the paper up and put it on the fire, sat down again, stood, paced around his parlour, made himself tea then let it go cold …

So he was pleased when the telephone rang in the ticket office, and he had something definite and concrete to do in answering it. He was even more pleased to find it was Norah.

'Teddy, how are you? I got your letter. What's happened?'

'Norah, thank you for telephoning. I don't know where to start.' Should he tell her first about the railway, or about Annie's sweetheart? The second calamity had eclipsed the first, in his head. But he knew that the railway problem was the one that other people would think was more important. He should start there.

'Start at the beginning, Teddy. I'm on Mrs Lovegood's telephone so I've plenty of time.'

'It's Annie. She's got herself a young man.' The words came out in a rush. Even though he'd intended telling Norah first about the railway. 'What will I do if she marries him? She'll stop working, I'll never see her again. I'll never see her anyway when the railway closes. I'll have no job and nowhere to live.'

'Woah, Teddy. Slow down. The railway closing?'

'In September.' He told her the news Mr Hornsby had brought. 'Everything will change, Norah.'

'And Annie? The young lady you like?'

'She's stepping out with a fellow called Bertram Watson-Clarke. His initials are like a toilet. I suppose it might have been Clarke-Watson. I didn't really listen to his name.'

'Oh Teddy, I'm sorry to hear that. From your letter it sounded like you and she had become good friends.'

'I thought we had. I thought she liked me.'

'But still, being friends does not mean she can't have boyfriends. And even if she marries this chap, she may still be able to be friends with you.'

'How will I ever see her, if she's married and the railway is closed?'

Norah sighed. 'I don't know, Teddy. We can't see the future. But even though we don't know what will happen, it doesn't mean we need to worry about it. Things have a habit of working out for the best, if you let them. There's plenty of time before the railway closes if it's not happening until September. And who knows? Annie might not keep seeing this chap. Even if she does, in the meantime you'll still see her on her way to and from work. Enjoy what you have now, and don't fret about what you might or might not have in the future.'

'All right. I'll try.'

'And, Teddy, I thought I might bring the children to visit you again when they're off school at Easter, if that's all right?'

He brightened up at the thought. Easter was only a couple of months away. 'I'd like that.'

'Well I must be going now. Remember, everything will be all right in the end. If it's not all right, it's not the end.'

He smiled. 'I'll remember that. Thank you.'

'Do you feel calmer now?'

'Yes. Thanks, Norah.'

'Off you go then. Cup of tea and then an early night. I bet you've not been sleeping.'

'Not really, no. Bye, then.'

'I'll write about the arrangements for Easter. Bye, Teddy.'

Chapter 11

Tilly

The unfamiliar deep-red duvet cover puzzled Tilly, as she gradually woke up the day after the gala ended, with the mother of all headaches. Gradually it all came back to her: the pub, Ken and Alan leaving, more drinks, that man – what was his name? Rob someone. Not wanting to walk home. Coffee – no, there'd been no coffee in the end. There'd been a kiss, he'd led her upstairs … Oh God. She'd practically jumped on him, hadn't she?

She opened her eyes, then closed them again quickly against the bright morning light, that had made her head throb even more. She'd seen enough to realise she was alone in the bed. Thank goodness for that, at least. She didn't have to roll over and see the stranger she'd had sex with a few hours before. What time was it anyway? There was a clock on the bedside table – it was gone nine. Oh God, what would her dad think? Her jeans were on the floor. She reached for them, found her phone in the pocket, noticed it was still on silent mode (she'd set it that way when working in the gala marquee) and that she had several missed calls and texts, all from Ken. She couldn't bear to listen to the messages or even read the texts, but instead sent him a quick text to say she was all right and would be home soon. *I spent the night with a friend.* What friend, he was bound to ask when she got back, but she'd face that later. She was not a teenager; she was a grown woman and capable of making her own decisions. And her own mistakes, she thought wryly.

She hauled herself out of bed and pulled on her clothes. The bathroom was across the landing. After using the loo and splashing some water on her face, she took a deep breath and went downstairs, ready for that awful, excruciating moment when she'd have to face Rob. Maybe, with luck, he'd have gone out leaving her a note, and she'd be able to slip away and forget the whole episode ever happened.

But no. He was in the kitchen, showered, dressed, and busy cooking a full English breakfast by the look of it. Coffee was brewing, bacon was sizzling, bread was toasting and a couple of eggs were awaiting their turn in the frying pan.

'Morning,' he said, as she entered the kitchen. 'Sit down. Breakfast in about five minutes. Help yourself to coffee, or there's tea in the pot.'

'Thanks.' She unhooked a mug from a mug tree and poured herself some tea, adding plenty of milk. A few gulps later, she felt her headache subside a little. Time to talk to Rob. Time to tell him … tell him what? That she didn't make a habit of this sort of thing. In fact, she'd never done it before. There'd been a couple of very short-lived relationships back in her university days, but she'd never before picked up a stranger and gone straight to bed with him. She couldn't believe even now that she'd done it. It had helped her forget her problems for a while, sure, but hadn't it also just added a new one?

'Bacon and egg OK? I just realised, I don't know if you're vegetarian or anything?' Rob turned towards her as he asked the question. He was holding a spatula and wearing an apron with 'World's Greatest Dad' emblazoned across the front. Oh

God. It was getting worse. He had a kid. Maybe more. Was he married?

'No, not veggie, yes, bacon and egg sounds lovely. Look, I'm not in the habit of this. I mean, I've never ...'

'Me neither.' He smiled. 'It was fun, though, wasn't it?'

She blushed. 'What I can remember of it, yes. But you ... are you ...' She gestured to his pinny.

He looked down, as though he'd forgotten what he was wearing. 'Oh! This. A present from my daughter. She's grown up – 22 now, working in Nottingham. A junior solicitor, specialising in divorce law, of all things.' He laughed. 'Wish she'd graduated a couple of years earlier. Might have saved a bit on solicitor's fees.'

She felt a rush of relief. 'So you're divorced?'

He nodded. 'Did I not mention it last night? To tell the truth, I can't remember.'

He hadn't cheated on his wife with her. And there were no little kids running around. He was, it seemed, free to have a relationship with her. But as soon as she thought that, she realised that was not what she wanted. The stresses of having a new man in her life were not, she guessed, what Jo would prescribe for her. She was not ready for it.

'I can't remember either. We talked about loads of things, but probably not the things we should have talked about, before ...'

'Before falling into bed together. Well then, now's our chance. Or maybe after eating.' He finished dishing out the food and handed her a huge plate. 'Kill or cure, I always say. It usually cures my hangovers.'

'Thanks.' She tucked in and felt better with every mouthful. She'd not eaten much the day before, she realised. There'd been little time. All that wine on an empty stomach. No wonder. Now then. How to tell Rob that last night was a one-off?

Tilly could not think of a way to begin the conversation she knew they needed to have, until breakfast was finished and the dishwasher loaded.

'Shall I walk you home?' Rob said. 'Or I could give you a lift if you like?'

'It's all right. I'd rather walk. On my own. To clear my head a little.' This was the moment. She took a deep breath. 'Look, Rob. I don't know how you feel about it, but I'm sorry. I had a lovely evening, and thanks for breakfast and everything, but I don't think … I mean … I'm not sure if …'

'You don't want to see me again?' He put his head on one side and gave a half-smile.

'That sounds harsh. You're a lovely bloke, Rob. But … I suppose I'm not really in the market, just yet.'

'That's all right. Neither am I, really. Last night was a bit of a surprise. A lovely one.'

She sighed with relief. 'Yes, it was. Let's … swap phone numbers. But for now, at least … just friends.'

'Perfect.' He took a notepad out of a drawer and they each scribbled down their phone numbers. Tilly tucked the scrap of paper with his number on into the back pocket of her jeans.

'I should get going.' Tilly shrugged on her jacket and went towards the front door. 'I'm not in the habit of doing this sort of thing, you know. Honestly.' Was that the third time she'd said it?

'It's OK. I get it.' He opened the door for her and gave her a peck on the cheek. 'Look after yourself, Tilly.'

Something about those parting words made a tide of emotion wash over her, and she turned away, too choked up to be able to bid him goodbye.

Tilly sent Ken another text as she walked up the hill, to let him know she was on her way. She half-expected, half-hoped that he'd have gone out to the railway for the day. A few hours to have a shower and change, and just spend some quiet time alone were just what she needed.

But he was at home and opened the door to her as she approached. He'd been watching for her through the kitchen window.

'Hi, Dad. Look, I'm sorry about—'

He held up a hand to silence her and ushered her through to the kitchen. 'Sit down. There's something I need to say to you.' Ken leaned back against the sink, staring at the floor as though mustering the right words. Tilly had only seen him like this a couple of times before, when as a teenager she'd deeply upset him. That time her headteacher had called him into school to tell him she'd been caught stealing a chocolate bar from the canteen, after she'd lost her dinner money. The time she'd refused to wear a cycle helmet because it spoilt her hairstyle. She knew she needed to wait, hear what he had to say, and apologise.

'You're a grown woman, Tilly. With your own life. I respect that.' His voice sounded shaky. She wasn't sure she'd ever seen him this angry. 'But, while you're living here, with me – and you're welcome to stay forever if you want to – you must treat me with respect too. And that means letting me know if you're not going to be coming home. Just a text. That's all it would take.'

Tilly felt a wave of guilt wash over her as he continued. 'Christ, I was worried sick when you weren't responding to texts and your phone was going straight to voicemail last night. God, I've lost Margaret, and last night I thought I'd lost you too …'

He shook his head. 'I was this close' – he held up his forefinger and thumb half an inch apart – '*this close* to calling the police and reporting you missing. But you're an adult and they probably wouldn't have done anything for a day or two.'

'I'm sorry, Dad, I was …'

Again, he held up a hand. 'You don't need to tell me where you were. You only needed to tell me you weren't coming back last night. I phoned round everyone whose numbers I had, that were in the pub last night, asking if they'd seen you leave. I heard you were still there when Sid and Martin left, and that you were talking to some chap Sid vaguely knows. I thought the worst, Tilly. Sid talked me out of calling the police, but of course he doesn't know how low you've been.' He sighed. 'After everything that's happened. How could you do it to me? *How?* One text, pet. That's all I needed. One simple text.'

Tilly hung her head. 'Yes. I'm so sorry, Dad. I guess I'd had one too many. I stayed with … a friend.'

'Stay with whoever you like, but let me know you're safe. Next time, text me.'

'There won't be a next time, Dad. I promise.' Tilly brushed away a tear. Her gesture seemed to melt Ken's heart. He pushed himself away from the sink where he'd been leaning and came over to where she was sitting, leaned over and wrapped his arms around her.

His love, his unconditional, unquestioning love after she'd been so stupid and so selfish, hit her hard in the heart. She crumpled against him and gave in to sobbing. Again. So many tears, so much grief.

'Shh, pet. It's all right. I'm here.' He held her tighter still, and in his arms she felt safe and loved, but also something new. Remorseful. He was right. How could she have done this to him? How could she have put him through this? She'd been through a lot lately, but so had he. And now she'd added to it. She didn't deserve him. She had to do something about it, to make it up to him. And there was only one thing she could do – sort herself out. Stop drinking. Stop thinking only of herself and her woes. Start living again.

*

Later that morning, Ken went off to Lower Berecombe. Tilly guessed he needed to get out of the house and concentrate on something other than her for a while. She took a shower, swallowed a couple of paracetamol tablets, drank a large quantity of coffee, and gradually began to feel more human.

She mooched around the house, put the TV on and watched ten minutes of a programme about finding holiday homes in the sun, then switched it off again. There was a neat stack of Michelhampton and Coombe Regis Railway Society magazines on a bookcase, and she spent a little time leafing through them. They were filled with articles written by society members, photos of the restoration work, and occasional grainy black-and-white photos of the railway in its heyday.

One article from a few years back, told the story of the glorious day when the railway had partly reopened in 2012. Tilly sat back and began reading that one in detail. It mentioned the society's chairman, Geoff Hill, who'd made a moving speech, and then Tilly smiled to see that Alan Harris had been the engine driver that day, driving a steam locomotive that was on loan from the Ffestiniog line in Wales.

The passion they all clearly had for this project touched her, and she wandered into the dining room, where the boxes of archived papers Ken had brought home still sat untouched on the polished table. Mum would have had a fit, she thought, noting how the slightly mouldy cardboard had already marked the wood. She fetched a dust sheet from the garage, spread that over the table as a tablecloth, and began pulling out the contents of the box, sorting them into piles: newspapers, letters, notebooks, magazines and general rubbish. A fair amount was of no interest – it looked like junk mail that had been delivered to the station over many years. She gathered that up and put it back in the box, ready to throw out.

Deep in the box was a framed cutting from a yellowed, old newspaper. A handwritten note at the bottom told her which newspaper it was – the *Dorset Herald* – and the date in 1895. She felt a tingle of excitement at the age of the article, as she wiped the glass with a tissue and read it. It was an account of the original opening of the railway. She found herself thinking that displayed alongside the account of the reopening in 2012, the two articles would make a good feature for Lynford station's museum.

This was something she could do, she realised. Something

to make it up to her dad. Something that would take her mind off the past and give her a way forward. This was it. She'd take up the challenge of dealing with this archive and rebuilding the museum. And she'd start right now.

Article in the *Dorset Herald*, 2 May 1895

The sun shone magnificently and the wind remained light for yesterday's opening of the long-awaited Michelhampton to Coombe Regis branch line. An estimated five hundred people gathered at Michelhampton station where the mayor made a short speech and cut a ribbon, thus opening the new platform that will serve the branch line. A cheer rang out from those who had gathered to witness the event. A full train, pulled by locomotive Coombe Traveller *built by Manning Wardle (one of three purchased for the line; the other two are named* Coombe Explorer *and* Coombe Wanderer*), departed the station to make the inaugural journey across the county to the coast.* Traveller *pulled four coaches, each comprised of a mix of first- and third-class compartments. The first-class accommodation is sumptuously upholstered in deep-red leather; their sides well served by large windows which on such a perfect day as yesterday afford spectacular views across the countryside.*

At a maximum speed of twenty miles per hour the train is not fast. One suspects that when the track-side vegetation is a little more overgrown in late summer, the passengers will be able to lean out and pluck blackberries while the train negotiates the numerous bends. There are many bridges over lane-ways, a beautiful viaduct, a blessedly short tunnel and numerous deep cuttings on the route. The track makes many tight turns, and I am given to understand that the twisty nature of the route is the reason a narrow gauge was chosen, for it is possible to manage much tighter turns using a two-foot gauge than could be accomplished with standard gauge.

The train stops at four stations – Blackford, Rayne's Cross, Lower Berecombe and Lynford – before it reaches its ultimate destination of Coombe Regis, where the station is perched atop a hill on the edge of the town. Views throughout are magnificent, and the vibrant green of springtime, the air thronging with birdsong and scented with hawthorn blossom, are replaced by the salty tang of the sea and the raucous cries of gulls on arrival at Coombe Regis. The town will no doubt receive many thousands of visitors this summer and every summer from here on. The coming of the railway has indeed opened up this picturesque little spot, and in time it will become a major destination for holidaymakers and day-trippers alike.

Chapter 12

Ted

The day after Ted met Bertram, as promised, Annie sought him out as she alighted from her morning train.

'Ted, I don't have to be in work until a quarter past nine today. We can have that chat we were going to have last night.'

'All right,' Ted said. The 08.42 was blowing its whistle, its driver desperate to be on his way. Since the announcement of the railway's closure, Bill seemed to want to just get his job done with no fuss and no chat. Perhaps he was as worried about his future prospects as Ted was. But Bill had a wife and children, and lived in a smart semi-detached house on the edge of Michelhampton. At least he knew who he was spending the rest of his life with, and where he'd be living. He had only to find himself a new job local to Michelhampton.

A few minutes later, with the token passed over, the train on its way, the signal set to stop ready for the next one and all passengers ushered out of the station, Ted went into the ladies' waiting room where Annie was waiting for him. It was a grey day with a chill wind, so unlike yesterday's promise of spring.

The weather matched his mood, Ted thought, as he sat opposite Annie and waited to hear what she had to say.

'So, now you've met Bertram.' She looked nervous, as though uncertain of what he would think.

'Your s-sweetheart.' The words came out as a statement, though Ted had intended them as a question.

'Well, I suppose in a way … we have been stepping out a few times. He collects me from work sometimes, and we go to the pictures in Michelhampton, or for a glass of gin and tonic in a hotel.'

'You like him.'

She twisted her mouth a little before answering. 'He's nice enough, I suppose. But—'

Ted interrupted. 'Why anyone needs a motorcar, I'll never understand. What's wrong with taking the train – let the engine do all the work while the passengers can sit back and relax, chat, or just look out of the window. If you're driving, I suppose you have to concentrate on the road ahead. It must be very tedious.' He couldn't help himself, but he knew it wasn't the motorcar that was upsetting him.

'Well, I suppose the railways don't go quite everywhere, do they?' She seemed irritated by his interruption.

'There's bicycles for everything else. If more people used the trains, they wouldn't be closing the railway, would they?'

'That's true.' Annie fiddled with her gloves that she'd removed, then looked up at Ted.

'Listen, Ted. There is something I must make clear to you. It isn't me … it's my father. He wants me to … spend time with Bertram. He's hoping, I suppose, that Bertram might … propose.' There were, he thought, tears in her eyes as she said this.

'Your father,' Ted repeated, not sure yet how to take in what she'd told him.

'Yes … there are reasons why Father's pushing us together. But look, nothing's certain. You and I are friends, aren't we? I've

111

enjoyed getting to know you these last couple of months, honestly I have. Let me tell you a little secret. Just between you and me, eh, Ted? You're the sort of person it's best to be totally honest and open with, I can see that.' Annie reached across to take his hand, but Ted found himself flinching away. A look of confusion crossed her face before she replaced it with that gleaming smile, the one that lit up the whole world. 'Ted, I like you so much more than I like Bertram.'

It took a while for these words to sink in. Ted mouthed the end of her sentence. *Like you so much more.* 'You do? Really?'

That smile again, bringing an answering smile to his own lips. 'Yes. It's true, I do. I probably shouldn't, but there's something about you ...' She cocked her head on one side and regarded him through half-closed eyes. 'You're sweet, kind, generous, honest and straightforward. You're a lovely man, Ted.'

'And I think you're lovely too,' he replied, blurting the words out and feeling the familiar blush rush up from his neck.

She reached again for his hand and this time he let her take it. 'So that's all right then. You're not to mind if I go out with Bertram now and again. My father is pushing me to spend time with him, and I don't want to argue with him. He has enough to worry about.'

Ted couldn't answer. From feeling in the depths of despair the previous evening, thinking she was lost to him, he now thought there was still a chance. If she liked him more than Bertram, then she wouldn't marry Bertram, would she? She was waiting for Ted to ask for her hand, that was clear. That was how ladies did these things. Norah had explained to him once, that it was generally up to the man to make all the moves, and up to the lady to make all the decisions. From what Annie had said, she'd made her decision.

But Ted couldn't propose to her yet. He'd need to make sure he was in a position where he could keep a wife. That was important. A man should not marry unless he was financially secure, earning enough for a wife and family, their future assured. And Annie was the kind of woman used to the finer things in life. She'd want a good, solid home with a pretty little garden in which to grow roses, a telephone line installed, a motorcar whether he liked it or not, so that he could take her out for picnics when he wasn't working. Working at what? That was the other question. No, he could not propose to her now, with such an uncertain future looming ahead. But he *would* propose, as soon as he was in a position to. And from what she'd just said, he was certain she'd accept. His heart sang.

'Ted? You've gone very quiet! Have I embarrassed you? I'm sorry, I didn't mean to.'

'No, not at all, I'm not embarrassed. I'm very happy.' Totally open and honest, she'd said. He'd always thought that was best too. No dissembling. Say what you mean and what you feel. If everyone did that, life would be so much simpler.

'Well, that's good, then!' Annie checked her wristwatch, a delicate gold piece on which the hands were so small Ted did not know how she could read it. 'Oh, goodness. I must be on my way. I shall see you this evening. Goodbye for now, Ted.' She stood, leaned over him and planted a kiss on his cheek.

*

It was about a week later that Ted spotted Annie's ring. A week in which he had floated around the station, doing his chores with a grin permanently plastered to his face, enjoying every moment of his brief chats twice a day with Annie, and dreaming of a future with her at his side every night. He'd written to Norah to tell her his news, and she'd replied that she was delighted for him but that he was right – he must make sure he was secure in a new job and a new home before proposing.

Now, Ted couldn't wait for September, for the railway to hurry up and close, freeing him up to start his new life so he could claim Annie's hand. What had seemed just a few days ago to be the end of the world now felt like an opportunity, and one he couldn't wait to meet head-on. As long as he could find a new job. But surely one would turn up – he felt so positive about life now, he was certain that the perfect job would materialise.

On Monday morning, Annie arrived on the 08.42 as usual. Ted had spent a long lonely weekend without her twice-daily visits to the station and was happy to get back to the usual weekday routine. But Annie seemed distracted as she alighted from the train, and hurried past him, saying only a quick, 'Hello, sorry, in a rush this morning,' as she passed through the station.

Never mind. He'd seen her beautiful face, and she'd be back just after five o'clock. He could last till then.

He'd made some cakes the previous evening. Sticky buns covered with icing. In one of their chats, she'd confessed to a sweet tooth, and he'd stored the detail away to surprise her one day. Today was the day. He'd offer her one when she arrived for her evening train.

He'd laid the cakes out on a tray in the ladies' waiting room, covered by a linen cloth. He expected no other female passengers, and as long as she arrived with a few minutes to spare there'd be time for her to take one.

She arrived at ten past five. 'Annie, hello! Please, come into the waiting room. I have a little surprise for you.' He held the door to the room open for her.

Annie looked a little flustered. 'A surprise? But why?'

'Just a little something to help you on your journey home today,' Ted replied, smiling.

'Oh, all right then!' She went into the waiting room.

He followed her in then whisked the cloth off the tray with a flourish. 'Please, help yourself! I made them myself.'

'Oh, Ted.' She smiled, and the room took on a golden glow despite the day outside being grey and damp. 'How lovely of you.' She peeled off her gloves to take one, and that was when he saw it.

A ring. A diamond flanked by a couple of sapphires, on the third finger of her left hand. A ring he'd not seen her wear before. A ring on the finger usually reserved for wedding and engagement rings. He drew in his breath sharply, and Annie looked up.

'What's the matter? Oh. This.' She'd seen what he was staring at and lifted her hand to gaze at the ring herself, as though she hadn't noticed it before. A blush rose to her cheeks. 'I'm going to need to explain this to you, aren't I?' She took a bite of her bun.

'Are you … are you engaged? To B-Bertram?' He could not believe it. There must be some other explanation. Perhaps it was her mother's ring, or grandmother's, and she was wearing it in memory. Norah wore their mother's rings sometimes. On her right hand.

'He … asked me to marry him, yes.' Annie sounded sorry about it. Not as sorry as Ted felt.

'But … why? I thought you said you didn't like him much.' As much as you like me, he wanted to add.

She sighed wearily. 'It's not always just about who you like, unfortunately. Sometimes it's about … who your father wants you to marry.'

Ted shook his head sadly, unable to believe the turn in his fortunes again. Just when he'd thought he had a future, that Clarke-Watson chap had snatched it all away. Well, he and Annie's father and his confounded expectations!

The whistle of the 17.21 train jolted him into life. 'The train, I must—'

'Of course, and I must …' She leapt to her feet, tugging on her gloves. 'Those buns were magnificent. Thank you. And … I'm sorry. Really I am.' She smiled, not her usual bright and cheerful smile but one tinged with sadness and regret, and ran out to the platform.

Ted followed, collecting his flag and cap. There was still a railway to run and trains to dispatch on time, even though his heart had been broken.

Chapter 13

Tilly

When Ken came home he seemed delighted to find Tilly at work in the dining room, a forgotten cup of tea cooling on the sideboard and piles of papers everywhere.

'You've made a start, then? Fantastic stuff!' He plonked down the box he was carrying beside the other one, that Tilly was now using for rubbish.

'Not there! Over there please, by the window, for anything not yet sorted.'

'How's it going, pet?'

'Well, as you say, I've made a start.' She put down the documents she was holding and gave him a hug. 'I'm sorry about last night. Super sorry. It was unforgivable. And you were right, Dad. This is something worthwhile for me to do, and quite absorbing, really. I think it'll be good for me. What time is it?'

'Just gone four.'

'Four! I'd have guessed it was about one-thirty.'

'I'll put the kettle on. Found anything interesting yet?'

'This.' She passed him the framed cutting and Ken sat down to read it.

'That's great! We could photocopy it, blow it up a bit, laminate and display that in the museum coach. When it's done up.'

'Yes, and I thought put it beside an account of the reopening. I found this too.' She passed him a copy of the Society's magazine from its early days in 1985, in which someone had written an article about his memories of travelling on the line as a child on a summer's day in the 1920s. He'd liked the tunnel best, it seemed, and had indeed leaned out of the window grabbing at foliage as the train negotiated bends, just as the *Dorset Herald* journalist had predicted.

'That's perfect,' Ken said, when he'd finished reading. 'You should show it to Alan, too. Before he was born, his mother used to bring his brothers and sisters here on holidays. I think his uncle used to work on the railway. It had closed by the time Alan was born, and there's some mystery – Alan never met his uncle and apparently his mother would never talk about him. I don't know the detail.'

*

As if to prove her worth to Ken, Tilly threw her heart and soul over the next few days into the job of sorting out the archives and researching the history of the railway. She'd had an idea to build up a display board that accounted for the history of the old railway, and another showing the history of the Society and the restoration efforts. There were plenty of opportunities for 'then and now' photos and articles side by side.

In among the boxes Ken brought home were Lynford station's logbooks, detailing every train that passed through and their timings. Someone had clearly been a bit of a stickler for detail, Tilly thought, as she piled up the logbooks in date order.

She'd also subscribed to websites that allowed you to view old newspapers online, and all were fully searchable. Searching for mentions of the railway in 1936, the year it closed, she'd come across various announcements, and had copied them to a folder on her laptop.

Announcement in the *Dorset Herald*, September 1936

The last day of operation of the beloved Michelhampton and Coombe Regis Railway is to be this Sunday, 20 September. The final service will depart Michelhampton at 11.05 a.m., and the last return service will depart Coombe Regis at 4.35 p.m. All trains will call at all intermediate stations.

Tickets may be bought in advance from any station, for those wishing to avail themselves of this last chance to travel on what must be one of the most scenic lines in the country. Its demise will be a great loss to the county.

Letter to the *Dorset Herald* – 28 September 1936

Sir

It is only a week since the closure of the Michelhampton and Coombe Regis Railway, but already our countryside feels too quiet, too still, lonely and unvisited. Can nothing be done to save the railway before the tracks are taken up and the assets sold off? Whilst I understand that the railway was not profitable for Southern Railway and that travelling between the towns and villages on its route is quicker by road, money and speed are not everything. The sublime scenery viewed from the railway's open carriages is surely worth far more and is worth saving. Is there not some public-spirited individual, some far-sighted philanthropic gentleman, some railway-loving local businessman, who might buy the railway in its entirety, and run it as a tourist attraction, perhaps during the summer months only? Is there really no business model for this line, under which it could be saved for the nation? If I had the money myself, I'd come forward, but unfortunately

I am not in that happy position. I write this letter in the hope that someone of suitable means will seriously consider the proposition.

Yours

Mr Walter Britten, Michelhampton

There was something so sad about that last one. Just a week after it closed people were already mourning its loss. In another snippet Tilly read about how the railway was broken up and its assets sold off at auction. Some railway carriages had been bought by local people and turned into garden sheds or summer houses. The Society had apparently bought several back and restored them, including the one used as a museum. She discovered that one of the steam engines that ran, the one that had been in continuous use on the gala weekend, was a replica. Built by Manning Wardle, the same company who had built the original engines, to the same design. They'd called it *Coombe Wanderer*, after one of the originals.

And what had happened to the people who'd worked on the railway, especially those such as stationmasters and their families, who'd lived in the station houses? Where had they moved to after the closure of the line?

*

The weekend after the gala, five days after Tilly's night with Rob, was when Jo was finally able to visit. Tilly had not allowed herself to get too excited this time, in case something happened and Jo was not able to come. She didn't want to risk being thrown into the depths of despair again, now that she was finally beginning to sort herself out. But everything went to plan, and by eight o'clock on Friday night Jo was sitting in Ken's living room, a glass of wine in hand, while Tilly finished preparing dinner. She was aware that Ken was speaking in a low voice, probably bringing

Jo up to date on Tilly's behaviour and recent state of mind. That was OK. She'd be updating Jo herself soon. And she knew Ken was acting out of love and concern for her. What he would tell Jo about her failure to come home last Monday night she didn't know. She still felt mortified by that.

*

On Saturday Tilly led Jo out on the long-planned walk along the cliffs. It was a blustery day, threatening rain, but Tilly was desperate to get out for some fresh air after too many days in the company of dusty boxes of papers in Ken's dining room.

'Rain can't hurt us,' Jo said, pulling on her mac. 'At least it can't hurt me. I'm a Yorkshire woman, remember? We'll just get wet, and then when we get back we can make hot chocolate and sit by the fireside. Now come on, mate. You've been promising me this. I get so few chances to go out for a decent walk since having the kids.'

They set off westwards, following the cliff path as it rose and fell over the contours of the land. Tilly had not been this way since her first few days here – since the day she'd ended up walking home from Beremouth swigging from a bottle of wine.

They walked in silence for a while, but then at the high point of the cliff, Jo stopped to admire the view. The sky was every shade of grey, but the clouds were high enough that they could see the coastline stretching out in both directions.

'It's better on a sunny day,' Tilly said, but Jo shook her head.

'I like it like this. It's more honest, somehow. It's as though the land's saying, this is how I feel today. I'm not in a good mood, and I'm letting you see it. I'm not pretending all's well.'

'That's deep!' Tilly laughed.

'It's rubbish. It's my way of saying, come on, mate, tell your Aunty Jo how you're feeling. Don't hold back. Your dad said you've had some ups and downs.'

'I have, yes.' Tilly turned away and continued walking.

'And? Anything I should know about?'

Life was always easier if she opened up to Jo, Tilly thought. 'Yeah. I suppose I should tell you about last Monday night.'

'Your dad said you didn't come home?'

Tilly took a deep breath and told the full story.

When she'd finished Jo was silent for a moment. 'Did he ... take advantage of you? Oh, Tilly, is this your "me too" moment? After all you've been through ...'

'No, not at all. It was me. I instigated it, and although I'd drunk a lot, I did know what I was doing.' Tilly shrugged. 'He was cute, and you know, for a short time I forgot all my problems.'

'You naughty girl!' Jo said in mock horror. 'But you don't want to see him again?'

'As a friend, only. Maybe. I don't want a relationship.'

'Fair enough. And how do you feel now about what you did?'

Tilly twisted her mouth. 'I think my only regret is that I was too drunk and too caught up in the moment to think to text Dad. That was unforgivable.'

'Yes. But he will forgive you, because your dad is amazing and lovely.'

It was a good job it was drizzling, so the moisture on her cheeks could be attributed to the rain, not tears. Yes, Ken was the best dad any woman could have. She was lucky, she knew.

'He's enjoying having you here,' Jo said. 'Have you talked to him, about everything that happened?'

'Most of it. I told him about the other miscarriages. And about Ian and Naomi.'

'That's good. Have you heard from Ian?'

'No. Only a text or two. And that's the way I want it.'

'Won't you have to talk to him about ... you know ... getting a divorce?'

'There are solicitors for that. I'll engage one, soon. When I feel I can walk into a solicitor's office and tell them what I need, without falling apart.'

'Aw, mate. Anything I can do to help, you know I will. I'd come with you if it'd help.'

'I know you would. And I-I appreciate it so much.' Tilly turned her face into the wind and let it whip her hair around her face. 'Shall we walk on? There's a pub down the hill in the next village.'

*

The weekend with Jo passed all too quickly and in no time at all she'd gone, and Tilly was alone with Ken again. But she felt more relaxed and happier than she'd been for some time.

'Done you good, having Jo here,' Ken said as they ate dinner the night after Jo had left. 'It'd be worth you finding some local friends, of your own age. Not just us oldies in the Society.'

Tilly nodded, thinking of Rob. A week had passed. Maybe in another week or two she'd suggest meeting up in the pub. For a drink, only. As a friend.

'And you're doing so well with the archives.' Ken smiled. 'Really pleased to see you getting stuck in. You know, I reckon if you took some of the photos and newspaper bits you've found, and went to see that Miss Pullen, I reckon she'd listen to you more than she does to us old men. Especially as you've already met her. You've got a bit of a connection already.'

'But she pushed me out of the door as soon as I mentioned the railway. I'm not sure she'd be too happy if I went to see her on railway business.' Tilly stared at her father.

He shrugged. 'It's the one thing we haven't tried – sending a young woman to her. You have people skills. Well, better ones than the rest of us old codgers. You might get somewhere. If we just understood what her problem was – does she want more money, does she want some other land in compensation, does she not really understand what we are doing …'

It would be a challenge. And it would make a change from the archive work. Tilly nodded. 'Well, I could give it a go, I suppose. Funny, isn't it, how some people just don't like change. There will always be people who'll find something to complain about. Even before the railway was built there were people objecting to it. I even found a letter to *The Times* objecting to the railway being built in the 1890s. Maybe I should do a display board about objectors?'

Ken laughed. 'Maybe you should, pet. For balance, eh?'

Letter to *The Times*, October 1893

Sir,

It is with the utmost horror that I write to your esteemed newspaper, having recently become acquainted with the plans to build a narrow-gauge railway through the sublime Dorset countryside, from Michelhampton down to the coast at Coombe Regis. As anyone who has travelled extensively through our green and pleasant land will know, Dorset is a county of extreme beauty where hills and valleys, streams and woodland jostle one another, competing to provide the most compelling vista. The railway will need to cut through or contour around those hills; bridge the valleys; forcing ugly scars across the countryside. Add to that the locomotives that will belch out dirty steam, blackening the hedgerows and frightening away the wildlife. The enterprise will bring nothing but a blight upon the landscape.

Coombe Regis is the most beautiful unspoilt village on the entire coastline. The reason it remains unspoilt, where so many of its neighbours have become built-up and over-developed, is because it is currently at least twenty-five miles from the nearest railway station and has only the roughest of road links. Travelling by carriage to Coombe Regis takes several uncomfortable hours. The best way to arrive is by boat, into its darling little port, but this is only possible when the weather is calm and the tide is high. It is the difficulties inherent in reaching the village that have allowed it to remain unspoilt.

If the proposed railway is completed, I fear it will bring an influx of day-trippers to the town. Proponents argue that it will bring prosperity, but I predict the opposite. There are at present two hotels, each catering for twenty or so guests; and those intrepid souls who undertake the arduous journey to reach the village each summer remain there for weeks or even months at a time, spending plenty of money with local businesses. In contrast, if a rail route is in place hordes of people from the lower classes will descend upon the little town, bringing with them a picnic to consume while sitting on the harbour wall. They will buy nothing beyond a postcard or two from the local shops, and perhaps a jug of ale at most from one of the inns before returning by the evening train. Their presence will keep away the traditional, long-term visitors. Coombe Regis's attraction lies in its remoteness, its peace and quiet, its solitude. As more and more people come to experience this, it will all be lost, and I for one will mourn its passing. Can nothing be done to halt this ill-advised enterprise before it is too late?

Yours, etc.

*

Tilly called on Ena Pullen the very next day. It was a half-hour drive to Ena's farmhouse – the route took her beyond Lower Berecombe, then along the lanes she remembered walking, and finally up the track to the farmhouse. As Tilly parked her car on the weed-infested gravel in front of the house, she glanced back over the valley and realised that in the distance she could just about see the village of Lynford, its newer estates sprawling up the hillside. Was that the station building itself, just beyond a copse of trees? During the season from here the occasional puff of steam might be visible on the horizon.

124

To one side of the front door was a window, with a grubby net curtain obscuring the view. If Tilly had a view like this, she certainly wouldn't put up net curtains. It wasn't as though there were any nosy neighbours nearby. The nearest house was at least a mile away, back in Lower Berecombe. Tilly knocked on the door, wondering how she would be greeted this time.

Ena had an amused expression on her face as she opened the door. 'Lost again, are you?'

Tilly plastered on her best smile. 'Not this time. But I must thank you again for helping me out last time I called. I was … in a bad way then. Better now.'

'Well, that's good. What brings you here today, then?'

Tilly took a deep breath. This was it. Her next words would probably bring the door slamming in her face. 'I'm working on the archives of the Michelhampton and Coombe Regis Railway and am trying to piece together the history of the railway, and those who worked for it. As your house is, er, near to the railway I wondered if you had any memories of it, or … anything …' It sounded lame, even to herself, and Tilly stood in silence for an agonising few seconds waiting for Ena to tell her to go away.

Ena's expression quickly changed. Her features hardened just as they had the last time Tilly had mentioned the railway. 'I've had letters and telephone calls and all sorts from that railway society. All asking me to sell my land. I won't sell, I tell you. So if you've come about that, you'd best go away.'

'Well, I'm really more interested in the history—'

'Oh, there's plenty I could tell you, but I think you should find it all out for yourself. Why should I make it any easier for you? I hate that railway. But there are things that ought to come to light. Then they'll realise why I won't sell up.'

Tilly shuffled on the doorstep. It was clear Ena was not going to invite her inside on this occasion. 'What things need to come to light?'

The old woman shook her head sadly. 'Bad things happened there. Terrible things.'

'What things, Miss Pullen? Do you remember them?'

'Ah no. I'm old, dear, but not that old. The line had closed by the time I was born. But my mother, the things she said about it.' Ena tutted her disapproval of whatever those things were.

'Will you tell me? I may be able to research more ...'

'That railway,' Ena said, 'was the death of my father.' She pinched her lips together.

'Death? How?' Tilly asked. It was the same thing Ena had said when Tilly was here before.

'That's for you to find out in your research. I don't know the whole truth of it. But that's what my mother always said. It killed him, that railway did, she said. I never knew him.'

'That's so sad, I'm sorry. Who was your father?'

'A good man. An innocent man, with his life ahead of him.'

Tilly realised that was all she was going to get out of Ena on this occasion. 'All right, I will see what I can find out. You know, there are boxes and boxes of old documents at Lynford station. I've been going through them. And then there's more I can find out on the internet. Would you like me to come back and talk to you again, when or if I find out more?'

'You might as well,' Ena replied, and then she gently pushed the door closed, signalling the interview was at an end.

Chapter 14

Ted

After Ted heard of Annie's engagement, things were not quite the same between them. She would still arrive in time for a chat, but their conversation was strained and forced. How did you talk to a woman you loved, a woman whom you knew was the only one for you, when she was engaged to someone else, someone she'd admitted she liked less than you? None of it made sense to Ted. Thank goodness, he thought, that Norah had written to make arrangements to visit at Easter, and that was not so very far off. He needed those long heart-to-heart chats that he could only have with his sister. Briefly, Annie had filled that role, but not now.

He could not help himself – he imagined now that everything he said to Annie might be repeated back to that Clarke-Watson chap, with his pinstriped suit and greased-back hair, and he'd laugh and sneer at the poor, simple stationmaster. Annie would try to defend Ted, but what could she say? The man was her fiancé. He was to be her husband.

Ted spent sleepless nights trying to work out a way around it. Should he go and speak to Annie's father? Should he confront the man, tell him not to interfere in his daughter's life, insist that Annie be allowed to choose who she wanted to marry herself? Annie had said there were 'reasons' her father was pushing her into a marriage with Clarke-Watson but hadn't said what those reasons were, and Ted couldn't begin to guess. But as he imagined himself, cap in hand, standing in front of Annie's father trying to make him relent and let her be free to follow her heart, he knew he couldn't do it. He'd stutter and stumble over his words. He'd make such a mess of it that her father would be all the more determined that Annie should marry the confident, obviously wealthy Clarke-Watson rather than the feeble, soon to be out of a job stationmaster that stood before him.

What else could Ted do? Talk to Clarke-Watson himself? Suggest that if he loved Annie, he'd release her from her obligations and let her marry whom she chose? Ted could almost hear the younger man's laughter as he imagined himself saying these words.

No. There was no way out of it, that Ted could see, unless Annie herself stood up to her father. But surely she loved her father, and wanted only to make him happy. What about *their* happiness, hers and Ted's? Did that not matter? The more he considered their situation, the more entangled in his thoughts he became. Life had seemed so much easier before he'd met Annie, but now he couldn't imagine life without her.

At last it was the Thursday before Easter, and Norah and the children were due to arrive. Ted had made the bedrooms ready for them – this time the boys were going to take his room, top to tail in his single bed – while he slept downstairs. He'd cleaned the kitchen and parlour and had the station and platform looking spick and span. He'd even persuaded Fred to wash his hair and brush his uniform for once. 'Can't be giving a poor impression of our little railway, now can we, Fred?' he'd said.

'What's the point?' Fred had complained. 'I'm out of a job soon. Who cares?'

'You're more likely to pick up another job quickly if people have seen you've done a good job here,' Ted admonished. 'So come on, for the last few months that we're up and running, buck your ideas up.'

It must have worked, for Fred did smarten himself up and work a little harder – only, however, when there was someone other than just Ted to see him. Ted didn't care. As long as the work was done. And he was pleased that for once he seemed to have found the right thing to say to encourage someone to do something they didn't want to. It wasn't a skill he normally excelled in.

Norah and the children arrived on the 16.45 from Michelhampton. Little Margot flung her arms around Ted's legs. 'Uncle Teddy! We're here *again* and it's not been a whole year! Mummy says we can go and feed the ducks. Will you come too? I'll show you the witch's ducking chair. It's where they punished bad witches. They didn't punish the good ones, Mummy said.'

'Margot, that's quite enough, let Uncle Teddy get a word in edgeways,' laughed Norah, as she pulled the child away and took her place, squeezing Ted tightly to her. 'You've had a tough old time since we were last here, you poor thing. You can tell me all about it this evening.'

Ted nodded, not quite meeting her eye, and ruffled Peter and Tom's hair. 'Hello, you two young scallywags.'

'Can we set the signals again? Can we wave the flag when the train's leaving? Can we drive the engine?' they both squealed at once.

'Perhaps, yes, and no,' answered Ted. 'In that order.'

'Oh, but I want to drive the train!' Tom said, sticking out his lower lip. 'There's a chap at school whose father is an engine driver. He's been allowed to ride on the footplate.'

'I'm not an engine driver. But I'll speak to my friend Bill Perkins, who is.'

That seemed to satisfy the boys, who cheered and began dragging their suitcases into the station house.

'Well, they're noisy! Are these your nephews, Ted?' He had not noticed Annie arriving for her train. She was standing just on the platform edge, smiling.

Norah stepped forward to shake Annie's hand. 'Yes, I'm Ted's sister, Norah, and those young men are my offspring. And this is Margot. You must be Annie. I've heard quite a bit about you.' Ted noticed a slight coldness in his sister's voice. It was not the usual warm tone she used when meeting someone for the first time. But then, she knew how hurt Ted was about Annie, and of course, his sister always took his side.

'And I've heard a lot about you, too. Lovely to meet you, Norah. Ted's a great friend.'

Ted found himself blushing, though why, he couldn't say. Norah meeting Annie – it was like two worlds colliding. Two parts of his life that hitherto had been kept separate; although the women were right, he'd spoken to each of them about the other. But for some reason, he'd never actually thought they'd meet. And now they were sitting on a bench on the platform, Margot on Norah's lap, chatting like old friends. He watched as Annie threw back her head and laughed at something Norah had said. Wouldn't it have been wonderful if he could have given Norah a sister-in-law? She'd often said she'd always wished she had one. But that would never happen now.

'Norah, I'll put the kettle on just as soon as the 17.21's been and gone. Can't trust it to Fred, I'm afraid. He's getting better, but still not up to dispatching a train on time. He's better off working in the goods yard.'

'That's all right. I'm in no hurry. You do what you need to do. We're all right here, aren't we, Annie? Now then, Ted said you were engaged. May I see your ring?'

Annie glanced at Ted before removing her glove and held out her hand tentatively towards Norah. 'Of course, here it is.'

Ted could not stand it any longer. He moved out of earshot, to the other end of the platform. There, in the distance, a puff of steam showed the train was on time and would be here in just a few minutes. Then it would take Annie away, and he'd be free to make tea for Norah and wrap himself in her wise, comforting words.

*

Once the last train of the day had been dispatched, the children were in bed, and the washing-up from supper completed, Norah flopped herself down on Ted's little sofa by the fireplace in the parlour.

'I'll make you some tea, shall I?' he asked, but she shook her head.

'No thanks, I'm not in need of tea. Just a rest, and to put my feet up.'

He pushed a footstool nearer so she could do just that.

'Are you very tired from your journey?' He sat down in his favourite armchair, on the other side of the fireplace. It was a chilly April evening and he'd got a good coal fire blazing in the grate.

'Not very. It's just that ... well, I've some news for you.' She smiled. 'How do you feel about having yet another niece or nephew? I'm pregnant again. This one's due in September.'

'Oh! Um, congratulations!' It's what he'd said when she'd told him about her previous babies, but he thought she'd said three was enough.

'Yes, it is congratulations, Teddy. We decided we wanted another. I'm hoping for a little girl to keep Margot company – the two boys do leave her out of things you know, but we'll be just as happy with another boy. Just think, when I bring the new baby to visit you, you'll be in some new place.'

He didn't want to think about that. This station house was what he associated with Norah's children. It was the only place he'd ever seen them.

'Oh, Teddy. Don't be sad. I'm sorry, perhaps I shouldn't have said that.' Norah reached across to him and placed a hand on his knee. 'Things will work out, you know they will. Now then, shall we talk about that first?'

He could only nod. His worries about the future felt at that moment like a tidal wave, about to engulf him. He realised too, that with a baby due in September, Norah would not be able to be on hand to help him then. He'd half-hoped she would offer to come and stay on her own, and help him settle in a new job and a new home. She had done just that when he first moved into the Lynford station house.

'First thing to do, is write to Southern Railway. Write to your area manager, what's his name?'

'Mr Hornsby.'

'Yes, Mr Hornsby. Write to him and ask if there are any stationmaster jobs available elsewhere in the area. Remind him you have fifteen years' experience. Would you be willing to work as a porter, or assistant stationmaster in a larger station, perhaps?'

Ted considered this. He'd been so proud to be promoted to stationmaster, and had assumed he'd stay at Lynford for all his working life. 'Not porter. That seems too lowly. But assistant stationmaster, I suppose so, yes.' Working for someone else. Doing as he was told, the way he tried to get Fred to do as he was told. It would be difficult. He was used to being his own boss.

'It'd only be for a while, until a stationmaster job came up again. So, as there are, what, five stations on this line that will close which means five stationmasters looking for other places, I'd suggest you get ahead of the others and write the letter soon. You're the longest serving, aren't you? Which means you will have a better chance than any of the others. And once that letter's in the post you'll feel that you've taken a big step forward.'

'Very well. I shall write it soon.'

'Well done, Teddy.' Norah stared into the fire for a while, picked up the poker and stirred the coals before she spoke again. 'Annie seems ... nice.'

'She is. She was. But she's en-engaged to that ... that man.' Ted could not make himself say Bertram Clarke-Watson's ridiculous name. Why couldn't he have a straightforward, no-nonsense name, like ... like Ted Morgan.

'You thought she might have had you, if you'd asked, didn't you?' Norah's voice was gentle, kind, soothing, and sympathetic.

To his shame, Ted felt tears pricking at the corners of his eyes as he nodded. He was a grown man of 40, yet he wanted to lay his head on his big sister's shoulder and cry his eyes out. Have her wrap her arms around him, pat his back and say there, there, and then go out and make it all better. But how could she? The only thing that would make this better would be if Annie broke off her engagement, Watson-Clarke or whoever he was moved far away, and Annie came back to him. How could Norah make all that happen?

'Teddy, dearest. I fear Annie is in a very difficult situation. She told me – she confided in me, to an extent. Her father wants her to marry this other chap. She prefers you, but she doesn't want to go against her father. Perhaps he has some money problems, I'd guess, though she didn't say for certain. Sometimes, people marry for duty, not for love.'

'But that seems so wrong!' Ted's understanding had always been that marriage was about love. Your job, that was about duty, but your personal life was your own, surely?

'I know, Teddy. But if she wants to please her father, there's nothing you can do. Maybe you'll find—'

'No! Don't tell me I'll find someone else. She's the one. The *only* one. All these years I never found anyone, and then Annie comes along and she's p-perfect, and she's all I want and I'd do *anything* for her, and she's engaged to someone else. Even though she told me she liked me better than him!' Ted had jumped to his feet and was pacing back and forth in the little parlour as he spoke.

'Oh, Teddy. Did she really say that?' Norah shook her head. Ted was not sure if it was in sadness or disapproval.

'She said she could tell I liked people to be open and honest. And I do! So she was open and honest with me, and told me that.'

'And was she open and honest when she told you she'd got engaged?' Norah asked, gently.

Ted remembered how he'd seen Annie's ring only when she took her gloves off to eat the sticky bun he'd made her. How she'd blushed and tried to hide it. Not open and honest then, no. But she was Annie. She'd not wanted to hurt him. That's why she'd hidden it. He opened and closed his mouth a few times but felt unable to put all that into words. Even to Norah.

Norah stood and caught Ted as he paced, stopping him, wrapping her arms around him. 'Ted, listen. It might help you to keep a diary. Like you did when you were little, remember? Write down how you feel, what worries you, and what you can do to make things better. Remember doing that?'

He did. When things were at their worst during his school days, Norah had suggested a diary. An external mind, she'd said. As you write it down, it'll help everything make sense, and help you understand what's important.

He nodded, and she smiled. 'Remember, Ted. The closure of this railway will not be the end of anything, it'll be the beginning of a new chapter in your life. One where you will make new friends and find new things to interest you. I firmly believe when you look back, in a few years' time, you'll see it as the best thing that ever happened to you.'

Ted shook his head and, as he did so, a tear fell.

'I know it's impossible to see it like that now, Teddy. But you need to … ride the storm. Hold fast to who you are. You'll come out the other side a better, happier man. I'll do all I can to help. Come, sit down again.'

She'd spoken comforting words, used a soothing tone, but for once, Norah had not been able to comfort or soothe him. He felt just as much in turmoil as he had since discovering Annie's engagement. But he nodded, sat down, and tried to hide his feelings, the way he knew other people did, when there was nothing to be gained from showing them.

*

The boys had been making themselves 'useful' that morning – offering to carry luggage for passengers, helping Fred in the goods yard, and Ted smiled to see how Fred enjoyed having someone around who was younger than him that he could boss about. It was after the 12.45 train to Coombe Regis had passed through, when Norah was inside making them all some lunch, that Tom came running along the platform to Ted.

'Uncle Teddy, Uncle Teddy! I just saw a sheep on the tracks. It ran along that way.' The boy pointed in the direction of Michelhampton.

Peter was close behind. 'The next train'll catch it on its cowcatcher, won't it? It doesn't matter if an animal's on the tracks. I told him but he won't listen.'

'Does it hurt the poor sheep if it's tossed aside by the cowcatcher, Uncle Teddy?'

'Well, yes, if the train's travelling at speed.'

Tom's lower lip began to tremble, while his brother scoffed. 'You're such a baby, Tom. It's only a sheep. There are loads of them around here, look.' He gestured to the fields around the station, dotted all about with white blobs, most of whom had smaller, lamb-sized blobs nearby.

At that moment Norah came out of the station house. 'Lunch is ready. Come on, boys, inside and wash your hands.'

'I'll be in shortly,' Ted said. 'I need to go and find an animal that's got onto the track.'

Tom smiled happily at this while Peter scowled. 'Can we come and help?' asked Peter.

'No, you go and have your lunch. I can't have children on the railway tracks.' Ted earned himself another scowl from Peter, but the boys did as they were told.

Ted walked off the end of the platform where it sloped down the short distance to the trackbed, and walked along. There was no train due in either direction for over an hour. Plenty of time to find this sheep, return it to its field, and get back in time for lunch.

He soon spotted where the sheep must have got onto the track – a broken section of fence between the line and the Pullens' farm. He'd send Fred to tell Mr Pullen to repair it. Or maybe he'd just come up here and do it himself; that was usually the quickest way of getting something done. The sheep was a hundred yards ahead of him, scampering along the line, darting from one side to the other as it looked for a means of escape. In the field, a lamb was bleating plaintively, following the progress of the sheep along the other side of the fence.

'Stupid thing,' Ted muttered. 'Just stand still and I'll get you back to your baby.' But the sheep seemed to want to find its own way home, by way of Michelhampton. Ted sighed. They were in the cutting now. Around the next bend was the tunnel. If it went in there it'd be even more spooked. Maybe, with luck, it would stop near the entrance and let him catch it.

But it went inside the tunnel. As he approached, he could see the poor creature, cowering halfway along. He crept closer, whispering in what he hoped was a soothing tone, and thankfully the animal stayed put. As Ted reached for it, he tripped – a few loose bricks from the tunnel wall were strewn beside the line. Something else that needed attention. It wouldn't be safe to leave that. He grabbed hold of the animal who struggled briefly, but then let herself be dragged out the way she'd come. The sheep had not yet been shorn so Ted could get a good hold of its fleece.

'Come on, let's be having *ewe*,' he said, smiling at his own joke. Once outside the tunnel and beyond the cutting he gripped the sheep under its forelegs and hauled it up and over the fence, where it immediately scampered off to rejoin its lamb.

Ted jogged back to the station, made his apologies to Norah and fetched a paraffin lamp. He went back to the tunnel to inspect the fallen masonry. It wasn't as bad as he'd feared. He pushed the bricks aside with his foot, made sure no more were loose. He'd tell Annie all about this little adventure when she arrived for her evening train.

And then he remembered again – Annie was engaged. Annie's future was with that Watson-Clarke chap, whatever his name was. There was no hope for her and Ted, and perhaps it would be better if he just let her go. If somehow he could just forget all about her. It would feel like tearing out a part of his soul, but if it was better for her that he did so, then it's what he must do.

He sat down, on one of the rails. He could lie down here, across the track, in the dark, and wait for the 13.50 to Michelhampton to come through. Fred would handle the signals. They'd wonder where he was, but they wouldn't let the train be late. It would puff through here at full speed, over his body, and then it would all be over. No more worries about a new job. No more upsets over Annie.

But no. It'd be Bill driving the train. And Norah who'd have to deal with the aftermath of his death. It wasn't fair. He couldn't do it to them. Besides, the train would probably derail if it hit something as large as a man, and then it'd be late to its destination.

He hauled himself to his feet, picking up a pointed stone from the trackbed. Crossing to the opposite tunnel wall, he used it to carve Annie's name across two bricks. *Annie Galbraith.*

Under it, on the next line of bricks, he carved the words, *I will love you forever. T.M.*

There. It was in writing now. It was real and unchanging, and no matter what Norah advised, he knew Annie was the only one for him, now and for always. Somehow, this cheered him a little. He knew his own mind. He knew what he wanted, even if he couldn't have it.

Chapter 15

Tilly

Tilly left Ena with her mind racing, and ideas for how to follow up on the little she'd gleaned. How had Ena's father died? What was his connection to the railway? Had he worked for it or just been a passenger? It had been the death of him, Ena had said, repeating her mother's words. Did that mean some tragic accident? Had he been run over by a train or something? If so, it must have happened very near the end of the railway's period of operation. Ena had said she was born after the railway ceased running. She recalled the story of the Lynford ghost – a man who'd died in the station building. Could that be Ena's father?

As Ena was clearly unwilling to say anything more, it was up to Tilly to go through the archives and discover the truth. It was the key to persuading her to sell that all-important strip of land, that much seemed certain.

Back home, she decided to concentrate on the last year the railway was in operation. She began Googling and searching online newspaper archives. She was becoming skilled at it, knowing what key words to put into the search boxes for best

138

results. It wasn't long before she found an account of the last day of the railway.

Article in the *Dorset Herald* – 21 September 1936

Despite heavy clouds hanging over the hills all day, the rain managed to hold off for the last day of operation of the Michelhampton and Coombe Regis Railway. Approximately 600 people turned up at Michelhampton to see the last train leave, and even more were there to greet its return. Enterprising local businesses had set up stalls selling refreshments and memorabilia, and appeared to be doing a roaring trade. Michelhampton station maintained a carnival atmosphere throughout the day, though one tinged with sadness when the final train pulled by locomotive Coombe Wanderer *made its final return and was then shunted into a siding along with the other locomotives, to await its fate, whatever that might be.*

The last services to and from Coombe Regis were packed to the rafters. If only a tenth that number had travelled the line regularly throughout the year, it might well have proved profitable enough to be kept open! But as one passenger remarked on the journey, the line cannot survive on quaintness alone.

Stations along the route were bedecked with bunting, and at each there was a small crowd paying their final respects to this much-loved railway line. Shepherds in fields waved as the train chuffed past. Motorcars near Rayne's Cross, where the railway and road run alongside each other for a while, tooted their horns. Everyone, it seemed, wanted to say farewell. Only cows in fields near Michelhampton were indifferent. At Coombe Regis, a brass band played 'The Last Post' as the return train pulled out of the station for the last time.

Staff employed by the railway are to be redundant from next week – their only remaining duties being to close up the stations and help with the selling-off of railway assets, scheduled for November. Some have worked on the railway for many years, so leaving it will be a wrench. One stationmaster, Mr Edward Morgan at Lynford station, said: 'This railway's been my life. It opened the very day I was born. I began work aged 15, as a porter at Rayne's Cross and then took the job as stationmaster here sixteen years ago. It's all I've ever known.'

As Stationmaster Morgan blew the whistle to allow the return train to depart, there was a definite sadness in his demeanour. He looked at the whistle after blowing it, shook his head, and placed the whistle in his pocket, having no further need of it.

Back at Michelhampton, as passengers disembarked from the last train, they stopped to peer at a wreath of bronze chrysanthemums that had been delivered by an unknown hand since the train departed in the morning. 'Perchance it is not dead, but sleepeth,' read the card pinned to the flowers.

Perchance, indeed. What a wonderful thing it would be if somehow the line could be reawakened for future generations to enjoy.

It sounded like a jolly occasion. Stationmaster Edward Morgan at Lynford station – hurray, she had a definite name for one of the staff! Tilly jotted it down. It was a good, solid, dependable kind of name. Perfect for a stationmaster. Something occurred to Tilly, and she fetched the detailed logs of the railway operations that had been in one of the boxes of archive material. She opened one of them at random, and studied the signature that appeared at the bottom of every page. The hand was tight and the writing spiked and hard to read, but it did seem to say, 'T. Morgan'. T, not E. Perhaps he called himself Ted, or Teddy.

In which case his initials were T.M. – and those were the initials at the end of the inscription inside the tunnel.

'So, Edward, or Ted Morgan, stationmaster of Lynford station in 1936 and for sixteen years prior to that: you loved someone called Annie Galbraith, did you? Who was *she*, I wonder? Did you marry her, in the end?' Tilly muttered to herself as she wrote notes and questions. More questions than answers, but it was intriguing.

*

140

A few days after meeting Ena, Tilly was sitting with Alan Harris in the tearooms at Lynford station, ready to interview him about his uncle, when her phone rang. It was an unknown number, and she answered hesitantly, expecting it to be either a spam call or, perhaps, a solicitor engaged by Ian calling about beginning divorce proceedings. It would only be a matter of time, surely, before all that got underway.

'Hey, Tilly. How are you? Rob Coogan here.'

Her stomach gave a lurch as she recognised his voice even before he'd given his name. She mouthed an apology to Alan and moved away to a quiet spot to take the call.

'Hi. I'm good, how are you?'

'Great. I was just phoning to see if … well, I was wondering about going to see the new Marvel superheroes movie. Not sure if you're into that kind of thing? But it's on in Michelhampton this week, so if you're at a loose end … we could have a drink after, if you like?'

Tilly was silent for a moment, considering. Was this a date? Did she want a date? No, but did she want an evening out? Yes.

'You still there?'

'Yes, sorry. I was just thinking. Not really into Marvel comic heroes but I do like to go to the cinema. Just one thing … this is just us going to the pictures, right? Not …'

'Not a date. It's OK. I remember what we agreed the other morning. It's just a trip out to the cinema with a friend. Deal?'

She laughed. 'Deal. Wednesday's good for me, or Thursday.'

'Thursday's perfect. Shall I pick you up?'

'I'll meet you there. Text me the time and cinema.'

'Will do. See you then.'

Tilly smiled as she saved his number to her phone. She didn't want a boyfriend, but she most certainly wanted a local friend, someone she could go out with now and again, and Rob looked perfect to fit the bill. She returned to Alan and opened her notebook at a blank page, ready to take some notes.

'Sorry about that. So, tell me all you can remember about what your mother said about the railway,' she said, her pen poised above the page.

'Straight in there, no beating about the bush,' Alan said, smiling. 'I like that. Well, I phoned my older brother and sister to see what they could remember. Margot was only little and doesn't remember much but Tom does. He said Mum used to bring them all – I had another brother, Peter, as well, but he died two years ago – to stay with our uncle, at least once a year. I never met our uncle. He died when I was a baby. I'm quite a bit younger than the others, the baby of the family, believe it or not.'

'And where did they stay?'

'Right here, it turns out! I hadn't realised. Our uncle was stationmaster here at Lynford.'

'He was Edward Morgan then!'

'Uncle Teddy, they called him. But Morgan was Mum's maiden name, so yes. How did you know his name?'

Tilly told Alan about the railway logbooks, and the inscription in the tunnel. 'Have you heard the name Annie Galbraith?' she asked.

He shook his head. 'Doesn't ring any bells.'

'Was your uncle married?'

'Not when my family used to visit. Tom said he was a single man then. Margot used to sleep upstairs in the spare room with Mum, and Peter and Tom slept on the floor in the sitting room – right here! There was no woman in the house. Mum used to do all the cooking when they visited.'

'What happened to him after the railway closed?'

'We don't know. Tom says the last visit they made was a few months before the railway closed. Mum was pregnant then, with me. Tom said he and Peter pestered Mum to take them back for the last day of operation, but I'd only just been born so there was no chance. And then after the closure, she just never mentioned him again. Tom said it was odd – when they'd ask about Uncle

Teddy she'd clam up, shake her head sadly and say nothing. After a while they stopped asking, and being kids, more or less forgot all about him.'

'That's very sad.'

'Yes, isn't it? I didn't even know of his existence until after I retired. I'd always had an interest in heritage railways, then I read in a railway magazine about the Society getting going with this restoration. I mentioned it to my brothers, and was so surprised when they said, "Oh yes, isn't that the railway we went on when we visited our uncle?" That connection is what drew me down here. Bit like your dad really – I'd lost my wife and wanted a project I could really get stuck into.' Alan gazed thoughtfully into the middle distance for a moment.

'I'm sorry about your wife,' Tilly said.

'It was ten years ago now. But I still miss her. Married to this place now, in a way.' Alan chuckled, slapping the wall of the tearoom. 'So, any of that any use to you in your research?'

'It all adds up. I'm trying to build up a picture of the people who lived and worked here. Your uncle was stationmaster for sixteen years.'

Alan nodded. 'Tom remembers a man wedded to his job. Obsessed with doing everything on time and by the book. Apparently, he once let Tom change a signal, and the lever was too stiff. The train was late leaving and Tom was mortified.'

'Aw, wasn't his fault though, if your uncle had left him in charge! Didn't something like that happen on the gala weekend?'

'Yes, indeed. Boys never change, do they?' Alan chuckled. 'Tom's other memory is of Uncle Teddy being late for lunch one day, because he'd been rescuing a sheep that had got onto the track.'

'He sounds like a kind man.'

'Yes, I think he was, according to my siblings.'

*

143

Later, with her tea drunk and plenty of notes written, Tilly had just about finished interviewing Alan when a shout came from the ticket office. 'Anyone got small hands?' It was one of the volunteers, Sid, who was repairing the wooden panelling behind the ticket counter where there'd been a leak in a pipe.

'Yours are very dainty,' Alan said with a wink.

Tilly grinned and went into the ticket office to see what was needed. 'Can I help?' she said, holding up her hands.

Sid pointed to the missing panelling. 'I'm trying to fit a new piece there, look, but it won't slot in place. There's something behind, stopping it, and I can't quite get at it with these great lumps of meat.' He held up his own gnarled hands. 'I can touch it but can't grasp it to pull it out.'

'I'll have a go.' Tilly knelt down beside the panelling, pushed up her sleeve and shoved her hand inside. It was a tight fit, but there, wedged behind a batten that the panelling was fixed to, was a package. She adjusted her position so she could reach further in and got her fingers around the top end of it, so she could pull it towards her. It budged a little, then suddenly slipped down. 'Bugger. Nearly had it.'

'There's a monkey wrench here – can you hook it out with that?' Sid said, but Tilly shook her head. She lay down on the floor and reached in again, from a lower position, and this time was able to get a firm grip on the package and pull it out, at the expense of a scratch along her forearm from the edge of the panelling.

'Here,' she said, passing the package up to Sid. It was the shape of a book, wrapped in a piece of brown paper that had clearly suffered some water damage from the leaking pipe – the reason the Society had needed to open up the panelling in the first place. Tilly hauled herself to her feet and brushed off her clothes, watching as Sid carefully removed the remains of the paper wrapping. Alan had come in too, to see what the commotion was about.

'A couple of notebooks. Here, you found it, you should be first

144

to take a look.' Sid handed the books back to Tilly. It was a small pile of exercise books, the type she remembered from schooldays. She felt a frisson of excitement as she carefully separated the pages of one and opened it. The writing was spiky, hard to read, but strangely familiar.

'Looks like a diary,' she said, looking at Alan. 'And if I'm not mistaken, that looks suspiciously like your uncle's handwriting.'

*

It was later that same day, when Tilly was back home and preparing a dinner for herself and Ken, that her phone rang again. She answered it without looking to see who it was.

'Hey, Tilly. How are you?'

The voice made her stomach lurch. After ... how long was it, since she'd spoken to her husband? Not since she'd been in Dorset. Not since ... She put down the potato she'd been peeling and the knife, and sat down at the kitchen table, forcing herself to sound as calm and nonchalant as possible as she answered. 'Ian! Well ... this is a surprise. I'm ... all right. You?'

'Fine, yes, fine. Look, I'll get straight to the point. We need to get divorce proceedings underway. I want to ... marry Naomi, as soon as possible. So that our child has two parents who are married. It'll make everything easier.'

'Sure.' It's all Tilly could think to say. He'd already made it clear that he intended staying with Naomi, because she could provide him with children, whereas Tilly had failed in this. Divorce – it seemed like a big step, but she realised it had to be done.

'So, I've engaged a solicitor. You should do the same. I think it's easier that way.'

'OK.'

'OK? Is that all you have to say? We're ending our fifteen-year marriage here and you're just saying OK?'

It was all she was allowing herself to say, even though inside she was raging at him. Her heart was pounding with the effort of staying calm. 'What do you want me to say, Ian?'

'I don't know. Show a bit of emotion, I suppose.'

Emotion? She was using every ounce of strength she had to hold back a torrent of abuse. He was the one who'd instigated their separation. He was the one with another woman, who must be heavily pregnant by now. And he wanted her to, what? Cry? Scream and shout? Beg for him to come back to her?

She remembered how he'd broken the news to her, on her last day of work. How he'd then gone to Naomi's, leaving her to 'celebrate' her redundancy on her own. It had all led to ... that event she still couldn't bring herself to think about, let alone talk about.

Her instinct was to scream at him, let him have all the emotion he wanted. Maybe it would make him feel better. Maybe he needed to hear her shout, so he could feel sorry for himself or feel sorry for her, so he could defend himself, and feel vindicated in his decision to leave her. She wasn't sure what he wanted. But she wasn't going to give him anything.

'Tilly? You still there?'

'I am, yes,' she said, making her voice as flat and cold as she possibly could.

'Well?'

'Well what?'

'Are you going to say anything more about it? Or is that it – you just walk away from our marriage?'

'You're the one who walked away, Ian. There's nothing to say. I'll engage a solicitor, as you suggested, and then we can leave it to them. Text me your solicitor's details to pass on. And then there's no need for you to ring me again.'

She hung up, before he had a chance to say anything more, and sat quietly, taking deep breaths until she felt in control. A moment later, her phone pinged with his solicitor's name and contact details. She saved the text then blocked Ian's number. It felt strangely cathartic. She'd had so little to do with him since that fateful day and wanted nothing more. Was this it then? Was she better? Stronger? Able to move on?

She returned to her potato peeling, then found to her surprise there were tears running down her cheeks again.

'Are you all right, pet?' Ken had walked in, back from his day at Lower Berecombe, and spotted her tears. 'Ah no. Crying again. Want a cuddle from your old dad?'

She fell gratefully into his arms. When was this going to stop, this constant need to collapse in a heap of tears? 'Sorry. I had a call from Ian and it's set me off again.'

'Good job I wasn't here. I'd have told him exactly what I think of him, for what he's done to you. Come on. You sit down, I'll finish those spuds. Let your dad look after you, eh?'

She brushed away the tears. 'No, it's all right. I'll do them. I mustn't let him get to me. I've blocked his number, anyway. He can't call again. But do you know any good solicitors? He wants us to get the divorce proceedings underway. And so do I. Sooner the better.'

'There are a couple in Coombe Regis and lots in Michelhampton. None I've dealt with, but I can ask around.'

* * *

'Did Alan give you some good information?' Ken asked Tilly later, as they worked together to clear up after dinner.

'Yes, he did. His uncle was the stationmaster at Lynford for many years. I think those books that we found in the ticket office may be his diaries. I'm going to start looking through them later.'

'Lovely, pet. You're doing so well – building up a history of the railway.'

'I'll get back to it all this evening. Take my mind off Ian.'

Ken nodded. 'I'll come and help.'

When the dishwasher was loaded and switched on, they went

together into the dining room. Ken picked up a pile of old editions of *Railway Magazine*. 'How about I scan through these? I'm assuming they've been kept by someone because they contain mentions of the line.'

'Great, thanks. I'm interested in anything about how the restoration got going as well.'

'Lots in the MCR Society magazine on that. I'll pull out a few.'

While Tilly began trying to carefully separate the stuck-together pages of Ted Morgan's diaries, Ken worked through the piles of magazines. He passed her a couple of articles, the magazines folded back at the right page ready for her to make a copy. They covered the formation of the MCR Society back in 1984, and then the purchase of Lynford station and a half-mile of trackbed, for just short of £100,000, in 2005.

'It was twenty years after its formation before the Society could start actual restoration works. A long time,' Tilly commented.

'Well yes. It took that long to raise the money. The Society couldn't get a mortgage to buy the station, of course. So – lots of jumble sales and raffles and manning stalls at church fetes. Quite an achievement, really. And then another seven years before they were able to start running trains at Lynford.'

'Amazing what you can do with a handful of volunteers, isn't it?' said Tilly. 'But listen to this, Dad. These notebooks are definitely Alan's uncle's diary.' She read out an undated entry from midway through one diary.

My dearest Annie spent some time chatting to me today, having arrived five and a half minutes early for her homeward train. I had everything ready for the arrival of the service, so was able to spend four minutes, possibly a little over, with her. She was wearing the green suit and coat that she looks so well in. Her shoes did not match. It is easier being a man and wearing black shoes and a black uniform, without having to choose outfits and worry about whether they are right together. But I digress. It is Annie I wanted to write about. I still feel the same for her. I think I will never feel any different, even if she treats me only as one would treat a pet dog. As long as she notices me, speaks to me and is kind to me, I will be happy. If ever she stopped travelling through Lynford each work day, I would be devastated. She is all I live for.

Tilly finished reading and looked up at her father.

'He had it bad, didn't he?' Ken said. 'Annie. Now wasn't that the name carved in the tunnel wall?'

'Yes, Annie Galbraith. Alan hadn't heard the name, but obviously she was the love of his uncle's life.'

'Did Alan say if his uncle married?'

'He doesn't know,' Tilly replied. 'Definitely not married at the time the railway was closed, but after that his brother says their mother never spoke about him again. Alan doesn't know what happened to him.' She waved the exercise book. 'Perhaps this will tell us. It's so tricky to read though.'

'You could also look for marriage records for them?'

'Great idea.' Tilly added it to her ever-expanding list. And what about Ena Pullen's father? Who was he? Tilly had not yet come across the name Pullen in her research, but he had to have some sort of connection to the railway, for it to have been the 'death of him', as Ena insisted it was.

149

Chapter 16

Ted

It had been raining heavily all day. Norah and the children left on a morning train; Norah giving Ted a huge squeeze as she said goodbye. 'I'd visit again, before the line closes, Teddy, but with the baby coming I don't think I'll be able to. But I'll telephone you every fortnight. Or more often – Charles has been talking about having our own telephone installed.'

Ted smiled. It would be good to think that Norah could be on the end of a telephone line at all times. 'That would be lovely.'

'And meanwhile, chin up, and get that letter to Mr Hornsby written.'

'I will.'

Norah bundled the children onto the train, admonishing the boys for leaning out of the window and getting themselves wet in the torrential rain, then she did exactly the same as she waved a last goodbye. Ted felt a pang of sadness as she left. It would be the last time she'd be able to visit him here. The last time the children would be here at Lynford. Ted wondered if they'd remember their visits at all when they grew up. It felt like the end of an era. When, and where, would he see her next?

The rain had grown steadily worse. Huge puddles were forming on the trackbed between the rails. When the 12.45 arrived, Bill reported flooding at Lower Berecombe. 'If it gets much worse, I'll not be able to get through. Should be all right from here to Coombe Regis, and I'll have a go at getting back again, but if the rain doesn't let up, it'll be the last service of the day, I reckon.'

Ted was shocked. In all his fifteen years as stationmaster he'd only twice known trains to be cancelled due to bad weather – once when heavy snow had drifted across the line at Rayne's Cross, and once when the line between Lower Berecombe and Lynford had flooded, in a storm like this one. It was the lowest point of the track, and if the water ran into the tunnel it was not safe for the train to pass through. There'd been talk of improving the drainage along that section of the line, but in recent years the railway company had not seemed to want to spend any money on maintenance. Of course, now he knew why. Ted supposed they'd known for a long time that the railway's days were numbered.

'I'll telephone the station at Lower Berecombe and see how bad things are,' Ted told Bill. It wouldn't do for a train to get stuck or slip on the rails. There was a climb out of Lower Berecombe, up onto the moors at Rayne's Cross. If trains were to be cancelled, it was best they were stranded at the ends of the line – either at Coombe Regis or Michelhampton.

As Bill's train pulled away, Ted went to the telephone and called Lower Berecombe. It was as Bill had said. Some floods, but all right for now. An hour later he gave the go-ahead for Bill's return journey. It might be the last train through.

A thought struck him. How would Annie get home? Maybe it was one of the days when Bertram collected her from work, rather than her catching the train. He hoped so. Otherwise she could be stranded in Lynford.

In the goods yard, the rain meant all work had to be suspended. Ted sent Fred home early, to the boy's delight.

Thirty minutes later the Lower Berecombe stationmaster telephoned with the news that the flooding there was now so bad no more trains could pass through until the rain stopped and the water drained away. Ted looked at the sky that seemed even blacker than it had been. Not much chance for the 17.21, then.

*

Annie came bursting in through the station door, shaking her umbrella which looked as though it had not done much to keep her dry on the short walk from the National Provincial Bank. 'Oof, what a day! It's coming down in stair-rods out there. I'm soaked!' She sat on a bench and stuck her wet feet out in front of her.

As usual, she was the only passenger to turn up for the 17.21. The only passenger whom Ted would have to inform of the cancellation. He straightened his stationmaster's cap, came out from behind the ticket-office counter, and stood in front of her.

'I'm sorry to have to inform you that due to inclement weather the 17.21 to Michelhampton has been cancelled.' It was the wording advised by the railway company's handbook, but sounded horribly formal when spoken aloud.

'Cancelled? Oh no! Why? What time is the next train?'

'The next one is due at 18.45,' Ted replied. 'There's flooding on the line at Lower Berecombe. The trains can't run until the water has drained away.'

Annie looked dubiously out of the window. Water was running down the ticket-office window in a sheet, due to a broken piece of guttering above. Something else Ted needed to fix himself because the railway company wouldn't, he realised, making a mental note.

'And is the next train likely to run on time?' Annie asked.

'If the rain stops soon, there's a chance.' A thought struck him. 'How about I make you something to eat, and then I'll telephone up the line and find out what the situation is.'

'I must get home tonight,' Annie said. 'But yes, it'd be lovely to have something to eat. I had to work through my lunch break today, as we were short-staffed in the bank.'

'You can use the station telephone if you need to tell your father you'll be late,' Ted offered. 'And I'll find you something dry for your feet.'

She smiled, her bright sunshine smile, which made him think the rain and the storm and the cancellations were all worth it, just for that smile. If only she wasn't engaged to that Bertram chap. He'd be so happy at the prospect of an hour in her company.

He showed her where the telephone was, then went to find her a towel, something dry for her feet, and to prepare some food. He returned with a cup of tea and a pair of oversized socks. 'Will you slip these on over your stockings, perhaps? To keep your feet warm.'

'Thank you. I have telephoned my father.'

'Please, come and sit in my parlour. It's warm in there, I have a good fire going.'

She followed him through, put her shoes near the fire to dry, and made herself comfortable on his sofa. She tucked her feet in his thick woollen socks under her as she cradled the mug of tea in both hands. She looked so at home. If only it *was* her home.

He prepared a quick supper of boiled potatoes and cold pork pie, which they ate with plates balanced on their knees in front of the fire. Annie asked why the line flooded and what could be done about it, and listened intently as Ted described how there was a little dip near Lower Berecombe, and if the stream overflowed its banks the water would run across a field and onto the track, settling on that low point. To solve it, he explained, the railway company would need to put in some proper drainage and bank up the side of the stream there so that flood waters were diverted away from the track.

'But of course, they won't do it now, not now the railway's due to close. At any rate, this is only the second flood I've known in nearly sixteen years working at this station.'

She tilted her head on one side and looked sadly at him. 'Such a shame you will have to move on. Nothing will be quite the same.'

She'd never looked more beautiful, he thought, than she did right now, sitting in his parlour with her feet tucked under her. 'I must check on the status of the next trains,' he said. He didn't want to drag himself away, but he was on duty still, and duty must come first. 'Please, stay here while I make a few telephone calls.'

Outside, the rain was still lashing down, and rumbles of thunder promised more to come. News from Lower Berecombe was as expected – no chance of any trains making it through the flooded part of the track for the rest of the day. A call to the area manager at Michelhampton confirmed that all services on the branch line were suspended until the following morning.

Ted returned to Annie with the unwelcome news.

'What shall I do?' she asked. 'Is there anyone driving to Michelhampton, perhaps?'

Ted shook his head. 'Not in this weather at this time of the evening, I shouldn't think. Perhaps you will need to spend a night in Lynford, at the Lynford Arms hotel?'

Annie made a face. 'I hate that place. Bertram took me there for dinner once. It was awful and the whole place feels dirty. I should hate to spend a night there. Is there really nowhere else?' She looked up beseechingly at Ted, her huge blue eyes like pools he could drown in.

'I know of nowhere else in Lynford ... perhaps Mrs Collins' guest house but she opens up only for the summer months ...'

'Do you have space here? I could curl up on this sofa ...'

Ted felt that familiar blush rise up his neck and across his face. Annie, spend the night in his station house?

'Yes, I have space ... I have a spare room upstairs, in fact ... but ... w-would it be quite p-proper?'

She giggled. 'Oh Ted, I have embarrassed you, haven't I? But look, we're not Victorians, we're grown adults, friends, and it's perfectly acceptable for one friend to stay with another, especially in exceptional circumstances like this. I should love to take your spare room for the night, if that's convenient.'

He smiled. 'Of course it's convenient. I shall make up the bed now.'

*

Ted wrote a hasty sign to post on the station door, advising any would-be passengers that all trains were cancelled until the following morning. Not that he expected there would be any passengers, but it was part of his duty. Then he locked the station door, passed through the parlour nodding at Annie, who still sat curled up on his sofa, leafing through a magazine she'd pulled out of her handbag. He went upstairs to the spare room, which had only been vacated by Norah and Margot that morning. Thankfully he had another set of sheets, and he made up the bed as quickly as he could, paying attention to making the corners as neat and tight as he could. He found a clean towel to leave out for her, drew the curtains and put fresh water into a pitcher beside the bed. If only he could put some flowers in a vase for her, but the rain would have flattened everything outside. When the room looked as neat and cosy as possible, he went back downstairs. He had no more duties that evening. Just a few hours to spend in Annie's company before they retired to bed.

In the parlour, Annie was still curled on the sofa, but she'd put her magazine down and was biting her lip, looking as though she was nervous about something. When she saw Ted she held out a hand to him and smiled, making room on the sofa beside her. 'Come. Sit with me. Let's chat. For once we have hours, don't we? No need to keep an eye on the train timetable! The storm has done us a favour, perhaps.'

He sat beside her, his senses tingling at being so close. His sofa was only a small two-seater, so her feet, still tucked beneath her, were pressed against his thigh. She'd kept hold of his hand too, so their joined hands rested on her ankle. They chatted easily, of this and that, the weather, local gossip, whether the new king should give up his lady friend Mrs Simpson or not. After a while she groaned a little. 'Mind if I stretch out my legs?'

'Not at all,' he replied, thinking she meant to stretch them in front of her, onto his footstool, but instead she twisted around sideways on the sofa and put her legs across his lap, her feet resting on the arm of the sofa. There was nowhere for his other hand to go, other than to rest on her shin. Her smooth silk-stockinged shin, warm to the touch. It felt so intimate. He blushed yet again, and knew that she saw he had, for she smiled and shook her head a little.

'This is cosy, isn't it?' she said.

'It is, y-yes,' he replied, with a little break in his voice. It was wonderful. A whole evening with Annie, this closeness, this familiarity. It was perfect.

'It's funny,' she went on, staring into the fire, 'I can't quite imagine sitting like this with Bertram.'

Her mention of Bertram acted like a jug of cold water thrown over Ted. He pushed her legs off his lap and stood up, pacing over to the fireplace then turned to face her.

'Annie this is wrong. You shouldn't be here. You are an engaged woman.'

She held out a hand to him again. 'I'm sorry. I shouldn't have mentioned Bertram. Let's pretend I didn't. Come back beside me, dear Ted.'

He shook his head. 'No. It is wrong. We can't forget about Bertram. He is the man you are … going to m-marry.'

She turned her face away and pulled out a delicate lace handkerchief that she'd had tucked up her sleeve. He realised with surprise there was a tear running down her cheek. Had he made her cry?

'What is wrong? What have I said wrong?' He wanted to sit beside her again, to take her in his arms and soothe away whatever had upset her.

'I wish I hadn't mentioned Bertram. I don't want to think about him.'

Ted frowned, trying to work out what to say to make things all right, to bring back that sense of cosiness they had briefly had. Before he could frame a question to ask, she spoke again.

'It's Father. It's all his fault.'

'Because he wants you to marry Bertram?'

'Yes. His business is in trouble. He's been struggling since the Great Depression. And Bertram's family business is doing well. His father is retiring and Bertram is taking over. If I marry him, the two businesses can merge, and Father will retire with plenty of money. If I don't marry Bertram, Father's business may well fail, and he could be made bankrupt. There. Now I've told you. That's why Father is making me marry Bertram.'

Ted wanted to write down her words and study them, to help him understand. He'd thought her father was a successful businessman, with plenty of money. Norah had guessed at money worries, he recalled.

'So what I'm saying is, dear Ted, that I don't want to marry Bertram but Father is putting such pressure on me to do it. To save his business. It's my duty. It's not what I want, but it's what I have to do, to save him from bankruptcy. The shame of it would kill him.'

Love versus duty. Just like the dilemma facing the King – pulled one way by his heart, the other by his sense of duty. He nodded, and then slowly sat down again next to her. She shuffled along, making more space for him, and he noticed that she was being careful this time that no part of her touched him. She was even leaning sideways a little so that their shoulders didn't touch.

'It is wrong, if you are being forced to marry someone you don't like,' he said carefully.

'I *like* Bertram well enough. He's a decent enough chap. I don't *love* him though.'

'Like him enough to be married to him?'

'Ah, that is the question. I had thought so. And then I got to know you.' She reached out and took his hand. 'Do you think we'd make a good couple, Ted? You and me. Me as a stationmaster's wife. Can you imagine it?'

Ted couldn't trust himself to answer. There was nothing he wanted more. Yet Annie, beautiful, bright Annie, how would she fit into a life in a provincial station? Even if somehow her father allowed it? He never would, though. Not if he needed that merger with Bertram's business to save his own.

'I hate him,' Annie suddenly burst out.

'Bertram?' Ted was shocked.

'No. My father. For putting me in this situation. It was all right, I thought, before I met you. But now it isn't all right. I won't do it. I won't, Ted! I'll break it off with Bertram. I'll tell Father he has to find some other way to sort out his financial mess. He can't just use me like this! It's not fair.' She was distraught now, dashing away her tears with the back of her hand.

Ted's heart was breaking for her. He reached out and pulled her towards him, twisting her around so that she was lying against him, and wrapped his arms around her, hoping that by holding her like this he was comforting her, taking away her pain.

'No,' he said. 'It isn't fair. You should … m-marry for love. Not for duty.' There. He'd said it.

'You'd marry me tomorrow if I was free, wouldn't you, dear old Ted?' she asked quietly.

He nodded, gazing into her eyes, feeling as though he would drown in them.

'Kiss me,' she said, lifting herself up a little.

He placed a kiss on her forehead, relishing the feel of her soft skin beneath his lips, but she shook her head. 'No, kiss me properly. The way you would if we were married. I want to know … how it feels.'

'Does Bertram not kiss you?' Ted asked, before he could stop himself.

158

'Let's forget all about Bertram tonight. I told you, I'm going to end it with him. Now, Ted. Kiss me.'

He leaned over to reach her, and softly, gently, placed his lips on hers. She was warm and soft and yielding. He put a hand under her head to help support her, and she snaked her arms up and around his neck, pulling him closer into her, deepening the kiss. On and on it went, until Ted felt he could stand no more, his body was on fire, every sinew and muscle and vein crying out for more of her …

At last she ended the kiss, panting a little, her face flushed. 'Well, Ted Morgan, that was quite a kiss! I think if we were to wed, our marriage would be a very happy one.'

'Will you, then?' he asked. 'Marry me, I mean?'

She cocked her head on one side. 'I will. But you must ask me properly, some other time. When I've sorted things with Bertram, and we've had chance to go on a few dates, perhaps. When you know … where you'll be working after September. And when my father's business is … more secure. Maybe he can merge with Bertie's business even without the marriage. I'll talk to him. I'll make him understand. Maybe … things will work out …'

'Should I speak to your f-father? Ask him for your hand?' Wasn't that how it was normally done? The idea filled him with horror but if it was the right thing to do, then he would do it.

She shook her head vehemently. 'Oh, no. That wouldn't do at all. You must leave it all to me.' She reached up to him again and kissed him once more, and all thoughts of Bertram and her father and her father's precarious finances flew out of Ted's mind.

*

Ted lay in his narrow, single bed a few hours later, unable to sleep, reliving every moment of that glorious evening. There'd been more kisses, laughter, discussion of whether it'd be a good idea to have a pet cat, and what flowers Annie would decorate the station with. She'd painted them a future, one that he could not wait to come about. It was going to happen. He just needed a new job, at another station in a larger town. They had not mentioned Bertram or Annie's father or his business again. It had felt to Ted as though they were in a warm cocoon, just the two of them, while the storm outside raged on. Nothing could touch them in his cosy little station house.

And then the thunder and lightning began. The storm seemed so close – just seconds between the flashes of lightning that lit up the room and crashes of thunder that seemed to shake the tiles on the roof. Ted lay on his back, listening to it, wondering whether Annie was asleep. Surely she couldn't be, not with this amount of thunder. She'd proclaimed herself delighted with her place in the spare room and had kissed him goodnight before closing the door. Not that he'd expected … of course he'd not expected anything more. The evening with her, the kisses and intimacy – they were all he could hope for, until she'd had chance to break things off with Bertram. It was only fair.

There was another, huge crash of thunder, and then the door to Ted's room flung open and Annie came in, wearing the old shirt he'd lent her as a nightdress, her hair loose about her shoulders, her eyes wide and frightened.

'Oh, Ted, I can't stand it! I was always afraid of storms. Silly, I know, but please … hold me?'

He pushed back his covers ready to get out of bed, but she crossed the small room before he could, and slipped into bed beside him. 'Hold me, Ted.'

He wrapped his arms around her, trying to keep his pelvis away so she could not feel the effect this was having on him. Lord, did she not know what she was doing?

But it seemed she did, for she pushed herself up against him, moaning softly, moving against him in an unbearably exquisite way, kissing him with a new depth of passion. 'Ted, Ted. Make

160

love to me. As if ... as if we were married. It's the only way ... to help me forget the storm.' She whispered between kisses.

'But should we? It's not proper ...'

'Oh, you and your *not proper*! I said before, we're adult, we're not Victorians. We're practically engaged, aren't we? We're going to be married. So what if we jump the gun a little? Don't push me away, Ted, please. I know you want me, as much as I want you, and you love me, don't you?'

He nodded.

'Well then. I want to know what it's like. With you.' And she wriggled beneath him, tugging up her shirt, pushing down his pyjamas and taking hold of him, and a moment later he was *there*, inside her, melting into her, the past and future all forgotten, and she was panting and moaning and clutching at his hair and he was moving up and down, in and out, finding a rhythm that seemed to please her as much as him, and working up to that final, explosive, exquisite moment when there was nothing else in the universe only the two of them becoming one.

Chapter 17

Tilly

Thursday came around quickly, and with it the trip to the cinema with Rob. The film was fun, full of special effects and a complex storyline that you probably needed to be a Marvel comic heroes geek to understand fully, but it was entertaining enough and Tilly left the cinema with a grin on her face.

'Fancy a drink then?' Rob asked, as they emerged onto a wet street in Michelhampton. 'There's a decent pub around the corner.'

'Sure. Just a sparkling water for me, though.' Tilly had borrowed Ken's car and driven herself to Michelhampton, meeting Rob in the cinema foyer. That way she couldn't be tempted to drink too much, and the evening wouldn't end up the way the last one with Rob had.

'Same here,' Rob said, leading her into a bright, modern bar where he ordered a large bottle of mineral water with two glasses. 'So, you liked the film?'

Tilly laughed. 'It was entertaining. Not sure I understood all of what was going on.'

'Have you seen the earlier ones in the series?'

'Nope.'

'Well, I could give you all the background … but you'd probably walk out on me after about forty minutes …' Rob grinned, then picked up his glass. 'Anyway, cheers. Thanks for coming with me. There's something unutterably sad about going to the cinema by yourself.'

'Cheers. And thanks for asking me.' She clinked her glass against his.

They chatted for an hour, laughing at each other's jokes and swapping life stories. Rob had married young, had one daughter, and divorced ten years previously. He was still friends with his ex, but in his words, 'We grew up and grew apart'. Tilly tried imagining a world in which she stayed friends with Ian, but couldn't. He'd hurt her too badly. There was no way back after how he'd treated her. She told Rob a little about her history, but not everything. Just that she'd been made redundant, and around the same time Ian had dropped his bombshell. She avoided mentioning the miscarriages, or what had happened after.

'Jeez. That all sounds like you had a tough time. And now you're living with your dad.'

'Yep. I had nowhere else to go. Well, I'd stayed with a friend for a while, and she'd have let me stay as long as I liked, but she's got a husband and two little kids and no spare room. Better to come down here.'

'Good old dad, eh?'

'He's the best. Mum died a couple of years ago, and I think he's enjoying my company. So it's mutually beneficial.' She rolled her eyes. 'But at 39 I probably ought to be thinking about moving out …'

He laughed. 'No hurry. Well, I've had a lovely evening. Thanks again for coming with me. Do it again sometime?'

She smiled, as she shrugged on her jacket. 'I'd like that. As Dad said, it's good for me to make some friends around here. Especially if I'm staying a while.'

163

'Do you think you will?'

'Right now, I can't think where else to go.' Or what else to do. The thought of going back to London and looking for a new job terrified her. Maybe she could find a new job locally, here in Dorset. But not yet. She wasn't ready. She'd give herself six months. Or more. There was plenty of redundancy money to last her a while yet. And she could feel herself healing, down here with the sea air and the cliff-top walks, the gentle life researching the railway, and friends like Rob to hang out with. This place was good for her.

*

The next day, Tilly applied herself to her research, trying to find out what had happened to Ena Pullen's father and to Ted Morgan. There was nothing in the boxes of archives, other than Ted's diaries that would help. But she'd vowed to read through the diaries in sequence, and Ted's writing was so hard to decipher, especially on the pages that had got wet and smudged, that she did not feel ready to do that yet.

Instead she went online and began once more searching newspaper archives from around the time the railway closed.

Two cups of tea later she struck lucky. How she'd missed this before, she did not know. A brief account of a death, at Lynford station, on the very last day of operation! She knew there'd been a death, but not that it had happened on the evening of the last day, presumably not long after the final train departed.

Article in the *Dorset Herald*, 22 September 1936
Police were called two nights ago to Lynford station, within hours of the station closing its doors for the last time. A man lay dead at the foot of the station house stairs, apparently having fallen from the top. Another man and a woman were present, and after questioning, the man was taken into custody on suspicion of foul play.

The Herald *understands that another witness states that he saw the second man who has not yet been named, push the dead man down the stairs after an altercation. He has not yet been charged, but the* Herald *understands that is likely to happen within the next twenty-four hours.*

All in all, it is a sad end to the railway's history.

Two men and a woman, and then another witness. Three men, then, and the woman. Tilly stared out of the window at the grey seas and sky, and pondered. Who would they be? It was likely that one of the men would be Ted Morgan. He was after all the stationmaster, and lived at Lynford station, so was the person most likely to be there. But was he the dead man, the arrested man, or the witness? And who was the woman?

What had Ena said – that the railway had been the death of her father? Was her father the dead man, the man found at the foot of the stairs, then? She shivered, imagining the Lynford station house, that steep, narrow staircase leading down from the tiny landing. She could imagine how a fall there, landing badly, could lead to a broken neck. Perhaps that was what had happened. But had the man fallen or been pushed? That was clearly what the police had wanted to find out, when they'd made their arrest.

Tilly searched further through the newspaper archive but could find nothing more about the case. The archive for the *Dorset Herald* was incomplete, and it seemed the story had not made the national papers. Maybe if she went to the Michelhampton Library they'd hold more copies. She Googled to find a number for the library and gave them a call.

The young male librarian who answered the phone had bad news for her. 'The *Dorset Herald* was taken over by another paper, the *Dorset Enquirer*, in autumn 1936. The other paper's archives were all lost in a fire in the Sixties. So you're right, there is a gap. It's such a shame.'

'Were there other local papers at that time?'

'I'll check, hold on.'

She heard the sound of him tapping a keyboard and realised he was probably using Google or the newspaper archive website, just as she could do herself.

'Hmm, no, it looks like there was only the *Herald* covering Michelhampton at that time. The place was a lot smaller than it is now. Is there anything else I can help you with?'

She thanked him and rang off. So, any reporting of whether the man had been charged with murder and what had happened, would have been reported in the *Enquirer* and those archives were lost.

Back to the diaries, then. Though if Ted Morgan had been either the dead man or the arrested man, there'd hardly be an entry about that day, would there? Besides, none of the entries were dated.

She turned to the first one and began reading. It felt intrusive, as though she was peering into his innermost thoughts. They sounded like the angsty outpourings of a tormented teen, rather than the words of a grown man. There were lots of mentions of his sister, Norah, who apparently had advised him to keep a journal and write everything down, to help him make sense of the world.

And there were constant mentions of Annie Galbraith, and his deep and apparently unrequited feelings for her.

Or *were* they unrequited? She read on and came across a passage that made her raise her eyebrows. Its tone was different somehow to the earlier entries. It sounded more like adult love than teenage infatuation.

Annie, Annie, Annie. You looked my way this morning, as you alighted from your train. You smiled, so sweetly, and I could tell you were thinking of that night, the night of the storm, that splendid, magnificent night. But I had to help the old gentleman alighting with his luggage, and when I'd dealt with him you were gone, and I had hours to wait until it was time to catch a glimpse of you again. When at last you arrived for your homeward train, it was with ten

166

minutes to spare, and we were able to sit in the waiting room and
talk, and I held your hand and wondered, as always, at its divine
softness and smoothness of skin. Oh, Annie. There will come a time,
I am sure now, when you will be mine, and I will be yours, and we
will be together. Where we will be living and what I will be doing
for a living, I do not know. But I will find something, I will find
a way, and then I will propose to you. I dare to hope, since that
night, that you will accept. And Annie, my Annie, I live for that day.

'That splendid, magnificent night,' Tilly repeated. 'What
happened then, eh, Ted? What did you and Annie get up to?'
Whatever it was, it seemed to have changed their relationship,
at least in Ted Morgan's eyes. Clearly by this date, whenever it
was – Ted had not dated his journal entries – he knew the railway
was due to close, and was looking for another job. Perhaps he'd
felt he must have a secure future before he could ask Annie to
be his wife.

When Ken arrived home, Tilly filled him in on her research,
especially the part about the death at the station on the last day.
Ken nodded. 'I'd heard rumours someone died there, but not
that it was murder. You know some people think the station is
haunted – occasionally volunteers have slept there overnight, and
often report on strange noises. I always said it was just the usual
sounds you get from an old building – pipes knocking, woodwork
creaking. You know what I mean. Maybe it's the ghost of this
fellow who was pushed down the stairs?' His eyes were twinkling.
Tilly gave him a playful punch. 'Knew you wouldn't take that
seriously. But it's interesting, isn't it? I need to find out who he
was, and what happened to the man who was arrested. That dead
man might be Ena Pullen's father, and that would explain why
she doesn't want the railway rebuilt.'
Ken nodded. 'So look for death reports of someone called
Pullen, around the time the railway closed, perhaps? She's

unmarried, isn't she, so her father's name would have been Pullen.'

'Good idea. I'm not too sure where to look up death records but there must be somewhere online.' Tilly noted it down. More work for another day. The more she researched, the more there seemed to be, still to do.

*

'Come up to Lower Berecombe with me today?' Ken asked Tilly, over breakfast the next morning. 'I want to show you the progress and ask your opinion on a few things.'

Tilly hadn't been to Lower Berecombe since the day after she'd arrived in Dorset, although she'd been to Lynford station many times. It would be good to see a station in an earlier stage of its restoration. She would actually pay attention to it this time, not like last time when she'd been in no fit state to care about the work being done. And it was a lovely day – warm and sunny, the kind of spring day that promised so much for the summer ahead. She dressed in jeans and an old T-shirt, and drove with Ken through the Dorset countryside that seemed to be leaping into life after the long winter.

Things had changed at Lower Berecombe. There'd been a lot of clearing up done – Ken had told her of the several skip-loads of rubbish that had been removed. A volunteer had repointed the brickwork of the station house, and the Society had paid a roofer to fix the broken tiles. Inside, the station was badly in need of restoration, but at least now it was tidy. Gone were the piles of rubbish, mouldy sofas and half-used tins of paint. Instead a set of garden chairs and table sat in the middle of the main room, and in the little kitchen area at the back was a kettle, mug tree and other tea-making facilities.

'We've got electricity here now,' Ken said proudly, 'so no need to use the Primus stove anymore. And we're on mains water, so we can even wash up properly.'

'Could do with replacing the sink though,' Tilly said, eyeing up the cracked and stained Belfast sink that was far too big for the tiny kitchen.

'Yes, that's what I was hoping you'd help with,' Ken said.

'Ripping out the sink?' Tilly's eyes widened. She was casually dressed but not ready for heavy-duty DIY.

'No, designing us a new kitchen. While we're intending to restore the rest of the building to how it would have been in the 1930s, we want a modern kitchen. There'll be no café here, unlike Lynford, as the place isn't big enough. But we want to be able to cater for volunteers, so they can heat up food, make tea and coffee, etc. A small fridge and a microwave, sink, and some storage space, I guess. Can you measure up and see if you can come up with a design to fit all that in and make the most of the space?'

Tilly smiled. 'Sure. I'll have a go.'

Ken patted her shoulder, handed her a tape measure, pencil and paper, and went outside to his shed. Tilly got straight to work, measuring the space and drawing a rough outline of the room on the pad of paper, marking the position of the door and window. And the mains water feed – she should mark that. There was a rotting cupboard under the old sink, so she knelt down to check if that was where the water pipe came in. Tugging open the door she gasped to find the cupboard occupied. A cat – the same tabby she'd seen on her first visit – was curled up on a stack of old newspapers. There was a sizable hole in the wall where the pipe entered, and that was presumably how the cat had got in.

'Aw, hello little one.' Tilly reached out a hand to stroke the cat's head. As she did so, the cat hauled itself up to a kind of crouching position.

'What's up, eh?' Tilly said. The cat looked uncomfortable, its belly swollen. As Tilly crouched down beside it the cat seemed to heave, pushing hard, and then …

'Oh my goodness, sweetie! You're giving birth!' She watched, astonished, as a kitten slithered out. The mother cat turned, sniffed it and began licking, clearing away the amniotic sac. The kitten snuffled and wriggled, and then the mother heaved once again and there was a second kitten.

Tilly was mesmerised, watching as another three kittens were born, one after the other, the mother barely making a sound. But she was exhausted after the last one, Tilly could see, for she collapsed down before licking that last kitten, who was still in its sac, wriggling. It would suffocate, Tilly thought, if the mother didn't see to it.

'Come on, girl, you've got a duty to do here,' she said, gently pushing the mother cat's nose towards its newest kitten. Thankfully the cat got the message and began licking, breaking the sac and stimulating the kitten to breathe.

'Is that the lot, then? Five? Well done, you,' whispered Tilly. The cat looked at her and miaowed slightly, as if thanking her for her help. The first couple of kittens, their fur already beginning to dry and fluff up, had crawled across the pile of newspapers in search of sustenance. Tilly gently moved them a little so that their mother could lie down, then she positioned them by their mother's underside where they quickly found teats and latched on. When all were feeding Tilly sat back, heaving a sigh of relief, and only then realised that tears were streaming down her face. This cat had managed to have five kittens, just like that, with no fuss. All healthy. And yet she, Tilly, had not managed to keep a pregnancy going despite three attempts. It felt so unfair. So very unfair. If just one of her pregnancies had lasted, she'd still be living in London now, with Ian and a baby. A baby she'd have loved, but would their marriage have lasted? Given that she now knew Ian had only stayed with her because he wanted children, she wasn't sure. Overall, she felt she was better off without him.

At the thought of Ian, Tilly wondered about Naomi's baby. It must be due very soon. He would be a father. Well, good luck to him.

She found a saucer and poured some milk from the carton Ken

had brought for cups of tea into it, then placed it beside the cat in the cupboard. The cat managed to twist a little so she could lap from it without disturbing her suckling kittens.

'Good girl. You're going to be a great mum to this lot, aren't you?'

She'd have been a good mum, too, Tilly thought. If only she'd had the chance to prove it.

Her next thought hit her like a sledgehammer, sending her stomach churning and her mind wheeling. That night with Rob – they hadn't used any protection, had they? She'd told him there was no need … She sat back on the floor, face in hands, feverishly calculating how long it had been since her last period. Oh God. Could it be true? Could she be pregnant? And if so, what then? What on earth would she do?

Chapter 18

Ted

Ted awoke alone on the morning after the storm. Annie had crept out at some point in the night, when he was asleep. He got up and peeped into the spare room, where she lay sleeping. His own bed was far too narrow for two to sleep comfortably, he knew, but still, he'd have preferred her to stay with him, entangled in his arms. He smiled to himself at the memory of their lovemaking. Who'd have thought this could ever happen? Annie Galbraith and poor old Ted Morgan! And he was going to marry her. She'd agreed, hadn't she? As soon as he knew where his future would be. There was still the problem of her father's finances, but she'd said that perhaps her father's and Clarke-Watson's businesses could merge anyway, hadn't she? Everyone would be happy in the end, and he and Annie most of all.

He dressed quickly and quietly and went downstairs to make tea. Should he bring her a cup in bed, or wait until she got up? Somehow it felt too intrusive, too intimate for him to go into her room while she slept. Why too intimate – after what they'd done – Ted couldn't have said. But somehow it just didn't seem quite proper.

He made a pot of tea, so there'd be plenty for her if she did come down soon. He took his own cup out onto the station platform and surveyed the line, up and down. The rain had ceased during the night, and the morning was bright and clear, with a freshness in the air. There were a few puddles on the trackbed, and the goods yard was a quagmire, but otherwise it looked to be business as usual here at Lynford. What of the other stations? He should go and make some telephone calls, he knew, but he didn't want to break the spell and end their perfect isolation just yet. He glanced at his watch. There was well over an hour before the first train was due, assuming they were able to run on time today. Forty minutes before Fred would turn up for work. Time enough to make some breakfast and rouse Annie. But first – those telephone calls. His sense of duty dictated that he should do those first.

Lower Berecombe's stationmaster reported that while there was still water on the trackbed, the rails were clear and the water was draining rapidly. There'd be no problem running the trains through there today. And the area manager confirmed they were expecting all trains to run to timetable.

One perfect night. That's all they'd had, but who knew – perhaps Annie would want to stay with him again sometimes, before they married. Ted could still not quite imagine being married and having Annie with him for good. But it would happen, of that he had no doubt. He whistled to himself as he prepared a breakfast of bacon and eggs and called up the stairs to let Annie know when it was ready.

She came down a few minutes later, having dressed and roughly pinned her hair up in its usual style. She smiled at him, shyly he thought, as she sat down opposite him at his tiny table in the kitchen, where he'd laid the breakfast things.

He smiled back, blushing, and suddenly realising he had no

idea how to talk to her today, on this *morning after*. Should he refer to what they'd done or ignore it? Ask her if she slept well? Ask her if she'd stay with him again?

'Trains are to run on time today,' he managed, at last.

'That's good,' she said, concentrating on her food.

He had a sudden, awful thought. Was she regretting what they'd done? Was she wishing she'd braved the storm in her own room? Or even wishing she'd gone to stay at the Lynford Arms after all. The worry felt as though it would engulf him. He had to know that she was happy with him, that she'd still marry him.

'Annie, is – is everything all right?' He gazed at her, but she did not raise her eyes to his.

'Yes, Ted. It is. There's nothing wrong. I'm glad we … did what we did.' And finally she looked up, just for a moment, and caught his eye.

The relief he felt was unbelievable, as though the weight of the universe had slid off his shoulders. He grinned. 'So am I, Annie. So am I.'

*

Annie kept out of sight when Fred arrived for work. It wouldn't do, she'd said, for him to guess she'd spent the night at the station. Ted set Fred to sweeping away the worst of the water that still lay across the goods yard, despite Fred's grumbling about the task.

'You're pretty cheerful today, Mr Morgan. Thought you'd be miserable what with all those cancellations yesterday mucking up your precious railway.'

'Couldn't be helped, lad. There was nothing I could do about it, so why would it make me miserable? Now get on with your work. We've a train through in a few minutes.' Ted went to set the signal, hand over the token, collect the morning papers from the train and exchange a few words with Bill. His usual routines restored, yet somehow today they felt different.

It was not the routines that were different. It was Ted himself, he realised.

When the 08.42 arrived, it felt odd for Annie not to alight from it. Instead, once the other passengers had gone, she came out of his parlour. 'I'll be on my way to work now. I'll ... speak to my father as soon as I can and tell him ... what we decided.'

He grinned broadly. 'Splendid! You have made me a very happy man, dear Annie. I will see you later, then,' he said, longing to kiss her goodbye but wary of Fred's beady eyes – the boy had come onto the platform to do a few chores.

'Er, not today.' She stared down at the platform. 'I've ... a lift home today.' She wiggled her fingers at him as a wave and was gone before he could say anything more. Her lift – was it with Bertram? He assumed so, as she'd never mentioned lifts home with anyone else. Would she take the opportunity to tell him the engagement was off? It would not be an easy conversation for her. But the sooner the better. Bertram, as well as Annie's father, needed to be told of the change of plan. So that as soon as he, Ted, had a new job lined up and his future secured, he could marry Annie and they would be together forever.

*

Write a diary, Norah had advised. Till today, he hadn't bothered much, just occasional jottings. But now he felt it might help to write a bit more. He had a lot churning around in his head that he needed to make sense of. It wouldn't hurt to try writing it down. He picked up the exercise book he'd begun using as a diary, and in the gaps between trains during the day he sat down behind the ticket-office counter and began to write.

He covered several pages detailing how he'd come to be where he was – how he'd got the job here in Lynford, how he'd worked hard to make this the best-run station in the whole of Southern Railway, how he'd employed Fred Wilson but despaired of ever making a decent porter out of him. And then he read back through what he'd written and tore the pages out in disgust. 'Boring. Irrelevant. These are not the problems I am facing,' he muttered, as he smoothed the next blank page ready to start again.

Begin with a list. *Problem one: the railway is closing and I shall lose my job. Problem two: I love Annie. She loves me back. But I need a solid job before she will accept me as her husband.* He sat back and read the lines again. Yes, that was a clear and concise summary of his worries. *Solution: Write to Mr Hornsby and ask for a new job to start as soon as possible.* An obvious solution. The sooner he had a new position, the better. Even one that started before the closure of the line. Norah had advised him to write, but it was yet another thing he had not yet done. Now was the time. He closed the notebook, found some Michelhampton and Coombe Regis Railway headed notepaper, and wrote the letter. It took a few attempts until he was happy with the wording, and he had to break off once or twice to see to his duties, but by four o'clock the letter was written.

Leaving Fred briefly in charge, he ran down to the post office, past the National Provincial Bank where Annie would be sitting at her desk filling in ledgers, and sent the letter. There. A step towards the solution.

At five o'clock he stood outside the front of the station, gazing up the lane towards the village centre. He could not see the bank's entrance, but he could see an Austin Seven motorcar parked opposite it, a man in a suit and a trilby leaning against it, smoking a cigarette. Bertram. With luck, Ted thought, the fellow would be getting some bad news that evening. He felt a pang of guilt at wishing misfortune on someone else, but it would be the right thing in the end. Annie didn't love Bertram. She loved Ted.

At five past five, Annie appeared, kissed Bertram on the cheek and got into the passenger seat. She was laughing, but was there a tenseness about her? Ted felt a wave of jealousy rise up through him. But perhaps she had to act as though everything was normal, for now, until she judged it was the right moment to break off her engagement. Give her time, he told himself. He trusted her.

Then when she'd spoken to Bertram, she'd speak to her father. Maybe she would already have Bertram's agreement to go ahead with the business merger without the marriage.

He ducked back inside the station before the car came past.

That evening, he wrote more in his diary. He wrote in detail of the night of the storm – was it really only the previous night? – and of what happened between them. It didn't help. It just made him want her more. Maybe tomorrow she'd tell him she'd broken things off with Bertram. He hoped her hand would be free of its ring again.

*

Ted kept his diary up over the next few days, rapidly filling the pages, but had very little chance to talk to Annie, as she seemed to rush through the station with no time to spare both morning and evening.

He had a reply to his letter to Mr Hornsby, saying that of course his name would be put forward should any stationmaster vacancies arise, but at the moment there were none. In any case Ted was expected to stay at Lynford until the closure of the line. After that he would be sent details of any vacancies within the railway company, and if he was prepared to move anywhere, there would probably be a job as a porter for him.

It was not the news he'd wanted, but he wrote it all down in his diary to try to get his thoughts into order.

One day, about a week after the fateful storm, Annie missed the 17.21 train, but turned up at the station ten minutes later. 'I stayed a little bit later at the bank on purpose, she said. I'll take the next train home. I can spend a little time with you, if you're free?'

Ted felt as though the sun and moon had risen together. 'Of course I am free, for you. I'll make us some tea. Please, go through to the parlour.' As she went through, Ted noticed Fred Wilson on the platform, frowning as he watched Annie enter Ted's private rooms.

'On with your work, lad,' Ted told him, but he felt the telltale blush rise up through his cheeks. Did it matter if Fred knew he was courting Annie? He hurried through to his kitchen to make the tea and returned to the parlour to find Annie sitting on the sofa, her shoes kicked off and feet curled under her as she had done on that night a week ago. His heart swelled to see her there, looking so much at home.

She had a notebook in her hand, and with a start, he realised it was his diary, that he'd left out after writing the last entry. She smiled and waved it at him. 'This is so sweet, Ted. You're writing all about me!'

'Er, that's to ... to help me ... to help me m-make sense of things,' he replied. He'd only ever spoken to Norah about his diaries. How could he explain the need for them to anyone else? But if Annie was to be his wife, she needed to understand him fully.

'Yes, I can see that. And I imagine it helps a lot to set it all down. I write in a journal too, sometimes. What a shame there's no other stationmaster's job available at present. Maybe something will come up.'

So she'd read the latest entry. Ted had to know where he stood with her. He dropped to one knee in front of her. 'Annie, will you m-marry me? Whether or not a stationmaster job comes up, I'll find a way to keep you, I p-promise I will. Annie, p-please make me the h-happiest man in the world, and say yes?'

She cocked her head on one side, smiled and reached out a hand to stroke his face. 'Oh Ted, you are the sweetest, most adorable man I have ever met. I would love to be your wife. But I can't say yes just yet. I'm afraid.'

His heart sank. 'Because I have no job offer yet?'

She bit her lip. 'Partly that. Ted, I spoke to my father. I asked if perhaps I did not need to marry Bertram to allow the businesses to merge. But he … became angry. Told me I was letting him down. That he'd be ruined without that merger. That the merger depended on goodwill between our families, and that if I broke off the engagement that would damage his relationship with Bertram. That … I was no daughter of his if I felt I could do that to him.'

'So that means …'

'I'm still engaged, for the moment.' She held out her hand to show him that the ring still sparkled on her finger. 'Father forbade me to say anything to Bertram. And until Father comes up with some other plan to save his business I daren't, in case Bertram calls off the merger and Father is made bankrupt. I'm so sorry, Ted.'

He nodded. 'I understand. I wish I was a rich man who could buy your father's business.'

'And I wish I didn't care as much about my father's fortunes. If I was more heartless, it'd all be a lot easier. Perhaps when you get a job and I know you'll be able to support the both of us, maybe then I'll feel more able to walk away from Father. Now, come and sit beside me.' She shuffled along to make space for him, and he sat down, relishing the chance to be near her again. 'Don't worry, dearest Ted.' She leaned over and kissed him, gently on the lips. 'It will all work out, you'll see. As soon as you have a job lined up, I promise I'll talk to Father again. By then maybe he'll have found some other way to pay off his debts.'

'I-I hope so,' was all Ted could say. He wanted to take her in his arms, kiss her, suggest that they run away together and let her father and Bertram simply deal with it. But she was right – they needed to take things slowly and do things in the right way, causing the least damage. All he could do was focus on finding a new job, and trust Annie to deal with freeing herself from her obligations.

Annie nodded at the diary that she'd balanced on the arm of the sofa. 'You should put that away somewhere safe. It wouldn't do for the wrong person to find it and read it.'

Ted followed her gaze to the parlour window, where Fred could be seen, still portering crates up and down the platform, every now and again glancing through the window at them. She was right. He would hate for someone like Fred to see the diary. The boy was not supposed to come into Ted's private rooms, although he sometimes came in to make himself some tea or to put his feet up during his lunch break, if it was raining outside.

'You need a good hiding place,' she said, looking about the room.

Ted nodded. 'I know just the place.' He stood up, went through to the ticket office where some wooden panelling separated the office from his parlour. One panel was loose and could be shuffled sideways behind the next one. There was a narrow gap behind the panelling, just big enough to hide the book.

Annie had followed him through, and watched as he hid the diary. 'Perfect. Just make sure no one else ever sees you put it in or take it out. Just you and I know it's there.' She caught hold of him and gave him a kiss – on the lips, but just a quick one, not the long lingering ones of the previous week. Ted longed to wrap his arms around her and pull her close, breathe in her scent, feel her softness pressed against him … But he was still on duty. He could not spend much longer with her today. That kiss, that little peck, would have to be enough for now. The next train to Michelhampton was due in ten minutes anyway.

Chapter 19

Tilly

All Tilly could think of for the rest of the day at Lower Berecombe was whether or not she was pregnant. Her stomach was churning. She felt nauseous – whether that was due to pregnancy or worry, she couldn't tell. If she was pregnant, oh God, she'd probably miscarry again. That was something she didn't think she could bear. It would send her under again, back to drinking too much, back to not wanting to live.

And if she didn't miscarry, if she had a baby, on her own … what then?

She could not work out how she felt about the possibility. She needed to take a test, and be certain, and then perhaps her feelings would be clearer. Right now, it was more than a bit over-whelming. She forced herself to focus for the day on the tasks at Lower Berecombe. She'd sketched a design for the kitchen area that she was pleased with – it would be perfect for a handful of volunteers to use when they worked there. She'd also used her phone to check out likely prices online. They only needed basic but durable units which could be bought locally, and her dad was perfectly capable of fitting them. Ken was delighted at her ballpark quote of just £600 to refit the kitchen, including floor and wall tiles.

'You're a star. That's a good bit under what I'd told the finance committee to budget for. Let's go shopping at the weekend, shall we?'

'Happy to,' she replied, and he smiled.

'Good to see my girl getting involved. Taking your mind off all the bad things that happened, isn't it? You're looking a bit perkier, too. I'm so glad.' He pulled her close into a hug, and she rested her head on his broad, strong shoulder. Yes, it was taking her mind off her old problems. But it looked as though she might have a new one gestating.

*

At last it was time to go home. Tilly asked Ken to drop her off by the small parade of shops in Coombe Regis, telling him she'd walk up the hill back home later. As soon as he'd gone, she dived into the nearest pharmacy and bought a pregnancy test kit. She bought some shampoo as well, and a pack of chocolate biscuits from the next-door grocery shop, in case Ken asked what she'd needed. And then she walked home, went straight to the bathroom and took the test.

Her heart gave a lurch when a second blue line appeared beside the first. It was positive. A whole set of new possible futures were unfolding in front of her. She was either going to have a baby or a miscarriage, and she had no idea how she would cope with either.

*

Ken was out that evening. They ate dinner, but then there was a pub quiz on, and he was in a team with Alan and some of the other volunteers from the railway, so he left her to the clearing

182

up. Tilly had been quiet throughout dinner, her mind on that white plastic stick that she'd hidden away in the drawer of her bedside cabinet. As soon as Ken had gone and the dishwasher was loaded, she reached automatically for a bottle of wine and the corkscrew. A drink or two, or three, would help her come to terms with things. Help her work out how she felt and what to do. She had the foil off and the corkscrew half wound in before she stopped.

'No. Can't do this, Tilly. You're pregnant.'

Pregnant. That big, fat word, applying to her. It was too much to get her head around. She unwound the corkscrew and put the wine bottle back in the rack, then reached for her phone, to call Jo.

Jo sounded a mix of delighted and aghast when she heard the news. 'Bloody hell, mate. That's ... amazing, that is. It was that bloke Rob then, was it? How do you feel about it?'

'I don't know. I really don't.' Tilly realised she'd been waiting for Jo to tell her how she felt. 'Terrified, I suppose, if I'm honest.'

'Have you told your dad?'

'Not yet.'

'Tell him. As soon as possible.'

'What will he say, though?' Would he be disgusted with her? He'd ask who the father was, and she'd have to say something ...

Jo laughed. 'Well I can't tell you – only he can tell you. But what I do know is, you need to tell him. He's lovely, your dad, and he'll support you in whatever you decide to do.'

'I'm not thinking of terminating it.' To tell the truth, Tilly hadn't thought at all about that option, but Jo's words 'whatever you decide' had made her realise that some people would assume that was the answer, given her situation. But no. She couldn't even contemplate that for a second. All those years of trying for a baby – she had to at least try to keep this pregnancy. Despite her terror that it might miscarry and put her through all that heartbreak all over again.

'Then he's got a chance of becoming the world's best granddad.

Tell him, Tilly. As soon as possible. You don't have to keep this to yourself.'

'W-what if I lose it?' Tilly's voice broke as she asked the question.

'Oh, mate. I know you must be scared but there's no reason that will happen again. And if the worst happens, your dad will be there for you through that, too. But maybe this time will be different. Be positive, Tilly. It's the best thing you can do for the baby right now.'

Positive.

Had she been positive with her previous pregnancies? Yes, during the first, ectopic one. But the others, perhaps she'd been too worried about miscarrying ... She must put those thoughts out of her head.

'OK. I'll tell him when he comes home. He's at a pub quiz right now.'

'Good. And Tils – I am here for you. Always. You know that, right?'

'Thanks, Jo. Love you.'

'Love you too, mate.'

*

Ken returned from the pub shortly after ten. Tilly had been sitting in the living room, with a cup of tea and a book that she couldn't concentrate on, waiting for him. She got up to meet him at the door.

'Good quiz? Did your team win?' She tried to keep her voice level though inside she was churning.

'A respectable second. We're happy with that. Have you had a good evening?'

'Quiet. Been thinking.'

'Oh yes? What about?' Ken hung up his jacket in its spot, beside her mother's old red coat, and followed her into the sitting room.

She sat on the sofa and he joined her. 'What's up, pet?'

'Something I need to tell you.'

'Good news or bad?' He sounded worried. There'd been so much bad news from her lately.

'Good, I guess, but scary in a way. Might shock you ...'

'I'm not easily shocked. Try me.' Ken reached out awkwardly and took her hand, patting it. He was trying to show his support, Tilly realised.

'OK. So the thing is ... it turns out ... I did a test. I'm ... well, I'm pregnant.'

'Pregnant! Oh, pet! That's ... well, first, how do *you* feel about it? And who ...'

'I'm ... kind of pleased. But mostly terrified, Dad. What if I lose it again?'

'But what if you don't? There's no reason to suggest you will.' Ken smiled. 'Tilly, I'm delighted for you. And anything I can do to help, I will. You know you have a home here. If you want to stay after the baby's born, that's fine too. But will you want to be with ... the father?'

Tilly shook her head. 'It was an accident, Dad. I guess I'd had a bit too much to drink and ended up ...' she blushed. This was not the sort of conversation it was easy to have with your parent however old you were. 'I ended up in bed with someone.'

'That night you didn't come home?' His voice was gentle, non-judgemental, and she loved him for it.

She nodded.

'Are you going to see the fellow again?'

'As a friend, yes. We already have met up – it was him I went to the cinema with last week. But I don't want him as a boyfriend.'

'Will you tell him?'

Tilly stared at her father. In all the conversations with Jo and now Ken, she hadn't once considered that question. Of course she needed to tell Rob. He deserved to know. How he'd feel about it, she had no idea. But it was his baby too ... and he might want to play a part in the child's upbringing. Assuming she got that far.

'Yes, I suppose I'll have to tell him.'

Ken nodded. 'And do you think he will … oh, you are going to call me old-fashioned. Do you think he will want to marry you? After your divorce comes through, I mean.'

'Dad, I don't want to marry him. He's a nice chap, and I think we could be friends, but neither of us want any romance. That night was a one-off. A fling.'

'A fling with consequences.' Ken smiled wryly at her.

'Yes. He might not want anything to do with the baby. Or he might want to stay in touch and help raise the child. I have no idea. And anyway, there's a long way to go first. There might not even be a baby, judging by my … record so far.' Her voice cracked on this last sentence, and she realised just how much she really wanted this baby. Even though she'd be a single parent, she wanted it with every part of her soul.

'Aw, pet.' Ken reached over and put his arms around her. As always, she felt comforted and strengthened by his presence. 'Whatever you need, whatever you want, I am here to help. You know that, love, don't you? There's space here for you if you want to stay, or if you decide to move out, I'll help with that too. Even if the baby's father takes no interest, you can rest assured the grandfather will take every interest imaginable.'

He sighed. 'I just wish your mum was here still. She'd be so excited, so happy for you.'

Tilly sniffed back a tear. 'She would, wouldn't she?'

*

In the morning, a text arrived on her phone, while Tilly was still lying in bed. It was from Ian. She'd blocked calls from him, but her phone still allowed texts through. She opened it nervously, hoping that whatever was in it would not endanger her fragile sense of stability. The message was short and to the point. She had the impression Ian had sent the same message to everyone on his contact list.

Baby born 2 a.m. A boy. All well.

Tilly put the phone down and lay back on her pillow. So Ian was now a father, of a baby boy. She wondered what they would call the child. Back in the heady exciting days of her first pregnancy, she and Ian had discussed names. 'Ryan for a boy, Lily for a girl,' Ian had said, and Tilly had agreed, liking both names. They were out there now – those two little children, her son Ryan and daughter Lily, that she'd never had.

She examined her feelings about Ian's baby, and was surprised to find she felt genuinely pleased for him and Naomi, that they'd had a successful pregnancy and a safe birth. They'd brought a child into the world, and she was sure they'd do a good job in bringing him up. As long as Ian didn't get bored of Naomi and look for someone else, of course. But why would he, now that he had what he said he'd always wanted?

She picked up her phone and sent a quick text back.

Congratulations. Glad all well.

What would he think when he heard of her pregnancy? She had no intention of telling him any time soon, but he would no doubt hear eventually … if she didn't miscarry again. Would he wonder if he should have stayed with her? She was thankful that he had not, now. Although the future felt uncertain, it was *her* future, hers and this baby's, and whatever happened, she would do her best to make it a good one. Funny how being given this one more thing to worry about, had actually had the opposite effect. Despite her ever-present fear of miscarrying, Tilly felt more at ease with herself than she had done for years.

187

Chapter 20

Ted

Ted's days were slipping back into the old, old routine. He had barely seen Annie. She'd rushed through the station each day, hardly stopping to talk, leaving him confused but still hopeful that she was now free, and if only he could find a decent job, she'd be his. A part of him wanted her to agree to marry him whether or not he had a good job and regardless of what her father wanted – surely if she loved him the way he loved her, she'd put him first and they'd find a way to manage, whatever job he had? But he trusted her to find the right moment to break things off with Bertram and accept him, Ted. If she needed to wait, then he would wait too. Whatever she wanted, he would do. Nothing was more important now than Annie's happiness.

'Is there any news?' he asked her one day, as she hurried through the station. Perhaps he shouldn't ask her directly, just like that. Perhaps other people would find a gentler way into the conversation, a way of leading a discussion around to what really needed to be talked about, but Ted didn't have those skills. If he wanted to know a thing, all he could do was ask it outright. And they only had a short time. Annie had arrived only five minutes before her homeward-bound train.

She smiled at him, a worried, distracted kind of smile, he thought, and reached out to touch his sleeve. There were other passengers on the platform, and Fred Wilson was lurking nearby. 'I-I am still waiting for the right moment to talk to Bertram. There are ... other considerations. It's not easy, dear Ted.'

She was right, but sometimes wasn't it easier just to face a problem head-on? If it was up to him, he'd have talked to both Bertram and her father at the earliest opportunity, the very day after their glorious night together. 'I know, but—' he began, but she held up a hand to interrupt him.

'It's our future, Ted. We have to ... play our cards right. Especially now that ... Ah, look. Here we are, my train is coming. You must wave your flag at it!' She stepped away from him, towards the platform edge.

The train arrived safely and Ted attended to his duties. When he blew his whistle for it to leave, he saw that Annie was leaning out of a window, her forearms resting on the lowered window. She blew him a kiss as the train puffed away. Her left hand, it was, that threw the kiss towards him. Her left hand, with that diamond and sapphire ring still snugly fitted on her third finger, mocking him as it glittered in the sunshine.

*

How he was supposed to make Annie happy when he never had the chance to talk to her, he didn't know. He'd been trying to catch her to ask her to stay for supper one evening. Or to come to see him on Saturday afternoon, when he could leave Fred Wilson in charge of the station (although he hated to do that, not quite trusting the boy) and take her out somewhere. Where, and to do what, he didn't know. For tea, perhaps, at the Lynford Arms hotel. But she said she'd hated that place, when she went there for dinner with

Bertram. He'd rather find somewhere that could be special just for them, that wasn't already sullied by association with her previous beau. Maybe he could take her on a trip to Coombe Regis, where they could stroll along the sea front and buy ice creams as they watched the waves break against the harbour wall. These were the things couples did when they were courting. Perhaps Annie would not give him an answer until he'd taken her out a few times. Perhaps they'd done everything backwards, spending a night together before they'd walked hand in hand along a promenade.

The more he thought about it the more he realised that was what was missing. An outing. A day off. A holiday. He never took a holiday. He was entitled to a day off each week, but he never took it. But this time he would. This weekend. It was four weeks since the night of the storm, and he felt it was time he and Annie spent some proper time together. Time in which they could talk, and enjoy each other's company, without him having to worry when the next train was due in.

Five minutes was all he needed – five minutes with her to ask her to come to Lynford on Saturday afternoon. If she could catch the 12.45 from Michelhampton, and sit in the second coach, he could jump on when it reached Lynford and join her for the remainder of the journey to Coombe Regis. Fred was capable of running the station for a few hours while he was out. Ted would have to trust him for once.

He had the chance the next morning, as she hurried through the station on her way to the bank. He caught hold of her arm.

'Annie, wait. Just two minutes. I've something to ask you.'

'Ted, I've still no answer for you,' she said. There was a tightness about her face and worry in her eyes.

'It's not that. Something else. Please Annie, wait two minutes.' He had to go then, and see to the train's departure, but thankfully she did wait until he had chance to ask her.

'A day out? Coombe Regis? Oh, I haven't been there for months! Yes, Ted. That would be lovely. And it would be a good opportunity for us to talk … I'll see you here at quarter past one on Saturday then.' She gave him a brief smile and was on her way.

Ted grinned, pleased that they had made a date, but then his face fell. *A good opportunity for us to talk*, she'd said. What did she mean by that? Was she having second thoughts, deciding that Bertram was her best option after all? Surely not. She loved him, Ted. He had to cling on to that. She no doubt wanted to talk about how and when to break the news to her father at last. He hardly dared to hope, but maybe … the moment would arise, he'd propose properly to her and she'd agree to marry him, by the end of Saturday. He allowed himself a little fantasy in which they became engaged, then another sudden storm blew up stranding her in Lynford with him once again …

*

Saturday eventually arrived. Ted had taken extra care with his appearance; combing and oiling his hair until it shone, brushing every last speck of dust from his uniform, and polishing his shoes to a high shine. The morning dragged slowly, as he went over for the hundredth time the duties that Fred Wilson needed to take over. The boy was, as ever, surly and insolent, uninterested in the work but rudely curious about Ted's afternoon off.

'You never takes time off, Mr Morgan. Got a lady friend, have you? That one I saw in your sitting room one day? She's a looker, all right. Wouldn't mind stepping out with her meself. Maybe I'll ask her, shall I? Maybe she'd choose me over you, what would you think to that, eh, Mr Morgan?'

'Less of your lip, lad. Now then, are you sure you know what you've got to do? I shall be back by seven o'clock, and I expect to see everything shipshape.'

'Shipshape? This is a station, not a boat!'

It was no good – no matter what Ted said or did, the boy never showed him any respect. Well, they wouldn't be working together for very much longer. The summer was progressing, and the railway would close in September. If not for that, Ted would have been trying to find a way to be rid of the lad.

At last it was time, and Ted was standing on the platform awaiting the arrival of the train from Michelhampton. He was still in his uniform, as it was the only smart outfit he owned, but he had left his stationmaster's cap inside and was wearing a woollen cap instead. Fred was on duty with flag and whistle. Ted had a momentary pang of worry – what if she wasn't on the train? What if she'd changed her mind? But everything was well, and she was there, in the second coach as they'd agreed. She was dressed in a loose, pale green frock, with a straw hat trimmed with white flowers. She had on a pair of white cotton gloves, so he could not see whether that accursed ring was still in place or not.

He jumped on the train as soon as it drew to a halt, to be out of Fred Wilson's prying eyes. 'Annie. Thank you for coming.' He took her hands and sat beside her.

She smiled. 'Did you think I'd stand you up? Of course not. I'm looking forward to not having to share you with the railway timetable.'

She could have him all to herself for the rest of her life, if only she'd say a definite yes to him, Ted thought. And today might be the day that she did so. A bubble of excitement rose up inside him at the thought.

At Coombe Regis they exited the train, walked through the station and out onto the High Street that ran down the hill towards the harbour. Ted caught hold of Annie's gloved hand. It seemed only natural to walk hand in hand. Here they were, stepping out together. She turned and gave him a half-smile, but left her hand in his.

It was a sunny day, with just a gentle breeze, and a few fluffy white clouds dancing above their heads. Ted wanted to savour every moment.

'Shall we walk down to the sea?' he said to Annie. 'And would you perhaps like an ice cream?' His nephews and niece always wanted ice cream. Perhaps it was the wrong thing to offer the woman you wanted to marry, but too late, the words were out.

'I should love an ice cream,' she replied to his relief. 'There's a shop opposite the harbour. We can go there.'

She knew the town better than he did. That was the problem of never taking a day off or going anywhere. Ted felt suddenly embarrassed by how small he'd allowed his world to become. Lynford station and the few shops and businesses in Lynford village. He never went anywhere else. That would all have to change.

Fifteen minutes later, each with an ice-cream cone wrapped in paper, they sat on a bench on the promenade facing out over the pretty little harbour. A couple of seagulls were hopping around by their feet, hoping for some wafer crumbs. This was how it would be when they married, Ted thought. He'd make sure he took his allowed days off, and every weekend they'd go somewhere special and eat ice cream in the sunshine.

Annie finished hers first. She dabbed at her mouth with her handkerchief, and then turned slightly on the bench so that she was facing him. 'Ted, that was lovely. And now we must talk.'

She took a deep breath as though summoning up the strength to continue. Ted's heart gave a lurch. He couldn't bear it if she was having second thoughts. If she told him she wanted to marry Bertram after all – that would be the end, for Ted. He wouldn't be able to go on, without her.

'The thing is, dear Ted, my father's financial situation is so uncertain I cannot rely on any help from him. And so I still dare not say yes to your proposal. Not until I know you have a safe, secure job, and you're able to keep me. Us.'

'I'm still trying … I think there'll be something, possibly in Michelhampton as a porter,' Ted began, but she held up her hand to silence him.

'I cannot be a porter's wife. The salary would not be enough to keep me and … our family.'

'We wouldn't need to start a family straight away, would we?' Ted felt himself blushing. To be sitting here, in public, talking about starting a family made him feel deeply uncomfortable.

'We would, Ted. We … already have.' She put a hand on her tummy. 'Ted, I'm … pregnant. With your child. That night, the storm – God, I never intended this to happen. It's made everything so difficult.'

'A baby? My baby?' He could not believe what he'd heard.

'Yes. Our baby. Dammit.' She looked away, and when she turned back to him there were tears in her eyes. Angry tears, he thought, rather than sad ones.

'I'm going to be a father?' He'd never thought that would happen. An image flashed through his mind – a tiny infant in his arms, wrapped in a white shawl, its face serene in sleep. Annie by his side, making sure he held the child securely, tucking the shawl around it.

'Yes. It's ruined everything.'

'Ruined?'

'Oh, Ted. I don't mean to be harsh. I didn't want this. I wanted you to get a good job, and then us to marry, and *then* we could have started a family. God, I wish we could go back to the night of the storm, and … not get so carried away, I suppose.'

He blushed again, at the reference to their night of lovemaking. 'It's my fault, I shouldn't have—'

She put a hand on his arm. 'You know perfectly well it was more me than you, Ted. Don't try to be the gentleman and take the blame. But anyway, here we are. A child out of wedlock. The shame of it …'

'But I *must* marry you now, before the baby comes! I must marry you immediately, to save your reputation!'

'No, Ted. There's no "must" about it.' Again she sighed, long and deep. 'I've got to work out what's best for this baby. If I tell

194

Father he might send me away, make me give up the baby and then make me marry Bertram anyway, for the sake of his business.'

'But if you tell him I will marry you ...'

She shook her head sadly. 'Not if you are without a job. Oh God. The situation is terrible. I ... I don't know what to do. I do want to be with you, Ted, but I can't see a way forward. If only you had an offer of a good place at a large station ... then maybe ... but we cannot marry if your income is not enough for us to have a reasonable standard of living.'

'Have you ... told your father?'

'About the baby? No.' She sighed. 'How can I? I'll have to, sooner or later, but ...' She shook her head. 'Oh, Ted. The situation is hopeless. If only things were different. If only money didn't matter. If only it was acceptable for an unmarried woman to have a child.'

'We'll find a way. I'll find a suitable job, I promise. I wish I could help more,' he whispered, and she smiled. But the smile did not reach her eyes, which glistened with unshed tears.

'There is nothing you can do, other than get a job. The rest is for me to deal with. Now then, shall we go for a stroll along to the beach?' She stood up and began walking along the promenade without waiting for an answer.

Ted followed, his mind tormented and confused. He needed Norah. He needed to write in his diary. How could he make sense of all that was happening to him?

*

It was a week after the trip to Coombe Regis when the closure of the railway line was officially announced in the local and national newspapers, along with news that the last day of operation was to be Sunday, 20 September. Ted had a letter from Southern Railway, containing details about the last day and the subsequent closure. Ted's employment was officially due to end a week after the last day. In that final week he was to oversee emptying the goods sheds, termination of contracts of junior employees – Fred already had a job lined up with a Michelhampton haulage company. From rail to road, for him. Ted was also instructed to empty the station house, vacating it by the end of the month at the latest so that it could be sold.

And still he had no other job. No other job meant no chance with Annie. It meant his child was in danger of being born out of wedlock. Or worse, given up for adoption if Annie's father sent her away.

Ted had stopped sleeping; instead spending hours tossing and turning, fretting about his future. He'd written a pleading letter once more to the area manager, Mr Hornsby, for help, and in response had received a list of vacancies within Southern Railway. All were for porter jobs, or ticket-office staff in the larger stations. There were still no stationmaster jobs available. He'd thought about trying other railway companies, but did not know who to write to. The idea of moving out of Dorset made him nervous, in any case. He knew nowhere else. If it wasn't for Annie, he'd have applied for one of the porter jobs and worked his way up again. But he needed a larger salary from the start, to support her and their baby.

Since the announcement of the line's closure, business had picked up. It was as though everyone wanted to make the most of it while they still could. Every weekend service was full and standing. Some weekday trains were busy too – with people eschewing the bus service for the train, for its last season. As a result, Ted barely saw Annie as she passed through each day, being too busy with other passengers.

As the summer progressed, the line became yet more busy, Ted became yet more stressed about finding a job, and Annie's figure began to fill out. One Friday afternoon she arrived early for her homeward train, and told Ted that it was her last day at work.

'I can't continue at the bank once the baby starts to show,' she said. 'It would be too difficult to explain. They won't allow an unmarried mother to work there anyway. So I have resigned.'

'I won't see you anymore, then?' Ted said, his heart sinking.

'You can telephone me at my father's house if you have any news about a job. This is the number.' She pressed a piece of paper into his hand.

'May I telephone you to ask you out again? Like our day at Coombe Regis?'

She regarded him for a moment before answering. 'Only if we are engaged. And that means only if you have a job. My father would not permit me to be seen out with a man if I am pregnant but not engaged.'

'Have you told him yet? About the baby?' She must have. How else would she explain her resignation from her job?

But she shook her head. 'No. I have told him the bank are laying off staff. I still … am frightened, to tell the truth, of what he will do. I can hide it from him a little longer, and maybe … you'll have a job offer in time …'

She walked away from him then and sat down on a bench on the platform. She took a book from her handbag and opened it to read. Ted watched her, realising this meant she was not interested in talking to him any longer.

He'd write in his journal that evening, he decided. He needed to try to make sense of it all. He needed Norah's wise words, but who knew when he would be able to see his sister again.

Chapter 21

Tilly

Over the next few weeks, as morning sickness kicked in and Tilly felt tired and emotional, she found herself appreciating more and more, if that was possible, the quiet, calm, steady presence of Ken. He was happy to fuss around her if she needed it or leave her alone if that's what she wanted. He took over the cooking after Tilly found certain smells of raw food made her gag. He brought her tea and ginger biscuits in bed every morning to help stave off the sickness. He drove up to Michelhampton in search of fresh pineapple, when the local shops were out of it and Tilly found herself craving it.

He was the perfect supportive housemate. She could talk to him about anything. And her fears that she might miscarry again were slowly diminishing, with each week that passed.

Although there was still the one thing they had not discussed. She kept telling herself she was waiting for the right moment. It came, eventually, one balmy evening when they were sitting outside in the garden in the sunshine.

'It's a gorgeous evening,' Tilly said. 'Remember when I first came and we had all those weeks of cold grey weather? Hard to imagine that now. I love it here in the summer.'

Ken smiled. 'I knew you would. You seem so much healthier, pet, than when you first arrived. The Dorset air's done you good.'

'I feel so much better,' she said.

'It's so good to see. When you arrived, oh pet, I was so worried. You were so depressed, you didn't seem to care what you did or what happened to you. It was like you were self-destructing, all that drinking and everything. Now you've got that little baby coming it's as though you've ... got more to live for.'

Tilly gazed at him for a moment. This was her chance, to tell him what had happened on that terrible day.

'Dad, I know you were worried. And you were right to be. I was in a bad way. Do you want me to tell you how I ended up at Jo's?'

He reached for her hand. 'Love, if it's going to help you for me to hear it, then tell me.'

And so Tilly took a deep breath, and while the sun sank into the sea and her father sat listening quietly, his hand squeezing hers as though to lend her strength, she told him the whole story.

The day after Ian told her their marriage was over, he'd brought Naomi round to their house. Tilly had spent the day watching TV, mopping up her tears.

'Oh. You're in,' he said to Tilly. 'I wasn't expecting ...'

'Where else would I be?' she replied. 'I've got no job. And this is still my home.'

'Right. Well. We'll, um go elsewhere,' he said, leading an embarrassed-looking Naomi, whose neat little baby-bump was unmistakable in the clingy black dress she was wearing, back to the front door.

Tilly had put herself to bed in the spare room, where she'd moved as soon as Ian had dropped his bombshell, and cried herself to sleep that night. In the morning she realised Ian had not come home. She went to make herself some tea and found there was no milk.

That was it. That was, for some reason she could not now work out, the final straw. No milk, and Ian had spent the night with Naomi, while he waited for her and her baby-less womb to move out. No milk. No chance of a decent cuppa to take the edge off her pain.

She'd opened the cupboard where they kept medicines and pulled out everything she could find. Half a packet of paracetamol, some ibuprofen, a couple of codeine tablets, some tablets for treating diarrhoea. And there was a half-bottle of whisky in the house somewhere. She gathered it all together, took it upstairs to the spare room, where the duvet was still crumpled and tear-stained from the night, and got into bed. Methodically she began swallowing pills, taking a swig of whisky after each. How many would it take? She had no idea. She vaguely hoped she'd just fall asleep and not wake up. That would be perfect. Blissful slumber forever, and a big fuck-you to Ian.

Halfway through she vomited. Most of it went over the side of the bed but plenty more over herself. Got to keep going, she told herself. No point stopping now. She forced more whisky down her throat, and that was the last thing she remembered.

*

Everything was white. Bright, glaring, uncomfortably white. That was her next conscious thought, though for a moment she wondered if she was truly conscious. Or had it worked – was this it? Was this the life beyond? A brutal, cramping pain in her stomach and the urge to vomit told her it wasn't. Gentle hands helped her sit up and lean over a cardboard dish. There were tubes attached to her, a needle in the back of her hand, something in her nose. She gagged – there was nothing to be sick on – and collapsed back against starched pillows.

200

'There now. Feeling any better? Have a sip of water, perhaps.'
A plastic cup was held to her lips and she took a sip, most of which trickled down the side of her face. She opened her eyes. The gentle hands belonged to a male nurse, whose name badge read 'Timothy'.

'Hello. Nice to see you with us,' he said, with a smile. 'If you're feeling up to it, your friend's outside. Desperate to see you, she is. May I tell her she can come in?'

'Wh-who is it?' Tilly asked, her voice coming out as a croak.

'Her name's Jo,' Timothy replied. 'You're here because of her.' He adjusted the drip in her hand, checked a urine bag (with horror Tilly realised she was also hooked up to a catheter) and then opened a door. Tilly realised she was in some sort of private room, presumably off a main ward.

'Oh thank God!' Jo rushed in, sat on the side of the bed and gathered Tilly into her arms. 'Oh my God, Tils. Thought you were going to … going to … God. Don't ever, EVER, fucking do that again, all right? Thank Christ you're still here.'

'Wh-what happened?' Tilly remembered there'd been no milk. And that pills and whisky had felt like a good alternative.

'Your dad rang me. He'd been trying to ring you all morning. You'd told him something about Ian leaving you? God, Tils, what's happening? You should have rung me. I'd have dropped everything … Your dad was worried you weren't answering, and he had a bad feeling, and so he asked me to go round. I found you … called the ambulance, and here you are.'

'Dad knows?'

Jo shook her head. 'No. I didn't want to tell him you were all right, in case … you weren't. Didn't want to tell him what you'd done. No parent should need to hear that. Fuck's sake, mate, I know things are crap, but *what were you thinking?*'

Tilly opened her mouth to answer, and realised there was no answer. She had not been thinking. She'd just … gone under. As though her life was a surfboard and the waves had been growing in intensity, and that last one – Ian leaving her – had knocked her off. She'd been submerged, underwater too long, and pills had felt like the only way out.

Jo reached over again and hugged Tilly, her long dark hair across Tilly's face, her tears wetting Tilly's neck. 'Tell me. What's Ian done?'

Tilly told her about Ian and Naomi, and watched as her best friend's jaw dropped wide open. 'The utter git! How could he! After all your years together, all you've been through. Bastard. Oh, mate, why on earth didn't you call me at once, that day? I'd have come straight over and drunk that Prosecco with you. After giving Ian a piece of my mind. Can't believe you've been holed up by yourself after that, for two days. No wonder you … Anyway, the thing is, you *don't have* to deal with it all by yourself, right? You've got me. And that lovely dad of yours. We'll look after you. Just *promise* me, Tils, you'll try to help yourself, too? Christ if I'd lost you today … I don't know how I'd have …' Jo pulled a wad of tissues from the box beside Tilly's bed and blew her nose loudly into them. Tilly reached out and took her hand, oddly feeling as though it was now she who needed to comfort Jo, and finding that was somehow easier than being the one needing comforting.

'Listen,' said Jo, her voice hoarse. 'You're coming to stay with me when you're out of here. I'm not going to take my eyes off you.'

'Thank you. You're the best friend anyone could ever have,' Tilly said. 'I suppose I should tell Ian.'

'Fuck Ian. He doesn't deserve to know. I'll pop round and collect a few things for you and tell him you're convalescing with me. I'll tell him you've had appendicitis or something, and have been operated on.'

'I think I was sick …'

'You were. I'll clean it up.'

'Can't tell Dad.'

Jo reached out and stroked Tilly's face, tucking a strand of hair behind her ear. 'We'll have to tell him something, Tils. He'll be so worried. I'll let him know you're all right, then it's up to you when or if you tell him the whole story.'

Tilly turned away and closed her eyes. She didn't even want to think about whether she wanted to tell her dad or not. It was all too much.

'Tired?'

'Feel like shit.'

'Not surprised. The doctors say it was a good thing you vomited in the bed. It was glugging that whisky that caused that. Got most of the pills out before they had chance to do much damage. You're going to be all right.' Jo took a deep, shuddering breath. 'You are one lucky lady, Tils.'

*

Ken was silent when she finished talking but retained his grip on her hand. A small muscle was clenching in his jaw, and Tilly knew he was struggling with his emotions. At last he sighed and shook his head sadly.

'Oh, pet. Jo just said she thought it had all got too much for you. Made it sound like a kind of breakdown. To think I could have lost you. That you were that bad. I … I had no idea.'

'I know,' she whispered. It was hard for her to believe she'd felt that was the only solution. She put a hand on her tiny bump. If things had been different, if Jo hadn't found her when she did, this little life inside her would never have had the chance to begin.

'Your friend Jo. *My* friend. I love that woman.'

'So do I, Dad.'

'Did you ever tell Ian?'

She shook her head. 'No. And I'm not going to. He thinks it was appendicitis, still. He gave up all his rights to the truth when he ended our marriage.'

He nodded. 'I think you're right not to tell him. None of his business, is it? Listen, pet. If ever you feel it's all too much and you can't cope, I mean God forbid but if anything went wrong with' – he nodded at her midriff – 'well, promise me you'd talk to me? Or talk to Jo? Don't keep it to yourself. Give us a chance to help you. A problem shared is a problem halved, don't they say?'

She stood and leaned over him to hug him tightly. 'Dad, I can't imagine ever considering it again. It's an old cliché, but I think it was a cry for help. And Jo and you have helped. As has Rob Coogan, in his way, and this little bundle of cells inside me. I'm … kind of … rebuilding myself, bit by bit.'

*

Tilly was three and a half months gone by her reckoning when she finally told Rob about the baby. She'd had a scan at twelve weeks that showed a healthy, good-sized foetus, wriggling around, sucking its thumb. She was past the point where miscarriages one and two had occurred, but her third miscarriage, the one that in many ways was the worst, had happened at fourteen weeks. Approaching that time, she'd barely been able to function, as the fear that it might all happen again threatened to engulf her. It was Ken who'd suggested she went out, to see a film, take her mind off things. And the only person locally she'd been to the cinema with was Rob, so it seemed natural to text him and suggest it. There was a new action film on she thought he might like, and she soon had an answer: yes, he'd love to go.

This time she let him collect her and drive them both to Michelhampton. Tilly had dressed in a loose shirt over jeans that no longer fastened. She'd have to buy some maternity clothes soon. The few she'd had from her last pregnancy had been left in Ian's house.

They had time to spare before the film and went for a drink in the same pub as on the previous cinema trip. 'You can have a glass of wine this time if you like,' Rob said, 'as you're not driving.'

'Um, actually I'd rather not,' she said. 'Just an orange juice for me, please.'

He frowned but got the drinks and sat down beside her, at the same table as last time. 'Have you given up alcohol? I hope it's not just that you felt you had too much that time when … we met.'

'No, it's not that.' This was it. This was the moment she needed to tell him about the consequences of that night. 'Listen, Rob. There's something I need to tell you. I should probably wait till after the film because you might want to just go home when you hear what it is, but … I think now's the time.'

She realised she was rambling. Better to just say it, get it out there. Taking a deep breath, she continued. 'So that, ahem, that night we spent together. My memory's a little hazy but I don't think we … used anything. And, well, I seem to be pregnant.' There. She'd said it. She picked up her drink and took a sip, not catching his eye, not yet ready to see his reaction.

'Pregnant?' he repeated, his voice half a whisper, half a croak.

'Yep.'

'Must be … three months?'

'Fourteen weeks, almost. I … um … had a miscarriage at fourteen weeks once. Bit scared that might happen again, if I'm honest.' She gave a nervous chuckle, then cursed herself for dropping that emotional bomb on him when he'd not yet had time to get his head around the fact she was pregnant. And 'bit scared' was the understatement of the century. Crippled with terror, more like.

'Ah no. Don't be scared of that. You'll be all right. But, gosh. Well. Hadn't really considered that I might … be a dad again. That's if … am I jumping ahead?'

'I'm definitely keeping it if that's what you're asking.'

'That's good.' He smiled, and there was relief in his expression. 'But … do you want me in the child's life? I mean, I'd love to, and I'll definitely pay my share and support you in whatever way you need. Of course. I hope you know that all goes without saying. I mean, it's a shock, haven't really taken it in. Oh God, I'm babbling, aren't I?'

She laughed. 'Yes, a little. It's hard to take in. Not sure I'm completely comfortable with it yet, not after having lost pregnancies before.'

'Pregnancies? More than one lost?'

She nodded. 'Three. Part of the reason my husband left me. He wanted children but I didn't seem able to provide them.'

He raised his eyebrows at this. 'I see why you're worried then. But there's no reason it'll go wrong this time, is there? If there's anything I can do …'

'Thanks, Rob. I guess you need some time to think about it. But I thought it's only fair you know, and that you hear it from me.'

'Thank you. I appreciate you telling me. Shall we go and see this film, then? I'm not entirely sure how well I'll be able to concentrate on it, but we might as well go!'

Tilly wasn't sure she'd be able to concentrate on it either. But telling Rob had felt like the right thing to do. He needed to know. It was his child too.

After all those years with Ian, it felt odd to think this virtual stranger, albeit someone who was fast becoming a friend, was as much involved in the making of her baby as she was.

But as she glanced across at Rob, his open, smiling face, his supportive, friendly demeanour, and she recalled his words offering whatever support she needed, she thought she could have done a lot worse in choosing a father for her child.

Chapter 22

Ted

Sunday, 20 September. The last day of opening. Ted rose at six o'clock, his usual time. He washed and dressed in his stationmaster's uniform as he had done every day for the last sixteen years. His shirt was clean, and the jacket and trousers newly brushed. He'd polished his buttons and shoes. By seven o'clock he'd had breakfast, donned his stationmaster's cap and opened the station. There was already a queue of people outside.

'Thought I'd get an early train today, just to Coombe Regis and back,' said one man. 'Expect tickets on the afternoon trains will be sold out.'

Ted didn't answer, but just hooked open the door and went behind the counter to start selling tickets. Why couldn't these people have made a point of using the railway before this summer? If they had, then perhaps it wouldn't be closing. And perhaps Annie would have agreed to marry him. He hated them. All of them – these passengers who wanted to travel today only because it was the last chance, but who'd let the railway decline until the company had had no choice but to close it.

'You're in a bad mood,' said the man who was going to Coombe Regis. 'Cheer up, mate. It should be a fun day. You'll have loads of people through here.'

A thought occurred to Ted. He had not seen Annie for over a month, not since she'd stopped work. He'd had two short letters from her, that asked after his health, confirmed that she was well but that there was no real news. They read as though her father was checking her mail. Perhaps he was. Ted had written back once, not quite knowing what to say. It had always been hard to put his feelings into words and it was even harder to do it on paper when he knew someone else was going to read it. It was different writing his diary, when he could ramble on knowing that no one else would ever read it. And what if her father was checking her incoming mail as well as her outgoing letters?

He was hoping that maybe Annie would take the train today, one last time. To commemorate the end of an era. To see him. The more he thought about it the more he convinced himself that that was what she would do. The thought cheered him a little. He had no idea what he'd say to her – he still had no job to go to – but just to see her beautiful face, to catch a glimpse of her stunning smile, to be in her company even if only for a few seconds, would make it all seem more bearable. How was she? The baby she was carrying – his baby – how big was it now? He longed to see her. If she didn't come today, he'd go to see her. Next week, once the station house was cleared. He needed to go to Michelhampton anyway, to find some cheap lodgings. And to find a job. In desperation, he'd scoured the local papers looking for anything he might do – but there'd been nothing suitable. Nothing he could even apply for; only adverts looking for skilled white-collar workers or tradespeople. He could learn new skills, but only if he could find an opening. And there were no railway jobs going.

The day passed in a haze of activity. There was always something to do – people wanting tickets, trains coming in and disgorging hordes of passengers, people wanting access to the platform to wave at the trains or take photographs. A couple of local businesses had set up stalls outside the station, selling tea made in an urn, slices of cake, paper cups of ale. Another stall was selling postcards printed with images of the railway and handing out balloons to every child. Ted kept a look out for Annie all day, but there was no sign of her. He could have missed her, he realised. With all the hundreds of people arriving and leaving on every train, she could have been on one and he might not have seen her. But surely if she'd come she would have searched him out?

Fred Wilson was busy too, helping with the signals and train dispatch duties. He was as surly as ever.

'Should have got more staff if you'd known it would be this busy,' he grumbled, as yet another train left the platform. 'Soon as the last one's gone, I'm off home.'

'No you're not, lad,' Ted replied. 'You're on duty till eight o'clock this evening. There'll be a lot of clearing up to do when it's all over, and I need you to help me do it. You'll be paid the overtime.'

'Huh. My last day, and finally I get the chance of some overtime pay.' Fred shrugged and went into the waiting room, where he sat down and lit up a cigarette. It wasn't time for his break, but Ted felt too tired and depressed to argue it with him.

'Stationmaster? Might I have a few words, please?' A small man wearing a trilby hat and with a camera hung around his neck had approached Ted. 'Albert Bundy, *Dorset Herald*. Do you have a few minutes to spare?'

'Er, yes, I suppose so,' Ted said. He'd never met anyone from the papers before.

'Excellent!' The reporter pulled a notepad and pencil from his pocket. 'If I could start with your name, and background, how long you've been working here, that sort of thing.'

Ted blinked, and for a moment felt lost for words. 'I'm T … I mean, Edward Morgan. Been here, um, sixteen years now.'

'And what does it mean to you, the closure of the railway?'

'It's the end. Of everything.' The words came out bitter, and Bundy looked startled by Ted's passion.

'The end. All right.' He made a note in his notebook. 'And what next, for Edward Morgan, stationmaster?'

Ted shook his head. 'I don't know. I've no job to go to. Another week closing things down here and then that's it. I'll lose my home, too.'

Bundy tilted his head on one side as he made more notes. 'That's very sad. Hope you find something.' He took a business card out of his pocket and handed it to Ted. 'Well look, maybe when you find a new job get in touch. I could do a "one year on" piece about how railway workers have fared since the closure. Hmm. Could be worth pitching. So, I'll write something up. *Dorset Herald*. Should be in tomorrow's edition. Nice to meet you, Mr Morgan.' He shook Ted's hand, then hurried off to interview people waiting for the next train.

Three questions. That was all the reporter had asked. Three questions to sum up the end of an era, the end of his lifelong association with the railway, the only thing he'd ever known.

*

It seemed fitting that the last ever train to depart Lynford station was the 17.21 to Michelhampton. The train that for the last year or more Ted had looked forward to, for it meant a glimpse of Annie. Not today, though. There'd been no sign of her. Today the train arrived from Coombe Regis packed to the rafters. The platform at Lynford was heaving – it seemed the entire village had turned out to see the last train depart. It was all Ted could do to battle his way through, yelling at people to stand back as he checked the doors were closed and that the train's guard could see him wave the flag.

With a whistle and an enormous cheer from the crowd, and a hearty wave from Bill Perkins, the last train left. Some of the people on the platform were dabbing handkerchiefs at their eyes. People Ted had never seen before, who'd probably hardly ever used the railway. Gradually they left, going back to their homes, many of them travelling in their own motorcars. The stalls outside the station packed up. All the cakes and postcards had sold, and the balloon seller popped the last of his balloons.

Fred was sullenly walking around the station collecting rubbish in a bucket. Burst balloons, discarded waxed paper cups that had held tea or beer, empty cigarette packets. 'Don't know why we bother,' he said. 'It's all closing.'

'We bother because for sixteen years I've ensured this station is neat and tidy, and I'm not stopping now. Get on with your work, lad. It's your last day. Your last couple of hours, then you're free of me forever.'

'Thank Christ for that,' muttered Fred, as he shuffled along the platform, kicking a cigarette butt onto the tracks.

Ted sighed, biting back the earful he longed to throw at that insolent lad. It wasn't worth it. Anything Fred didn't do today Ted would easily be able to do over the next few days. He had another week, and no trains to dispatch.

At last everyone had left, except Fred who was finishing up in the goods yard. The light was beginning to fail as Ted closed the station doors and locked up, for the last time. He stood for a moment with his hand on the ticket-office counter, and gazed at the station clock, that he'd religiously wound and kept accurate for so many years. What would happen to the station, and everything in it? He supposed the railway company would sell it all off, in an auction. Who'd buy that clock, or the bench on the platform where Annie had so often sat, or the chairs in the ladies' waiting room, or the goods sheds, or even the station house itself?

Who'd buy any of it? The whole lot should be bulldozed, Ted thought. He slapped his hand down hard on the counter. All those years working here, keeping everything perfect, and for nothing. It was all over.

He felt as though he was drowning. The uncertainty. No job. No more station. No more home, in a few days. No Annie.

He recognised the feeling, when it was all too much. He needed help. He needed someone with a calm, wise voice, to reassure him there was a way forward. Norah. He needed his sister, Norah.

Immediately he went into the ticket office and lifted the telephone. He'd call her now. At least, he'd call her neighbour, and ask her to fetch Norah. His hands were shaking as he dialled the number. It took so long for the dial to click its way back after each number.

And then it rang and rang and rang and there was no answer. No answer at all. He remembered then that Norah had said in her most recent letter that she would be unable to telephone him on the last day, as her neighbour had been admitted to hospital and so she had no access to a telephone.

If he could not speak to Norah then he had to speak to Annie. No one else could calm him. He dug out the slip of paper she'd given him with her home telephone number on and, barely able to focus, dialled her number. She had to be at home. He could not bear it if she wasn't. He needed her.

The number rang several times, and Ted felt panic rising with every unanswered ring. He'd never felt like this before – so lost, totally at sea, panicking and unable to cope with life. Even in those dark days of school, when he'd been bullied, when he'd not yet learned any techniques for coping with stress or change – even then he'd never felt this bad.

At last there was a click, and a cultured male voice, with no trace of a Dorset accent, answered. 'Galbraith residence. Who's calling, please?'

Not Annie. Why couldn't Annie have answered? Mustering every last speck of his social skills, Ted forced himself to speak, keeping his voice as steady as he could. 'This is Edward Morgan, from Lynford station. Is Miss Galbraith available to come to the telephone, please?'

'Ah, Morgan. I've heard a bit about you. No, Anne cannot come to the telephone now. She is out for the evening. With her fiancé.'

'Fiancé? D-do you mean … B-Bertram …' Ted struggled to recall Bertram's last name. His mind was spinning. Had she *still* not had chance to tell her father the engagement was off? After all this time?

'Bertram Clarke-Watson. Yes, I do mean him. But listen, Morgan, now that I've got the chance to speak with you, I want to tell you something and I want you to listen. If you've got designs on my daughter, you need to think again. You've turned her head, somehow, and made her think she has a choice in who she marries. But let me tell you this, son. She has no choice. She will marry Clarke-Watson. And you, if you're any kind of a gentleman, will step aside to allow her to do just that. You hear me?'

'I-I hear you, sir … but …' Did her father know about the baby? If she hadn't told him she'd ended the engagement, Ted could only assume she hadn't told him about her pregnancy yet either. Surely she would have to, soon. It was clear though, that she had spoken to her father about him in some respect – her father had at least heard of Ted.

'There are no buts. She tells me you might have a job at a larger station. But I'm telling you, no matter what size the station, no daughter of mine is marrying a stationmaster. Clarke-Watson's a man of business. He's a fine head for business on his shoulders. He's going places. If his company and mine were to merge, we'd be the largest insurance company in the county. He's building a new house, outside Michelhampton. And he's arranging to buy an apartment in London. You can't compete. Besides, I like Clarke-Watson. I don't know you from Adam.'

'I-I could come and meet you …' As the father of Annie's child, surely he'd have to meet Mr Galbraith, the child's grandfather, sooner or later? An image flashed through his mind of a christening: Annie holding the child in a long white robe, Ted standing proudly at her side, Annie's father smiling indulgently on the opposite side of the font.

The image dissipated when Mr Galbraith spoke again. 'You'll stay away, Morgan. Stay well away from Anne. And don't call this number ever again, you hear me?'

With that, the line went dead. Ted slumped into the nearest chair. It was over. Everything was over. Everything was finished. There was no way forward for him now. He leaned back, his head against the wall of the ticket office, his hands hanging loosely at his sides, staring at the ceiling. It needed a coat of paint, he realised, surprising himself with such a mundane thought at such a traumatic time. No one would ever paint it now. No one would care. It was all over.

Chapter 23

Tilly

A couple of weeks later marked the third anniversary of Tilly's mother's death, and the first she'd spent with her father. She'd intended to come down to be with him for the first anniversary, but she'd been recovering from one of her miscarriages. And then having missed the first, although she'd phoned him and remembered her mum in her own way, it hadn't seemed right to be with him on the second anniversary. But here she was now, for the third, and they'd planned to go and lay flowers on her mother's memorial plaque, in the churchyard where her ashes had been buried.

It had been cancer, the dreaded 'C' word, that had taken away Tilly's mum. An aggressive form of cancer of the colon. Margaret had been one of those people who didn't like to 'bother the doctor with little upsets' as she'd so often said. So when she had 'a bit of a tummy ache' and 'some trouble on the toilet' as she'd put it, she'd dismissed it as nothing to worry about, caused by something she'd eaten. It was only when Ken, concerned by her rapid weight loss and her clear discomfort, frog-marched her to the doctor's surgery one day that she was diagnosed. By then the cancer had already spread but was considered possibly still treatable. She had a round of chemotherapy followed by surgery, but then came the unwelcome news, relayed to Tilly by her father on the phone, his words punctuated by anguished sobs, that there was secondary cancer elsewhere in her body, and that only palliative care was possible now.

'Put Mum on,' Tilly had said, feeling her world collapsing around her. It was only two months since her ectopic pregnancy. Mum had been so supportive through that, despite being so ill herself. Tilly had refused to consider the cancer would be terminal. It was her mum, she'd survive, she'd have the surgery and come through it, she had to! But no, her dad's words meant she had to face her worst fears.

'Mum? Dad just told me … I can't believe it. Oh, Mum!'

'Shh, love. It's all right. I've had a good life. Look at me, I'm 64, that's not a bad innings. You're not to fret about it. It's not good for you, not so soon after your … troubles.'

'But, Mum, 64 is no age. Can't they—'

'No, love. There's nothing more. They'll make sure I'm comfortable and that it doesn't hurt. These painkillers are marvellous. I feel perfectly all right, you know! They're going to send round Macmillan nurses later on, to help your dad. I don't want you to worry about it. I keep telling Ken that, too. He's worrying for nothing. We should be making the most of the time we have left together.'

'Yes, we should. Can I come down to visit this weekend?'

'Of course, love. Any time.'

She'd gone, she remembered, every weekend possible from then until … the end. Ian came with her only once. Mum had declined rapidly, and rather than being a few months as Tilly and her father had expected, it was only three weeks before Margaret was moved into a hospice, and seven days later she died, with Tilly and Ken at her side, holding a hand each as she breathed her last. There was a vase of freesias, Margaret's favourites, scenting the room. A radio was playing in the room, tuned to Classic FM, where some lovely, peaceful music accompanied her on her final journey. Tilly had always meant to write to the radio station and find out what they were playing at the moment of her mother's death, but somehow never got around to it. She'd left the hospice with Ken that day, and driven him home, all the while his head was shaking as he repeated, 'What am I going to do without her? I never thought she'd go first, never.' It was going to take him a long time to adjust to life alone, Tilly realised.

She stayed with him two days, left for a week to return to work, then came back for two more days either side of Margaret's funeral. Ian accompanied her only for a day. She stocked up Ken's fridge and freezer with ready meals, his cupboard with packs of pasta and tins of beans, made sure all his washing was done and offered to come back in a couple of weeks to help clear out Margaret's things.

Ken had shaken his head. 'No, pet. It's all right. I'll do all that myself … when I feel up to it. Right now, I'd rather leave it all be. It feels too final to take it away. I can't, just yet.'

She'd hugged him. 'There's no rush. When you're ready, if you want help, call me.'

They'd spoken twice a week on the phone since then, but somehow she'd only managed to visit one more time, although Ken had been up to London to see her on several occasions. Then her own problems had escalated, and she'd hidden the second two miscarriages from him, not wanting him to experience any more loss.

But now he knew. Now he knew everything, and he was dealing with it, and more than that, he was helping her deal with it too.

And Margaret's things were still in their places, in the house.

*

217

Tilly found her father sitting at the breakfast table, a slice of toast half eaten on his plate, staring out of the window. It was a bright, sunny day, although a strong breeze was blowing, whipping up waves on the sea below.

'Your mum loved this kind of weather,' he said, as Tilly put a hand on his shoulder, acknowledging the importance of the day. 'She always wanted to go for walks along the cliffs, feel the wind in her hair and come back with rosy cheeks.'

'We could do that today, in her memory, if you like.'

'I'd like that, pet. After we've been to the graveyard.'

Margaret's remains had been cremated, and in a corner of the churchyard there were a number of plaques set in the ground, marking the place where ashes had been buried. Tilly hadn't been here since the day she'd accompanied Ken to bury the ashes, a couple of months after the cremation. The vicar had said a few prayers as they stood around the prepared hole in the ground. Tilly remembered how as Ken had upended the box, tipping them in, a gust of wind had caught them and blown a handful of ashes back towards them. As though Mum's reaching out and giving us one last hug, Tilly had thought, her eyes full of tears. She'd felt too choked up to be able to repeat that thought to Ken, and the little ceremony had ended quickly with the vicar being the only person who spoke, other than Ken's muttered thanks as he shook the clergyman's hand afterwards.

Today, with breakfast over, Tilly drove Ken first to a florist's shop where they collected a shallow planter Ken had ordered a few days earlier. It was filled with petunias, lobelia and white alyssum. 'Your mum loved these. Simple garden border plants.'

'Beautiful,' Tilly commented. 'It should last a few months, if we come back often enough to look after it.'

They drove on to the churchyard, that was set halfway up the hill on the other side of town. From the corner where Margaret's ashes were buried there was a spectacular view over Coombe Regis, its little harbour and, of course, the endless sea.

'Mum would have loved this view,' Tilly commented as they made their way along the lines of memorial plaques to Margaret's, which was engraved simply with her name and dates of birth and death.

Her name was near the top of the stone. 'Space for me underneath, when the time comes,' Ken had said, when he ordered the plaque.

'She would, yes,' he said now, gazing at it before placing the planter down just above the plaque. They stood together in silence for a few minutes, each lost in their own thoughts.

What would you think to this pregnancy, eh, Mum? Tilly found herself silently asking. Her mum would have been delighted, she thought. She'd have said something slightly inappropriate, such as, 'Well you're not getting any younger, Tilly my girl, so it's best you crack on by whatever means necessary.' Tilly would have laughed and come up with some playful insult to throw back at her, and the whole thing would have ended with her mum putting the kettle on. She smiled at the little fantasy and placed a hand on her small but unmistakable bump.

'Ready to go for that walk, then?' Ken asked, and Tilly nodded. A sunny, blowy walk along the cliffs, punctuated by a rest on the bench at the highest point where they would share the flask of tea Ken had made, was the perfect way to mark the occasion.

And it was. A little while later they were sitting on the bench, sipping tea from plastic cups. Tilly leaned against her father, feeling his warmth and strength seeping into her. She'd lost her mum, her husband, her job and three pregnancies. But not her life, thanks to Jo, and not her future, thanks to her dad and this new little life just starting inside her. She felt as though her life was being reborn, here on the Dorset coast.

She glanced at Ken, who was staring out to sea, a distant, longing look in his eye. He was missing Margaret still, so much. Three years was no time after the forty they'd been married. Would he ever feel he could move on? Margaret's coat still hung there, on the peg in the hallway, where it always had. If or when the day came that he felt he could remove it – give it to charity or even just store it away – then she'd know he was moving on at last. Maybe getting past this third anniversary would help.

'Dad?'

'Yes, pet?'

'Would you mind if … I stayed with you until after the baby is born? I know it's months away but …'

He turned to smile at her. 'Of course. You can stay as long as you like. I want you to stay. Your mum would have wanted that too.'

'Thanks, Dad.' He wrapped an arm around her shoulders and she snuggled into him.

'This is your home as long as you want it, Tillikins.'

'Dad, you're really going to have to stop calling me that. Especially when the baby comes along. I can't have a baby name myself when I'm a mum, can I?'

He smiled fondly at her. 'I called you that from the moment you were born, pet.'

Chapter 24

Ted

There was a frantic tapping at the glass of the station door. Ted lifted his head wearily. The railway was closed – didn't they all know it? What idiot was trying to get into the station now? He hauled himself to his feet, ready to give whoever it was short shrift, but then he caught a glimpse of a familiar red coat through the ticket-office window. Annie! She'd come after all! She was not with that Watson-Clarke fellow, despite what her father had said.

He ran clumsily across the room, knocking a stack of paperwork off the counter in his haste to open the door and let her in. He fumbled with the lock but at last it was open and she stumbled inside, falling immediately into his arms.

'Ted! Oh Ted!' She was out of breath, as though she'd been running.

His own despair forgotten, he held her tight, revelling in the scent of her perfume, the softness of her, the brush of her hair against his face. 'Shh, Annie, I'm here. It's all right.'

'Ted, my darling. It's over, it's all over …'

'Over?' For a terrible moment he thought she meant it was over between them, or that her pregnancy had somehow gone wrong.

She looked up at him. There were tears in her eyes but also a wildness, a recklessness he hadn't seen before. 'I mean my engagement. I told him. I told Bertram it was over. My father had insisted I go out today with Bertram. I wanted to come here, to be with you on the last day, but I had no choice. Ted, I wanted to be here so much!'

'It was a g-good day,' he said. 'A lot of people came.'

'That's good. But Ted, I told Bertram about the baby. I didn't tell him whose it was. And I told him I wouldn't marry him. He got angry. So angry – I've never seen him like that! He scared me. We were in the car – he'd pulled over when I told him, and he was shouting at me and calling me … all sorts of horrid things.'

'Did he hurt you?' Ted asked. He could feel rage rising at the thought of that fellow abusing his darling Annie. He gently pushed her away to look for evidence. If Watson-Clarke had harmed a single hair of her head, Ted couldn't be responsible for his actions if he ever saw the other man again.

'He grabbed my arm, bruised me, I thought he was going to slap me but he didn't …'

'I hate him. How dare he. I'll … I'll …' Ted's fists involuntarily formed themselves into balls.

'I got out of the car. I ran. I flagged down a van; the driver dropped me here.' Annie stroked Ted's arm, as though trying to calm him. 'I told him I was going to marry you, Ted. And I am.'

'But what about your father?' Ted couldn't help himself – the question slipped out even as a rising tide of joy rose up within him, quashing the anger he'd felt a moment ago.

'I don't care anymore. I think we should marry, as soon as possible, and go away somewhere.'

'Where?' Ted's world had been Lynford for so long. He couldn't imagine where else they would go, although of course he knew he had to move soon. Within a week.

'Anywhere. Away from here. Out of Dorset. Out of reach of

my father and Bertram.' She clutched at his hands and gazed up at him. She'd never looked so beautiful. He wanted to say yes, of course, let's go now, today, immediately. But his sense of duty held him back. He was employed for another week. He must work that week, and be paid for it. He – they – needed the money. And then he must find another job that would keep them both.

'Ted? What do you say? Do you still want me?' Her voice sounded small and uncertain.

He pulled her towards him once more and wrapped his arms around her. 'Of course I do. I love you, Annie. I always have and I always will. I would do anything for you. I'd lay down my life for you, and for our child.'

She smiled. 'It won't come to that, dear Ted. So I will tell Father, and if he throws me out, well, then I shall come back here and be with you. We can stay here for as long as you're allowed, and then we will go away. I have a little money. Not much but enough to live on for a month or two, and you'll find work in that time. We'll be together, which is what matters most. And we will live happily ever after.'

He let her words soak into him. Why shouldn't things work out as she'd said? They had every chance. They had a future – they only needed to reach out and grab hold of it, and make it happen. He rested his cheek on the top of her head, and then as she shifted, lifting her face to his, he met her lips with his and they kissed, long and deep, just as they had on that long-ago night of the storm.

And then, out of the corner of his eye, he saw movement outside the station once more, through the now-unlocked station door. A figure outside, his hands cupped around his face as he peered through the window, his eyes wide with shock, his mouth open as he roared with fury at what he was witnessing.

The door crashed open and Ted and Annie jumped apart, putting a couple of feet between themselves. Ted was horrified.

How much had the man seen? Watson-Clarke's face was red, furious, a vein pulsating on his temple.

'What the hell do you think you are doing? Who is this? Oh, it's that weedy stationmaster. Out of a job as of today, aren't you? What were you doing, pawing at my fiancée?'

'Bertie, please …' Annie began, clutching at his arm. But he shook her off. Ted stood mutely, his head bowed as though his lips were still on hers, the way they had been a moment ago. That perfect moment just now, the dream of them running away together evaporated like steam on the wind.

'Get off, Annie. I see how it is. This is the fellow, isn't it? The one who's knocked you up. It is, isn't it? This pathetic excuse for a man. Look, he can't even say anything in his defence. Mute, is he?' Bertram stabbed at Ted's chest hard with his forefinger. Ted's instincts wanted him to push back, but something told him it'd be wise not to provoke the man. He took a step backwards but still said nothing.

Annie sobbed. 'Bertie, leave him. He's … just a friend. A good friend. I didn't know where to go, so I came here.'

'You're saying it's not him? He's not your lover?'

'He's … just a friend,' she repeated. Ted stared at her, and she gazed back, a look of pleading in her eyes. She wanted him to keep quiet, he realised. She was hoping he'd back her up, say they were just friends, deny that he was the father of her baby. Could he do it? He determined to play along, if he could. She knew this Watson-Clarke fellow, and would know how best to handle this situation.

'That right, is it?' The man stepped forward, nose to nose with Ted who was backed against the ticket-office wall now. 'You're just her *friend*, are you? Never been anything more to her than that? Never kissed her, taken her to your bed, *done* her?' He spat these last words out.

The provocation was too much. Ted raised a hand to wipe away spittle that had landed on his cheek, and then slowly, carefully, placed his hands against the other man's chest, fighting to keep himself under control. 'You are standing too close. You are making me feel uncomfortable,' he said, keeping his voice as steady and quiet as he could manage. Annie looked like she was holding her breath.

'Uncomfortable? I can make you feel a lot more *uncomfortable* yet, buddy. Answer my question. Answer it!' Bertram's voice had risen to a screech, and Ted flinched involuntarily.

He pushed Bertram away again. 'I am her friend, yes. And I hope to marry her one day. And the baby she carries is mine.' There. The truth was out, and saying it brought Ted a sense of freedom, no matter what happened next.

'Why, you utter bastard! If I had a gun, I'd shoot you now, right here. What did you do, force yourself on her? She felt sorry for you, I expect, you being such a pathetic excuse for a man, and you saw your chance and took advantage of her? I should take you outside now, and give you a right pasting, you unspeakable cad!'

'It wasn't like that at all. I love her. She loves me too.' Ted kept his voice quiet and steady still, hoping to defuse the situation, but it didn't work. His calm tone seemed only to inflame Bertram further.

'Love? How dare you speak of love! The woman is my fiancée, or at least she was. Now I have to decide whether I want to take on some other man's brat. You should be begging me to keep her and the child. You have no way of providing for her, do you? The railway's closed, hasn't it? You're out of a job, buddy, and she's got expensive tastes.'

'I love her,' Ted said once more. Wasn't that enough of an explanation? Bertram roared with rage and grabbed him by the collar, slamming him against the wall, causing Ted's prized station-master's certificate to fall and smash. It was hard to determine which caused him the most pain: the ruin of the certificate or the assault.

'Bertie, please, leave him alone. Just go,' Annie cried, clutching at the other man's arm, attempting to pull him away from Ted.

'Let go, woman. This is for us men to resolve. Outside, buddy.'

'No. I won't fight you. I don't want to hurt you.' Ted shook his head. He could feel his self-control ebbing away with every breath. He was bigger than the other man – taller, and strong from all the manual work in the goods yard. But whether he'd win a fight was another matter. Something about the fury in Watson-Clarke's eyes, or whatever stupid name the man went by, told him the fight would not be a clean one. This wasn't what he wanted. Suddenly it all felt too much. He wanted to back away, to be alone, writing in his journal to try to make sense of things. Or speaking to Norah who would advise on the best way to deal with all this.

'But just maybe I want to hurt you, hmm?' Bertram spat. He grabbed hold of Ted's lapels. Ted twisted, shaking him off, and moved out of the ticket office, into his sitting room. Anything to get away from the man.

'Leave me be,' he said, his voice emerging as a growl.

The other man had followed him in. 'Leave you be? Why? You took my woman and knocked her up. You need to pay for that, buddy.'

Annie pushed past Bertram and stood beside Ted, taking hold of his hand. The gesture lent him strength for which he was grateful. 'Don't let him upset you,' she whispered. 'Don't let him fight you.'

'Out of the way, Annie. This is nothing to do with you,' Bertram said, once more squaring up to Ted.

Ted watched as Annie's mouth fell open. 'Nothing to do with me? How dare you say that! It's my baby. It's everything to do with me! And I've made my decision. I'm not marrying you, Bertie. I'm marrying Ted, come what may. So now I think you should leave and stop threatening him!'

Bertram turned and sneered at her. 'If I walk out of here, you are left with no choice but him. A life of poverty, with a pathetic excuse for a man. A baby a year until your body is worn out. Your father will be bankrupt so he won't be able to help even if he was minded to, you realise that, don't you? You might think you care for him but how long will that last, when you find yourself with no money and no status?' He gazed around the room. 'So this is where you'll live? Or would live, if the railway wasn't closing? I guess the company will be selling this place. You'll live somewhere even smaller, even poorer.' He was silent a moment and Ted could see a thought occurring to him. 'So, is this where it happened, then? Right here, on that sofa?'

'No, no. Not at all. Bertram, please leave.' Annie's voice was wobbly now, fear showing beneath her anger as she plucked at the man's arm in an attempt to lead him back to the public parts of the station. Ted felt his whole body shake with fury. He'd always been fussy about who he let into his private space – only people he trusted and liked. Just Norah, the children, and Annie. This man was violating his home and Ted was finding it hard to keep control.

'Not here? Where then?' Bertram crossed the room and opened the door that led to the little staircase. 'Up here, then? Let me see. I want to see the place where my fiancée lost her innocence. She wouldn't give it to *me*, oh no. She saved it for a miserable git like you.' He began to climb the stairs.

'Don't go up there. It's private,' Ted said, his voice low, gruff. He felt like a volcano about to erupt.

'I'll go wherever the fuck I want, buddy,' Bertram said, over his shoulder. 'Here? This tiny single bed with a grubby cover? Here's where it happened? You fucked her here?'

That was it – the last straw. The use of that vulgar word in relation to their one perfect night. Ted could not take any more. He bounded up the stairs after him, shouting. 'Get out! Get out of my house! Stop using that word about her. We made *love*. We love each other! Get out!' He tore at Bertram, pulling him out of the bedroom. Annie followed them up, screaming at them to stop.

'Get out!' was all Ted could keep yelling.

'Go down,' Annie shouted. 'This is Ted's home.'

'And you're nicely at home here too are you, you slut?' Bertram spat in her face. Ted wanted to hit him for that but there was no room to take a swing. The tiny landing wasn't big enough for the three of them. Bertram tried to push past Ted to see into the other bedroom. Ted scrabbled at him, trying to stop him. Annie was wedged between them. Ted could feel her soft body pressed against him. She was battering her fists at them – at both of them – screaming in panic that she couldn't breathe, that she was scared she'd fall.

'What's going on?'

The voice called up from below. It was Fred Wilson, peering up at them from the foot of the stairs. As Ted turned to look, Annie screamed again and he felt her stumble, he felt her lash out randomly in her panic. He reached and grabbed, anything to stop her tumbling down those steep, lethal stairs, anything to keep her safe, but the scream was one of pure terror, and now it was coming from his own lungs …

Chapter 25

Tilly

Tilly had a couple of days completely free, and there was an appalling weather forecast as an Atlantic storm was due to pass over. There was plenty of food in the bungalow, and no reason to go out. Time to sit down with her laptop and try to make inroads into the research she knew she needed to do.

This suspicious death, at Lynford station. Who had died and what had happened after? She re-read the short newspaper article she'd already found, that gave no names, just that a man was found dead at the bottom of the stairs and there were three witnesses. Two other men and a woman.

'Who were you, poor dead man?' Tilly asked her laptop, as she paid for twenty-four-hour access to a newspaper archive site, and set to work searching for any mention of 'Lynford', 'murder' around the date of the closure of the railway and afterwards.

She carefully read every article she found, and gradually the picture became clear. A man named Bertram Clarke-Watson had died of a broken neck, after falling down the stairs. A witness named Frederick Wilson who had been a station porter accused Ted Morgan of having pushed Clarke-Watson, during a fight. Tilly added Wilson's name to her list of railway employees. And the woman present had been Annie Galbraith, as Tilly had already suspected.

Ted Morgan had been charged with murder, following the witness statement from Frederick Wilson, although Annie Galbraith's statement had been more ambiguous.

'The men were fighting,' she said, according to a reporter who'd managed to grab an interview with her as she emerged from the police station after giving her statement, 'because Bertram was jealous of the time I spent with Ted. I'd been engaged to Bertram but had broken it off. He wanted us to get back together. But Ted didn't push him. They tussled, and Bertram fell, and oh! He bounced down the stairs, tumbling over and over and then … he just lay there, and I knew from the angle of his head he must have broken his neck.'

A crime of passion, it appears, the reporter summed up. One that has left the former stationmaster charged with murder, awaiting trial that is likely to happen early next year. Meanwhile, he is to be remanded in custody.

So Ted's love, Annie, had been engaged to someone else! That explained some of the angst-ridden entries in Ted's journal. The other man had never been mentioned by name, but it was clear that Ted had known of the engagement and felt embittered by it. Tilly pulled out one of Ted's journals and re-read a passage she'd already seen.

I am not good enough for her, and HE is, I suppose. He is rich and drives a motorcar and is a businessman. Her father is in favour of the match as it will allow their businesses to merge. He would never approve of someone like me, someone who will soon have no job. Why does the approval of a parent matter? I must ask Norah this. She will explain. Our parents were gone before she married, and so I suppose no one needed to approve her choice of husband. She asked me once, I recall, if I was happy that she was marrying Charles Harris and I did not know how to answer, for the important thing was whether or not she and Charles were happy. Why was it anything to do with me?

But Annie's choice of husband IS to do with me, for if she marries him then I do not see what else there is in life for me. It would be different if the railway was not to close, and if she was to keep her job so that I would see her every day. I could manage on that, as a stray dog manages on scraps. But the railway's days are numbered and I may never see her again. That I cannot bear to think about.

But she'd broken off the engagement, it seemed. Had she then accepted Ted?

A thought occurred to Tilly. Ena Pullen's words about the railway being the death of her father. Was her father Bertram Clarke-Watson, then? And if so, who was her mother? Ena had said the railway closed before she was born. She was unmarried and her surname was Pullen. So no. Clarke-Watson could not be her father. It did not add up.

She looked back at Ted's diary. At the start of what she guessed was the first notebook, Ted had written that it was on Norah's advice that he was going to write down his thoughts and feelings, as that might help him make sense of them. 'You had a good sister there, Ted,' Tilly said. 'I wonder if she was able to help you after you were arrested.'

She guessed not. Alan had said that his siblings reported that after the railway closed, their mother would not tolerate any mention of it, or of their uncle. In the end they'd stopped asking and had almost forgotten him. Had Norah thought Ted was guilty of murder and wanted to cut all ties, perhaps? Tilly could not think of any other explanation. It was sad. Ted did not come across as a murderer, in what she'd read of his diaries so far. He sounded more like a lovestruck teenager. Tilly was inclined to think that Clarke-Watson must have fallen by accident rather than pushed on purpose, as the porter Frederick Wilson had implied.

What would the jury have decided, when it went to trial? Tilly imagined a distraught Annie Galbraith testifying for the defence, insisting that the fall was entirely an accident, that perhaps it was

Clarke-Watson's own fault, maybe he'd even started the fight. And would her word have swayed the jury more than Frederick Wilson's word?

Who was this Frederick Wilson? Tilly wanted to know more about him. She searched for more articles about the closure of the railway and in one found a mention of *the young porter at Lynford station, barely out of childhood, who now needs to find alternative employment.* Barely out of childhood – probably in his late teens then. Surely the jury would believe Annie over him? Next job then, was to find reports of the trial.

*

That evening, Tilly updated Ken over dinner on everything she had found out, and what her next lines of enquiry would be. He nodded his approval but she could tell that his mind was elsewhere. He wandered out of the kitchen as she cleared up after they'd eaten, and when the dishwasher was loaded she went in search of him, to see if he wanted a cup of tea.

Tilly found her dad standing in the little room that had been her mother's crafting room. The sewing machine was still set up on the table, with a little pile of patchwork squares beside it, as though Margaret would come back at any moment to get on with her project. Tilly stood beside Ken and leaned her head against his arm.

'I miss her still, so much,' she said, and Ken nodded.

'I was wondering, perhaps if we clear out this room, it might make a little nursery, for when the nipper comes along.' Ken picked up the half-finished piece of patchwork. 'No idea what I'll do with all this stuff though. I mean, look at this. So pretty. I couldn't throw it out.'

Tilly took it from him. Margaret had been machining diamond shapes together in a classic 'tumbling blocks' design. It was in shades of minty green and very attractive. 'Maybe I should have a go at finishing it. What was she making?'

'A bed quilt, I think.'

'Maybe I'd just try for a cot quilt,' Tilly said quietly. 'It's almost big enough already, then.'

'It could be your mum's present to the baby.'

Tilly looked at her father and saw there were tears in his eyes. 'Yes, that feels like the perfect legacy.'

Ken shook himself. 'Right then. Let's do this. I'll start clearing it out as soon as I can. You put aside anything you want to keep. We'll go shopping for paint and, you know, baby furniture – a cot and whatnot – tomorrow.'

Tilly patted her bump and smiled. 'We'd like that, Dad. Very much.'

'It's time, pet. Time for me to start clearing Margaret's things. I've not been able to do it, but now that there's someone else needing the space, I think I can.'

'She'd want this, Dad. She'd have wanted the baby in here.' The room faced southwest, with a view across the sea. Cool in the mornings but with impressive views of winter sunsets. Perfect for a baby, Tilly thought. And right next to her own room. It was all feeling more and more real.

'You're right. It's as though I can feel her telling me, "Now come on, Ken, get rid of my old junk at last."' He sniffed. 'And so I shall. Will you help me, pet?'

'Course I will, Dad,' Tilly replied. 'We can start tomorrow morning if you want.'

'Yes. Can't start right now. The rugby's on in a minute. Munster are playing Glasgow.'

Tilly laughed. 'Everything goes on hold while the rugby's on, as Mum always used to say.'

'Yes, she did say that. Well clearing this will be easier with you alongside me. Thanks, pet.' Ken gave her a hug.

'Fancy a cup of tea while you watch the match, Dad?'

He smiled and nodded.

Chapter 26

Ted

Annie was screaming, ear-piercing screams that made Ted feel as though his heart was being wrenched from his body. He ran down the stairs after her and gathered her into his arms. Just a short while ago, in what now felt like a different universe, it had been *he* who was unable to cope with events, he who'd not known how to handle the situation. And now it was the other way around – he was the strong one. His actions just now, at the top of the stairs, had proved it, hadn't they?

He looked at the man lying twisted and broken at the bottom of the stairs. Bertram's neck was at a horribly unnatural angle. His eyes were open and staring, horrified, at them.

'What have we done?' Annie screamed, pulling herself away from Ted as she knelt beside the inert body. 'He's … oh my God! He's dead! Bertie's dead!' As if she could no longer bear to look at her one-time fiancé she turned away and buried her face in her hands, sobbing, her shoulders heaving.

Ted realised that Fred was still there, standing gaping at the scene before him. How long had he been in the station house?

How much had he seen and heard? He stood and took a step towards the boy. 'F-Fred, it's not what you think ...'

'If that fella's dead, then this is a matter for the police,' Fred announced, pulling himself upright. 'I saw what happened. I saw it all and I'll tell it all, too.' Before Ted could say anything more the lad marched self-importantly out to the ticket office, and Ted heard him lift the receiver to make a telephone call.

'Dead, dead,' Annie was saying, rocking herself back and forward where she knelt beside the body.

'Shh, Annie. It'll be all right. I'll make it all right,' Ted soothed, sitting behind her and once more wrapping his arms around her, hoping that somehow he could absorb all the horror of the situation from her. But the fact remained that a dead man lay in his sitting room, and the cause of his death was the fight at the top of the stairs. And they'd been fighting over Annie.

As he held her, he could feel the unmistakable swell of her belly, in which his child nestled. He spread out his hand over it and felt a small movement beneath his fingers – the baby fidgeting, twisting, making itself comfortable. It was incredible to think that was his child, his and Annie's, a little person in its own right, moving independently, making its own decisions. Suddenly everything became crystal clear to Ted. Whatever happened, however this tragedy played out, the most important thing was to protect Annie and their child. Nothing else mattered. Nothing at all.

'You'll be all right,' he whispered, pressing his face against hers. 'It'll be all right for you and our child, Annie. Trust me.'

'Oh Ted, Ted, what are we going to do?' she moaned.

'Shh. Don't you worry. Leave it to me.'

Fred poked his head into the sitting room. 'Police are coming. You can't go nowhere, or do nothing, they said. You got to stay right here till they come. I'm gonna wait outside till they come. Can't stand to look at that.' He nodded at the corpse and ducked out again. Ted heard the ticket-office door slam.

There was nothing more to do but wait and do his best to

comfort Annie and work out exactly what he needed to do and say to ensure her safety and the future of their child.

It was only ten minutes before the local Lynford policeman turned up on his bicycle. Ted had persuaded Annie to move to the sofa, and there they had sat, arms around each other, while they waited.

The policeman, Sergeant Potter, a red-faced man who both of them knew well, took one look at the body of Bertram that still lay in a tangle at the bottom of the stairs. 'I shall have to call in reinforcements,' he said pompously. 'I shall use your telephone to do so.' He went out to the ticket office to make the call, then returned to Ted's sitting room. Fred Wilson came in behind him but seemed too agitated to come in the room where the glassy-eyed corpse still lay.

'It's all right, lad,' Sergeant Potter said to Fred. 'You've done your duty in calling the police. You can go home if you like, and I'll be round tomorrow to obtain your witness statement.'

The boy heaved a sigh of relief and left the room. Ted heard his footsteps running down the road away from the station. If only he and Annie could run, too! But he had to stay, and face whatever was coming, and do what he could to make things right for Annie and the baby.

Potter sat on an armchair opposite Ted, notebook and pencil in hand. 'Now then, Mr Morgan. Tell me in full detail everything that happened here this evening.'

This was it. Everything rested on Ted getting this right. He took a deep breath.

'Miss Galbraith came here to see me. Mr Watson-Clarke followed. We f-fought. We were fighting at the top of the stairs, when Mr Watson-Clarke f-fell.'

'The deceased's name is Watson Clarke?'

'Bertram Clarke-Watson,' Annie corrected him, dully.

Potter jotted down some notes. 'Hmm. You were fighting. I must ask you, Morgan, and you must reply truthfully. Did you push this Clarke-Watson fellow down the stairs on purpose?'

'I did not want to fight him,' Ted replied. 'But he wanted to fight. He said ... things about Annie that I could not accept. We fought. At the top of the stairs. And then I-I pushed him, to get him away from her. I pushed him, and he fell. I-I didn't mean for him to fall. I just wanted to p-protect her.'

Annie was staring at him with an open mouth as he made his confession. Ted dared not look at her.

Sergeant Potter nodded. 'That ties in with what young Fred Wilson said on the telephone. That you shoved the man with some force, after a lot of shouting.' He cleared his throat. 'I need to ask – why were you fighting?'

'I love her.' Ted reached a hand to Annie who took it and squeezed, lending him strength. No need to say anything about the baby.

The policeman nodded. 'Must say I can't imagine you fighting, Morgan. Not your way at all. But then, if you love this young lady, then I suppose that might change the way you behave. And today was the last day the railway was open, wasn't it? I imagine emotions could be running high.'

Ted swallowed, and nodded, but didn't trust himself to say anything more. He glanced over to the body. It lay facing into the room, towards the sofa, the eyes still open and staring accusingly at him.

Sergeant Potter must have noticed, for he rose and picked up a rug that lay folded on a footstool and draped it over the body.

'Morgan, I am sorry but whatever the extenuating circumstances I shall have to take you in for questioning. As soon as the police van from Michelhampton arrives, you'll need to come with us there. I'm afraid until we've completed investigations we shall have to hold you, on suspicion of manslaughter.'

At least he'd said manslaughter and not murder. There was the death penalty for murder. Ted swallowed hard and nodded his understanding.

The sergeant closed his notebook. 'Well. While we wait for the other constables, I suggest we all have a nice cup of tea. What do you say, Morgan? Perhaps Miss Galbraith could make herself useful?'

Annie stared at him but then stood and went out to the kitchen to make the tea without a word. While she was out of the room Sergeant Potter pontificated on the effects of the closure of the railway on Lynford's businesses. With a man lying dead not five feet away. Ted barely listened. It was all too surreal for words.

At long last the police van arrived from Michelhampton, bringing two more policemen. Right behind it was an ambulance, and Bertram's body was swiftly loaded onto it, once the police had examined the scene and taken a few photographs. With the ambulance and body gone, Sergeant Potter took a brief statement from Annie.

'There was a fight. We were all at the top of the stairs. I-I don't quite know how Bertram fell,' she said.

'It's all right, my dear,' Potter said. 'We will find out all the details from Fred Wilson. If he was at the foot of the stairs, he was in a better position to see all that happened anyway.' He patted Annie's knee. 'You need trouble yourself no further. Now then, how are you to get home this evening?'

'I-I'll telephone my father. He has a motorcar.'

'Good idea. I suppose you can stay here until he comes. Now then, Morgan. Let's be having you.' He recited Ted's rights to remain silent and pulled out a pair of handcuffs. Ted held out his wrists and allowed the policeman to put them on. The metal felt cold and uncomfortable against his skin.

'Annie!' She looked up at him, her eyes wide and shocked, filled with tears. 'Look after yourself, won't you? And look after … the child. Whatever happens … th-that's the most important thing. Do *whatever is best* for him or her. Whatever that entails. Promise me.'

She nodded. 'I promise, Ted, but you'll be all right. It'll be put down to a terrible accident. Won't it, Sergeant?'

'That'll be for the courts to decide, I expect,' said Potter. 'Come along, Morgan.' He took a firm hold of Ted's elbow and led him out of the room, through the ticket office to the front of the station, where the police van was waiting.

Ted glanced over his shoulder and said a silent farewell to the place that had been his home and his life for sixteen years. This was not how he had imagined leaving it. But then, he'd never quite been able to imagine leaving the place for the last time. Whatever happened now, to the station and the railway, no longer mattered. None of it was important, after all. All that mattered was Annie and the child she was carrying.

Chapter 27

Tilly

As she'd promised, the next day Tilly put her research on hold and helped her father clear out Margaret's things. They started with the crafts room, boxing up stuff that could go to charity shops and advertising unwanted larger items on Freecycle. 'Someone might make use of it, pet, and she'd like to think that,' Ken said. Anything for Freecycle they moved out to the garage. Tilly kept a lot of her mother's sewing things – the machine, her work basket, that half-finished patchwork project – but threw out most of the bags full of scrap fabric and half-used skeins of wool.

By the time they'd finished, mid-afternoon, the room was almost bare. Only a large chest of drawers and an armchair were left, and a large framed painting of crashing waves that Tilly had always loved.

'So, all ready for decorating,' Ken said, looking around the empty room.

'Yes. I'll go and buy some paint tomorrow. You all right, Dad, now that it's gone?'

He nodded. 'It's only stuff, isn't it? It's not *her*. She's still right here, where she belongs.' He touched his chest, then left the room.

Tilly didn't follow him, thinking perhaps he needed some time to collect himself. Instead she sat on the armchair, her hands folded across her bump, and tried to envisage the room as a nursery. A cot in the corner, this armchair opposite but angled towards the window. The chest of drawers over there, with a changing mat on top. It was big enough to function as a changing table. She'd paint it a pale yellow, she decided, the kind of colour that picks up sunshine and magnifies it. Some bright patterned curtains. The carpet was a neutral beige, in good condition as it had only been put down when her parents moved in. She'd clean it and keep it.

'This will be your room soon, little one,' she said, smiling. As long as her pregnancy lasted.

After a few minutes she heard Ken passing the door a few times, and went out to see what he was doing. He was hauling sacks of clothes out to the car. 'Decided to start on my wardrobe,' he said, in explanation. 'I could do with some more space, and Margaret's clothes were taking up three quarters of it.'

'I'll give you a hand, Dad.'

Before long, all Margaret's clothes were bagged and ready to be taken to the charity shop or clothes recycling point. On the last pass, Ken stopped beside the hall cupboard and put his sack down. He unhooked Margaret's red coat from its peg, held it to his face for a moment, and then quietly folded it into the sack with the rest.

*

The date for Tilly's second scan approached. She'd had one at twelve weeks, and although all had been well, she had still not been able to relax. With her last pregnancy, all had been well at twelve weeks but then she miscarried at fourteen. This time she had tried not to look too far ahead until she had the second scan at eighteen weeks. At that stage, she told herself, it was not too far off being a viable foetus. Hadn't some premature babies survived after being born at just twenty-three weeks or so?

So when the scan approached Tilly felt nervous, but at the same time excited. Ken offered to come with her but she declined. Every other woman at the clinic would have a husband or partner with her. It felt wrong to be there with a parent.

She'd planned to go alone, but at the last minute, on the day of the scan, she called Rob. She wanted someone alongside her, she realised. Just in case there was any bad news.

'Hi. Er, it's fine if you say no, but I just wondered ... I have an antenatal scan today and if you'd like to come along ...'

'I'd love to,' he said quietly. 'I'm honoured that you've asked me.'

She dressed in her new, super-stretchy maternity leggings and a long, loose top, and drove herself to the clinic at Michelhampton hospital in good time for the scan, feeling apprehensive about what it might show, scared there'd be some abnormality. After all, she was eighteen weeks gone now but still hadn't felt the baby move ... Her palms were sweaty and there was a tight knot in her stomach as she took a seat in the waiting room.

Rob arrived five minutes later, having come straight from his job in a Michelhampton sports centre. He kissed her cheek and grinned happily as he sat beside her.

'Been a long time since I was at a pregnancy scan,' he said. 'Never thought it'd happen again. I really am chuffed to bits that you asked me to come along.'

'You're the father,' she said. 'God, I am desperate for the loo.' A nurse had given her a plastic cup and asked her to drink two or three cupfuls of water before the scan. 'A full bladder pushes the baby up out of the pelvis, so we get a better picture,' she'd explained.

'You're not the only one,' Rob said, suppressing a chuckle as another couple emerged after their scan and the woman rushed straight into the ladies' leaving her partner clutching and cooing over their scan photo. He kept up a stream of gentle banter as they waited, and his good humour rubbed off on Tilly, making her feel more relaxed than she'd been when she arrived.

At last it was Tilly's turn. As she went into the room for the scan, the radiographer, a grey-haired woman with a round face, smiled at her.

'Mrs Thomson, is it? And Mr Thomson, if you could sit there please.'

'Ah, I'm not Mr Thomson, I'm just …'

'He's the father,' Tilly cut in. 'And please just call me Tilly.' She should drop the name Thomson, she thought, and revert to her maiden name, Hutchings.

'Rightio. Well, hop up onto the couch there, and if you could pull your top up and your leggings down a bit …' The poor woman seemed confused about Tilly's circumstances but oddly, Tilly found she didn't mind at all. Families came in all shapes and sizes these days, didn't they?

'Sure.' She grinned at the radiographer and did as she was asked. Lying on her back she was amazed at how large her bump was now. This was the furthest she'd got with any pregnancy. The woman smeared gel over her and then got on with the scan. A screen was mounted high up so that Tilly could see what the scan was picking up.

'Breathe, love,' said the radiographer and Tilly realised she'd been holding her breath. But there it was, her baby, wriggling slightly, looking like a proper little human now rather than the odd-shaped creature with an oversized head she'd seen at the previous scan. This time he or she looked like an actual baby.

'Want to know its sex?' asked the woman, and Tilly thought for a moment. Did she? Or would it be better to wait until the child was born.

'No, I think I'd rather not.' Better not get too attached, just in case.

243

'OK. Well, everything looks good, size is right on the average, good strong heartbeat. Do you want a photo?'

'Yes, please.'

Rob reached for her hand and squeezed it. 'Isn't that great news?'

Tilly looked at him with tears in her eyes and managed to simply nod in reply.

The radiographer printed off a photo, handed Tilly some blue tissue to wipe off the gel, and it was over. All good. No more scans now – the next time she'd see her baby would be after the birth. That thought gave Tilly a jolt of nervousness and excitement.

'Thanks so much,' she said to the woman, as she took her scan photo and smiled at the image of her snub-nosed baby, its tiny hands clearly defined, its knees drawn up to its chest.

'Not at all, love. You take care, now. Have you felt it move yet?'

Tilly shook her head.

'Might be a bit early yet. But you will soon. Like a fluttering in your belly. Funny sort of feeling. But once you feel it the first time, that's it, there's no end to it until the baby's born. Good luck, love. There's a loo just to your left if you're desperate.'

Tilly went, and it was as she was washing her hands after that she felt it. Exactly as the radiographer had described – a fluttering, as though there was a butterfly trapped inside. She put a hand on her belly. 'Is that you, little one? Letting me know you're there?' She left the hospital arm in arm with Rob and with her scan picture in her handbag, a hand still on her bump waiting for more evidence her baby was alive and kicking, and a huge smile on her face.

*

Ken had a bad cold, and was giving the railway a miss for a couple of days while he got over it. Tilly was nursing him – at least as much as he was allowing himself to be fussed over. She had installed him in the sitting room, stretched on the sofa with a rug over him, a cup of tea on a side table and the TV remote control and some reading material to hand.

'You're to shout out if you need anything more,' she told him. 'I'll be in the dining room doing some research.'

'Thanks, pet.' Ken sighed. 'Your mum used to do all this if I was sick.'

'I know. She was an excellent nurse.'

'It's nice to feel looked after, when you're under the weather.'

Tilly nodded. He'd done a wonderful job cosseting her since she'd come to live with him, and even more so since she'd got pregnant and told him about her problems. It was nice to be able to pay a little back, now that she was feeling more on top of things. Her lovely dad. She'd do anything for him. She tucked the blanket around him and went to get on with her research.

She wanted to read more of Ted Morgan's diaries. She sat down with the notebooks, and her own jotter pad and a pen. She decided to read through, making notes of important points, and perhaps type it all up later on. As always it was a bit of a struggle getting to grips with the small, spiky handwriting but once she'd got going it became easier.

There were pages and pages of yet more angst-ridden outpourings about Annie, and worries about the closure of the railway. Lots about Annie being engaged to Bertram Clarke-Watson. And then the news that her engagement was off, and Ted's elation, and his up-and-down emotions as he debated with himself whether she would ever consider taking him as a husband, and whether he should ask her, given that he would soon be out of a job.

I must wait until my future is secure and I have another job lined up, he wrote. *I must be certain that I can provide for her.*

And then an account of a day out, a trip to Coombe Regis, ice creams eaten sitting on the harbour wall. Tilly smiled as she read this. It may have been over eighty years ago but the simple pleasures of a day at the seaside still held true. She read on, and then her mouth fell open in surprise as Ted recounted a conversation he'd had with Annie as they ate their ice creams.

I am to be a father. Annie is carrying my child. I keep having to say those words over and over to myself, either aloud if no one is near or in my head if there is a danger of being overheard. Annie and I have created a new person, one that I will meet in a few short months. This changes everything. It means I MUST marry her, as soon as possible.

But Annie says there is no 'must' about it, and that she will not agree to a wedding yet, not while I do not have a secure future. She wanted me to find a job with good pay and then for us to marry and start a family, but things have gone backwards and the family is to be started first ... She would prefer to live in a town or a city, so I need a job at a larger station. She needs me to be on a good salary, to be able to provide for her and our child, so she is free from her father whose financial problems were what made her agree to marry HIM. I will find a good job, do whatever it takes, for her to be mine, and for our baby.

Our baby. I cannot quite absorb that concept.

Tilly put the diary down for a moment and stared into space, trying to process all that she had learned. So Ted was the father of Annie's baby. That meant Alan Harris had a cousin somewhere. Did he know? She assumed not. He'd never mentioned one. If Annie and Ted hadn't married, then it meant that Annie had a baby 'out of wedlock', back in the 1930s when it would have been seriously frowned upon. How had she coped?

There was more on the following pages, in the same vein, and then details about the preparation for the last day of the railway's operation. Tilly made plenty of notes of this. A display board detailing the final day of operation would be good, she thought. She already had seen newspaper articles about it and perhaps could track down some photographs.

And of course, there were the tragic events at Lynford station, that also happened on that last day. Tilly had reached the point in Ted's diary when he was writing on the night before the last day. He'd been arrested the following evening. She turned the page expecting there to be no more, and was surprised to see more pages filled in, but in a different hand. A swirly, large, confident handwriting, that somehow looked more feminine. Written in pencil, smudged here and there as though the writer had been crying.

And what that final diary entry contained, made Tilly gasp with shock. This changed everything.

Chapter 28

Annie

Months had passed since the railway closed, since that terrible night at the station house. Annie found it hard to think about what had happened then. She rubbed her swollen belly absently. It would not be long now till the baby came. Life had been difficult during these last few months. Her father had been furious when she phoned him that night and asked him to fetch her. Shocked when she'd told him on the journey home of the death of Bertram, and then furious once more when she'd informed him that she was pregnant.

'Jumped the gun, did you?' her father had asked, through gritted teeth as he drove, too fast Annie thought, through the country lanes leading back to Michelhampton.

She realised she had a choice now. She could let her father think the baby was Bertram's. Maybe it'd be easier that way? But no. The time for lies and deceit was over. She should tell him the truth. 'No, Father. It's not Bertram's.'

'Whose, then?' He spat the words out, spraying flecks of spittle over the windscreen of the car.

'Ted Morgan's. The man I love,' she replied, keeping her voice as steady as she could.

'That no-good stationmaster? Who's out of a job? He telephoned me earlier. If I'd known ...' He thumped the steering wheel, sending the car careering across the road and almost into the hedge before he yanked the wheel straight again.

'I love him, Father,' she said again, quietly.

'But he's been arrested for killing Clarke-Watson, you say? How the hell is my business going to survive now, without him? You've ruined me, girl. Ruined yourself, as well.'

Annie had not responded to this, turning her face away. She'd always known he'd be angry. Of course he would. It was an impossible situation to be in. But she found it hard to stomach that he cared more about the future of his business than that Bertie, a man he'd always said he admired and liked, was dead. Or that he was going to be a grandfather.

By the time they reached home, he'd calmed down. Parking the car on the street outside their house, he turned to her again. 'So, my girl, I have been thinking, and I have come up with a solution to this unholy mess.'

She stared at him and opened the car door. 'Tell me when we are inside.'

'No. Sit here and listen to me. First, does anyone else know about this baby?'

'N-no. I've kept it hidden. I can't hide it for much longer though.'

'So only Morgan and Clarke-Watson knew?'

'Yes.'

'Then we will tell everyone that the baby is Clarke-Watson's. That you couldn't wait until you were married. It's more respectable, more understandable. His parents will then be more sympathetic, and his father will hopefully allow the merger to progress anyway. Your situation might elicit sympathy from the wider world too. When you register the child's birth, you can leave the father's name blank.'

'But when Ted is released, I shall marry him, and the truth will have to come out …' Annie couldn't believe what she was hearing. Or that she was being kept outside, while she heard it, after all that had happened that evening. She wasn't sure she could cope with much more.

Her father laughed hollowly. '*When* he's released? I think you mean *if*, my girl. We'll cross that bridge if or when we come to it. You'll tell people the baby is Bertram's, if you have any sense. If you do not, I shall have no choice but to disown you. You'll be sent away to have this baby, give it up for adoption, and then you'll be on your own.' He opened his own car door and climbed out. 'And that's my final word on it.'

*

A couple of days later she'd been summoned to Michelhampton police station, to give a full statement of what had happened at Lynford. It had been a difficult interview. Apparently, Fred Wilson was insisting that he'd witnessed the whole thing, and had seen Ted push Bertram down the stairs, deliberately. The charge was to be one of murder. Annie was asked to clarify, once again, exactly what she had seen.

'I'm sure it *wasn't* deliberate,' she told the police inspector, carefully, forcing herself to look the man in the eye as she spoke. 'They were fighting, I mean, Mr Clarke-Watson was fighting Mr Morgan. Mr Morgan was trying to defend himself.'

'Perhaps he pushed Mr Clarke-Watson away? Perhaps he pushed too hard, is that what happened, Miss Galbraith?'

'He didn't mean to, I'm sure he didn't,' she repeated, sounding lame even to herself. But whatever she said, she knew she didn't sound convincing. She couldn't stop herself from crying – both for Bertie who despite everything didn't deserve what had happened to him, and for poor dear Ted, whose only crime was of loving her too much.

'You must be very upset,' the inspector said, patting her hand. 'You've had a terrible shock. It's good that Mr Wilson was there to witness the attack. It means you aren't the only witness, and when it all goes to trial, perhaps the prosecution won't even need to call you. I understand you are in a, ahem, delicate condition? Better that you be left alone, and not have to go through the ordeal of the trial. I'll make a note, and let the legal teams know. So very sad that Mr Clarke-Watson will never know his child.'

'It's all right, I can testify,' she said weakly, but the inspector just smiled condescendingly at her, loaned her his handkerchief and made his note.

'You've been very helpful.' He stood and helped her shrug her jacket on. 'Now my advice to you is to go home to your father and forget all about this unpleasant episode. We can't bring back Mr Clarke-Watson, unfortunately. And let us hope that Mr Morgan is never released from prison, after what he's done. Perhaps when you've had the baby adopted you might be able to find yourself a new suitor and put all this unpleasantness behind you. Good luck, Miss Galbraith.'

She'd wanted to hit him. How dare he *hope* that Ted would never be released! The case had not even gone to trial yet. But she'd bitten back any retort and had simply walked out of the police station with as much dignity as she could muster.

*

With Bertram dead, his father had briefly come out of retirement to run the business and had quickly agreed to merge it with Annie's father's business after all and let Mr Galbraith run things. 'Well, that worked out at least,' her father said. 'The old man had no wish to try to find a new front man, and there was I, ready and willing.' But the Clarke-Watsons were not interested in their grandchild. They preferred to keep the whole existence of the child as hushed up as possible, and assumed that Annie would give the child up for adoption as soon as it was born.

Annie's father had said the same thing. 'You'll live here quietly until the baby arrives, then it'll be put up for adoption. And then once that's all over with, I'll see if I can find someone to take you off my hands. Won't be as good a match as Clarke-Watson was, mind you. You really messed that one up. You'll never be fully welcome in decent society again.'

Annie found she didn't care anymore what her father or anyone else thought. As so often, her thoughts turned to Ted, who was still locked up in Michelhampton police station, charged with murder after Fred Wilson's statement and his own confession, and awaiting trial.

She had agonised over whether to write to Norah and tell her about the baby, and about what happened on that terrible night. In the end she had written a brief note, telling Norah how sorry she was at Ted's arrest and saying that she was certain the fall had been an accident and that Ted wasn't to blame. She'd had a terse response. Norah apparently blamed Annie for her brother's predicament, and she'd told Annie not to visit Ted in prison as he awaited trial. 'You will make things harder for him if you go,' Norah had written. 'If you care at all for him, stay away.'

Annie had stayed away, although it broke her heart to think of Ted alone, confused and depressed about what was happening to him. She wanted to take him in her arms, tell him she could make it all right again, and then take him away from there, away to a little station house with roses around the door just as they had dreamed of. But that could never happen now. That dream was gone, and she was astute enough to realise it. The best she could do was keep her promise to Ted, to do whatever was best for their child. Which meant keeping the baby and finding some way to give it a happy and secure future.

*

The day on which Annie had met George was, in every other way, unremarkable. Her father had been out at work, the autumn sun was shining brightly in a crisp blue sky and Annie had decided she could not bear being in her father's house another minute. She owned a loose-fitting winter coat that covered her growing bump and would continue to do so for a while yet. She donned it, along with a hat that didn't match but would have to do and set off on a walk heading towards Michelhampton Park.

The glory of the day had lifted her spirits a little from the dark places they'd been since the day of the accident, and she smiled to herself as she strode along through the park, kicking up piles of autumn leaves. There was a man, sitting on a bench opposite the park fountain. He'd been watching her, she realised. He looked young, about her age, maybe a little older. He had a soft, kind face. She flashed him a smile, and he stood as she passed by.

'Please, won't you sit down? It's a beautiful day, isn't it? I was watching a couple of robins, who were bathing in the edge of the fountain. Maybe they'll come back, to entertain us again.'

'I'd like that,' she replied, and sat on the bench beside him. He had sandy hair, blue eyes, and a gentle smile. He reminded her a little of Ted, and her heart gave a lurch.

But he had none of Ted's shyness, and within minutes they were chatting like old friends, arranging to meet up again a few days later. The man's name was George Pullen, and he was a farmer's son, with prospects of taking over a sizable property of arable land from his parents, in due course. She'd treated him to one of her best smiles, and had seen his face light up in response as it had its usual effect.

*

Now, heavily pregnant and only a couple of weeks away from giving birth, Annie smiled at the memory of the day she met George Pullen. An auspicious day, for sure. They'd seen each other every week since then, and she'd found herself able to talk to him about anything. He knew it all. He knew about the baby – well, now that she was nearly at her due date and was the size of a small whale, of course he did! He knew about Bertram and Ted, and about the fight. He believed the story that Bertram was the child's father, but he knew of Annie's feelings for Ted. With the trial only a week away she had not been able to keep any of it secret, and in any case, she found she did not want to. George had become her confidant, her best friend. He was steady, gentle and loyal, and now that her old friends had dropped her, not wanting to be associated with a 'fallen woman', she'd come to rely on George's company more and more.

George had proposed, in a way. 'If the worst happens,' he'd said hesitantly one day when they were alone in her father's sitting room, 'and Ted Morgan is found guilty, then please, I hope you'd consider taking me instead. I could be this child's father.'

'Oh, George,' she'd replied, reaching out to touch his cheek. 'You are so sweet and such a good friend. But I cannot say yes. Not while there's still a chance with Ted …'

'Of course not, dear Annie. I just want you to know … that I could be your backup plan, as it were. If you would consider me, and if Ted Morgan isn't free, then … I am yours. There will be no need for your baby to be adopted.'

She'd smiled, and dabbed at her eyes, unable to say anything more. She was lucky to have found him, she knew. But Ted would need her to be waiting for him, if he was found not guilty. And she would be there for him.

Her father approved of George; at least as far as he approved of anything she did these days. 'Best you'll get, in your situation,' he'd said gruffly, and left it at that. Annie had the impression he just wanted shot of her, once and for all, so she could bring no more shame on him. Well, one way or another he'd get his way. If Ted was by some miracle released, she would suggest that they

254

go far away as soon as possible, and make a life for themselves far from Michelhampton. They'd live in poverty but they'd be together, and they'd be happy. And if Ted wasn't released – then there was George. Her backstop.

She'd written to Ted briefly just once, in defiance of Norah's request. She'd had a letter in return – a short, sad little letter that told her he'd sunk deep into depression and closed himself off from the world, but which repeated his last words to her as he'd been taken away in handcuffs: *Look after our child. Do whatever is best for him or her.*

The best option for their child was a secure future. That was something only George could offer her, if Ted was found guilty.

She'd been asked if she would testify for the defence, despite the fact that the trial date coincided with her due date. The prosecution were only calling Fred Wilson as a witness. She'd reluctantly agreed – maybe she'd be able to convince the jury that Bertram's fall had been entirely accidental. But it would be difficult, so very difficult to stand there in the witness box in front of the judge and tell an outright lie.

*

At last the trial began. Annie was desperate to go and watch, to sit in the public gallery, and see for herself how Ted was. Perhaps her presence would lend him strength. Or, on second thoughts, perhaps it would upset him. Norah had asked her to stay away from him. But she'd been told by the lawyer that she could not attend, as she was due to be called as a witness. Then on day two of the trial, her pains started. Her father took her to the Michelhampton hospital and deposited her at the entrance to the maternity ward, clutching at her belly, holding a small suitcase containing nightdresses, toiletries, and the few items for the baby that she had managed to collect.

The child was a girl, born after many hours of pain and

screaming, which left Annie vowing she would have no more children, no matter whom she married. Later, she cradled the baby in her arms, named her Ena, and kissed her soft, downy head.

'You'll be an only child as you grow up, little Ena, just like I was. But you'll have your mummy with you to love you all your life. I won't go off and die when you're little like my mother did. And I'll make sure your daddy is a kind and gentle man, whoever he ends up being. You won't be bullied, the way I was by my father.'

Ena just grimaced and turned her little head towards Annie's breast, searching for sustenance. Annie helped the child latch on, and then relaxed back against the hospital pillows, imagining Ted's expression of rapture when – or if – he saw his daughter for the first time.

*

Annie came home from hospital with baby Ena three days later. Her first visitor was George, who brought her flowers, chocolates, and a baby's layette in white, trimmed with lemon-coloured lace.

'It's beautiful!' Annie exclaimed, from where she lay on the sitting room couch. Ena was in a pram that her father had grudgingly bought, in the corner of the room. Thankfully she was asleep at the moment. Annie had had no idea how hard looking after such a tiny person could be.

'Your daughter is beautiful,' said George, peering into the pram with an expression of wonder and awe on his face.

He'd be a doting father, Annie suddenly realised. He'd love and cherish any child he brought up, whether they were his own or not.

George came to sit near her and took her hand. 'The trial came to a conclusion today,' he said gently. 'The jury didn't deliberate for long. I came here as soon as I heard the verdict.'

'Oh, oh my goodness,' Annie whispered. She'd missed the whole thing, being in hospital giving birth. Her heart beat faster as she realised she was about to find out which of the two possible futures was to be hers and Ena's. Let it be a future with Ted, she prayed silently. Let him have been found not guilty, free to leave, free to take her and Ena away. But something in George's tone told her that fantasy was not to be.

'I'm very sorry,' George said, rubbing his thumb in circles across the back of her hand. 'I know how much you care for Mr Morgan. But I'm afraid he was … found guilty of murder.'

'Guilty!' Her heart flipped over. The worst possible outcome. The very worst. She tried to say something more but no words would come. Ted, convicted of murder. How could that be true? 'Oh, George, it can't be, tell me it's not true!'

'I'm so sorry, dear Annie. It seemed the jury set a lot of store by the evidence from the station porter, who said Morgan had pushed Mr Clarke-Watson down the stairs deliberately. Morgan's sister was present, and testified as a character witness, but as she was not present at the scene and, well, she cried so much while she was on the stand that she was quickly excused.' He frowned slightly. 'I know you always said it was an accident.'

'Yes, it w-was an accident, I'm sure. Ted never meant to hurt Bertram. I'm sure of that. Oh, George, I should have testified! I should have insisted! They should have delayed it for me.' Would her testimony have changed things? Maybe it would have, but not necessarily for the better, she realised. She wasn't sure it would have stood up to cross-examination. She glanced at Ena, sleeping peacefully in her cot. She was the most important thing in all this. Ted had said that.

She pulled out a handkerchief and dabbed away her tears. 'What will happen to Ted now?'

'I'm afraid he'll be hanged for it.' George moved to sit beside her on the sofa and wrapped a comforting arm around her shoulders. 'Oh, my love. I am so very sorry about it all.'

Hanged. The word hit Annie like a stab to the heart. Hanged. So final. And it was her fault – all her fault. Her actions had led to this point. If she'd testified, if she hadn't let him confess to pushing Bertram, if she hadn't let Bertram follow her to Lynford on that fateful night, if she hadn't stayed there on the night of the storm … Ted would be free. Not awaiting the hangman's noose. And their baby …

She made a snap decision. The only decision left to her, now that Ted was to be hanged. A decision that would allow her to keep her promise to him.

'Ena will never know her true father,' she said carefully, raising her eyes slowly to gaze deep into George's. 'But she can know another father, if there's a man who would still consider taking her, and her mother, on.'

George gasped. 'Oh, my sweet, are you saying yes to me? Are you really? I never thought … so soon after … but yes, I would be honoured and privileged to be your husband!'

With an enormous effort she pushed Ted out of her mind and forced herself to smile, watching how the effect of it lit up his face, in just the same way it had once lit up Ted's. 'And I would be honoured to be your wife.' Ted would approve, she thought. This arrangement would provide the best possible future for Ena, just as she'd promised Ted, and now, keeping her promise was all she could do for him.

Chapter 29

Tilly

Before she shared what she'd discovered in that last entry in Ted Morgan's diaries, Tilly thought she should find the whole truth. All of it – what happened to Ted after his arrest, what became of Annie Galbraith and her baby. Once she had worked it all out, she could gather everyone together and tell them what she'd uncovered. She put the diaries to one side, opened up her laptop and began searching newspaper archives again, typing 'Edward Morgan', 'trial' and 'Lynford' into the search box. There must be a write up of it somewhere. Ted had been arrested on suspicion of murder, after all.

At last, Tilly found a brief account of Ted Morgan's trial, tucked away at the bottom of a page of a national newspaper. As she read the article her heart sank in dismay. Frederick Wilson had testified, saying that he'd seen the defendant tussle with the deceased, and that Mr Morgan had purposely pushed Mr Clarke-Watson down the stairs. Wilson had, the paper said, run to the unfortunate man's aid, only to discover his neck was broken and he was dead. He'd then tried to comfort the deceased man's fiancée and had also telephoned the police.

There was no mention of any testimony from Annie Galbraith.

Tilly opened a new browser tab on her laptop, and searched a site that listed births, marriages and deaths, for the name 'Galbraith'. There was just one in the Michelhampton area – a girl, born to Anne Galbraith, and given the name Ena.

And there was the truth, that Tilly had already begun to guess at. Ena Pullen must be Annie and Ted's child. How then did she end up with the surname Pullen? Annie must have married. Tilly ran a few more searches and yes, there it was, a wedding between Anne Galbraith and a George Pullen, in Michelhampton not long after the birth of Ena. George must have been a good man, devoted to Annie, to take on another man's child in those days, Tilly thought.

She remembered that Ena said her mother blamed the railway for the death of her father. Tilly went back to the newspaper report and read the last few paragraphs.

'Oh, Ted, you poor thing,' she whispered, as she read that the stationmaster had been found guilty of murder and sentenced to death by hanging. 'What a sad end.'

She found a tear running down her cheek. She'd grown to like Ted very much, through reading his diaries. He came across as a kind, simple man who wanted very little from life – just to be able to be with the woman he loved.

Why hadn't Annie testified? She could have saved him, possibly.

Tilly noted down all the details she'd found and then realised that Ena had been born on the very day that Ted had been found guilty. Perhaps that was why Annie had not testified? If she'd been in hospital, in labour, she would not have been able to attend court. Would they not have delayed the hearing to wait for her? Or perhaps for some reason they'd discounted her evidence before the trial. Whatever the reason, it was clear that Annie had moved on pretty quickly, marrying George Pullen so soon after the trial, and presumably before Ted's hanging.

Maybe Ena knew more. It was time to go and see her again. But first Tilly should talk to Alan.

*

'I don't know why you think my presence will help this woman change her mind about the railway,' Alan muttered, as Tilly drove him and her father to Ena Pullen's house. She had telephoned Ena and asked if she could visit again, to outline the results of her research. And she'd asked permission to bring 'two members of the railway restoration society' with her. Ena had grumbled a bit but then agreed. But whether she'd invite them all inside, or turn them away on the doorstep, was yet to be seen.

Ken knew the results of Tilly's research, but Alan didn't. It was going to be a tricky, but interesting, encounter.

It was a beautiful sunny day when Tilly drove into Ena Pullen's farmyard and parked in front of the barn, as she had on her previous visit. She climbed out of the car, stretching her back. Now that her pregnancy was further progressed, she was beginning to feel some aches and pains. But she welcomed them – they were proof the baby was still there, growing, and that every day was a step nearer to becoming a parent at last.

Alan and Ken followed her to the farmhouse door, where she rang the bell. 'I still think it's a bit heavy-handed,' Alan said, 'three of us turning up at once.'

Tilly began to answer, but at that moment the door opened and Ena peered around, unsmiling. 'You're here. Better come in, then. I'll put the kettle on.'

'Let me help,' Tilly said, following Ena to the kitchen. Her father and Alan scuffed their shoes on the mat and shuffled along the hallway, like two naughty schoolboys. They were nervous about what reception they'd get from Ena, and Tilly knew Alan was worried she'd become even further opposed to the railway if they played their cards wrongly in this meeting.

261

A little later, with introductions out of the way and a pot of tea brewing, they sat around the kitchen table and Tilly began telling Ena what she'd discovered.

'Your mother was Annie Galbraith, I believe,' she began.

Ena nodded. 'Yes, and she was a fine woman. Very beautiful when she was young. I wish I'd taken after her, but she always said I was more like my father.'

'Your father. You told me when I was here before, that the reason you were against the railway reopening was because your mother told you it had caused the death of your father.'

Ena sniffed. 'That's right. It was the death of him, she always said, though she wouldn't tell me what she meant. She'd tell me when I was grown-up, she said. And then she died, you know. When I was 17. And my father – adopted father, that is – died not long after, and I've been here ever since. My friend Sheila moved in with me. We ran the farm together for years. Sheila died about ten years ago, and I sold off most of my land and retired at 70.' She sat a little straighter in her chair, clearly proud of her achievements.

'That's impressive, running a farm till that age,' Ken said. 'I retired at 60.'

'What did you do?' Ena asked.

'Area manager for a railway company. I managed half a dozen stations. Glorified stationmaster, really.'

'Which makes me a stationmaster's daughter,' Tilly said. 'Just like you, Ena, I suppose.' She smiled at the older woman.

Ena twisted in her seat and stared at Tilly. 'What do you mean? My father wasn't a stationmaster. He was a businessman. A very successful one, even though he was so young. Who knows what he could have been, if he'd lived?'

It was Tilly's turn to stare. 'Who are you talking about?'

'My father, of course. Bertram Clarke-Watson. Who died before I was born.'

Tilly glanced over at Alan, who'd sat quietly throughout, a

frown on his face. 'Ena,' she said gently, 'I don't believe Mr Clarke-Watson was your father.'

'Of course he was. My mother had been engaged to him. She must have jumped the gun a little, and fell pregnant with me. You know how it is. Obviously.' She nodded at Tilly's rather obvious bump and then at her bare ring finger.

'Ena, look at this a moment, would you?' Tilly brought out the final notebook of Ted Morgan's diary, the one in which Annie had written the true events of that fateful night. 'Is that your mother's handwriting?'

'Ye-es, looks like it,' Ena said. She flipped back a few pages, then jabbed at Ted's spiky hand. 'That's not, though.'

'No, that's Edward Morgan's handwriting. He was Lynford's stationmaster.'

'Never heard of the fellow.'

'He was my uncle,' Alan said, and gazed at Ena, still frowning slightly. Tilly gave him a small smile. He was beginning to put two and two together.

'Ena, did your mother tell you how your father died?' Tilly asked, gently.

'No, she never did.' The old woman looked at Tilly with watery eyes. 'Did you find something out?'

'I did, yes. It's all in here.' Tilly tapped the diary. 'It seems that while your mother was engaged to Bertram Clarke-Watson, she spent a night at Lynford station when she could not get home due to a huge storm. Somehow ...' Tilly hesitated, wondering how best to put it. 'Somehow, she ended up in bed with Edward Morgan. He was very much in love with her, and it seems she cared for him too.'

'She slept with another man while she was engaged? I can't believe she was sleeping with two men before she was married!'

'She broke off the engagement with Mr Clarke-Watson. And as far as I can work out, she only slept with one man – Ted Morgan – and only that once.'

263

'Are you saying … that I'm the result of that night?'

'Yes. It's all in here. According to Ted's diary, Annie told him he was the father of her child.'

'So how did he die – this Ted Morgan? My real father, if what you are telling me is true, though I'm not at all sure it is …'

Tilly paused for a moment before she answered. 'I think first you should read your mother's words for yourself.' Tilly pushed the diary across the table. 'But I must warn you, some of this may come as a shock.'

Ena stood and fetched a pair of glasses from a drawer, then sat down again. She picked up the diary and read it carefully. Tilly found herself holding her breath, looking from Ken to Alan as Ena read it. Alan was still frowning and biting his lip. It was the first time he'd heard any of this story, and Tilly knew he must be bursting with questions.

Sunday, 20 September 1936

I am waiting in the station house at Lynford. It is the day the last trains ran, the day the station closed for good, and the day that Bertram Clarke-Watson, my fiancé, died from a fall down the stairs. My father is driving now from Michelhampton to collect me, so I only have a short time to set down the truth. Ted, dear Ted Morgan, always said that writing things down helped him make sense of things, helped him understand what was important, and get things straight in his mind. So I too shall try it. It shall also be a confession, though one I hope no one will read.

There was a fight, tonight. I had told Bertram about Ted's baby that I am carrying and broken off our engagement. He was angry and followed me here. He picked the fight with Ted, at the top of the stairs. Ted did not want to fight. I went upstairs too, to try to stop them, and at one point I lost my footing. I thought I was going to fall, but Ted reached for me and held tightly on to me, saving me from falling. It was at that moment that I suddenly saw that if only it could be Bertram who fell, as an accident, then maybe Ted

264

and I could have a future together after all. At that exact moment I admit that I wanted Bertram dead. And so I lashed out. Holding on to Ted I shoved back against Bertram with all my strength, and down he went.

I had not expected that boy, Frederick Wilson, to be a witness. I don't know what he saw or thinks he saw, or what evidence he will give. I thought we would be able to tell the police it was a tragic accident. But Ted has shouldered the blame, confessing to the police to having pushed Bertram. He told me that I must take care of our child, that our child is the most important consideration, no matter what. So I know I must keep quiet about my part in Bertram's death. I can only say there was a fight and that he fell, and I do not know quite how it happened. Because if I confess the truth then I will go to prison and our child will be born in prison, and that is not giving him or her a good life, as I promised Ted when he was taken away. I have a choice of either exonerating Ted or keeping my promise to him. I cannot do both. It is a terrible choice to make, but I must do what Ted, my own love, wants.

Annie Galbraith

At last Ena finished reading and put the book down with a little gasp. Alan reached for it. 'May I read it too, now? Ted Morgan was my uncle.'

'Yes, you said that ...' Ena replied, and then as though a light bulb had switched on in her head, she looked up at him. 'You're my cousin, then. I never had a cousin.'

'Neither did I,' Alan said, softly. 'There were four of us, Ena. Three left. One day I hope my brother and sister can meet you too. They remember your father. I never met him, being the youngest. I was only a baby when he died.'

'You're my cousin,' she said again.

Alan reached across the table and took her hand. 'Yes. Pleased to meet you, cousin.'

'You need to read that, now,' Ena said, pointing to the diary.

'The poor man. And Mother … how could she …' Alan picked up the diary and began reading while Ken looked over his shoulder. Ken already knew the gist of the story but had not yet read it in detail.

'She loved him, didn't she?' Ena said. 'Ted, I mean. What happened to him?'

'It took me a while to find out, as the *Dorset Herald* archives were lost years ago in a fire. But I eventually found something.'

'Go on,' Ena said.

Tilly glanced at Alan. He was still reading the diary, but he quickly finished and put it down. 'So did Annie Galbraith keep her promise to my uncle, in the end?'

Tilly took a deep breath. 'She did. The case went to trial. The porter, Fred Wilson, who Annie mentions in the diary, stated that he'd seen a fight and seen Ted Morgan push the other man down the stairs, on purpose. Annie didn't testify at the trial. She was in hospital, giving birth to you, Ena.'

'So Ted Morgan was found guilty?'

'Yes. And then a few months later, he was hanged for murder.'

'Oh my.' Ena clapped a hand to her mouth.

Alan stared at Tilly. 'No wonder my mother wouldn't talk about him, if she thought he was guilty of murder. The most unforgivable crime, she always said. And hanged for it. But in this book, it's clear he didn't do it.' He looked sideways at Ena.

'She should have testified! She should have told the truth.' Ena thumped the table. 'The poor man! She always told me it was her fiancé who was my father. Clarke-Watson. She never told me she'd broken it off, never told me about Ted Morgan, or any of the rest of it. She lied to me!'

'She'd made a promise to Ted Morgan. I'm sure she did everything with your best interests at heart.' Tilly patted the older woman's arm. But Ena shook her head.

'No, whatever she did, she did for one person only. And that was Annie. She was a selfish woman. She was bitter, too. I think

266

she'd wanted better for herself than to be a farmer's wife. I always suspected she'd only married my father – I mean George Pullen – because with a small baby no one else would have her. Her mother had died when she was a teenager, and her father was by all accounts a strict, old-fashioned man, who I suppose would have been furious at her for getting pregnant outside of marriage. My father – George, I mean, I will always call him father and he was a good man –adored her. She could do no wrong in his eyes, but even as a child I could see she treated him badly. Always nagging him, saying she wondered what she'd ever seen in him, saying he was lucky she stayed and didn't leave him for someone better. Then she'd look at me and mutter something about it being all my fault, and she'd stare across at Lynford and say, "That bloody railway, that was the start of it all". So now it all makes sense.' Ena picked up the diary, turned to Annie's words and then went backwards, frowning at the difficult handwriting of her biological father. 'Look how much he cared for her. He was besotted.'

'Yes, he was,' Tilly replied. 'And she loved him too – you can tell from that last diary entry that she wrote. It must have been difficult for her, being pregnant and unmarried, back then. There was a real stigma attached to it in those days. Engaged to one man but pregnant by another, who she obviously loved. I do feel sorry for her.'

'But then she found someone else in the end,' Ken said. 'Your stepfather, Ena.'

'I suppose she did what she thought was best,' said Ena, grudgingly. 'She had something about her, that made men fall at her feet. Well, whatever it was, I never inherited it, and perhaps I've been happier for it. I was never interested in men, anyway. Neither was Sheila.'

Alan grinned. 'Good on you, cousin.'

Ena smiled, shyly at first and then broadening. Her face lit up when she smiled, Tilly thought. Not just her face. Ena had one of those smiles that seemed to light up the room. It was a pity she used it so rarely.

'We should shake hands properly, cousin,' Ena said. 'And I'm afraid I've forgotten what you said your name was?'

Alan stood and came round to Ena's side of the table. 'I'm Alan Harris. Stand up then, and give me a hug. We should have grown up together. We could have been great friends.' He cleared his throat. 'We still could.'

Tilly watched, her breath held, as Ena stood up and wrapped her arms around Alan. She barely reached to his shoulder, but he bent his head down so that his cheek rested on the top of her head. They stayed like that for a moment. Tilly reached for her father's hand. He'd been quiet throughout, but she saw now there was a glistening in his eye as he watched the cousins' reunion.

At last they broke apart, and Ena sat down again, looking flushed and slightly embarrassed. Alan on the other hand was still grinning broadly.

'So, cousin Ena, may I ask you what your feelings are about the railway restoration project now?'

Tilly held her breath again. What a direct question! How would Ena take it? She could easily be offended that Alan would use his kinship with her to attempt to change her mind.

But it seemed she had nothing to fear. Ena threw back her head and laughed. A young, tinkling laugh that was a joy to hear. Soon they were all joining in, chuckling away, looking at each other and waiting to hear how Ena would answer.

'Oh dear me, cousin Alan! I can't very well refuse to sell up now, can I? Not now I know my father spent his life working on that railway and loved it as much as he loved my mother. After all, I suppose it's what he would have wanted, the poor dear man.'

Chapter 30

Annie

The wedding was a quiet one, six weeks after Ena's birth, in a registry office, with just George's parents and Annie's father in attendance, and the baby in a carrycot in the corner. It was not the wedding Annie had dreamed of all her life – no frothy white dress, no bridesmaids or page boys, no choir or peal of bells. She wore a blue dress that she'd had for a couple of years, and held a simple bunch of flowers tied with a white ribbon. Thankfully the baby weight had fallen off her quickly and some of her old clothes still fitted.

She'd sighed as she'd dressed for her wedding, thinking of Ted, languishing in his cell for a crime he hadn't committed. Her eyes filled with tears as she imagined how different her wedding day would have been, had she not got pregnant and if she'd had the courage to stand up to her father and choose Ted over Bertram. But as she stood in front of the registrar with George standing at her side, his eyes filled with love, she rose to the occasion, gave him a bright smile and determined that she'd make the best of it. She had her beautiful daughter, a man who adored her and would be a good father. They would be well enough off. Most importantly she was keeping her promise to Ted. George's parents had decided to retire from farming, and their wedding gift to the couple was to be their farm. They had bought a neat bungalow on the edge of Michelhampton, and had already moved out. George and Annie were going straight to the farm after the wedding breakfast.

'We'll have a honeymoon later,' George had said. 'When Ena is old enough to be left with someone else, and we can be alone together. I can't wait to show you the farm!'

Annie was also looking forward to seeing her new home, too. She'd never yet been to visit, what with Ena being so young. She'd heard the farmhouse was a big one, with six bedrooms and two large reception rooms – a very different proposition to living in a cramped station house. George had a motorcar and had promised to teach her to drive. She'd need to, he said, for the farm was quite isolated. Isolation would suit Annie, she thought. She no longer wanted to see anyone. A quiet life away from the world with her daughter, mourning the loss of Ted, was all she had to look forward to. All she deserved.

The post-wedding meal was as quiet an affair as the wedding itself had been. Tea and sandwiches in a Lyon's Corner House. Annie's father had refused to pay for a proper reception in a hotel. 'Will you make a speech?' Annie asked him.

'I don't see any need, do you?' he replied. 'You're married now, and we can put all this unpleasantness behind us. You've landed on your feet with George Pullen, that's for sure. You've got somewhere to live, and somewhere to bring up that child. I'm pleased about all that. I'm pleased too, that my business is prosperous again, thanks to the merger. Be thankful, Annie. Things might not have turned out this way.' He cleared his throat. 'Though if you'd been a more sensible kind of girl, you could have been married to Bertram Clarke-Watson by now, and let me tell you, that wedding would have been a much bigger affair than this one.'

With that, he pushed back his chair, nodded to George's parents and shook George's hand. 'Well, I must be off. My business can't be left unattended any longer, you see. Best wishes, and all that.'

All this unpleasantness. Annie bit her lip to stop herself from screaming at him that he could not dismiss the loss of the only man she'd ever love as 'unpleasantness'. Thank goodness one result of marrying George was that she'd be free from her father, with no real need to ever see him again.

'We'll be going too,' said George's mother. 'I hope you'll be very happy in the old farmhouse, Annie. Come and see us next week, tell us how you're getting on. And bring our lovely little step-granddaughter with you, of course.'

'We will, thanks, Mum,' George said, helping her on with her coat and kissing her cheek. 'Bye, then.'

And then there were just the two of them left.

'So, shall we go?' asked George. 'Or would you like to, I don't know, take a drive somewhere first?'

'I think I'd like to see my new home,' Annie said. 'Besides it'll soon be time to feed Ena.' The truth was it had been such a strain holding herself together for the day, and not crumpling in tears with thoughts of Ted, that now she just wanted to be alone for a while.

'Very well, we'll go straight there,' said George, smiling as he helped Annie to her feet, and then lifted the carrycot in which Ena had lay sleeping throughout the meal. 'Come on little flower. Come and see your new home. Daddy's going to decorate a bedroom for you and build you a cot and a rocking horse and a playhouse. When you're older, Daddy will buy you a pony of your own.'

Annie gave a small smile on hearing this. Despite her misery and guilt, she realised her daughter would have a father who loved her dearly. She was giving Ena the best possible life – keeping her promise to Ted. Even though keeping that promise meant that Ted would pay the ultimate price. For the thousandth time Annie wondered if she should perhaps come forward after all, admit her own guilt, insist on a retrial and allow Ted to be freed. But then *she* would be the one in prison. And if she, Annie, were executed what then would become of baby Ena? Her coming forward would not be doing whatever was best for their child, as Ted had wanted. It had been an impossible dilemma. She'd made her choice, telling herself it was best for Ena and therefore what Ted wanted, but she could not help but endlessly question it. Would she ever be free of her sense of guilt? Maybe over time, in George's remote farmhouse the memories would fade and her anguish would lessen as she built a new life for Ena. It was all she could hope for.

George had parked his motorcar, an old Rover, just around the corner. As she climbed in, Annie couldn't help but remember the Austin that Bertram had collected her from her job at the bank in. Those days felt like a lifetime ago. She watched as George strapped the carrycot onto the back seat and then climbed in the front.

'Ready?' he said. 'Let's go home, then.'

It was a forty-minute drive, south from Michelhampton, through Blackford and Lower Berecombe and then along a narrow lane between high hedges. 'This is all our land,' George said proudly as they drove the last couple of miles.

Annie recognised the area. The old railway line, now dismantled, was not far away. Not far away at all. They'd driven past Lower Berecombe station, and she'd remembered all those times she'd passed through it on her way to or from Lynford. And now they were driving over a bridge, that she realised with a jolt crossed the old trackbed. George turned off the lane and along a track that rose gradually uphill, and there it was. West End Farm. A large, rambling brick-built farmhouse, with two barns behind and a neatly tended garden to one side. The house was larger than Annie had imagined, and the whole farm was better maintained than she'd dared dream. But as she got out of the car and turned to gaze around her, it was the view across the valley below that made her gasp.

'Marvellous, isn't it?' said George, as he stood beside her, his arm around her waist.

'It's … oh God. It's … terrible!' Annie stifled a sob and turned her face away. To think she would have to live with this view for the rest of her life! There was a clear uninterrupted view of several miles of the old railway line winding its way through the gently rolling hills. And in the distance, just visible past a copse of trees, was the edge of Lynford village, where the station house roof stood out clearly against the skyline.

Every day, as she looked out of her windows, she would be able to see the place where Ted had lived. The place where she'd become pregnant. The place where Bertram had died. The scene of her crime. She would never be able to forget it. Her sense of guilt would never diminish. The view from her front door would be a constant reminder of her past; of the unforgivable wrongs she'd done.

*

A few weeks after they married, George silently passed a newspaper across the lunch table to Annie, and placed his finger on a brief paragraph at the bottom of the page. Annie read it in silence, then pushed back her chair, walked out of the room and out through the front door of the farmhouse. There she stood, on the doorstep, gazing at the view she'd been averting her eyes from for the last seven months. The view across the valley, past the copse, towards Lynford. The view of the little station, its roof line silhouetted against the sky, a curl of smoke emitting from its chimney as was usual since the station house had been sold and converted into a private home.

'Oh, Ted,' Annie whispered, as a solitary tear ran down her face. 'Oh, my darling Ted.'

George had come to stand beside her, and he laid a gentle

arm across her shoulders, tugging her towards him. She shrugged him off. 'Leave me alone, George. Just … I don't know. Go out, leave me.'

He held his hands up as though in surrender. 'I'm sorry. Just thought you might need comforting.'

'Comforting? How could you comfort me? He's … he's dead. Hanged. And … it's all my fault. I should have … I could have testified. I could have insisted. I should have told them … it wasn't him, it was … Oh God. Ted … Ted tried to stop me falling, he pulled me back and I … I should have told them this. Why didn't you tell me to tell them the truth? Why didn't you make me? Why didn't I … oh God. And now it's too late. I could have stopped all this! And you want to … *comfort* me? There's no comfort to be had in all this. None at all.'

She spat out the last words, and went back inside, upstairs, into Ena's nursery where the little girl was asleep in her cot. The nursery was at the front of the house, its window affording an even better view across to Lynford station. Annie stood there, hands on the windowsill, forcing herself to keep her eyes on the place where Ted had lived, as a kind of penance. Why now, why now, when the news of Ted's hanging had been reported, why only *now* did she fully realise what she'd done? Why hadn't she realised before that she could have – should have – done something? Even after he was convicted, she could have stopped him being hanged. She could have told the truth and taken the punishment herself. They'd have sent her for trial, and maybe decided on a manslaughter charge. Ted would have been released. He wouldn't have been hanged. He'd have been able to raise their child, somehow. It was all her fault. That poor, dear man, who'd never hurt anyone, who was the father of her child, for goodness' sake! That dear, darling man, whom she had loved, and whom she'd sent to his death. It was all her doing. She'd done it for Ena, sure, but in keeping her promise to Ted she might as well have been the one to put the noose around his neck.

And George – boring, weak old George, with his rough farmer's hands, his staid, old-fashioned ways, and his farm in the country with *that* outlook to ensure she could never forget what she'd done – how had she ended up with him? He'd been there, besotted by her, able to give her a home away from her father, able to provide for Ena. It had been the easy way out. But she didn't love him. Not like she'd loved Ted. She'd never love him like that. She'd never love *anyone* like that.

She sobbed, collapsing onto the floor by the window, her head buried in her arms, her body heaving as she felt the full impact of what she'd done, what she'd allowed to happen.

Her crying awoke Ena, who began kicking and wailing in her cot. Annie hauled herself to her feet, wiped her eyes on her sleeve and picked up her daughter, carrying her back to the window.

'Look over there, Ena. See that distant house, with the smoke coming from the chimney? See it, do you? That was where you were started. Where your daddy lived. And that place was the death of him, as well.' As she said the words, she found herself hardening. Good job the railway had closed. There could be no Michelhampton and Coombe Regis Railway, not without Ted Morgan at Lynford station. Thank goodness all the land had been sold off, so the railway could never be reopened. Even George had bought a stretch of railway land, at the top of two of his fields. The railway was gone for good. She was glad of that. But Ted was also gone. He too, could never return.

She resolved to one day tell Ena the whole truth about her true father – but not until the child was grown and fully able to understand the sacrifice Ted had made, and the reasons behind Annie's actions. Until then the story about Bertram Clarke-Watson being Ena's father would suffice.

Annie nuzzled her face against Ena's. 'Your daddy, your *real* daddy, was a good, kind and gentle man, Ena. Just you and me now, against the world. Just you and me.' Out of the corner of her eye she saw George, who'd been hesitating in the doorway of the nursery, shake his head sadly and turn away.

Chapter 31

Tilly

It was mid-December. Tilly only had a couple of weeks to go until her due date and her baby-bump was now enormous. Ken had declared it, 'The perfect Christmas present!' and Tilly could hardly wait to meet the new member of their little family.

Life was very busy. Between getting ready for the baby and planning Christmas with Ken, she'd also been hard at work planning the Christmas gala at Lynford station. Her museum, housed in a couple of restored railway carriages, was complete and had proved popular. There were all sorts of events and activities planned for the gala weekend – mulled wine and mince pies to be sold in the café; carol-singers dressed in late-Victorian costume; steam trains running up to the end of the line where Alan Harris was dressed as Father Christmas and installed in a grotto, handing out presents to children. The station had been decorated with garlands of holly and ivy with a huge Christmas tree erected outside, festooned with hundreds of multi-coloured lights. 'Not entirely period,' Ken had said as he switched it on, 'but much safer than candles and pretty darned impressive though I say it myself.'

It did look good, Tilly thought, as she inspected the station on the evening before the gala. Everything was ready. The weather forecast was good, the local press were lined up to visit, there'd been plenty of advertising and they had sold hundreds of advance tickets for the train and grotto. In fact, many time-slots were fully booked.

'It's all down to you, pet,' Ken had said, as she updated her bookings spreadsheet. 'You've done a fantastic job organising this gala. It's going to be our most successful one yet.'

Tilly was pleased with what she'd achieved. It had gone well, and she'd enjoyed these last few months. She had a purpose – well, two purposes really. One working with the railway, and one growing her baby. She felt fulfilled, in a way she never had during her marriage. She'd built a life for herself here in Coombe Regis, and although living with her father wasn't her long-term plan, she was happy with him for now, and he was happy to have her, and there was no need to look beyond the next few months. She'd learned, at last, to surf the waves rather than let herself get swamped. She'd learned to manage her own reaction to external events. 'You can't control what happens to you, mate,' wise old Jo had said. 'You can only control how you respond to it.'

And there was so much to look forward to. As Tilly walked through the ticket office, reattaching a garland of greenery that had come loose at one end, her thoughts drifted back to that day early in the year when her father had fetched her from Jo's and brought her to Dorset. She'd felt then that there was nothing to live for. But now there was so much! In the immediate future: the gala and a visit from Jo who was due to arrive in the morning. In a couple of weeks' time: the arrival of this baby who right now was vigorously kicking as though he or she couldn't wait to meet her. In the long term, who knew? A deeper friendship with Rob, perhaps, as they bonded over their baby.

'Looks perfect, pet.' Ken had followed her into the ticket office. It was dark outside, and the Christmas tree looked spectacular lit up against the backdrop of the goods shed and museum coaches. More lights were strung along the platform. It seemed a shame to switch them off, but it was time to lock up and go home for a meal and a rest before the big day tomorrow.

Saturday, the first day of the Christmas gala weekend, dawned bright and sunny, with a light frost making everything sparkle. Tilly rolled out of bed and stretched her back, rubbing her hands over her tightly swollen belly. 'Don't you be having any ideas about coming early, little one,' she said. 'Hang on in there a bit longer. I've too much to do.'

She showered and dressed and met Ken in the kitchen for a fry-up breakfast to set them up for the day. 'All right, pet?' he asked. 'If you get too tired, let me know and I'll drive you home.'

'I'll be fine, Dad. I'll just sit down somewhere quiet and rest if I need to. Or Jo will bring me back.'

'Ah yes, good old Jo. I'm looking forward to seeing her again.'

'So am I,' Tilly replied. And she really was. Jo had done so much to help her, and this visit felt as though she'd be able to show how much of Jo's advice she'd taken on board.

It wasn't long before they were at Lynford station, switching on the Christmas lights, helping Alan get togged up as Santa Claus, arranging the hundreds of mince pies onto trays in the café, making sure all the volunteers knew what they were doing. Tilly unlocked the museum coaches and checked they were clean and tidy, ready for an influx of visitors. She was proud of the displays that told the story of the railway from its conception through to its closure, and then its rebirth as a tourist attraction. And her research into the railway's staff had paid off – there were pictures and profiles of several of them, including, of course, Ted Morgan. Alan had asked his siblings and they'd searched through their mother's photo albums, eventually finding a grainy black-and-white image of a gentle-looking man standing to attention in a stationmaster's uniform, flanked by two small boys. 'My brothers

– Peter and Tom,' Alan had told her. She reached out a hand to touch the enlarged copy of the photo that she'd put up on display.

'Well, Ted. You'd be proud of this station today, I think. And proud of your daughter, too.'

Ena was due to visit the gala later on and was to be treated as guest of honour. She'd certainly changed her outlook towards the railway since learning the truth about her parentage.

*

At last it was time to open up, and the morning passed in a whirl of activity. Tilly had no specific job to do, beyond helping to check tickets at the entrance and generally making sure that everything was running smoothly. Jo arrived on time and hugged her tightly.

'You're looking so well, mate! Look at the size of you, you're like a bus!'

'Cheers, Jo. Looking good yourself.'

'Ah, no offence meant. Big is good, when you've only – what? a fortnight to go?'

'About that, yes. Oh, it's so good to see you again, Jo! Come on, let me show you around.' Tilly grabbed Jo's hand and began weaving through the crowds – not easy with a belly the size of a bus as Jo had put it – towards the platform. A train was waiting at the platform, pulled by the replica *Coombe Wanderer* which was gently steaming away as people climbed on and found their seats.

'Dad! Jo's here,' called Tilly, pulling Jo towards the engine's cab where Ken was working as the fireman, shovelling coal into the firebox.

'Hello, love,' Ken shouted back. 'Can't hug you, sorry, not in this state.' He was wearing a set of blue overalls, covered in coal dust and smuts. His face and hands were also blackened. Fireman was the dirtiest job on the railway, but Ken always enjoyed doing it.

'You want to ride on this train? Or come and have a mince pie?'

'Oh, mince pie, please. I'm starving. Early start and all that.'

They settled into a corner of the frantically busy café. Tilly was grateful to spend some time sitting down and drinking tea while they caught up with each other's news.

A few minutes later, just as Jo was telling Tilly what her plans for Christmas were, Tilly looked up to see a familiar figure approaching their table, carrying a tea and a mince pie. She grinned as he approached. She'd invited him, but hadn't been sure that he would come.

'Hey, Tilly. Good to see you. May I join you?'

'Yes, sure! Jo, this is Rob Coogan. Rob, my oldest friend, Jo.'

Jo's eyes widened as she took in the name, but she smiled and shook his hand. 'Good to meet you, Rob.'

'You too, Jo. How's it going, Tilly?'

'Really well, thanks. Look at all the people! We're fully booked on the trains this afternoon, but still people are coming just to look around and hopefully spend a bit of money.'

Rob pulled a spare chair to their table and sat down. 'That's great, but I really meant how's the pregnancy going? Not long now, is it? I wondered if … there's anything you need? Anything I can help with? I want to help out, however I can. If you'll let me.'

'Thanks, Rob. Everything's going well. I guess if you want to, you could chip in to help buy the pushchair. I'd like one of those rugged three-wheeled ones, that I could take along the cliff path …'

'You mentioned wanting one of those when we met up last weekend. It's in the boot of my car, I'll drop it off this week.'

Tilly leaned over and hugged him. 'Wow, thanks so much for buying it!'

'No problem. As long as you'll let me push it occasionally, with the little person in it …'

'Of course! And you'll be the first to know, when the baby comes.'

He swallowed, and there was a suspicious glistening in his eye. 'Thank you, Tilly. Well, I should leave you two to it. I want

280

to check out the museum displays. Someone told me they were awesome. Have you seen them yet?'

Jo laughed. 'You do know they are Tils's work, mate?'

Rob laughed. 'Course I do. She's spoken of little else for months! Well, I'd best take a look. Catch you later.'

'He seems nice,' Jo said, when Rob had left.

'He is. I think he'll be a good dad, and a good friend.'

'Nothing more?'

Tilly shook her head. 'Unlikely.' Then she grinned. 'But you never know, I suppose.'

Jo laughed. 'No, you never know. But there's no need to try to predict the future, is there? Concentrate on the now, not the myriad possibles that may or may not occur. Right now, you're happy, aren't you?'

'Very,' Tilly agreed. And she was. Happier than she'd ever been.

There was a commotion in the ticket office, and Tilly got up to see what was going on. Ena had arrived, and with her was Geoff Hill, the chairman of the restoration society. The local press had come, too.

'Ena! So good to see you,' Tilly said, giving the older woman a kiss on both cheeks. 'Would you like to look around first before we get down to business?'

'Oh, I think I'd rather get the business out of the way first, and then relax. Especially as this lot are here, wanting photographs and whatnot.' She indicated the reporter and photographer.

'OK, well we have a space set up in what used to be the ladies' waiting room,' Tilly said, and she led the party into the room, where earlier Ken had positioned a table and a few chairs. Jo followed her in. The room was festooned with seasonal garlands and fairy lights, with a small Christmas tree set in front of the fireplace. Tilly had originally wanted to light a coal fire in here for the gala, but in the end had decided against it, on the grounds that with small children running around excitedly it could be a health and safety risk.

Ena sat at the desk, along with Geoff Hill, who took some papers out of a cardboard folder and laid them on the table in front of her. The photographer set himself up opposite and began taking snaps.

'Miss Pullen, it is with the utmost pleasure that I present you with this document for signing, today,' Geoff began, sounding rather pompous, Tilly thought. Still, it was a big day for the railway and why not make an occasion of it?

'Your signature is required here, and here,' Geoff went on, pointing out the spaces. 'I'll sign on behalf of the railway, and then Tilly can act as witness.' He took a fountain pen out of his jacket pocket, unscrewed its lid and tested it on a piece of scrap paper before handing it to Ena.

She took the pen with a smile and posed with it in her hand for the photographer.

'Miss Pullen, you've finally agreed to sell an important strip of land – part of the old trackbed – to the Michelhampton and Coombe Regis Railway Society,' the reporter said. 'Can you tell us what persuaded you to sell up?'

'I'd never thought I would sell my land to the restoration society,' she said. 'But then I learned my birth father was for many years the stationmaster right here in Lynford, and the railway was his life. So this seemed the right thing to do.' She leaned over the paper and scrawled her signature, then handed the pen back to Geoff.

'Is it true, Miss Pullen, that your father was involved in the death of a man here and was later hanged for it?' the reporter blurted out.

Tilly watched as Ena slowly raised her eyes to the reporter's and fixed him with a stern look. 'There was a death here at the station, yes. My father was wrongly accused and erroneously convicted of murder, on the basis of a fabricated witness statement. I have begun proceedings to re-open the case and am confident that he will receive a posthumous pardon when I present the new evidence that has emerged. I'll grant you a full interview on that subject at a later date, if you guarantee your paper will help me tell the true story and clear his name.'

'We'd be delighted to, Miss Pullen.' The reporter jotted something on his notepad, then turned to the society's chairman. 'Mr Hill, what will the acquisition of this strip of land mean for the railway?'

'It means a great deal, and we are extremely grateful Miss Pullen has agreed to sell. We will be able to complete laying track from this station right through to Lower Berecombe, thus restoring over seven miles of the original railway. In time we will also be able to go beyond Lower Berecombe, to Rayne's Cross to terminate at the Old Station pub. This is a very exciting time for the railway and marks the beginning of a new era of its rebirth. When the railway closed, a local businessman left a wreath of bronze chrysanthemums at Michelhampton station, along with a card reading, "Perchance it is not dead, but sleepeth". With this purchase of land, I think it is fair to say the railway is awakening fully, at last.' With that, Geoff sat back and smiled, proud of his speech which the reporter had recorded.

'Wow!' Jo said quietly, in Tilly's ear. 'You made all this happen, didn't you?'

'Well, I helped,' Tilly said.

'She did more than help. It's all down to her,' said Ken, who'd come into the room, still wearing his boiler suit. Behind him Tilly spotted Rob, standing in the doorway watching the proceedings with interest.

To her surprise, Geoff then turned to Tilly. 'And now, Tilly, on behalf of the society, I'd like to thank you for all your efforts – getting to grips with our archives, setting up the museum and organising this event. You have been amazing.' He nodded to Ken who dipped out of the room and returned seconds later holding a huge bouquet of flowers and a Moses basket tied with a massive bow and containing all sorts of items for the baby. 'This is from the Society, as a token of thanks for all your hard work.'

'Oh! Goodness! Thank you!' Tilly clapped a hand to her mouth, as Jo gently pushed her forward to receive her present. Everyone clapped, and Rob gave a little cheer.

'And something else, Tilly,' said Geoff, after she'd handed the flowers to Jo to hold, and exclaimed over the beautiful baby things. 'When you've had your baby, when you're ready and if you want it, we'd like to offer you a paid job with the railway, as our archivist, events coordinator and publicist. It can be part-time – just a couple of days a week or whatever you want it to be. We'll work out an hourly rate and pay accordingly. We'd very much like you to be part of the permanent team.'

Tilly looked around the room. All eyes were on her. Ken's smile was broad and hopeful, and he nodded slightly at her. This was his doing, she realised. He'd have persuaded the committee to offer her this job. And suddenly she realised it was what she wanted. A job where she could pick and choose her hours, work from home, stay living down here in Dorset spending time with her dad. What a place to bring up a baby. What a great way to build some independence and bring in a little money, while doing work she'd come to thoroughly enjoy.

She nodded. 'I would love that. Thank you very much.'

And again, the room erupted in applause and cheers. Ena crossed the room to shake her hand. 'From one stationmaster's daughter to another, may I be the first to congratulate you on your new job.'

'Thank you,' Tilly said, then on impulse pulled the older woman in for a hug. 'Thank you so much.'

'And now,' announced Geoff Hill, 'I'd like to offer Miss Pullen a chance to take a ride on the *Coombe Wanderer*, to see her cousin Alan Harris' – here, he broke off for a moment, spotting a child peering around the door – 'who is currently, ahem, helping Santa at the end of the track.'

'I'd like that very much,' said Ena, with a smile.

Tilly smiled too. The railway had a bright future ahead. And so did she.

Epilogue

Article on the *Dorset Enquirer* Website

Edward Morgan, who worked as stationmaster at Lynford station during the 1920s and 1930s until the closure of the line in 1936, and who was convicted and hanged for murder in 1937, has been granted a posthumous pardon after his case was reviewed by the Criminal Cases Review Commission. New evidence was found at Lynford station during restoration work, and Mr Morgan's daughter Ena Pullen was instrumental in bringing the case before the commission and securing her father's pardon. The stationmaster is commemorated in a plaque mounted on the restored platform at Lynford.

In a statement to this paper, Miss Pullen said: 'I am delighted that my father has received a posthumous pardon. I am proud to be his daughter and pleased that he is remembered at Lynford station where he lived for much of his life.'

Last year, Miss Pullen sold a strip of land to the Michelhampton and Coombe Regis Railway Society, which has allowed the company to link Lynford and Lower Berecombe stations. The extended line is due to open to visitors at the August bank holiday weekend.

If you enjoyed *The Stationmaster's Daughter*, why not try *The Pearl Locket*?

Author's Note

Many years ago, way back in the mid-1980s, my brother Nigel moved to Barnstaple in north Devon. He had always been a 'railway enthusiast' as he termed it, or 'trainspotter' as I would tease him, being an annoying younger sister. Not long after moving he became involved with the Lynton and Barnstaple Railway Association, set up to attempt to restore a highly picturesque narrow-gauge railway that had linked the two towns from the 1890s until closing in the 1930s. Sounds familiar? This novel is indeed based heavily on that railway, although I wanted to fictionalise the places to give me more freedom in the storytelling. I relocated my railway to Dorset because it's my home county and its beauty is often overlooked by people keen to rush on down to Devon and Cornwall.

The real-life L&BR managed to buy their first station, Woody Bay, perched high on Exmoor with magnificent views, in the mid-1990s. I remember visiting it early on, when there was a daunting amount of work required to restore it to its former glory. I donated the first visitor book used at the station. All my family have also helped lay a bit of track there, and there's a track-side memorial to our father that my brother built. In 2003 Woody Bay opened to the public, with trains running from 2004. A second station, Chelfham, was also acquired by the society and is being restored, but there is a long distance between this and Woody Bay, so no chance yet of linking the two, whether or not all local landowners agree to sell their sections of trackbed!

Nigel spends most of his days off doing voluntary work at either Woody Bay or Chelfham. From what seemed to his rather cynical sister back in the early 1990s as pie in the sky, a railway has been reborn and the L&BR has become a major tourist attraction in north Devon. It's well worth a visit if you are ever in the area. I'm proud of what the society has achieved, especially my brother's part in it.

I borrowed a lot of ideas from the L&BR when writing this novel. Nigel kept lending me books about it, and the website at https://www.lynton-rail.co.uk contains a wealth of detail and photographs. The company Manning Wardle existed, and built the locomotives used in the original L&BR. Its name lives on and is now owned by the L&BR. Much of my description of the last day of operation of the railway was taken from reports of the closure of the L&BR, including the detail of a wreath of bronze chrysanthemums, left by a businessman at Barnstaple Town station with the inscription: *Perchance it is not dead, but sleepeth.*

Acknowledgements

I usually start by thanking my editor, but for this novel I feel I should begin with my brother, Nigel Thompson. I would definitely never have thought of writing this book without his thirty-year involvement in the real-life Lynton and Barnstaple Railway Association. He and I also brainstormed early ideas for the story. (He wanted me to use a fifty-something male railway volunteer as the principle character – ie himself! I vetoed this, though Tilly's father Ken is a volunteer and does play a large part in the novel.) So, thanks so much, Nidge, for your input, the loan of the books, and your comments on the first draft.

Now to my editor, Celia Lomas, who really got the story I was trying to tell, and helped shape it from its rather geeky first draft into something I hope people will enjoy reading. Thank you, Celia. I am going to miss working with you. Thanks also to Kate Mills and everyone else at HQ who worked on this novel.

Thanks are also due to my husband Ignatius McGurl and son Fionn McGurl, who as always acted as beta readers and provided valuable feedback. Brutally honest, in the case of Ignatius's feedback. Thanks, dearest.

Sue Barnard, a writing friend who along with her husband is a member of the Lynton and Barnstaple Railway Association, read and commented on a later version of the novel – thank you, too, for your input.

Finally, thanks to all my readers. I stopped working at the day job during the writing of this novel, to become a full-time novelist. It's your support that made that possible and your comments that keep me going. Cheers!

Turn the page for an enchanting extract of
The Forgotten Secret ...

Chapter 1

Clare, February 2016

We rounded a corner, turned off the narrow country lane and onto a gravel track, drove past a little copse of birch trees and there it was. Clonamurty Farm, County Meath, Ireland. Old, tired, dilapidated and in urgent need of repair. But it was mine. All mine, and *only* mine, or soon would be. A little shudder of excitement ran through me, and I turned my face away so that Paul, my husband, would not see the smile that had crept onto my face.

I think it was in that moment that I first realised my life could change, for the better. If only I was brave enough to seize the day.

'What a godforsaken mess of a place. Good job this is a hire car. That track'll be trashing the tyres,' Paul grumbled, as he parked the car beside a rusty old piece of farm machinery that had waist-high thistles growing up through it.

'I expect it could be renovated, with a bit of money and a lot of effort,' I said. Already I could see its potential. With the weeds cleared, the stonework repointed, the rotten windowsills replaced and painted, and a new porch built around the front door it would be beautiful. A lazy Labrador sunning himself in the yard and a couple of cats nonchalantly strolling around owning the place would complete the picture.

As if I'd conjured them up, two tabbies appeared around the corner, mewing loudly, tails held high, coming to see who we were and whether we had any food for them, I suspected. I smiled to see them, and bent down, hand outstretched, to make their acquaintance.

'Clare, for God's sake don't touch them. They'll be ridden with fleas and Lord knows what else.'

'Aw, they're fine. Aren't you, my pretties? Who's been looking after you then, since your daddy died?' I felt a pang of worry for these poor, beautiful creatures. Though they weren't especially thin, and their coats seemed in good condition.

'Their *daddy*. Oh grow up, will you?' Paul stomped away from me, towards the front door, and fished in his pocket for the key we'd picked up from the solicitor in nearby Blackstown. Actually the solicitor, Mr Greve, had handed the key to me. It was my uncle Pádraig who'd left me the farm in his will, after all. But Paul had reached out and snatched the key before I'd had the chance to take it. The farm wasn't quite mine yet. I needed to wait for probate to be completed, but we'd had the chance to come over to Ireland for a weekend to view the property and make a decision about what to do with it.

I followed Paul across the weed-infested gravel to the peeling, blue-painted front door, and watched as he wrestled with the lock. 'Damn key doesn't fit. That idiot solicitor's given us the wrong one.'

I peered through a filthy window beside the front door. 'Paul, there are boxes and stuff leaning against this door. I reckon Uncle Pádraig didn't use it. Maybe that key's for another door, round the back, perhaps?'

'The solicitor would have told us if it was,' Paul said, continuing to try to force the key into the lock. I left him to it and walked around the side of the house to the back of the building. There was a door at the side, which looked well used. A pair of wellington boots, filled with rain water, stood beside the step. I called Paul, and he came around the house, his lips pinched thin. He never liked to be proved wrong.

The key fitted this door and we entered the house. It smelled musty and unaired. It had been last decorated at some point in the 1970s, I'd say. I tried to bring to mind my memories of the house, from visits to Uncle Pádraig and Aunt Lily when I was a child, but it was a long time ago and I'd been very young then. My maternal grandmother – Granny Irish as I called her – lived here too in those days. I have clear memories of one of my cousins: David (or Daithí as he renamed himself after he became a committed Republican), hazy memories of his two older brothers but only vague impressions of a large rambling house. I have better memories of the barn where I used to love playing hide-and-seek with David among the bales of straw. Sadly, David and his brothers had all died young, which was why the farmhouse had been passed down to me.

The door led into a corridor, with a grubby kitchen off to the right and a boot-room to the left. Straight ahead a wedged-open door led to the main hallway, which in turn led to the blocked-off front door, the sitting room and dining room. This area looked familiar. There'd been a grandfather clock – I looked around and yes, it was still there! – standing in the hallway. A memory surfaced of listening to it chiming the hour when I was supposed to be asleep upstairs. I'd count the chimes, willing it to chime thirteen like the clock in my favourite book – *Tom's Midnight Garden* – and was always disappointed when it stopped at twelve.

We peered into each room. Upstairs there were four bedrooms, a box-room and a bathroom. All felt a little damp, as though it had been months since they'd been aired or heated. As with the downstairs rooms, the decor was horribly dated. I expected Paul to make sneering comments about the state of the place – and to be fair, it was in a total mess – but he surprised me by commenting favourably on the layout, the size of the rooms, the amount of light that flooded through the large front windows. 'It could be quite a house, this,' he said.

'It certainly could,' I replied. 'And we could come for holidays, let the boys use it and perhaps rent it as a holiday home in between, after we've done it up.' I could see it now. Long, lazy weeks, using this house as a base to explore this part of Ireland. It was within easy reach of Dublin and the east coast, and the surrounding countryside of rolling farmland was peacefully attractive.

'Don't be ridiculous. We can't do this place up. We live in London. And why on earth would anyone want to come here for a holiday? There's nothing to do. No. Like I said earlier, we'll sell it to some developer or other, and I have plans for what to do with the money.'

'Can we at least discuss it?' I couldn't believe he was dismissing the idea of keeping the farm, just like that.

'What's to discuss? I've made up my mind. As soon as probate comes through, I'll put it on the market. We can find suitable estate agents to handle it for us while we're here.' He smiled at me – a smile that did not reach his eyes but which told me the matter was closed. 'Come on. Let's go and find somewhere we can have a cup of tea. I've got to get out of this depressing house.' Paul turned and walked along the passage towards the back door. Somewhere upstairs a door banged, as though the farmhouse was voicing its own disapproval of his words.

As I followed Paul out, knowing there was no point arguing with him when he was in this kind of mood, I realised that he would not be able to do anything without my say-so. The house and all its outbuildings, Uncle Pádraig's entire estate, had been left to me. Not to Paul, just to me. So if I wanted, I could refuse to sell it, and there'd be nothing Paul could do about it. Except to moan and snipe and make my life a misery, of course.

It hadn't always been like this. We'd been married twenty-five years. He swept me off my feet when I first met him. I was fresh out of university with a degree in textile design but not enough talent to make it as a designer, and was working in a shoe shop by day and a pub by night to make ends meet. It was not what I'd dreamed of for myself.

Then one day, the best-looking man I'd ever set eyes on came into the pub and ordered himself a gin and tonic, and 'whatever you're having, love'. Usually I turned down these offers – the bar staff were not allowed to drink alcohol while on shift although we were allowed to accept soft drinks from customers. But this time, something about his sparkly eyes that seemed to look deep into the heart of me, something about his melodious voice and cultivated manner, something about his sharp suit and immaculate shirt made me accept, and then spend the rest of the evening between customers (it was a quiet night) leaning on the bar chatting to him.

He was in the area for a work conference, staying in a hotel just up the road, but couldn't stand the company of his colleagues another moment so had escaped from the hotel bar and into the nearest pub. By the end of the evening we'd swapped phone numbers and agreed to meet up the following day when I wasn't working, for a drink. He turned up that second night with a gift of the best box of chocolates I'd ever had, and a perfect single stem red rose in a plastic tube. My previous boyfriends had all been impoverished arts students. No one had ever treated me like that before.

He used to sing that Human League song to me – you know the one: 'Don't You Want Me, Baby'. I wasn't exactly working as a waitress in a cocktail bar when he met me, but pretty close. And he liked to tell people he'd pulled me up, out of the gutter. 'Who knows where she'd have ended up without me, eh?' he'd say, patting my arm while I grimaced and tried not to wonder the same thing.

Paul had been kind in those early days. Thoughtful, considerate, and nothing was too much trouble for him. He was always planning extravagant little treats for me – a surprise picnic on the banks of the Thames, a hamper complete with bright white linen napkins all packed and ready in his car; tickets to Wimbledon centre court on the ladies' final day; a night away in the Manoir aux Quat'Saisons. All would be sprung on me as a surprise.

It was exciting, but looking back, perhaps slightly unnerving in the way that it left me with no control over my life. I'd have to cancel any plans I had made myself, to go along with his surprises. And any twinge of resentment I felt would turn quickly into guilt – how could I resent him doing such lovely things for me? When I told my friends of his latest surprise treat, they'd all sigh and tell me how lucky I was, and ask could I clone him for them.

Gradually I'd stopped making my own plans, at least not without checking with Paul that it'd be all right for me to see my parents, or spend a day shopping with a girlfriend, in case he had something up his sleeve for us. And so as Paul and I became closer, my old friends had drifted away as I'd rarely seemed to have time to see them and had cancelled on them too many times.

We left the farm in silence, and got back in the car to return to Blackstown in search of a café. I spent the journey wondering what plans Paul had made for the money if we sold the farm. Perhaps he'd surprise me, the way he so often used to, and present me with round-the-world cruise tickets, or keys to a luxury holiday home in Tuscany.

It was the sort of thing he might have done in the early days of our relationship. He'd stopped the surprises after the boys were born – it wasn't so easy to swan off on weekends away with toddlers in tow. But the boys were in their twenties now and had left home – Matt had a job and Jon was a student. Perhaps Paul did want to rekindle the spirit of our early relationship. I resolved to try to keep an open mind about the farm, but I would certainly want to know his plans before I agreed to sell it.

There's something funny about being at my stage of life. OK, spare the jokes about the big change, but being 49 and having the big five-oh looming on the horizon does make you re-evaluate who you are, what your life is like, and whether you've achieved your life's dreams or not. Ever since my last birthday I'd been doing a lot of navel-gazing. What had I done with my life? I'd brought up two wonderful sons. That had to count as my greatest achievement.

I say 'I' had brought them up although of course it was both of us. Paul wasn't as hands-on as I was – it was always me who took them to Scouts, attended school sports day, sat with them overnight when they were ill. But then, Paul would always say his role was to be the breadwinner, mine was to be the mother and homemaker.

I've tried to list more achievements beyond being the mother of well-adjusted, fabulous young men, but frankly I can't think of any. We have a beautiful house – that's down to me. Maybe that can count? I decorated it from top to bottom, made all the curtains, renovated beautiful old furniture for it. I did several years of upholstery evening classes and have reupholstered chairs, sofas and a chaise longue. But all this doesn't feel like something that could go on my gravestone, does it? *Here lies Clare Farrell, mourned by husband, sons and several overstuffed armchairs.*

We arrived in Blackstown, and Paul reversed the car into a parking space outside a cosy-looking tea shop. I shook myself out of my thoughts. They were only making me bitter. Who knew, perhaps he did have plans for the proceeds of the sale of the farm that would help rekindle our relationship. Surely a marriage of over twenty-five years was worth fighting for? I should give him a chance.

'Well? Does this place look OK to you?' he asked, as he unclipped his seatbelt.

I smiled back as we entered the café. 'Perfect. I fancy tea and a cake. That chocolate fudge cake looks to die for.' Huge slices, thick and gooey, just how I liked it. I was salivating already.

'Not watching your figure then? You used to be so slim,' Paul replied. He approached the counter and ordered two teas and one slice of carrot cake – his favourite, but something I can't stand. 'No, love, that's all,' he said, when the waitress asked if he wanted anything else. 'The wife's on a diet.'

I opened my mouth to protest but Paul gave me a warning look. I realised if I said anything he'd grab me by the arm and drag me back to the car, where we'd have a row followed by stony silence for the rest of the day. And I wouldn't get my cup of tea. Easier, as on so many other occasions, to stay quiet, accept the tea and put up with the lack of cake.

It was so often like this. Once more I wondered whether I'd ever have the courage to leave him. But was this kind of treatment grounds enough for a separation? It sounded so trivial, didn't it – *I'm leaving him because he won't let me eat cake and I've had enough of it.* Well, today wasn't the day I'd be leaving him, that was for certain, so I smiled sweetly, sat at a table by the window, meekly drank my cup of tea and watched Paul eat his carrot cake with a fork, commenting occasionally on how good it was.

Chapter 2

Ellen, July 1919

Three good things had happened that day, Ellen O'Brien thought, as she walked home to the cottage she shared with her father. Firstly, she'd found a sixpence on the road leading out of Blackstown. Sixpence was the perfect amount of money to find. A penny wouldn't buy much, and a shilling or more she'd feel obliged to hand in somewhere, or give it to Da to buy food. But a sixpence she felt she could keep. It hadn't lasted long though, as she'd called in at O'Flanaghan's sweetshop and bought a bag of barley-drops. She'd always had a sweet tooth and even though she was now a grown woman of eighteen she still could not resist the velvety feel of melting sugar in her mouth.

The second good thing was the one that most people would say was the most important of the three. She'd got herself a job, as upstairs maid for Mrs Emily Carlton, in the big house. Da had been nagging her to get a job and bring in some money to help. There was only the two of them now in the cottage since one by one her brothers had gone across the seas to America, Canada and England. Da was getting old and appeared less able (or less willing, as Ellen sometimes thought, uncharitably) to work, and had said he needed Ellen to start earning. She'd been keeping house for him for five years now, since Mammy had died during that long, cold winter when the whole of Europe had been at war.

But it was the third good thing to happen that Ellen rated as the best and most exciting; the event she'd been looking forward to for months. It was the news that at long last Jimmy Gallagher was home from school. For good, this time. He was the same age as her, just two months older, and had been away at a boarding school for years, coming home only for the long summer holidays.

It was Mrs O'Flanaghan at the sweetshop who'd told her the news. The old woman remembered how Ellen and Jimmy would call in for a pennyworth of sweets on a Friday after school, back in those long-ago childhood days when they both attended the National School and had been best friends. Jimmy had passed his exams now, and finished high school. 'Set to become a lawyer, if he goes off to university and studies some more, so he is,' said Mrs O'Flanaghan. 'But first he'll help his daddy with the harvest. And maybe he'll decide to stay on and become a farmer. Those Gallaghers have such high hopes for him, but I'm after thinking he's a simple soul at heart, and will be content to stay here in Blackstown now.'

Ellen certainly hoped so. She calculated when would be the soonest that she could go over to Clonamurty Farm to see Jimmy. Not today – it was already late for her to be getting home to cook the tea. Tomorrow, then. Sunday, after church, if she didn't see him in church. She was not due to start at Mrs Carlton's until Monday.

Ellen rounded the corner and turned off the lane, up the rutted track that led to her home. It was looking more and more dilapidated, she thought, sadly. Back when Mammy was alive, Da would never have let the thatch get into such a state, sagging in the middle and letting water in over the kitchen. The gate was hanging off its hinges, and the front door was waterlogged and swollen, its paint long since peeled away.

'Hello, boy,' Ellen said to Digger, the elderly wolfhound who had hauled himself to his feet, wagging his tail at her approach. She fondled his ears. 'Daddy in, is he? I've news for him, so I have.'

Digger pushed his muzzle into her hand, and she remembered the pack of barley sugars. She gave him one, which he ate with a crunch, and then she pushed open the door to the cottage.

'Da? I'm back.' Mr O'Brien was sitting in his worn-out armchair beside the kitchen range, his head lolling back, mouth open, snoring loudly.

'I'll make you a cup of tea, will I?' Ellen didn't wait for an answer, but began setting the kettle to boil, clattering around a little so as to wake him naturally.

It worked. 'Eh, what?' he said, sitting upright and blinking to focus on her. 'Ah, tis you, Mary-Ellen. Late, aren't you?'

'Not really. I have good news, Da. I'm after getting myself a job, up at Carlton House. I'm to start on Monday. Ten shillings a week.'

'Ah, that's grand, lass. Keep two yourself and the rest towards the housekeeping. You'll be back each day to cook for me?'

Ellen shook her head. 'The job's live-in, Da. I'll get a day off every Sunday and will come home then.'

Her father pursed his lips. 'Who'll cook for me, then?'

Ellen was silent for a moment. 'I'll make you pies on Sunday that'll last the week.'

'And what of potatoes? I'll have to cook my own, will I?'

'Da, you wanted me to find a job. And now I have. You'll be grand.'

Seamus O'Brien grunted. 'Cooking me own tea. Women's work, that is.'

Ellen ignored him. She was used to his grumps, and knew he was more than capable of boiling a few potatoes. She poured water into the teapot. Should she tell Da about Jimmy being home? A smile played about her lips as she thought of Jimmy, and imagined meeting up with him tomorrow.

'What's that you're so pleased about, girl? Your new job?'

'Aye, that, and the fact that Jimmy Gallagher's home, so I heard.' The words slipped out unbidden.

'Michael Gallagher's lad, from Clonamurty?'

'That's him, Da. I was at the National with him, remember?'

Seamus O'Brien shook his head. 'Don't be getting ideas. Them Gallaghers are too good for the likes of us. They'll be looking for a lass with money for their Jimmy. Not a kitchen maid, like you.'

'Upstairs maid,' Ellen said quietly. But her father's words stung. Was she really too lowly for Jimmy? Not that she thought of him as a potential suitor, or at least, she tried not to. These last few years they'd only seen each other a half-dozen times each summer and Christmas, when he'd come home for school holidays. She'd thought their friendship was strong, and that Jimmy liked her company as much as she liked his, but what now? Now they were both grown, both adults, would he still like her? Or was she just a childhood friend, someone to think back on fondly?

She didn't know. She wouldn't know until she saw him again and had the chance to judge his reaction on seeing her. She hoped if nothing else they would still be friends, still share a few easy-going, laughter-filled days together like they always had. One day, she supposed, he would find himself a sweetheart and that would be hard for Ellen to deal with, but she would smile and wish him well. Occasionally she had dared fantasise that she would become his sweetheart, but her father was probably right. His parents would want someone better for him, and who could blame them?

He'd almost certainly be at Mass tomorrow. She'd find out then, for better or for worse, whether his last year at school had changed him or not.

Jimmy was indeed at Mass. She saw him walk in with his parents and younger brother, so tall now, so handsome! His dark-blond hair, too long across his forehead so that he had to keep flicking it back. A smattering of freckles across his nose – faded now compared to what he'd had as a child. His broad chest and long, elegant hands. She felt a flutter in her stomach. Would he want to know her anymore? She tried to catch his eye, carefully, as she didn't want her father to see her doing it. But he didn't notice her, or if he did, he made no sign.

The service, led by Father O'Riordan, was interminably long. The priest was getting on in years, and Ellen often thought he was simply going through the motions rather than truly finding joy in the presence of God. His sermon, as it did so often, rambled on, touching on several topics but not fully exploring any. Ten seconds after it was over Ellen could not have said what it was about. The only thing for certain was that she had learned nothing from it, despite listening intently.

When she went up to receive the Holy Sacrament, she once more tried to catch Jimmy's eye, but he was at the far end of a pew on the other side of church, and did not go up for communion. That was odd. To be in church and not receive communion? He must have something on his mind he wished to confess to the priest, and had not had the chance to do so before Mass, she thought.

At last the service was over. She walked out with her father, feeling a strange mixture of delight at having seen Jimmy again but disappointment that he had not acknowledged her in any way. At the door of the church her father stopped to say a few words to the priest, and she caught sight of Jimmy once more, over the priest's shoulder, standing a little way off.

He was looking right at her, smiling slightly, and making a surreptitious hand signal, fingers splayed then closed, not raising his hand at all. Anyone watching would have thought he was just stretching his finger joints.

But Ellen knew different, and the sight of that gesture filled her with joy. It was part of their old childhood sign language – a set of signs they'd made up so they could signal to each other in class without the teacher realising. There were signs for 'see you

303

after school by the old oak', 'watch out, the teacher's coming', 'I have sweets, want to share them?' Jimmy had made the sign for 'see you after school'. She was puzzled for a moment but quickly realised he must mean 'after church'. She signalled back 'yes' (a waggling thumb) and had to suppress a snort of laughter when he replied with the sign for 'want to share my sweets?' accompanied by a lopsided cheeky grin.

As soon as her father had finished speaking to the priest, she made some excuse about having left something in the church. 'I'll see you back at home, Da,' she said. 'Couple of things I need to do, then I'll be back to cook the Sunday dinner.'

'Aye, well, don't be long, girl,' he replied, his mouth downturned as it so often was these days. He walked off, not looking back, and as soon as he'd turned the corner and was out of sight Ellen darted off through the churchyard in the opposite direction, to the old oak that stood on the edge of a field beside the river. It was near the National School, and had been the place where she and Jimmy always met up after school when they were children.

He was there now, waiting for her. 'Well! Here we are, then,' he said, smiling broadly. She was not sure whether to hug him, kiss his cheek, or shake his hand. In the past she'd have thrown herself at him, arms round his neck, legs around his waist if her skirts were loose enough and she was sure he could take her weight. But they were grown-up now, and surely that wasn't seemly behaviour? She was still dithering when he resolved the issue for her – holding out his arms and taking her two hands in his. 'Well,' he said again, 'you're all grown-up now, Mary-Ellen, so you are!'

'Still just Ellen, to you, though,' she replied. There were altogether too many Marys around the place without adding to them by using her full name.

'The lovely Ellen,' Jimmy said, bringing a blush to her cheek. 'You've changed.'

'How?'

'More beautiful than ever,' he said, so quietly she wondered if perhaps she hadn't heard him properly. When she didn't reply, he let go of her hands, took her arm and began walking through the park. 'Aren't you going to ask me how my last year in school was?'

'How was it?'

'Boring as all hell.'

Ellen gasped to hear him use such a word, and Jimmy laughed. 'The teachers taught me nothing. Nothing at all. But I studied enough to pass my exams, so the old man's pleased with me. Now I've the whole summer at home to help with the harvest and decide whether I want to go on to university and become a lawyer, or stay here and become a farmer. Wildly different choices, aren't they?'

Ellen nodded, willing him to say he wanted to stay in Blackstown. 'What will you do?'

'Ah, my sweet Ellen. Sometimes fate has a way of deciding things for us. Sometimes something becomes so important to a person that they actually have no choice. They just have to follow where their heart leads them, no matter what.' He gazed at her as he said these last words. For a moment she thought he was going to pull her into his arms and kiss her, right there, in the middle of the park, where other folk were strolling and might see, and might recognise them and tell her father! But she'd take that risk. Her heart surged. Surely he was saying that she was the most important thing in his life, the thing his heart would insist he follow?

But his next words changed everything. 'Ellen, let me tell you what happened this year at school. The teachers taught me nothing but I learned plenty, anyway. One of the old boys organised a club, called the Dunnersby Debaters. But we weren't a debating society. We were there to learn Irish history, the real history, not the English version the masters taught. We learned the Irish language. We heard all about Wolfe Tone, and the 1798 rebellion, and all the other attempts to rise up against our oppressors.

We learned exactly what happened in the 1916 Easter uprising, and why we must not let those efforts die in vain. Ireland *must have* home rule. One way or another, we must find a way to achieve it. I joined the Fianna Éireann too, and learned to shoot, so when the time comes I'll be ready.'

His eyes were blazing as he made this speech. She could see the passion surging through him like wildfire. They'd spoken before, a year or two ago, about the prospect of Irish independence, but had mostly been repeating what they'd heard their parents say. Ellen had never been sure whether it would be good for Ireland or not – would the country not be worse off if it threw off its connections to its powerful, wealthy neighbour and branched out on its own? Was it not better to be a little part of a bigger nation, than a small, poor nation that was independent?

But clearly Jimmy had made up his mind the other way. What would that mean for him? What would it mean for her, and the future she hardly dared dream about, a future with Jimmy at her side?

Dear Reader,

Thank you so much for taking the time to read this book – we hope you enjoyed it! If you did, we'd be so appreciative if you left a review.

Here at HQ Digital we are dedicated to publishing fiction that will keep you turning the pages into the early hours. We publish a variety of genres, from heartwarming romance, to thrilling crime and sweeping historical fiction.

To find out more about our books, enter competitions and discover exclusive content, please join our community of readers by following us at:

🐦 *@HQDigitalUK*

🅕 *facebook.com/HQDigitalUK*

Are you a budding writer?
We're also looking for authors to join the HQ Digital family!
Please submit your manuscript to:

HQDigital@harpercollins.co.uk.

Hope to hear from you soon!